## PRAISE FOR *FAREW*



"Moving effortlessly from Paris to Dresden to Shanghai, Wagenstein masterfully chronicles the lives of European émigrés and refugees in WWII Shanghai. . . . Impressive in his ability to move from the small details of individual displaced lives to a larger panorama of international intrigue, . . . Wagenstein brings to life a largely unknown chapter of Nazi persecution."

—*Publishers Weekly*

"Although unknown in the United States, Angel "Jacky" Wagenstein is one of Bulgaria's greatest modern writers. In *Farewell, Shanghai*, he has constructed a fascinating and profoundly moving roman à clef. . . . *Farewell, Shanghai* is a worthy addition to the stories true and just short of true that chronicle human destinies strewn like flotsam and jetsam in the great storm of World War II."

—*The Advocate* (Baton Rouge, LA)

"Based on real people and terrifyingly true events, Wagenstein's gripping tale (and its excellent translation into English) exposes the less-discussed but just as horrific history of the Nazi regime in China."

—*Historical Novels Review*

"Gripping. . . . A fascinating story that effectively tells about the tragic events that beset those Jews who managed to reach Shanghai in 1938 and 1939 before World War II began."

—*National Jewish Post*

"*Farewell, Shanghai* is a major contribution to the literature about World War II and an outstanding novel."

—*The Reporter* (Broome County, NY)

"Vividly cinematic. . . . [A] profound examination of the radically different ways humans react to moral challenges."

—*The Tennessean*

ALSO BY ANGEL WAGENSTEIN

*Isaac's Torah*

# FAREWELL, SHANGHAI

{ *a novel* } ANGEL WAGENSTEIN

*Translated by*

ELIZABETH FRANK *and*
DELIANA SIMEONOVA

HANDSEL BOOKS
an imprint of
Other Press • New York

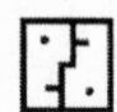

This work has been translated with the support of the National Culture Fund of the Ministry of Culture of the Republic of Bulgaria.

Originally published as *Sbogom, Shanghai*



First softcover printing 2008
ISBN-13: 978-1-59051-308-8

Production Editor: Mira S. Park
Text design: Natalya Balnova

This book was set in 11.7 pt Bembo by Alpha Design & Composition of Pittsfield, New Hampshire.

10 9 8 7 6 5 4 3 2 1

 Printed in the United States of America on acid-free paper. For information write to Other Press LLC, 2 Park Avenue, 24th Floor, New York, NY 10016. Or visit our Web site: www.otherpress.com.

Library of Congress Cataloging-in-Publication Data

Wagenstein, Angel.
[Sbogom, Shankhai. English]
Farewell, Shanghai / Angel Wagenstein ; translated by Elizabeth Frank and Deliana Simeonova.
p. cm.
ISBN-13: 978-1-59051-254-8 (hardcover : alk. paper)
ISBN-10: 1-59051-254-5 (hardcover : alk. paper) 1. Jews–China–Shanghai–Fiction. 2. Jews–China–Shanghai–Social conditions–20th century–Fiction. 3. World War, 1939-1945–Fiction. I. Frank, Elizabeth.Simeonova, Deliana. II. Simeonova, Deliana. III. Title.
PG1039.33.A37A3513 2007
891.8'134—dc22

2007007361

IN MEMORY OF MANFRED DURNIOK,
THE MAN WHO FIRST OPENED CHINA'S PAGES TO ME.

# FAREWELL, SHANGHAI

EMERGING FROM A DESERT OF CLEARED-AWAY RUINS, *the modernist edifice of the Philharmonic—almost windowless, its exterior walls and roof marked by frivolous curves—stood by itself, yellow and unaesthetic, in that border section of the great city called West Berlin. Some people called it Free Berlin. But let's not argue: the names of things never express their real nature.*

*Not far away stood the Wall. Not the Great Wall of China, in the East, but the other one, in the West. This Wall, less imposing, and not exactly built for the ages, divided peoples and worlds, ideas and ideals, memories and judgments not only about what had happened but also about what might have happened if a certain black cat hadn't crossed the road right under your nose. Opinions about this or that varied: from one side of the Wall, things looked one way; from the other side, well, another.*

*I sat down in the third row all the way to the right, in the semi-darkness of the thoroughly empty hall. The sole source of light came from the weak glow of the obligatory emergency exits; even the stage, where, at this early morning hour, a rehearsal was taking place, was gloomy and oppressive. They were doing a run-through of Tchaikovsky's Concerto for Violin and Orchestra; the conductor, Herbert von Karajan, must have gotten up on the wrong side of the bed, because under his breath he never stopped grumbling—was he ever sour and irritable. Something was going wrong with the rehearsal; twice he had left the stage in a huff, and, after awhile, come back, limping—apparently his knees hurt him.*

*His latest return didn't immediately silence the whisperings of the musicians. In one corner, someone tittered; somewhere else you could hear the provocative plinking of a violin string, followed by subdued remarks and laughter. What he overheard I don't know—there, where I was sitting, at the low end of the hall, muffled conversations only made their way through the space like an indistinct susurrus, but the maestro, seized with fury, started shrieking, yes, yes, that's the word, literally shrieking, his voice breaking into a light and ridiculous falsetto:*

*"Haven't I already forbidden you to speak Chinese?! Haven't I?!"*

*He was really a hothead, this great Austrian, and, if we do say so ourselves, something of an hysteric, in that he demanded absolute obedience during rehearsals and didn't tolerate even the slightest horseplay. Above all not this morning, when everything seemed off and wrong. Probably he suspected that his musicians were smirking at him or scheming against him, deliberately resorting to this incomprehensible "Chinese" that so obviously annoyed him. Especially since among the musicians—some of the absolute best in Europe—there wasn't even one who was in the least Chinese.*

*With his baton he tapped the desk several times and raised his hands, but from the beginning it was clear that, once again, things weren't going well. Karajan let fly an obscenity, and angrily broke the baton. That's it exactly: he broke it as if it were a match, like a teacher at the end of his rope who breaks his pencil in two. Somebody ran to fetch him another. Apparently this must have been some kind of regular ritual because nobody was in the least astonished at this fire-brigade readiness to get him a new baton, on the double.*

*While he was angrily tossing away the two halves of the broken stick, the maestro made a slight turn toward the hall and that's when he noticed me. Shading his eyes with his palm, he stared out into the semi-darkness and cried out in a tone not only unwelcoming but, as a matter of fact, quite threatening:*

*"You over there, who are you?"*

*I answered.*

*He didn't react: he neither ordered me to stay nor threw me out, but went back without a word, banging the desk with his brand new baton.*

*"Attention! From the beginning!" Then, a minute later he was shrieking again, "Stop, stop, stop!"*

*What a madhouse! The* Concerto for Violin and Orchestra *was clearly not going to be played that day.*

*The soloist, with a serene and absent air, withdrew to the back, where he sat down on an empty chair. With his violin on his knee, he emanated neither boredom nor irritation: he was just waiting patiently for the storm to pass. From where I was sitting I could see his long, immaculately white hair and his long, pale face, but the light wasn't strong enough for me to make out his features. Nevertheless he was the one I was interested in; he was the one I wanted to talk to. M.D., the film producer, had brought me to the concert hall, promising to stop by toward the end of the rehearsal in order to introduce me to this world-famous celebrity. Because it was him I needed: the violinist Theodore Weissberg.*

*Of course you have the right to ask: Who, in actual fact, are you? And what, beyond a banal meeting, was I searching for in that empty concert hall on that gray Berlin morning?*

*I wasn't looking for anything in particular; I just wanted quite simply to learn more about certain details and compare some contradictory pieces of evidence about certain events. From true stories of long ago, now almost forgotten, which some people might find strange and implausible. But is there anything more implausible than History? I mean History with a capital H, the science of the past, not its expurgated version, simplified and polished for kids in school, but the kind that's full of contradictions and unanswerable questions, illogical, often absurd, the fruit of accident or millions upon millions of contingencies—just like life itself, and like the obscure depths of being, where certain creatures devour others, and prosaic aspirations spread out their tentacles and suck out the marrow of noble ideals, although on the surface everything seems predictable, orderly, and reasonable—more or less like a set of math problems neatly solved for high school seniors.*

*And so, who am I? Neither a hero nor a victim. An anonymous supernumerary in the crowd scenes of a play. A supporting player without the right to speak. This is why I don't want to impose my opinions and judgments, my own point of view. These always distort things depending on where you happen to situate yourself. The same phenomenon or event, observed by different people from different angles, looks different. Someone will say: things didn't happen like this, but like that. And he'll be right. And so will those who see it a bit differently. Everything depends on whether you're on stage or in the audience, whether you take part in the events or glimpse them through a keyhole, which reduces your field of observation to a miserable slit. It also depends on the things you remember and those you forget. Some people have the ability to remember astonishing details from the war, but forget at the same time what started it. Others remember the name of the grocer they knew as kids, but forget who was prime minister at that time. People are different. Each one has the right to his own memories and his own amnesia without anyone's meddling in his affairs.*

*This is why, at times, I prefer to stay on the sidelines, and keep myself out of the picture. To be frank, I don't want to take part in the crowd scenes, to say nothing of the heartrending monologues—I just want to be a spectator, seated in the half-darkness of the auditorium, in the third row. Because things exist in spite of our points of view—they are what they are. Those who are color-blind can't make out colors; others are blind and don't see anything at all; still others are deaf or rather barely detect frequencies high and low. We human beings are all different, but things—colors and sounds—exist outside of ourselves, completely independent of whether we question them or challenge them or even judge them in different ways. They just* are.

*So, pardon me, but you won't see me again or recognize me in the empty hall, though I do beg your indulgence if now and again a bias of my own, some sympathy or revulsion, rises to the surface, like blood that oozes through the bandage and hints at the open wound it covers. This happens apart from me, completely by itself.*

*That's at least what I'm trying to say now, as I begin my tale about Hongku, a suburb of Shanghai—a harbor town at the mouth of the Yangtse river.*

*Hongku, Shanghai District: a little-known chapter in the chronicle of Jewish tragedy during the Second World War.*

*This historic opus unfolded amid the Babel of a new Babylon, in which Chinese neighborhoods choking with overpopulation were intertwined with the luxurious quarters of the "International Settlements"—or "concessions," according to semi-colonial statute—with their first-class hotels and restaurants barred to the Chinese, their English gentlemen's clubs on Bubbling Well Road just off Waterside Boulevard, their sailors' pubs on Avenue Edward VII beside the cottages and the fancy stores of "Frenchtown" Rue Lafayette, avenues Joffre, Foch, and "Cardinal Mercier," and the kaleidoscopic Yatze Road, with its side streets and little Chinese shops stuffed with jewelry and statuettes of fake gold, ivory, and amber. And also with the stinking bordellos of the Nantao and Chapei quarters or the densely populated, rat-and-disease infested marshes on the other side of the river, in Pootung.*

*Having endured the first Japanese invasion of 1932, nearly wiped out by Japanese aircraft in 1937, and long occupied by Japanese troops, the city continued to wallow in luxury and insouciance, not only along Nankin Boulevard, ablaze with the razzle-dazzle of a million blinding lights, but also in the dark desperation of the slums, with their unemployment and dead-end poverty.*

*It was only during the first year of the occupation that the city sanitation agency finally cleared from the streets the corpses of thirty thousand people dead from hunger and disease—all this in the shade of the imposing twenty-two-story Broadway palace where in one night the diplomatic representative of Nazi Germany, Baron Ottomar von Dammbach, lost eighty thousand Shanghai dollars at poker to Sir Elias Ezdra, a Sephardic Jew of the so-called "Baghdadi," or Jews who had settled along the Silk Road as early as the eleventh century. After the Opium War and the Treaty of Nankin, in 1842, when the English annexed Hong Kong and began construction of the Shanghai harbor on the Yangtse delta, the Baghdadi quickly attained important economic positions in the region. Almost a century later, their banks and brokerage houses were supplying tin, rubber, and quinine to the Third Reich, which, when it had need of it, was not repelled by Jewish money. As for the Baghdadi themselves, owners of the Shanghai Banking Corporation, Yokohama Specie Bank, or Sassoon House, they had nothing against their proper German partners as long as they brought with them the guarantee of solid profits.*

*Shanghai—today one of the gigantic gateways of the new China, open to the whole world—was, during the 1930s and the years of World War II, from its eruption in the West and Europe on September 1, 1939, all through Pearl Harbor and Hiroshima in the Far East, until the morning of September 2, 1945, when Japan formally surrendered, a nexus of economic, political, and military interests, diplomatic intrigues, and personal ambitions—a meeting place for the criminal world, inter-*

*national adventurers, spies, and profiteers, people uprooted and hunted, and those in search of strong sensations or easy money. The Chinese, those real masters of this ancient land, were deeply sunk in worry—some over their bowl of rice, others, collaborators and puppets of the Japanese occupier, over complicated manipulations for keeping and battening on what they'd plundered from their own people. And all this against the background of the roar, sometimes distant, sometimes near, of an endless bloody war on multiple fronts between the pro-Japanese Chinese Republic, led by the puppet Wang Chingwei, the Nationalist divisions of Chiang Kai-shek, and the People's Liberation Army of the communists, led by Mao Tse-Tung.*

*Shanghai—site of glamor and poverty, of the endless humiliation of barefoot coolies with their rickshaws and of little prostitutes with their drunken sailors, of the East's porcelain tenderness and military brutality, of opium and human degradation. But also the last lifesaving shore, a symbol of desperate hope for survival. Because during those years, while great democracies looked with indifference on the genocide being prepared by the Hitlerists, Shanghai, with its limited status as an open city, was the only place that could give shelter and an extremely expensive salvation to around twenty thousand German and Austrian Jews, many of them intellectuals, and to another 3,800 Jews from various other occupied countries, who managed to get there before the thick smoke of the crematoria could engulf all of Europe.*

*Hongku is the name of the section that was turned into their ghetto.*

*Shanghai is the name of the city of their damnation—and their deliverance.*

## *Instead of an Introduction to Joseph Haydn's Symphony No. 45, called the "Farewell"*

Night was falling. The meager light of sunset, veiled by the thin river mist above Huangpu, barely pierced the half-destroyed steel plant in the dusk. The sky was still glowing through broken windows and walls with big cracks—the work of shock waves. Tilted concrete columns and iron beams cast shadows that swayed between hurricane lamps and Chinese paper lanterns carried by human silhouettes barely distinguishable in the gloaming. Those who came from the outside stepped over knocked-out gates or directly through fissures in the collapsed walls and piles of brick.

Like a scene out of the theater of the absurd, down the dark iron stairways poured people from every direction, in outfits that, given the setting, were unusual or, rather, just out of place. A whole world of memories came back to life, in which women were dressed in the fashions of yesteryear, formal evening gowns that, in all likelihood, they hadn't worn in ages, with small coquettish hats and veils from the years before the Great War—ensembles like those worn to a state concert at the Musikverein of Vienna or to a palace reception in the Berlin Charlottenburg. Some men were wearing clothes that long ago served as evening dress; here and there you could spot a man in an antiquated dinner jacket, quite often in combination with duck trousers, and next to him there were still others sporting sandals on bare feet and the torn cotton clothes of dockworkers or streetsweepers.

The newcomers hung their lamps and paper lanterns on iron stakes, odds and ends of machines and whatever else they could find. But the space, a cavernous factory interior with rails on which at some time in the past railway wagons would arrive, was too vast to be lit up by these blinking flamelets, which resembled fireflies lost in the black maw of the factory.

People were greeting each other with a festive rituality, just like after Sunday mass or a wedding. Here and there someone would bow to kiss a lady's hand, though if an outside observer were to have taken a closer look, even in the dim light he would have noticed her torn lace gloves, through which the tips of her fingers peeped out, stained with the indelible blacking of dyeworks in leather factories or workshops for the spinning of raw silk.

And still all of this near-parody of rituality evoked a certain genuinely joyful excitement and the anticipation that something important and grand was about to happen.

So people continued to fill up the hangar, and in the silence, slightly tense and ceremonious, only their steps could be heard, and, sometimes, whispers or quiet laughter.

At the end of the space an improvised platform had been raised, above which, in the warm humid currents of air stinking of slime and rotten fish, there waved a transparent banner with a greeting written in big red letters:

**WELCOME! GOD BLESS AMERICA!**

Decorations consisting of crossed, handmade American flags, colored also by hand on pieces of rice paper or cotton, were reminiscent of something like the opening of a series of football games between two provincial colleges.

But it was hardly a collegiate competition—far from it!

On the platform was arranged a hodgepodge of chairs and music stands cobbled together from wooden planks, and downstairs, in the empty space intersected by the rails, roughly made benches had also been set up, among which the newcomers confusedly passed each other in order to find a seat. At the very front a few rows of benches remained empty, apparently reserved for VIPs.

And here they are, the distinguished guests—fifty or so American marines and their commanding officer, feet clanking on the iron floor, making their way with an upbeat military stride ridiculous for this place through portals that had been blasted out by explosions and turned into twisted scraps of sheet iron.

The people in evening gowns or factory workers' clothes stood up to applaud the guests and the sound of their clapping echoed thunderously throughout the enormous space. The American boys had probably not been expecting such a welcome in this not-very-ordinary factory setting, since they were nodding with some perplexity left and right before taking their seats on the front benches.

One American captain in turn, his hands raised high, was clapping in all directions at the mixture of tuxedos and rags. And you couldn't understand who in fact were the heroes of this strange ceremony—the Americans or the inhabitants of these ruins.

A badly dressed man with silver hair above his high forehead, a wax-pale face, and the aura of someone who had spent his years with a microscope or in the white silence of a hospital received the captain, and, with a restrained bow, quietly introduced himself in English:

"Professor Sigmund Mandel from the autonomous government of Hongku. Welcome, sir. Please, follow me, your seat is in the front row."

Delicately escorting the captain, he stopped, however, on the way in order to introduce to him a Japanese officer from the sanitation services who was smoking with a cupped hand, and sitting by himself at the end of a bench.

"Allow me, sir, to introduce the colonel. He has the special distinction of . . . how shall I put it? . . . of making it possible for this day to happen."

Lost in thought, the short Japanese with round, thick glasses came to life, jumping to his feet with a start, while trying to let his cigarette drop unnoticed and step on it, his face remaining gloomy and unfathomable. He clicked his heels and saluted in a military fashion despite the fact that his rank was higher than that of the American captain. The latter looked at him in surprise and didn't salute him back. The American was right: after the capitulation of Japan on September 2nd on the deck of the American cruiser *Missouri*, the place of a Japanese officer, even one stripped of his epaulettes, was, if not before a military tribunal, at least in a prisoner-of-war camp.

The captain continued on his way and Professor Mandel smiled a bit confusedly to the Japanese man before following his exalted American guest.

A minute later, as if they were waiting for the American officer to take his seat, on the platform appeared probably the shabbiest philharmonicists in the world—gotten up in the same mix of ragged tuxedos and duck work togs as everybody else.

One of the musicians came forward. Holding his violin tightly under his arm, his long hair falling almost to his shoulders, he bowed a little stiffly and made an awkward sign with his hand for the applause to stop. He announced with a voice so quiet with emotion that from below people started shushing for silence:

"The Shanghai chamber orchestra of the Dresden Philharmonic will perform in honor of our distinguished American guests the "Farewell" Symphony No. 45 by Joseph Haydn."

Someone tried to applaud again, but a general and stern "Shhhh!" nipped this particular desire in the bud.

In the ensuing silence, solemn and full of anticipation, the orchestra players passed a little candle to each other, lighting with its flame their own candles, each attached to a handmade music stand.

The American boys from the Marines exchanged looks; it was hardly likely that at home in Illinois or Minnesota they'd had much of a chance to attend a performance of Joseph Haydn's Symphony No. 45.

It was a symphony, written in other times and according to other human dimensions, that had been performed in glitzy palace halls and on vainglorious stages. Now it was going to sound a little stranger and maybe a bit sadder than Haydn had wanted it—in this half-destroyed and deserted factory in Hongku, Shanghai District.

The violinist, who had also undertaken the role of master of ceremonies, and had been famous some time ago on the stages of Europe and America as the virtuoso Theodore Weissberg, patiently waited for the conclusion of this mysterious ritual of the candles, as predetermined by Haydn himself, before he continued:

"Parts: *Allegro assai, Adagio, Allegretto, Presto-Adagio.*"

Theodore Weissberg sat down in front of his music stand, waited for an instant, and then nodded his head.

The first chords of the "Farewell" Symphony resounded.

This was not an ordinary concert: the people stuffed in the belly of the former steel plant, the early evening with its smell of swamp and rotten fish, were bidding farewell to Shanghai. . . .

# PART ONE

# 1

IT WAS EARLY IN the evening of November 10, 1938.

The concert in the great hall had begun. The mild light of the crystal chandeliers, dimmed as far as possible, only intensified the bright sparkling flames of the candles attached to the solid red mahogany music stands. Theodore Weissberg was in an immaculate tuxedo—in fact, as is correct at such concerts, all the other members of the Dresden Philharmonic were in tuxedos as well.

Dressed in formal evening clothes, the audience in both the orchestra seats and the boxes was holding its breath. This Symphony No. 45 in F sharp minor is rarely performed, and it had not been easy to get tickets.

On this particular evening, four SS officers had installed themselves in the center box, where long before the Weimar Republic, in the time of the iron chancellor, fürst Otto von Schönhausen, a.k.a. Bismarck, the Hohenzollerns and their entourage used to sit. In the audience's eyes, it was an important sign of the profound changes that had taken place in Germany. The highest-ranking among the officers was Hauptsturmführer Lothar Hassler, a very handsome man, blond and blue-eyed, as if he'd been cut out from one of the torn posters left over from the Berlin Olympics and still hanging on city walls, of the all-conquering Aryan nation. Something about him recalled the masculine, Viking-warrior-type profiles of Leni Riefenstahl's film characters.

The most junior officer, possibly an aide-de-camp or something of that kind, tilted toward Hassler, obligingly offering the open program.

"*Allegro assai.* I think it means 'rather jolly.'"

"I hope so," Hassler murmured gloomily. "Tonight I hope it will be 'rather jolly.'"

He knew what he was talking about, the Hauptsturmführer; he spoke little, but he always had the exact word for the exact thing.

While the Haydn symphony was pouring out its light and tender "farewell," the last of the naive were also saying farewell to their comfortable illusions about good old Germany—this winter's tale that, in just a few weeks or so, would kick out like dirty kittens the Nazi bums who had just by chance grabbed hold of power.

For it was on exactly this night—the evening of November 10, 1938, Wednesday going on Thursday—that history would bestow the name Krystallnacht—"The Night of Broken Glass" —and this referred not to the crystal chandeliers of the Dresden Konzerthaus, but to the crystal tinkling of broken Jewish shop windows.

Jolly fellows, bloated with beer, were smashing shop windows all over Germany and Austria, which, to the unparalleled enthusiasm of the local population, had recently been annexed. Broken glass windows, under stomping boots, clinked and crunched during this jolly crystal night.

Terrified old Jews hauled out of their beds were being dragged down the streets with cardboard signs hung on their chests: *JUDE.*

Synagogues were burning—on Fasanenstrasse and Oranienburgerstrasse in Berlin, above Schwedenplatz in Vienna, and in Leipzig, Munich, Frankfurt, and Stuttgart. All through that November night of elegant concerts burned another two hundred synagogues.

*Allegro assai*—rather jolly!

Lothar Hassler lifted the small opera glasses to his eyes. His gaze swept across the hushed audience and, coming to rest at the box just opposite, lingered on the face of a young woman with golden-copper hair softly illuminated by the barely flickering chandeliers. This was the mezzo-soprano Elisabeth Müller-Weissberg, famous not only in Germany but also on the stages of Carnegie Hall, and wife of the violinist to whom in a moment the bright circles of the opera glasses now shifted.

They remained on him for a long time while the officer examined with curiosity this world-renowned celebrity, a member of the Prussian Academy of Arts, while along the Hauptstrasse there flowed an improvised evening procession by torchlight. The crowd was singing merrily, and at the front, in time to the song, drums were booming:

*Auf der Heide blut en Blü-melein*
*Ein! Zwei!*
*Und das heisst E-e-rika . . . .*

Exactly there, at the corner, where you could find the famous bookstore Meersohn & Sons, some gay blade came up with the idea of making a bonfire out of the books. Marx, Heine, Freud, Feuchtwanger, Stefan Zweig, Thomas and Heinrich Mann, Bertolt Brecht and Anna Seghers, Friedrich Wolf and Leonhard Frank, Baruch Spinoza and Marcel Proust, Franz Kafka and Henri Bergson all made excellent kindling. Einstein with his quantum structure of radiation threw off a spray of sparks, flying afterward above the flames with his covers spread like wings.

Don't think that these pork butchers and *lumpen* sots have any idea who you are, Albert. We know—we know very well. Maybe over there, where you managed to slip away just in the nick of time, you might feel sad about what's happening in your former motherland, but we feel cheerful—after all, you yourself say that everything is relative. We're working according to your Jewish formula, Alberto, sorry, but excuse us! Our Energy to smash you equals the Masses that support us, multiplied by the Speed of Light squared, with which we will conquer the world. This is the situation, dear Albert, so farewell! It's time now to find out at last who are the real masters of Germany—the Jews or us!

$E=mc^2$ fell right into the center of the galaxy of fire and shot out a myriad of mirthful sparks.

# 2

TWO ORCHESTRA PLAYERS, THE oboist and the horn player, collected their scores, blew out their candles, and silently left the stage, this being the ritual whenever Haydn's "Farewell" Symphony is performed. But much to their surprise, waiting for them in the wings were some uniformed stormtroopers, who unceremoniously grabbed the musicians and pulled them outside. The two naturally tried to resist and find out what was going on, but some big-shot superior officer with stretched-out breeches and shiny boots put a finger to his smiling lips: *shhh*, quiet now, don't disturb the concert! And there was no malice in his expression —only a kindhearted, almost friendly look. After all, dear friends, as you yourself understand, this isn't some madhouse of a Jewish synagogue, but a classy concert hall, so let's have, as people say, mutual respect!

Theodore Weissberg, without lifting his bow from the strings, saw through the flames of the candles how, backstage, the brown-shirted thugs were dragging away the two musicians, and threw a confused look at the next violin.

Other musicians had also noticed what was going on, because a slight, almost imperceptible movement shivered through the orchestra. Even so, the concert continued.

For the contrabass and the violoncello, it was their turn now.

The two orchestra players could obviously already guess what was waiting for them, but a concert is, after all, a concert: each of their movements was being followed by the silent, unsuspecting audience. They collected their scores, blew out the candles at their stands, and, throwing a worried and questioning look at the first violin, slipped away a little uncertainly.

Backstage, the story of their colleagues almost repeated itself: "Shhhh! Silence! Respect the Aryan composers!"

The low-ranking officer hovered over the ear of Lothar Hassler:

"It's really scandalous that all these symphony players are Jews!"

"No, not all. Some don't even suspect that their grandmothers are Jews. It's all right. They'll find out. What's really scandalous is how we let Germany be turned into a synagogue. . . . Quiet. It's his turn now."

The violinist Theodore Weissberg, considered by music critics both here and across the ocean to be one of Germany's most gifted virtuosos, gathered his score, blew out the last candle, and, a little stiffly, walked out. This then was the finale of Joseph Haydn's Symphony No. 45 in F sharp minor—called the "Farewell." After that the stage plunged into darkness.

Some time passed in meditative silence before the crystal chandeliers blazed up and the hall exploded with applause. But the orchestra players did not return to take a bow.

This was the last concert of the Dresden Philharmonic.

# 3

UNTIL THE LUNAR NEW year there were still two months to go. Only then could one expect the Japanese authorities to relax their grip, and for relatives to be able at last to visit one another. It was November, according to the Julian calendar. Rotten weather. You could even call it dog's weather, if from the southernmost neighborhoods Longhua and Nanshih to the northern borders of the enormous town, that is to Chapei and Hongku, the stray dogs hadn't long ago been eaten.

The air was chilly and humid, with the sticky smells of frying, canals, and muck. The sea breeze brought no freshness, but rather the stench of the innumerable swamps at the mouth of the river Huangpu, left arm of the great Yangtse, through which the transoceanic ships reached their destinations.

It was getting dark. The hundreds of junks that circled in leisurely fashion around the ship hulls ominously towering above them were already lighting up their paper lanterns. Countless flickering little lights were reflected, lengthened and swinging, in the thick foul waters greasy with oil spots and whole islands of floating filth. Outcrying each other in a language they apparently considered English, hawkers from the junks offered for sale everything they had at their disposal—from vegetables, fruit, and fish to amulets and small gods carved out of buffalo horn and jade.

Leaning over the ship's railing, bored transit passengers stared down from above, not even coming down to the shore, since not only were they alarmed by rumors about pickpockets and professional con artists, but also in an hour or so they would continue their voyage south toward Singapore, Hong Kong, and Macao, and to points even more distant—Manila and Bombay. And the passengers for whom this was the final destination and who were disembarking down the gangplanks of the firmly moored ships weren't in the least concerned with souvenirs, let alone fruit and vegetables. They were primarily passengers from the regular lines of the shipping company in Kobe that ferried back and forth between the continent and the islands Japanese civilians who were constantly on the move—merchants, bank clerks, and representatives from the newly opened branches of big Tokyo firms. Some officials, met by liveried chauffeurs and deputies from the consulates or major banks, were en route to the airport in Longhua in order to continue their journey to the interior by air—to Peking, or even further, to Manchukuo, now controlled by the Japanese. Later, when it became clear that the supply of military vessels was becoming depleted, the steamships carried troop reinforcements for the occupation authorities, here and there with some bespectacled pipsqueak officer full of Samurai confidence.

Far above the docks and the warehouses, the low yellow buildings of Japanese headquarters and the port administration, the shipping agencies, customs and border police, above the cranes and the mountains of packing crates and cargo, beyond the heavy black waters of the river lit up with junks and their swinging lights, the cloudy sky reflected the blurred orange radiance of the hotels and offices situated along the luxurious riverside boulevard known as the Bund. Toward it streamed the dazzling radiance of the International Concession, which the people from the junks had never seen, although ever since childhood they had heard legends about that other, distant, and unknown world of the boulevards.

For they, the people of the junks, were born on the water and lived on the water, while, at the mouth of the river, the shades of their ancestors waded up to their knees in the swampy waters of the rice paddies without their ever having seen up close even once in their lives the splendiferous buildings in English colonial style, the gambling houses, the tennis courts, the gentlemen's clubs, the hotels and the restaurants, in front of whose entrances towering Sikhs in snow-white turbans, curved daggers hanging ominously from their sashes, their legs imperiously spread apart, stood guard.

He was thinking along these lines as he leaned against the ship's rail, chewing his dead Russian "papirosa" cigarette with its thick paper tip, the captain of the rusty and, at least from its external appearance, quite neglected coastal freighter *Chelyabinsk*, which had experienced, so it seemed, both the Russo-Japanese war of 1905 and the rout at Tsushima as well as the dramatic turns of the October revolution in its Far Eastern version.

The *Chelyabinsk*, like a slow-moving suburban streetcar creeping along one and the same closed route, was coming from the mouth of the Mekong, where it had been laded with raw rubber from the French plantations of southern Indochina. In Shanghai it was taking on cotton and unprocessed silk that it had to unload in the north in Da-Liang—or Dalnyi, in Russian—before leaving it to its long journey along the Transiberian railway. The captain was gazing indifferently at the dockers who were running upward along the gangplanks carrying huge loads beneath which only their bony feet jutted out, and who were scrambling down again toward the waterfront shouldering flat crates of coarse Siberian cedar, each with its identical, printed sign: *Uralmash—USSR.*

He did not become particularly concerned when one of the dockers dropped his load and collapsed unconscious on the wet oily deck, probably from hunger, since in only two hours he would receive his fifty Shanghai cents, enough—actually more than enough—for a small bowl of rice with a few leaves of fried leek and a tin cup of green tea. The captain quietly and impassively issued instructions and two sailors carried away the fellow who had fainted to the cabin with a red cross indicated on its oval iron door.

Half an hour later two dockers exited the cabin and no one, neither on board the ship nor on the quai, paid the slightest attention to this minor incident. The two began to make their way down the gangplank, carrying their *Uralmash* crates, and the infusion of one docker more into the swarming, sweat- and onion-stinking anthill of nameless and faceless humanity didn't change a thing about the huge, multimillion, and chaotic equation of dead-end poverty and immense wealth called Shanghai. Every morning the municipal authorities collected from the streets those who had died of hunger, and one candidate more or less for a similar fate meant nothing as far as the statistics were concerned.

It's been said already that the month was November. The tenth of November, Wednesday going on Thursday. The year: 1938.

Until the outbreak of the Great War in the West, there were nine months and twenty days to go.

# 4

HILDE PULLED THE CURTAINS apart at the window and was disappointed at what she saw. She herself didn't know exactly what she had expected, but the view was really very different from both the tourist posters and the hopes of those who had believed in them. The landscape was gloomy, with sooty facades and laundry hung out to dry. Opposite, down below—so low that the hotel seemed perched on top of Mont Blanc—there stretched an infinity of railroad tracks, a crisscrossing tangle of arrows, wires, and signals, abandoned trains and one small lonely locomotive that, from here, looked like a child's toy and was huffing and puffing and lazily chugging hither and yon. The small hotel was just decent enough for travelers with a modest per diem—a hotel with two stars, one of which was burning out.

From here one could see neither the Eiffel Tower, nor Montmartre, nor the Arc de Triomphe, nor the dark silvery surface of the Seine spreading across the town and reflecting the sky. She knew everything even without having seen it: the boulevard Saint-Michel, the Louvre, and Notre Dame; she even felt as if she were personally acquainted with the proprietor of the corner bistro below. She had never been to Paris, but while she was studying French language and literature at Humboldt University in her enraptured, almost voluptuous way—an undertaking that, in the midst of her studies, came to a crashing end on account of the total exhaustion of the miserable inheritance left her by her parents—she had leafed through this amazing city; she had imagined it. She had longed to see it in its real glamor and not just reflected in books and movies, to breathe its air, to hear its sounds, to lick it and savor its taste, to drink a cup of coffee at the corner bistro with that fellow she had dreamed up—the man from Provence who was friendly in a neighborly sort of way: "Good morning, Mademoiselle Hilde—the usual? Coffee and croissant, that's right, isn't it, Mademoiselle Hilde?"

Despite her momentary chagrin with the view from the hotel window, she was in fact happy to be here, happy that she had escaped at least for a while the suffocating atmosphere of Berlin, that barnyard of Europe, as Ehrenburg had called it. For the time being, she had left behind the worries, the rumors, the futile acting classes, the idiots who want you to sleep with them in exchange for a small part with two lines, the wandering around during crowd scenes, when you haven't got the slightest idea why you're supposed to go back a hundred times simply to pass again and again in front of the camera. All day for five Reichsmarks with a costume they give you, and six and a half with your own clothes, that is, if they're right for the film, about which you know nothing and which probably you'll never even see. And with the crew's everlasting efforts to inadvertently brush up against your tush and flirt with you, and the extra's eternal hope that one day you'll be noticed and the director, comfortably seated in his canvas chair, will wave his finger, call his assistant, and quietly ask, "That one over there, the blonde. Who is she?" And then all this nonsense would fall into place and, taking its logical and destined path, inevitably open your way to a great career in the movies. Except that nothing like that ever happened to any of the extras.

Although, actually, it had happened once, and quite unexpectedly at that, and it's why she had woken up this morning not in her garret in the Berlin Grünewald, but in Paris.

There was a cautious knock on the door; through the chink appeared the bald head of Werner Gauke, the legendary one-armed UFA photographer.

He had lost his arm in the First World War at Verdun, but this had made him no less skilled in the métier of the art-photographer, whose amazing photo sketches—masterly balancing acts of light and shadow—were not infrequently exhibited in the windows of Friedrichstrasse and Kurfürstendam and reproduced in prestigious magazines. He was, furthermore, notorious (to the disbelief of the unenlightened) as a great womanizer.

"Are we ready, doll? Take all three costumes, we're gonna knock ourselves out today. I've called a cab. See you downstairs—coffee's waiting."

"Just a shower and I'll be there."

"Ten minutes, doll! Kiss-kiss."

He smacked the air and slipped out.

Her first disappointment accompanied her downstairs, to the bistro: the proprietor was no make-believe guy from Provence, but a bloated matron, probably a former prostitute who had invested her savings, earned from treading the Paris sidewalks, in this small establishment. And the cheap workers' coffee, richly redolent of chicory, was served not in a cup, but a soup bowl, and was hardly better than the average ersatz coffee in the Babelsberg buffets near the UFA studios. The only exception was the croissants. But this is why Paris will always be Paris—to have its Eiffel Tower, Moulin Rouge, and croissants!

Afterward they got to work. Look down! Lean on the parapet. More—more! Looser, not like a statue! Stretch out now on the bench—more, so your titties stick out! Move to your right, doll—you're blocking the Obelisk!

Dear Werner, round, rather stout with age, loaded down with cameras and lenses in leather cases hanging from his neck, constantly wiping with an enormous handkerchief in his only hand the sweaty baldness of his head, was investing all his unattainable photographer's imagination in the exemplary accomplishment of the task assigned him. And the task was no more and no less than an expressive series of photos of a German beauty with Paris as the background.

Hilde, quite by chance, had become the object of these efforts.

After 1933, all the movie studios, from UFA to Bavaria Film to TOBIS to Terra, were put under the control of the Nazi Ministry of Propaganda, in other words, the gimp Joseph Paul Goebbels, who looked more like a professional card-sharp than a Reichsminister. Thrown to the winds was the leftist "Union of Popular Cinema," led in its seminal years by, among other luminaries, the likes of Heinrich Mann, Bertolt Brecht, Käte Kollwitz, and Béla Balázs. Hollywood in time had sucked in Ernst Lubitsch and Georg Pabst, just as it did Emil Jannings, Lia de Putti, Pola Negri, Elisabeth Bergner, Greta Garbo, Peter Lorre, and Billy Wilder. A long time before that the legendary "Blue Angel," Marlene Dietrich, together with her director Sternberg, had set their sails toward Beverly Hills. Fritz Lang, immediately after the coming of the Nazis, disappeared into thin air only to show up again in France, where he made his famous *Liliom*.

The German screen was orphaned; the great epoch of *Kule Wampe*, *Doctor Mabuse*, *Metropolis*, and *Street Without Joy* had passed.

Classic German cinema was dead.

Then rose the star of Leni Riefenstahl.

The career of this mediocre thirty-year-old actress and passionate sportswoman had started with the "mountain" films—neither good nor bad, though all the same *Storm over Montblanc* had penetrated even the depths of Soviet Russia. Every artist has his shining moment, and if he doesn't miss it, the road to success and glory lies ahead. Her own shining moment was the Nuremberg Congress of the National Socialist Party in 1934. It was then that she shot *The Triumph of the Will.* This was a work both pompous and pathetic, resembling to a certain extent many Soviet documentary films of that time, but with substitute azimuths—race instead of class. A new series of films by the freshly initiated party favorite soon followed, with the big hit, *Our Wehrmacht*, becoming a cult classic and conclusively shaping the aesthetic parameters of Nazism. Leni Riefenstahl took an active part in the creation of that cliché, which turned into a state norm: the image of the German warrior, strong and invincible, not muscular like an African gorilla but touched with a slightly feminine Nordic beauty. The model aroused national pride and no one paid attention to the fact that this Aryan matrix no sooner fit the Führer himself than it did Goering, Himmler, or Bormann. Perhaps a number of handsome men from the Nazi elite conformed in part to the model, but most often rumor had it that they were gay.

The Berlin Olympics gave a new fillip to her career with *Festival of the Nations*, a soul-stirring tribute to Aryan blood. The African-American Jessie Owens, legendary Olympic athlete and champion in everything he did, cast something of a shadow over the infinite and beautiful power of the white race, but, no problem—artists know that shadow emphasizes ever more strongly the brightness of the light. The colossal success of the film, especially among the Nazi elite, inspired Riefenstahl to a followup: in 1938, almost on the threshold of war, she got busy with the second series: *Festival of Beauty*.

And this was Hilde's shining moment.

For she was a remarkably beautiful young woman, slim, blue-eyed, and blonde, symbolizing the image of the German mother of the future with her healthy German children, a typical representative of the Master Race—exactly the one stipulated by the idealized model. The guys in the crew, pinching her here and there, would whisper compliments in her ear about her eyes—pure Scandinavian lakes and such nonsense; the makeup artists already knew the beautiful extra and would kiss her on the cheek: "Our Valkyrie's back again!"

With looks like these remarked by everyone, small wonder that one day the creator of *Festival of Beauty* happened to notice her.

"What's your name?" asked Leni Riefenstahl, tenderly drawing her finger along the line of Hilde's lips.

The young woman burned with embarrassment. All the same, whether the great Riefenstahl was a lesbian or simply expressing motherly sympathy, what happened was what every girl extra dreams of: the director had picked her out from the anonymous crowd, and summoned her forth.

She swallowed before responding. "Hilde Braun."

"You're gorgeous, Hilde. I'm going to need you. Call me when you get back from Paris."

"From Paris?" said Hilde, not understanding.

Probably no one yet knew why Riefenstahl had suddenly decided to insert in her *Festival of Beauty* a series of snapshots of a typical German woman situated against a Paris background. Maybe someone had planted this idea in her mind, or instinct, typical of artists, had suddenly suggested an intimate and very possible future. For the breath of impending war was blowing in the wind. And Arthur Neville Chamberlain, the British prime minister, of whom no one could say with certainty whether he was a sly dog or an idiot, had, in Munich, already consigned Europe to her doom.

One way or another, Fräulein Hilde Braun still received a contract and an advance of five hundred *Reichsmarks*, an enormous sum to her, for her permission for unlimited use of the photographs in the film as well as on the pages of the Nazi *Der Stürmer*, the newspaper of the real Aryan—according to the ads.

# 5

HILDE WAS RUNNING UP the endless steps toward Sacré-Coeur. They hadn't taken the small Montmartre funicular because here and there on the steps Werner kept getting struck by genius ideas for photographs. She stopped and turned in order to wait for her rather portly cavalier, who, in addition to himself, had to shlep the full set of cameras and lenses. For this he had no assistant—a clear sign of the Reich's successful efforts to save the foreign currency it needed so badly. Finally, Werner caught up with her, and breathing heavily, wiped the beads of perspiration from his forehead.

"So, is our little doll satisfied?" he finally managed to ask.

Hilde threw a radiant look over Paris, like a conqueror about to capture this city as it sank into the thin haze of the horizon. Veiled in the pale pink of sunset appeared the barest hint of the Eiffel Tower, the Seine and its bridges, the Île de la Cité with Notre-Dame, the Obelisk, the Madeleine. . . . Boundless, eternal, vain, sinful, at once intimate and haughty—Paris! Evening drew near, and, wrapped in a mantle of transparent mist, the city prepared for its nocturnal rites.

In a sincere impulse, Hilde planted a kiss on the photographer's cheek, but he said good-naturedly, "Not like that! That's how you kiss your old uncle. I think I deserve something better. After all, it was me who pitched the idea of Paris to Leni Riefenstahl. Me and nobody else. And here's why: I had something in mind; I've had my eye on you for a long time."

He tried to kiss her on the lips, but Hilde, quick as a little fish, slipped away from his embrace and gaily ran up the steps toward the church, which was white as sugar.

High up she put her elbows on the stone parapet; the great city spread itself out below. Then she felt the photographer's hand on her arm, and, next to her face, his hot breath. She didn't withdraw her hand, but just looked at him in surprise and again gazed down at the city.

"I envy people who've got Paris as a hometown. I don't have one. Or rather, I almost don't have one. I guess Stuttgart was the nicest thing about my childhood. But that was over a long time ago, and forever. I haven't been there for ten years now; I don't even know if my parents' grave is still there. Then this gray and repulsive Berlin. Every day the train to Potsdam. Then Babelsberg . . . then. . . ."

"Then the UFA studios, the one-armed Werner Gauke. . . ."

She gently caressed his hand, which was still lying on hers. Perhaps through this gesture she wanted to express her friendly feelings toward him and that for her his disability didn't matter.

"Yes," she agreed. "UFA, Werner Gauke. 'The Magus of Photographic Chiaroscuro.' Isn't that what they write? But they don't write that he's my only friend inside those disgusting soundstages stinking of glue and paint where everything is a celluloid lie."

"That's how it is sometimes. A lie in twenty-four images a second. Though not always. Do you know what they call the proportions of the screen? 'The Golden Section.' In great films it really does become golden, my girl!" he said, adding with neither rhyme nor reason, "Your section is golden too. I think I could fall head over heels in love with you, like a teenager."

"Please don't. Because I can't. I'm afraid I can't fall in love with anyone. Ever."

"Don't hurry. You're only twenty-three. . . ."

"At twenty-three one knows everything worth knowing. What you learn during the rest of your life is just details."

# 6

THEY HAD DINNER RIGHT then and there behind the church at a small restaurant for tourists. The area was congested with artists who, under visitors' eyes, had been drawing the same thing year after year: the Sacré-Coeur basilica, a souvenir from Paris for ten francs. Considering their craftsmanship, it's small wonder that Van Gogh was canonized as a saint—the steep little street where the restaurant was located was called St. Vincent.

Hilde picked at her food with her fork, took a sip of wine, and picked at her food again. "You drink a lot and you don't eat!" said Werner, in a schoolmasterish tone.

Not to be outdone, she fired back, "And you eat a lot and don't drink!"

She was preoccupied with something; her thoughts were somewhere else, apparently, than with the pot of legendary *coq au vin.*

After awhile she added indifferently, "You still haven't told me about your wife, your children. How many do you have—two, three?"

"Two. Do you insist on hearing about them?"

"Not particularly. But I know my fellow countrymen well. Right now, at—" she looked at her small wristwatch—"nine twenty-six p.m., solid German middle-aged burgers start telling their young women companions, whom they've destined for the sack, how lonely they feel at home, and how much their wives, otherwise kind and faithful, don't understand them. . . . Or something like that."

The photographer laughed sincerely:

"You're Satan!"

"Yes, I am. Do I smell like sulfur?"

"Don't play-act now. You smell like *Mon Boudoir* perfume—which I gave you as a gift this morning, didn't I? Otherwise, of course I'm attached to my family. But this has never stopped me from taking in the surrounding landscape. Does that bother you?"

"In general, no. But you're at least honest. Usually men lie, before they succeed in getting . . . that thing."

He cast a long look at her, as if he wanted to read the answer in her face before asking the question.

"Am I going to get 'that thing'?"

"Look now, my dear Werner. My dear friend! On the table before us there's a rooster in wine. But in this case the rooster is you, and the wine we've drunk is enough for us to start talking nonsense to each other. Let's go. I'm tired."

# 7

IT WAS ALREADY LATE at night. The small hotel room was lit up only by the orange glow of the bedside lamp. Hilde, in her pajamas, was reading a book when the door opened and Werner sneaked inside. He alone, the one-armed man from Verdun, was capable of simultaneously holding a bottle of champagne tightly under his arm and carrying two glasses in his one hand.

"May I?"

Hilde answered indifferently:

"You ask after you've already come in."

As if he hadn't heard her, he sat down carefully on the corner of the bed, silently put the glasses on the night table, then drew the bottle from under his arm, which was missing up to the elbow, and poured.

She didn't drink from the glass he handed her, but put it on the table. She also carefully took the glass out of his hand and set it down next to hers.

"Listen, Werner. Werner Gauke, world-famous photographer and my only friend. Listen clearly now. Because tomorrow you're going back to Berlin."

"As far as I know, we're both going."

"You're not well-informed. Only you are going back. I'm staying. I don't want to be an Aryan model for the artistic insights of Leni Riefenstahl. Do I smell like sulfur now?"

"You smell like *Mon Boudoir.* Have you thought carefully about what you're doing?"

"About everything. From the first to the last letter of the moral code."

"Besides the moral, there is also the penal code."

"It has power over only those who are in its hands."

"You're right. Won't we see you again in Babelsberg?"

"Between friends? No. Never again. To start with, I have five hundred marks. I earned them today by honest labor and the negatives will stay with you. For the glory of *Der Stürmer.* Later on we'll see."

The photographer thought for a while, drew his hand over his face, and sighed:

"You've put me in a fine fix with the bosses. That stupid idea about the Paris background was mine."

"I'm sorry, but this is the very least I could do for you. I could have gotten you into an even deeper fix, but I felt sorry for you. You see, I'm a Jew."

At first, the photographer didn't understand what she was saying, but a second later he literally jumped from his seat.

"What? What did you say?"

"You heard me: I'm a Jew, through both my mother and father."

Her words slowly penetrated his brain. Then Werner suddenly burst into sincere laughter. "Come on! You're joking!"

"Exactly, my dear Werner. A Jewish joke about Isidor, who converted and changed his name to Siegfried. And there isn't a Hilde Braun any more than there's a Hildebrand or a Brunhilde

Braun. My given name is Rachel Braunfeld. My father decided on it after my parents moved to Stuttgart. During the Austro-Hungarian period, his business in Vienna had been 'Braunfeld Hats, By Appointment to the Royal Court.' Then, after the empire broke up, things changed. He went bankrupt and so my parents found themselves in Stuttgart. There they loved neither Jewish hats nor old-fashioned purveyors to the court. And so, to survive, my family converted. We Braunfelds became Brauns. And I'm an in-between product of Judaism and Christianity who has nothing to do with your great Aryan nation."

# 8

THE TWO OF THEM stood in front of the sleeping-coach, under the sooty vaults of the Gare de l'Est.

Hilde was the first to break the silence.

"You're the one with more experience. What do people say to each other in these situations?"

"Nice things to say good-bye."

"Okay. I knew you were a great photographer and a number-one studio ladykiller, and that you're a genius in both areas. Now I've found out what a terrific guy you are as well. Excuse me if all of this causes you a big headache. But *c'est la vie*. Thank you, I'll remember you. Now it's your turn."

"Yes, it's my turn . . . I have no words for the little number you've played on the entire Aryan nation. I won't say anything to Leni Riefenstahl—let her continue to believe in goodness and Germany's destiny to remake the world. I'll remember you too. You're the most magnificent girl I've ever met, and the first I failed to bed."

From the inside pocket of his coat he took out his wallet, pressed it against his chest with the remaining part of his amputated arm, and with skillful fingers started going through it.

He put something in the small pocket of her coat.

"This is a check for two thousand francs. They gave it to me for emergencies. You're the emergency. In fact, I'd even say you're a natural disaster. Take it, I'll settle it with them one way or another—I'm an old studio fox. Now you can kiss me good-bye."

She embraced him and kissed him warmly on the cheek, saying hurriedly, "I know, I know, this is how you kiss your old uncle. But the world is full of lovers, while good old uncles are so rare! I love you!"

The engine whistle blew, and the conductor called out to the sleeping-car passengers to board the train.

"I wish you success, Hilde . . . or whatever your name is. It won't be easy but you'll manage. I feel it. Now wait here on the platform—I'll try to make you happy by waving a handkerchief from the window."

When Werner pulled the compartment window down and leaned outside, she wasn't there anymore. He discovered her in the crowd, making her way toward the station exit.

"Hilde!" he cried, and repeated even louder, "Hilde!"

She didn't turn, but only raised her hand and waved good-bye. Then she disappeared into the crowd.

# 9

YOU COULDN'T SAY THAT Elisabeth, the wife of violinist Theodore Weissberg, who had seemingly disappeared off the face of the earth, was beautiful in the usual sense of the word; to a certain extent, her features were quite irregular. But she had a majestic, noble, proud bearing all the more striking when she walked, enveloped in her magnificent long blue fox coat, which had no doubt cost a fortune. Such a lady, especially when she was moving along the snow-covered street, was no ordinary sight even in luxurious Dresden, which had seen enough aristocrats whose ancient lineage had brought them straight to the Zwinger—museum of German museums. She was really an impressive woman, this Madame Elisabeth Müller-Weissberg!

Wet snow was falling and instantly melting on the asphalt. Taxis were few, gas rationing having made this service barely within reach. She was in a hurry—couldn't wait her turn at the taxi line and started off on foot, since for her this was going to be a momentous day.

After running long and fruitlessly from one department to another, she had finally, with the assistance of the influential director of the State Opera, received an appointment with the Nazi boss Hassler. From telephone conversations with his aide she had been left with the impression that the Hauptsturmführer had postponed the appointment on purpose, in this way giving it special importance and meaning.

No more than she did the wives of the other arrested Dresden Philharmonic players know anything about the fate of their husbands. All their attempts to find them had crashed against the wall of cold but polite silence on the part of the imperial police administration, which claimed to know nothing about this question. Finally someone whispered to Mrs. Müller-Weissberg that the solution to the mystery was hidden not with the police, and not even with the lower ranks of the Gestapo, but in the town's party elite and, more precisely, with the SS chiefs.

Today she had to see this Lothar Hassler, who had made himself out to be as important and inaccessible as a Punjabi prince on a white elephant.

She stopped in front of an imposing building in a heavy, late-nineteenth-century baroque style, apparently now a military institution, and walked directly toward the uniformed guards at the entrance. She said where she was going and gave her name, and the man in the glass booth picked up the phone and after a moment politely let her enter under the enormous eagle viciously clutching a wreath of gilded oak leaves, with a swastika in the center.

With complete self-confidence she crossed the bustling hall, which, with its marble mosaics and columns, was more like a prestigious old banking house than the site of Nazi headquarters, and walked toward the wide stairway. And it wasn't merely one or two people who turned to look at her admiringly. The singer Müller-Weissberg was quite famous, a fact that became obvious through those officers who, saluting her with respect, stopped or gave way.

The usual bureaucratic procedures with the aide, secretary, and so on were quickly dispatched, and Elisabeth found herself in an enormous office covered in thick oak paneling that, darkened by time, made the place somber and unfriendly. With its heavy desk at one end, oak conference table on massive legs, and corner armchairs and sofa upholstered in green leather, this salon, which was quite cold for the heating season, now at its peak, was telling her that though this office had once belonged to a big fish, it was presently occupied by the new conquerors of Germany. The aide, who had let her enter ahead of him, clicked his heels and announced:

"Mrs. Müller-Weissberg, on your orders."

Lothar Hassler stood up from his desk and hastily stubbed his cigarette out in the ashtray.

Not nearly as self-assured as before, she stepped into the somber office, as Hassler moved in her direction.

"It's a special pleasure for me, Madame."

He bent to kiss her hand, but she uneasily withdrew it, looking around with the feeling that she had fallen into a trap.

The officer was looking at her with his watery eyes without altering his slightly ironic expression, with its expectation that she would speak first.

But she remained silent, knowing neither how nor when to start.

"Let me—" he said finally, extending his arms to help her take off her costly blue fox coat.

The woman hesitated, but still removed it, and he threw it carelessly over the back of an armchair.

Then, gesturing, he invited her to sit by the small low table where a crystal carafe with cognac and two glasses had already been laid out. Hassler poured and raised his glass in a silent, hospitable toast, but Elisabeth did not touch hers.

"Let's get straight to the point, Mr. Hassler," she finally resolved to say, thus abruptly diving right into the deep end. "Where is my husband?"

"As the saying goes, 'take the bull by the horns'? Good. I'm an admirer of yours. You know it, too. And I would do anything within my powers to prove it to you."

She gave him a look full of hope. "I would be most grateful. Please, release him."

"I would like to do that—because of you, dear Madame. Very personally because of you. We are not adventurers who frivolously waste the talents of the nation. We believe in the people of spirit, without whom, we, the politicians, are merely empty sound, wind and mist. . . . But your husband's case isn't so simple."

"Why? Isn't he, in your opinion, one of the . . . as you deign to put it . . . 'talents of the nation'?"

"In this case it doesn't matter. Because he is a Jew. A Jew pure and simple, so all other considerations are beside the point. The documents indisputably prove his non-Aryan origin."

"He has never concealed it. And is this why you let me come here, so that you could tell me this? Where is he?"

"Indeed. Where is he. . . ? I don't know. I've ordered a search. In any case, without interfering in such an intimate matter, I would advise you to think about the future of your marriage. I understand the difficulties from a moral standpoint, but things in our country have radically changed. Personal morality cannot be placed above the interests of the nation. A divorce would be of benefit to both of you, believe me. And to your prestige, your career. You are an Aryan and he—"

"A Jew, as you've already pointed out. But this problem is nobody's business but ours!"

"But it's also the business of the new Germany, dear Madame—of its state policy," he said softly. "You can feel yourself what's blowing in the wind. It's true, we regret the scandal of that November night last fall, but we can't always succeed in containing the legitimate rage of the crowds."

"I think you're not even trying. All this is done by your people."

"My people? You're judging us too harshly. Is the village priest responsible if someone from the congregation gets drunk as a pig and smashes his neighbor's window with a bottle?"

"Let's leave the village priests alone, Mr. Hassler. You invited me here so that we could agree on the conditions of his release."

Lothar Hassler smiled nicely.

"You are putting it imprecisely, my dear. When we spoke on the phone, I referred to 'means.' Let's discuss the 'means.' The 'conditions' are dictated by us. Unless. . . ."

Elisabeth hesitated for a moment, then opened her expensive crocodile bag and silently poured its contents on the small table.

There were a number of valuable pieces of massive gold jewelry, a dozen antique gold coins, rings, a platinum crucifix encrusted with diamonds, a turquoise diadem, a pearl necklace, and insignificant trifles of ivory and gold.

Without even glancing at this small treasure, Lothar Hassler kept his searching eyes fixed on the woman. Then carelessly, almost with disgust, he started going through the precious objects with his finger.

"Is this your estimation of your husband's worth? I wouldn't say he's a Paganini, but still. . . ."

She looked at him in confusion, then took off her wedding ring and threw it on the table. The ring made a concentric circle before landing with a clink on the glass.

"I don't have anything else. This is it. And I hope you choke on it!"

"Why all this rudeness? I wouldn't have expected it from a lady who has sung at Carnegie Hall. But as you wish, Madame."

Lothar Hassler went to his desk, took out two passports from a drawer, and threw them on the table—next to the family treasures and the wedding ring.

"Well then, rudeness for rudeness. Here are two passports. Permission to leave the borders of the Reich, valid for four months, during which you will need to arrange your affairs and get the hell out of here with your Jew! But in return for his freedom I want. . . ."

The officer walked around the table to Elisabeth, roughly pulled her up and pressed her close. She detected the slight odor of his recently smoked cigarette as well as the lavender scent of his "Carriage Post" aftershave.

"In exchange for his freedom—I want you! Everything has a price and you have to pay it . . . and not just with trinkets."

Elisabeth, frozen to the spot, turned pale as wax. She threw a quick, instinctive look toward the leather-upholstered door, perhaps with the hope that at this instant the aide would come in, bringing sudden salvation and an unforeseen miracle. But there was no miracle. Even the phone didn't ring.

Lothar Hassler, without taking his eyes from her or hurrying, stuck his hand into her cleavage, and searched for her breasts.

Elisabeth, again with desperation, looked at the door, but neither the secretary nor the aide came in.

Nor would they ever appear.

# 10

HILDE WAS WALKING, OR rather sauntering along the Left Bank, chewing an impressive hunk of baguette with gusto. It's only tourists who, when they eat in such a carefree way, don't worry about running into people they know.

Particular reasons for being carefree, however, Hilde didn't have. For three weeks already she'd been waiting for a response from police headquarters to her application for an extension of her *Droit de sejour*—permission to stay in the country. But cold silence was all she'd gotten so far, despite her explicit statement that she was a Jew threatened by the Third Reich's anti-Semitic laws. Her visa would soon expire, and illegal stays in France were severely prosecuted—if, of course, the unwanted immigrant got caught by the authorities. Paris, even without her, was swarming with people with expired visas, fake documents, or none at all, but the situation would become really disheartening if the French police were to take the fugitive to the border under military escort and hand her over to the German authorities. By now this had become a banal, almost everyday occurrence, and in her case virtually no one there would shed a tear if she were to throw herself into the arms of the Gestapo and contritely beg forgiveness for having acted in such a harebrained way.

It was late spring. Down below the waters of the Seine lazily glided, carrying small purring ships and heavily laden barges. Along the whole length of the embankment, artists on stone parapets showed their watercolors; secondhand booksellers displayed not only books yellow with age but also Christmas cards from the last century, posters with brands of cocoa and liqueur forgotten since childhood or old enamel signs with a pointed finger showing the way to the *pissoirs*. No doubt there are collectors of every kind of nonsense. Especially if they buy it in Paris.

She wandered along the Quai-Voltaire; on the opposite bank the Louvre rose up in its full splendor. The setting sun was red and anxious, heralding a windy dawn. The windowpanes of the great museum across the river blazed as if on fire and the river reflected their glimmering flames while the small waves swayed and put them out.

If Hilde had been a bit more interested in politics, she would have known that even without this bloody sunset, Europe's tomorrow looked quite windy.

The dress rehearsal for the upcoming war—the brutal civil butchery in Spain—had ended with the victory of the fascist Falange over the republican People's Front. The international brigades—a shining moment of international solidarity with the Republic—suffered a heavy defeat and the French camps north of the Pyrenees were crowded with beaten and retreating units speaking every language under the sun. Meanwhile, amid the turmoil, Nazi Germany had consecutively devoured Austria and Czechoslovakia to the absentminded and indifferent silence of the West.

Yet, in both the West and the East, people still remembered the proverb, "Appetite comes with eating." That's why all the

European countries were silently amassing troops at their borders, taking special security measures, and quietly mobilizing their reserves, while everyone proclaimed in unison that international treaties were being honored, things were under control, and there was no military tension. Just like the song: *Tout va très bien, madame la marquise. . . .*

The general population for its part knew very well the story of the marquise in question, who was constantly being reassured that everything was all right despite the fact that the estate was in flames, because everywhere people were stocking up on food, fuel, and blood plasma.

And if anyone still harbored the illusion that the conflict would be limited to Europe through diplomatic compromise and tossing the Reich insignificant morsels of territory, it was enough just to browse through the newspapers to find out what was happening in the Far East. There for a long time already, since the annexation of Korea in fact, Japan had permanently installed itself on the continent, and since the beginning of the thirties had put its foot as well on Manchuria, creating the new country Manchukuo. The puppet Puyi from the Chinese royal dynasty had granted the Japanese full and indivisible rule over these territories, which bordered the Soviet ally—the People's Republic of Mongolia.

The confrontations at Lake Hanka in July 1938 and at Khalkin Gol ten months later between units from the Far East Red Army and the Kuangtung Sixth Japanese Army under the command of the general Rippo Ogisu—bloody collisions reported for the time being by the international telegraph agencies as border incidents—could be considered the prelude to a possible upcoming war. Down below, in Southeast Asia, French Indochina was burning with anti-colonial riots led by a certain member, hitherto unknown, of the French Communist Party, a regular at the Montparnasse cafés and the prisons in Saigon and Bangkok, the poet and the journalist Nguyen Tat Thanh, a.k.a. Ho Chi Minh.

Lightning was tearing apart the brittle peace under the sky; Eurasia was on edge in expectation of the storm. But Hilde had no interest in all of this. Politics was the last thing on her mind.

She continued her walk further to the Quai des Grands-Augustins. After veering toward one of the bridges over the Île de la Cité, she stopped and stared at the simultaneously mighty and graceful architectural masses of Notre-Dame, with the Gothic sun above the central portal, its multicolored stained-glass windows, and its two towers.

School memories of Quasimodo, Esmeralda, and all that. . . .

Staying like this for a long time, gazing at the medieval temple while nibbling on her bread, she was startled by a mild and warm voice. "I hereby offer you the Cathedral. It's all yours!"

She hadn't noticed when he'd moved up beside her, leaning on his elbows—this young brown-haired and dark-skinned southerner with a broad peasant face and high cheekbones—perhaps a cousin of the Provençal guy from the invented bistro. In his expression and bearing there was something youthfully open and joyful.

"Thank you. You're very generous."

"Oh, it's nothing at all. Are you American?"

With her mouth full, she shook her head no.

"Swedish? No, I know—Dutch. You're Dutch, aren't you? Do you speak French at all?"

"When they were speaking French at Sans-Souci, you guys in Provence were mooing with your cows."

"So you're German, I see. But give me one more try: you don't approve of Hitler, do you?"

"Can't stand him."

"Thank God! *Röslein, Röslein rot, Röslein auf den Heiden,*" he sang, while Hilde choked on a bite of her snack.

"Are you German yourself?"

"God forbid. Just a Czech. By the way, I want to say that when Kafka was writing German in Prague, you guys in Saxony were also mooing with your cows. Do you know that there actually is such a small town—I mean, Prague? Actually I'm talking nonsense. You just occupied it, didn't you?"

"Not me. Just then I was at the movies."

"Great! We'll have dinner together and you'll tell me the story of the film."

"You're really fresh!"

"That's the way we are, we Poles."

She laughed. "Didn't you say you were Czech?"

"Is that what I said? Don't be petty now!"

"And what for example is your name?"

"Mine?" He looked at the sky and his face beamed when he remembered: "Vladek!"

"A made-up name."

"How'd you guess? And your name, Fräulein?"

"Hilde."

"Word of honor?"

"Why? Do they hide their names here?"

"Here foreigners hide everything. Name, real address, nationality, girlfriend, political beliefs. Everything! If the authorities here insist on knowing everything about you, the most important thing is to hide it. Because from their end you always expect them to pull a dirty trick. Generally, in Paris, there are a million humanoids expecting dirty tricks. American visas, permit extensions, new I.D. documents, passes, right to work, naturalization, political asylum. The biggest waiting room in Europe. And another million who've already lost hope and don't expect anything anymore. Nothing but grief! You, for example, are desperately waiting for a money transfer because you're broke."

"How'd you guess?"

"Rich tourists don't eat dry baguette. Without even butter and ham. It doesn't matter. You said you'd have dinner with me, didn't you?"

"I said nothing of the kind."

"Well, say it then."

This dark man with the face of a peasant had begun to amuse her. She laughed and said, "Of course we'll have dinner. Do I have a choice?"

He carefully took the bread from her hands and threw it in the river. "After all, let the fish also feel like German tourists in Paris."

# 11

THEY HAD DINNER SOMEWHERE in the Latin Quarter. Under the striped tent the little tables were crowded so closely together on the sidewalk that it was only with difficulty that the waiters pushed their way through them.

Hilde observed with aversion how her companion separated an oyster from its shell and lifted it to her mouth. She immediately spat out the slimy morsel and took a quick sip of wine, while her new acquaintance with the youthful face, Czech or Polish or who knows what, rolled with laughter.

It all ended with a compromise: while Hilde was staring out at people, cars, and noisy groups of tourists, she was served with a portion of impossibly bloody lamb. This time she overcame her personal gastronomic preferences and the disgust evoked by the practically raw meat, and dug into it with the fierceness of a cannibal.

Then, imperceptibly, a group began to gather. Unfamiliar people pulled up chairs to their table; new tables clustered together and new chairs clustered at the tables. Apparently this was a place for people to meet, most of them young and speaking some Slavic language or other—maybe Polish or Czech, or maybe Russian—Hilde couldn't tell one from the other. Sometimes Spanish words cropped up in their conversation; out of the Spanish linguistic whirlpool she was able to identify the names of Spanish towns—Teruel, Madrid, Alicante. . . .

She wasn't so uninformed that she didn't know what it was all about. Until not so long ago the newspapers had been teeming with names of this kind, and the German radio stations had gone into raptures describing the heroic deeds of Luftwaffe aces in dogfights with Soviet pilots—with those on both sides officially considered "volunteers." Someone now said something and then unexpectedly broke into tears, apparently the effect of alcohol. The young people were no doubt suffering, and drinking up their last *sou* before heading off to their homelands, legally or illegally.

Even so, they were all terribly kind to her, flirting with her and constantly filling her glass with wine.

The group of friends was just passing by the pont Alexander-III when Hilde, feeling truly joyful and carefree, took off her shoes, which had been hurting her after her long day of wandering, and began to walk barefoot. Her new friend, whom she called by his first name, Vladek—which he had invented—took them out of her hands and threw them in the river. She couldn't even manage a protest before he took off his own shoes too and tossed them over the parapet, exclaiming, "This is how we walk, barefoot on the burning coals of life!"

A minute later a rain of shoes began falling from the pont Alexander-III, as the desperate and beaten defenders of the Spanish Republic, who, at this hour, had lost the battle, also insisted on walking barefoot on the burning coals of life.

From the quai below, under the bridge, the bums shouted out, "Hey, you up there, are you crazy?"

"Yes, we're crazy," someone explained.

"Then come on down here with us!"

"Got any wine?"

"Got any cigarettes?"

The deal struck, a bottle of cheap wine was soon being passed from hand to hand, and under the arches of the bridge, which gave shelter to both bums and young *compañeros* just back from the civil war, little points of light played on the reflected waters of the Seine.

It was already past two when someone sang the Marseillaise. Apparently it was time to take the Bastille.

"I'm tired," shyly said Hilde, who had no more strength for revolutionary acts.

Vladek took her by the hand and the two of them slipped away unnoticed up the steep stone stairway.

"Where do you live?" he asked, once they had reached the bridge.

She looked around helplessly.

"Far away, somewhere in Ivry."

"It's too late for the last metro, and too early for the first one. Let's not spend our money on taxis. You'll sleep at my place. I live close by. It's a small attic but we'll find you a place. Or are you scared?"

"I'm not scared," Hilde said bravely.

"That's how it should be. We don't violate drunken women."

"I'm not drunk!"

"Of course you're drunk. Sober people don't throw their shoes in the water."

"You threw them."

"Is that what happened? Don't start quibbling now."

So the two of them, barefoot and holding hands, crossed the bridge, deserted at that hour.

# 12

HILDE STARTED LIVING WITH the strange young man who continued to conceal his name and nationality. But it was all right: she felt safe with him, and his carefree manner or maybe just his seemingly happy-go-lucky attitude she found contagious. She also liked it that he couldn't stand her German name and called her Röslein—Little Rose. What wasn't clear, however, was what he was living on or what he was doing in Paris. In any case he was evidently waiting for something about which she didn't even dare to inquire. As a general rule she never asked him about anything, knowing in advance that to avoid answering he'd come up with a juvenile joke.

Only once, nestled in his arms against the cold, she cautiously asked the question that she'd been keeping inside for a long time: "What language were you speaking that night in the restaurant?"

"Portuguese," he answered without hesitation.

"Nonsense! It was some kind of Slavic language."

"Really?" he said, surprised. "I've always considered it Portuguese."

She was about to express her linguistic doubts but he stopped her mouth with a kiss.

After they went to the neighborhood cinema to see Jean Gabin in *Pépé le Moko*, she remembered the weekly newsreels in which they were still unraveling the Spanish theme and asked, "You aren't an Anarchist, are you?"

"No," he replied. "A polyglot."

This was obviously not the whole truth, as she would find out much later. But by that time she had long since stopped asking questions.

It had been a week since Hilde had moved in with the young man whose name, at least for now, was Vladek. She was walking down the street, embracing with both arms a big paper bag with a loaf of bread, a bottle of wine, two raw beef steaks, and a head of lettuce. The housework was her responsibility while her young champion disappeared for hours to conduct his mysterious affairs.

She climbed the spiral stairway toward the attic. Such were the stairways in half of Paris—old, uncomfortable, and ill-kept—so she was surprised to see that the door to the small apartment was wide open. "Vladek!" she called out, but when there was no answer she cautiously looked inside.

And inside there was complete havoc: underwear thrown all over the place, drawers pulled open, papers scattered, the mattress on the floor where Vladek slept torn inside out and flung in the corner with its seaweed gutted out. Even the small suitcase she had brought with her from Germany with only enough stuff for a three-day business trip was wide open, its lining torn. It was as if a tornado had stormed through the small attic and swept up everything in its way.

Petrified, Hilde stood by the door, hugging her paper bag with groceries and unable to comprehend what could have happened.

Behind her she heard the heavy breathing of the fat concierge, who was climbing the stairs with difficulty.

"*Et voilà, mademoiselle!* Really, they're such idiots, those guys from the police. They turned everything upside down!"

"Why?"asked Hilde, almost fainting.

"You think they give you explanations? I found out in any case that the young gentleman had escaped from a camp for prisoners of war or some such place. Poor soul, he didn't even have documents. They took him away, and that was it. But I don't believe he's a thief or a criminal. So polite and nice."

There was something a little disingenuous about the way she spoke. Concierges around the world tend not to have such solidarity with tenants who have dealings with the police. She took a deep breath and then delicately added, "You will remain here or . . . ? Because today Mr. Leblanc stopped by. He said he was going to disconnect your electricity and gas. He said the young gentleman hadn't paid his rent for two months and. . . ."

"No, I'm not staying," Hilde said firmly, even though she hadn't the slightest idea where she would go. Probably back to that small hotel whose second star was flickering out. "What does the young gentleman owe?"

"A hundred and ninety-two francs, mademoiselle."

She reached into her thinning wallet and offered two bank notes. "You can keep the change."

"Thank you, mademoiselle. Excuse me, but—"

The concierge peered down the spiral staircase and when she didn't see anyone who might be eavesdropping, she asked confidentially, "Excuse me, but could the gentleman by some chance be a German spy?"

"No," answered Hilde. "A polyglot."

The door lady nodded with sympathy, full of understanding.

# 13

ALONG THE SHUSAN BOULEVARD, two parallel rickshaws were moving in dangerous proximity to each other, while the bare feet of the coolies rhythmically and sonorously slapped against the oily wet asphalt. Without losing each other, the pair skillfully maneuvered in and out of the leftward stream of other rickshaws, bicycles, and rare automobiles. Traffic in Shanghai moved to the left, the English having imposed their rules here too. In one of the rickshaws was seated, with a relaxed and important air, a young Chinese man in a white silk shantung suit, white Panama hat, and white shoes. His legs were crossed in a lordly manner, and he held a thin little fan with which he refreshed himself. The parallel rickshaw was carrying his luggage—a big leather trunk pasted according to fashion with every imaginable label from hotels and international resorts, which the owners of the luggage, as a rule, had never set foot in. This was indeed prestigious, a sign of high social status, although here, for a long time now, such a sight had ceased to impress anyone; here, every day, rich Chinese businessmen would arrive from Burma, Surinam, Macao. And visitors from the United States weren't rare either. Those who had managed to put aside a small fortune from the numerous bars, restaurants, secret and open brothels, and gambling houses of San Francisco and Los Angeles were returning to the land of their ancestors with the idea of getting up a little business on the side.

The coolie hauling the luggage kept throwing curious glances at the passenger in the other rickshaw. What times these are, dear mother! Men have become women and wave at themselves with small fragrant sandalwood fans just like some general's concubine. And women are engaged in men's affairs, hang out in bars and even go off to war. Girls of marriageable age have stopped binding their feet in wooden molds, as they used to, and tottering about like sparrows. Well, to put it squarely, it's not so bad they no longer follow this tradition! Because then when they get old and their feet turn into painful stubs, the young have to carry them to the pagoda. Don't tell me, little mister! You think I don't know what it's like to carry an old lady with feet like stubs? Didn't I carry my old mother on my back to burn a few celestial vapors in the Lunghua pagoda? But then, in those days, men were men and the Chinese, Chinese. In those days they knew that you wore white clothes for mourning and that white is the color of death. They knew it from the time they were kids! And you, little mister, are wearing white clothes as if your mother had died. And are merrily gaping at everything as if your mother hadn't died. Pfoo!

Running with broad, equal strides beside the other rickshaw and moving his lips soundlessly but vehemently, the ragged coolie thus conducted his imaginary dialogue with the important gentleman in the white silk shantung suit, while the latter waved his fan without the slightest suspicion that someone had entered into a dramatic dispute with him about modern times.

Before the intersection where Shusan crossed North Sichuan Road, the rickshaws slowed down and the coolies expertly stiffened their feet forward to check momentum. The rickshaws came to a smooth stop and lined up one behind the other beside the pavement in front of a red building of indifferent height—a ground floor with a low second story above. The house was like a borrowed Chinese word in the English language, squeezed tightly between massive stone buildings in the colonial style. But there was something dear and old-fashioned about its solitude, with the Chinese-style angles in the corners of the roof, which was covered in green enamel tiles, the miniature windows on the upper floor, and the golden-yellow tracery of the wooden grids before them, which further emphasized the sour-cherry redness of the house.

On the side there were three vertical Chinese characters in blinking neon. Along the commercial streets of Shanghai everything had to blink day and night, to sparkle, to attract attention with its varied colors. Horizontal and considerably more modest was the sign in Latin script: FOTO *AGFA*. How this would sound in Chinese remains unknown, but it was, more or less, the content of the three blinking signs.

The door was shut, and there was a notice hanging on the window in English and Chinese: "Closed." Probably lunch-break, which, during the summer, given the humid and sticky heat in this place, lasted until five, when a breeze would blow in from the sea. The dignified and oh-so-important Chinese gentleman, who had descended from the rickshaw, insistently rang the bell, and as he waited for the door to open, cast a look at the shop window. There, looking out at him with lovelorn eyes, were Robert Taylor, Greta Garbo, and Fred Astaire with Ginger Rogers, painted by hand in a manner impossible to describe, almost unrecognizable in their candy colors. Surrounding them there was a whole series of smaller individual and group portraits, specimens of the photo studio's virtuosity in giving color to anemic black and white photographs. The Chinese customers loved that: What was the point, after all, of wasting money if a photograph couldn't be more colorful than and different from life itself?!

The door opened with a melodious ring to reveal a blond giant with watery blue eyes, and a puffy face shining with sweat. His hair was disheveled, in fact his whole appearance suggested the seediness of a lost European, sunk and degraded in drunkenness—a sight not infrequent in these latitudes. Apparently the man had been dragged away from his afternoon nap, because he yawned noisily.

"Good afternoon, sir. I am bringing the merchandise," said the Chinese gentleman in English, taking off his Panama hat and bowing respectfully, but with, of course, dignified restraint.

"Ah, yes, the merchandise. . . . Well then, bring it in so we can take a look at it!"

There followed an indifferent yawn.

The passenger made a sign with his hand and the coolie who was transporting the luggage, despite his disagreement with the views of the man in white, grabbed the suitcase with servile readiness, and carried it at a run inside. His intensely obsequious steps were a demonstration of his extra-special effort and meant, naturally, to increase the tip. The passenger handed over to each of the coolies a crumpled, oily banknote and with an imperious gesture signaled them to get lost.

But getting lost was exactly what the coolies didn't do; there flared up one of those shrieking quarrels carefully refined over generations in which it was averred that the money was incredibly skimpy, that both the coolies had run as required while the *masta-masta* was not paying as required. *Masta-masta* in Chinese phonetic perception sounded like "mister" or "master" and the local barefoot coolies used it with the deep and unfaltering conviction that they spoke English. And this la-di-da *masta-masta* in turn and in almost the same squabbling register gave the news that they were sons of turtles and grandsons of frogs, greedy thieves and the lowest cheats. Then he angrily thrust into their outstretched palms one more coin. Blooming with smiles, the two bowed and disappeared with their rickshaws, smirking with satisfaction that they had outsmarted the foreigner.

# 14

THE TWO OF THEM, the newcomer and the large blond man, entered the place, which was dimly lit from the drawn cane blinds. The ceiling fan toiled diligently away like an airplane propeller, but its rotation only spun the humid hot air without cooling it down. The host absentmindedly looked up and down the street, then locked the door, checking whether the "Closed" sign was correctly positioned toward the outside. Only after that did he silently open his gigantic, shovel-like arms and embrace the Chinese man. It wasn't easy for them to kiss each other on both cheeks; the European was too tall and had to bend over, and the too-short Chinese was forced to stand on his tiptoes. But with effort and good will this ceremony was performed, with the taller man even patronizingly patting the Chinese man on the back the way you pat a good and obedient child.

"Did you check well for a tail?" asked the host. "Because those guys from the Kempeitai are ferocious and it isn't just in the toilets that they've stuck their spies."

"Kempeitai" was a word that caused almost mystical terror. This was the name of the occupier's secret police, the Japanese Gestapo—a pack of fiends as far as the outlawed anti-Japanese student movements as well as the viciously persecuted secret nationalist and communist organizations in the occupied Chinese territories were concerned.

"What do you think? Was it just by chance last night that I lost a hundred dollars at mah-jongg? What a shame! And you won't even guess who the winner was. Saneioshi-san himself."

Captain Masaki Saneioshi was the chief of the local Shanghai Kempeitai, an absolute monster who broke living bones and hung his victims head down, a cynical taker of bribes and an incurable gambler.

"Saneioshi?!"exclaimed the European. "You're crazy to put yourself right under their noses!"

"Why not? Do I smell bad? Even Saneioshi most courteously offered me his personal automobile late in the night to take me to the Park Hotel. Those boys, the ones from the Kempeitai, oh they're really quite splendid. I even think that in the very near future they're going to try to engage me as an informer. If Major Smedley from the American mission doesn't come running first."

"I'll be proud to know you," said the blond man, sourly.

"You can start being proud right now. If you help me take the suitcase upstairs."

Huffing and puffing, the big blond fellow dragged the trunk upstairs along the narrow half-lit stairway. And while the Chinese man was relaxing in the bamboo rocking chair, swinging back and forth and waving at himself with the fan, the other fellow, squatting uncomfortably and gasping, opened the trunk.

Inside there were no personal items—only a flat box of rough Siberian cedar, stamped with the black stenciled letters: *Uralmash —USSR.*

It was no easy thing to undo the tightly nailed cover until the fine packing shavings became visible. A little later on the floor were carefully spread out, as if for an exhibition, radio lamps, condensers and resistors, coils, an ammeter, a modulator, and all the other small items needed to assemble a shortwave radio.

The Chinese gentleman kept on silently rocking in his rocking chair while the other man diligently examined the parts, caressing them with tenderness or simply removing particles of dust and straw. Finally he even kissed a radio lamp, held it up high like the torch of the Statue of Liberty, and solemnly recited in a tone suggesting a great historic proclamation:

"Finally! 'Tungsram,' UX-210!"

But when he failed to receive a response to his enthusiasm, he dropped his arm and continued in a businesslike manner, "So what's the story with the decoder?"

"On the way," briefly replied the Chinese. "They had 'Ramsay' send a message via Frankfurt to the firm. The Boss has promised."

"There they promise with ease but deliver with difficulty. And did 'Ramsay' tell them about my explicit demand that the cryptographer have shorthand and a command of languages? It's an absolute necessity."

"Of course. Absolutely. Don't you also want him to have a command of classical ballet, archeology, and trigonometry? Or something on an even grander scale?"

The big man said with killing irony, "Listen, you've always impressed me with your exceptional intelligence! And there's nothing smarter in the world than a smart Chinese. If we're talking about ideas on a grand scale, he's full of them. He sacrificed one million people for the construction of the Great Wall, which in the final count didn't defend the Chinese from a Mongolian invasion, but the Mongolians from a Chinese invasion. Then when he doesn't know what to do with it, he declares it a tourist site."

The other fellow was calmly swinging back and forth, and even yawned, perhaps from the lack of oxygen.

"There's someone even smarter: a smart German. I'm not talking about you—you're a sleepy Saxon. The smart German periodically comes up with the idea of starting a terrible war, even though deep in his soul he feels he'll lose it. Like the one that'll break out within the month. But let's not quibble. Tell me, what's up?"

"What's up? At this very moment in Shanghai, do you realize how many regional radio stations there are? You won't believe it—62! At every micron of the frequency scale in the range of 39 to 60 meters, there's a station. It makes your head spin! In French, English, German, Chinese, Japanese. Even Hindi and Farsi! And if you knew the information they spew out from dusk till dawn. Where they get it, I don't know, but they can yak away freely because the signal doesn't even reach Nankin. However, twelve thousand kilometers from here, they'd give their left ball to have it. If we clue them in on the fact that you can already hear the German transmitter quite well at 15 MHz in Xinxiang, they'll positively faint. Because to keep their guys informed at the base in Tangshan, those Nazi knuckleheads openly exchange, without codes or safeguards of any kind, everything in Berlin that's supposedly top secret. *Streng Geheim.* Is it ever not! Now can you say something smart?"

By all means this was a piece of news. Or at least this was what the European was thinking as he cast a pioneer's look of wonder at the builder of Chinese walls.

At Üteborg, not far from Potsdam, there was a polygon in which, under the strictest secrecy, military-technical experiments were conducted on new fuels for airplanes, and the construction of rockets and reactive engines. It was believed, not without reason, that there would soon be developed here new and thus far undreamt-of parameters to modern war. This is also why these experiments stirred up not only an unconcealed and ever-increasing appetite for information on the part of Russian intelligence but also the curiosity of the English and the Americans too. Far ahead of the others, the German scientists had achieved innovative and substantial successes in this area and it was now turning out that what could not be learned directly from the source could be discovered at least in part in Tangshan, built and serviced by German specialists as a twin to the polygon in Üteborg.

At the same time the Kuomintang government, according to certain intercepted radio communications, had employed seventy Nazi high military advisors, with General von Seeck in charge. It also became known that the ex-Gruppenführer of the assault unit "Berlin-Brandenburg," Walter Stenes, was in charge of directing an operational group of German specialists participating in joint projects with "I.G.Farben" on the development and introduction of military-chemical substances with the code names *Weisskreuz*, *Grünkreuz*, *Blaukreuz*, and *Gelbkreuz*. To meet the needs of the nationalists from Kuomintang, another German group was developing an extremely effective light Czech weapon, which here, in its Chinese variant, received the name "Chang Djundjang"—the real name of General Chiang Kai-shek. The importance and the reputation of these Nazi specialists and advisors had considerably grown after Chiang Kai-shek's American military advisor—the renowned pilot Charles Augustus

Lindberg, who had been the first to fly nonstop over the Atlantic Ocean—openly expressed his sympathy and unreserved support for National Socialism. And it was clear even to children that Lindberg was not a political loner and that he expressed the attitudes of certain influential circles in the States. In Tokyo they closed their eyes to this activity, after the prime minister, Prince Konoe, and Kinkazu Sayonji, foreign policy advisor to the cabinet, received the personal assurance of Hitler's ambassador, Major-General Eugen Ott, that it was not directed at Japan. In this case it could constitute a potential danger only for Mao's communists and the Soviet Union. And these were good tidings that served everyone—from Tokyo and Berlin to Washington.

The Chinese gentleman, however, hardly burned with excitement at this information; as far as he was concerned, it was yesterday's news.

"So what then?" he repeated.

"The sky has to be milked! Milked, milked, like a Swiss cow! And that's why I need someone with shorthand and languages. The nineteenth century, my dear and highly respected mandarin, ended thirty-eight years ago. But at the Center they drink till the first rooster, wake up late, and sleep through the changes in the calendar. They don't give us things by hand anymore; it's indirect information that needs to be analyzed. To milk and to analyze the milking, to milk and . . . how to put it. . . ."

"To analyze the milking," said the Chinese man helpfully.

"That's it exactly. And those guys over there are waiting for everything to be served up to them like Cantonese duck. Garnished with water chestnuts!"

He gave a wave of his hand, sighed, and went to the refrigerator. There, amid the almost entirely melted ice, snugly lay a bottle of original Moskovskaya vodka. In Shanghai this drink was not actually an exotic rarity. Though rather expensive in comparison with turbid-looking rice brandy, it had been served for quite some time now in the numerous Russian restaurants and pubs set up for the long-settled high and low ranks of the defeated Far East White Army of Admiral Alexander Vassilievich Kolchak, who had been shot in Irkutsk.

The two of them raised a silent toast and in the Russian manner poured the vodka straight down their throats, swallowing it in one breath.

Shivering from the strong drink, the Chinese man wiped his lips with his palm and said, "Apropos the Cantonese duck garnished with water chestnuts, what're you doing tonight?"

In the dossier of the big blond man on file in the city headquarters of the Kempeitai at Bridge House, among other things was written: Kleinbauer, Alfred Gottfried, German national. Legal. Photo shop Agfa, North Sichuan Blvd. Tel: 24-11. Drinks. Lives alone. In Shanghai since 1929. From G. no signs of unreliability.

From the dossier it wasn't clear what "G." meant—Germany or even Gestapo. In this case it didn't much matter: for the secret services around the world at that time the two names were synonymous. Moreover it had not been noted that since 1929, the photographer in question had cooperated as a radio operator with the Shanghai correspondent of the newspaper *Frankfurter Zeitung,* a certain Doctor Richard Sorge, charming salon lion, conqueror of women's hearts, outrageous cynic, and bon vivant. This doctor had recently spread his sails in the direction of Tokyo, carrying away with him, under the code name

"Ramsay," the whole household inventory. In Shanghai a parallel structure had to remain behind and function; thus the orphaned photo shop had to be furnished again with the small kitchen utensils required for the short-wave sector.

The dossier of the Chinese gentleman was considerably clearer: Cheng Suzhin. Born Shaosin, Hangshou, 1912. University degree, English and Chinese philology. Journalist at *China Daily Post*. Tel. 27-35, Park Hotel. Well-disposed toward Japan. Reliable. Maintains friendly relations with Japanese officers and businessmen. References: Hisao Masayoshi from the Rengo Tsushin press agency.

But this dossier also had minute inaccuracies: you'd never know from it that it referred to the second carrier who during that November night had descended the ladder of the Chelyabinsk, shouldering the wooden crate with spare tractor parts from *Uralmash-USSR*. According to official information, however, at that time the *China Daily Post* correspondent Mr. Cheng Suzhin was to be found a hundred kilometers away from Shanghai, a special envoy on a long mission to Tangshan. There he was doing research on a problem crucial for China, namely the production, processing, and export of rice, with the newspaper publishing every Monday without fail his extensive and erudite reports on the subject. Mr. Hisao Masayoshi, a man above suspicion, from the Shanghai bureau of the prestigious Japanese press agency Rengo Tsushin, could testify that two days ago at the Shanghai port he had personally met his friend Suzhin, who had returned on the luxury liner *Yokohama Maru* after a long absence.

By the way, a rumor was going around that somewhere in the region of Tangshan, from whence hailed Mr. Cheng Suzhin, there was a top secret military polygon where they were testing new fuels for reactive engines, as well as chemical weapons for military use. This, however, no one could confirm or deny. In response to the professional curiosity of his Japanese friend, Suzhin had not only displayed complete ignorance on the subject, but emphasized as well his marked indifference.

# 15

FOR A MAN AND a woman to sit in a small pastry shop and dream of happiness is probably not such a bad thing, but the camp prisoners in Dachau were sick to death of this particular tango, because it was the favorite song of Scharführer S.S. Hansi Steinbrenner, who later, in survivors' memoirs, was called "The Terror of Dachau." With this "small pastry shop" the pitiful orchestra, composed mainly of the remnants of the Dresden Philharmonic, accompanied to work every morning exactly at seven the Strafkompanie Sieben—the terrible Seventh Correctional Unit.

To which Hansi would merrily hum the song, conducting it himself with his billy-club, by means of which he would, from time to time, and with a precise sense of rhythm, rain down blows on the back of whoever was falling behind:

*In einer kleinen Konditorei*
*Da saßen wir zwei*
*Und träumten vom Glück. . . .*[1]

Dachau was a small, insignificant town in Upper Bavaria with about twenty thousand residents—small merchants, a few brew-

---

[1]"In a small pastry shop/We two were sitting/Dreaming of happiness."

ers and landowners, and workers in the paper industry. There was nothing remarkable about it and no one in the world would have known the least thing about its existence if on March 22, 1933, less than three months after Hitler became Chancellor of the Reich, there hadn't opened the first Nazi concentration camp. At this point it was quite primitive, with an undeveloped system of internal operations, and an unclear profile, still miles away from its future as a death factory. In comparison to Auschwitz, Maidanek, and Treblinka—still unborn in the historic imagination of National Socialism—with their millions annihilated, Dachau's modest career started quietly, almost imperceptibly. On the last day of its existence, twelve years later, on April 29, 1945, when the American tanks swept in, it was able to chalk up to its credit only sixty-six thousand dead.

But this was a figure for the future. For the time being the camp was a penal institution to which were sent, quite randomly and according to the personal whims and pretexts of this or that higher-up, some of those who couldn't be prosecuted by the regular courts for the crime of being a Jew, social democrat, communist, or crook who, having served his time, was nevertheless unworthy of being integrated into the new German society.

All of this was pondered a hundred times over but never fully understood by the violinist Theodore Weissberg, not to mention that, strictly speaking, he had never felt himself to be, in the full sense of the word, a Jew. Like the majority of German intellectuals of Jewish origin at that time, he had visited the synagogue only for the weddings of his relatives' or colleagues' children. For exactly the same reason he had also happened to attend Evangelical or Catholic rituals. His mother tongue was German, and he was a complete and, one could even say, perfect product of German civilization who in fact rarely remembered that he was a Jew. Until he was reminded of it.

At this point he was privileged: instead of heavy slave labor on highway construction, he got to play twice a day about the small pastry shop and the couple who dream of happiness: once in the morning, when it was time to go to work in obligatory lockstep, and once again twelve hours later, when the camp prisoners returned, barely dragging their feet with exhaustion. The rest of the time he had to carry buckets of water from the barracks to the work site or just ramble around the camp, according to orders.

Theodore Weissberg was a fragile man, delicate and considerate toward everyone. From his words and behavior you could tell that he'd received a good bourgeois upbringing, at home, in the family of a very successful lawyer. The rough and sometimes quite spicy jokes of the camp prisoners—in many cases workers, small craftsmen, miners from the trade unions, and other modest existences—stung him; he withdrew into himself and was looked upon by his comrades in fortune as a conceited intellectual. But it wasn't that the violin player was conceited—far from it. It was simply that he wasn't good for anything besides that which completely possessed him and that which he in turn possessed to perfection: music.

Except for his colleagues in the little camp orchestra, with whom he fully shared feelings of mutual solidarity, there was only one other person toward whom Theodore felt disposed to be friendly and trusting, and even grateful: Shlomo Finkelstein. This was a short-legged little guy, almost a dwarf, fat and bald, of distant Galician origin, who had done nominal time for petty crimes—pickpocketing, selling contraband cigarettes, and making too frequent visits to department stores, where he would forget to pay for the merchandise stuffed in the lining of his excessively long coat. He would tell Jewish jokes with a colorful Jewish accent, and this took no special effort on his part; it was how he spoke anyway. The camp prisoners would oftentimes make him the target of their jokes and laugh at him, but instead of being offended, he would laugh with everyone else at both his height and his way of speaking. So this Shlomo Finkelstein, a semi-literate petty crook, as paradoxical as it may sound, became, with his simple goodheartedness and readiness to do any kind of favor, the confidant of the aristocratic violinist, helping him wash the oily bucket, sweep out the sleeping quarters, or carry the impossible thirty-kilogram bags of potatoes from the truck to the kitchen. Camp inmates usually hate the guy whom the bosses love, and vice versa, but Shlomo was well regarded by both sides—the object of amusement, the court jester, to whom everything was forgiven in advance.

The days and the months flowed by heavily and monotonously, with no news from Elisabeth (in contrast to normal prisons with legal regulations, here correspondence was forbidden), and the hour-long morning and evening roll-calls, always with the small three-times cursed pastry shop and the constantly perfected art of not stirring up in Hansi Steinbrenner the desire to hit you on the back with his club to the exact rhythm of the tango.

This, by the way, was what happened to the flautist Simon Zinner, a good but temperamental musician, who in the past had typically performed Mozart's flute and piano works in luxurious venues. One time this Zinner simply couldn't stand the scene with the rhythmical blows of the club on the back of a former miner so ill with silicosis he could barely stand on his feet. Putting aside his flute, he grabbed the club with his strong arms and let go on Hansi himself. Opening his eyes wide, this fellow couldn't believe at first what was happening, couldn't even react immediately and defend his dignity as a big shot. But then he found a way—and how!

The Seventh Correctional Unit was set out until midnight without water or dinner on the beaten-down parade ground. Exactly at midnight, Hansi Steinbrenner, with the same club, and to the rhythm of the tango that the orchestra hadn't once stopped playing for the last five hours, smashed an iron beam down on the fingers of the flautist Simon Zinner and turned them into a bloody pulp.

Theodore Weissberg vomited and fainted.

When he came to himself with the help of the generous Shlomo, who had carried him to the bunks in the small barrack, the violinist for a long time couldn't rid himself of the feeling of guilt that he'd been playing music while that beast had been shattering his colleague's fingers.

One morning at the beginning of July, while the orchestra was accompanying the camp prisoners to work, someone patted Theodore on the shoulder. The violinist was startled and his bow drew a shrieking falsetto from the strings. Behind his back stood Hansi, who, in an unexpectedly friendly tone, said, "It that you, Weissberg? Don't jump; they're not going to butcher you. Go to the commandant's office. On the double! And you others—keep at it! The music . . . more upbeat—this isn't a funeral! Come on, shitheads, left-right! Left-right! . . . *In einer Konditorei . . . Da saßen wir zwei . . . Und träumten vom Glück. . . .*"

He sang and was actually doing the conducting himself while Theodore, perplexed and haunted by vague fears, made his away across the parade ground toward the office of the Dachau high command.

# 16

SOUNDS OF A PIANO flowed through the spacious living room, which was bathed in mild light. Elisabeth was playing quietly for herself. The furniture, the heavy carpets, the tall Chinese vases, the crystal, the silver candelabra—everything in this home spoke of wealth that had been accumulated not exactly since yesterday. And there was something pretentious, perhaps bourgeois in a German sort of way, about this pedantic, even fussy order, in which there wasn't a single crease in the tablecloth, or a magazine accidentally dropped on the carpet, or an open, unfinished book on the sofa, or a soiled ashtray, or folds falling unevenly in the curtains.

She failed to notice Theodore Weissberg, who, entering behind her back, would, in other circumstances, have looked a bit ridiculous—face long unshaven, hair cropped short, dressed in a rumpled and unbuttoned concert tuxedo in which once upon a time they had arrested him, a sleeve torn in God knows what kind of police van or regional detention center. Appearing this way he looked more like a rich bonvivant, a drunken habitué of nightspots, who has finally decided to return to the family hearth, rather than a camp inmate just liberated from Dachau.

Leaning against the arched portal, Theodore silently listened to the piano.

His wife, suddenly sensing someone's presence in the room, stopped playing, turned around, and gave out a muffled cry. "My God!"

She leapt up and threw herself upon her husband, though he delicately pushed her away. "Don't touch me, darling. First, every stitch of clothing has to go into the incinerator, and me—into the bathtub. If you had any idea what a lice-ridden hell I've come from!"

With her palm, Elisabeth tenderly stroked his cheek.

"My darling, my poor darling!"

Theodore in turn silently stroked her face with the back of his hand.

And now, here he is—the virtuoso Theodore Weissberg: unrecognizable. Freshly bathed and shaved, wrapped in a fluffy white bathrobe, with slippers on his bare feet, he poured champagne into two crystal glasses.

"To your health, my dear. To you! For having held up. And for this unexpected happy ending."

She gazed at him with sad amazement, took barely a sip from the glass, and then intently looked at him again with her big green eyes.

"Is that what you think? Listen, Theodore, listen, my darling nitwit. Listen to me: I knocked on certain doors and the only thing I realized was that nothing has come to a happy ending. In fact it hasn't even begun yet. We've got to get out of here. As soon as possible, while it's still possible!"

Theodore laughed. "My brave little lead soldier! To leave Germany, our Germany, because of a random gang of misfits who'll fall out of power tomorrow? Never!"

Elisabeth swayed desperately, sprang to her feet, took a few steps, and again fell back into the armchair. She nervously lit a cigarette and only after that said, "My God, you haven't understood a thing! What's happening here is not the casual whim of a dozen Munich drunks; it's going to last a long time, Theodore. This is a well thought-out government policy."

"I am a violinist, not a politician."

"They don't give a hoot if you're a violinist. In fact they couldn't care less!"

"Well, I don't care about them! And apart from that, what about your contracts? A day will come when the misunderstanding with my musicians will be all straightened out and they'll be released. Then we'll have to reconstitute the orchestra. To leave it after building it up for so many years? And our colleagues and friends and this home? To leave everything behind? And run away. . . . Where?"

Elisabeth deeply inhaled the smoke from her cigarette, waving it aside with an abrupt movement of her hand. "Contracts . . . colleagues . . . home. . . . Our world has collapsed, Theodore. You've got to understand this. Now their world is taking over."

"I asked you, where to run *to*? Where, for the love of God? I'm a Jew."

"So I've heard—somewhere else, in fact, at a very prestigious place. And?"

"Only, my dear, that no one is giving entry visas to German Jews. Haven't you heard? So get it out of your head. All harbors are closed to us. All!"

"Not all. There is one still open. The last one, they told me: Shanghai."

Theodore opened his mouth, but said nothing. Only with difficulty did he realize what he was being told. "You're crazy," he said finally, almost stuttering. "Shanghai? Is that what you said? You really *have* lost your mind! Shanghai, at the end of the world? And exactly at this moment when, in the camp, I had the distinct feeling that someone had placed a sheltering hand over me? No, no, really—someone was silently protecting me, I could feel it every day. Why did they release me before the others? I'm asking you—why? I don't get it, but they even returned my violin to me, and the wallet with the money, and the wedding ring. They almost apologized for the misunderstanding! By the way, where is *your* ring?"

Elisabeth looked at her hand, as if seeing it for the first time. "Oh yes, my ring. I lost it, I think," she said indifferently.

Theodore gave his wife a peculiar, intense look, a deep vertical wrinkle appearing between his furrowing eyebrows and a blue vein cutting through his high pale forehead. Elisabeth's heart froze with horror at the very thought that some suspicion had caused this strange anxiety in her husband. But he took her hand and gently touched it with his lips.

"Losing a ring has no particular significance," he said finally. "A possession like any other. But it suggests something, perhaps. I'm superstitious, you know. I believe in the signs of destiny. Elisabeth, my dear. Listen and understand me correctly. If I'm forced . . . yes, that's it exactly: I don't want it, but if I'm forced to look to distant roads for survival, you're not obliged to follow me. I don't have the right to ask this from you. You are German; without me your life would probably turn out differently. Maybe more happily. If I'm forced to leave . . . at least for now . . . at least till this complete idiocy goes away, you must stay here. As a good spirit—in this country, on this street, in this home. This makes sense. It's true that, for me, it will be the same as splitting away a part of myself—my right hand, my heart . . . but I do not have the right to deny you a normal life, a career. . . . To expose you to danger. You are under no obligation to endure the ordeals of my tribe. . . . To carry someone else's cross. Are you listening to me, Elisabeth?"

She didn't answer immediately, but eventually drew her gaze away from the point where she had fixed it, as if her thoughts were not here, but infinitely far away.

"Yes, I'm listening to you. And listening very carefully. You haven't read the Bible. Of course, you haven't. You know, it's not so bad for a person to take a look at it now and again. Now listen to me, my dear."

She reached out and from the table took up a handsome volume, which was nevertheless incredibly thin, probably because of the special paper it had been printed on, the pride of Leipzig publishing. Apparently she had consulted it recently, because between its pages a tram ticket had been inserted.

She opened the book exactly there, at the ticket. Glancing through the text, she found the place she wanted and calmly read: And Ruth said, Entreat me not to leave thee, *or* to return from following after thee: for whither thou goest, I will go; and where thou lodgest, I will lodge: thy people shall be my people, and thy God my God: Where thou diest, will I die, and there will I be buried: the Lord do so to me, and more also, if *ought* but death part thee and me.

She read this with an even voice, but tears streamed down her cheeks.

# 17

THE UNPREPOSSESSING CORRIDOR, WITH its cold neon light, was jammed with women—young and old, well and badly dressed, bearing the signature of withering and fallen society ladies or girls from the lower classes. Hung throughout the corridor, photographs of film stars and framed posters advertising popular French films spoke colorfully of the long and glorious history of the movie studio.

Hilde was leaning against the wall and waiting, aloof from the surrounding din. Her thoughts kept going back to Vladek. This rambunctious young man had disappeared without leaving a message, a sign, or a trace. He had probably been deported—the usual procedure in such cases. But where to? Which country? Vladek, speaking some Slavic language, which he considered—would you believe it?!—Portuguese!

Finally the door at the end opened, a man in a shirt and wide black suspenders made way for a weeping girl to step outside, took the cigar out of his mouth, and nervously shouted to the people standing in the corridor:

"Hey there—silence! This isn't a bazaar! Silence! Next!"

When the door closed, those who'd been waiting gathered around the one who'd just come out.

"What are they asking for? What are the requirements?"

"It's all bullshit. They don't know themselves what they want. Don't waste your time with these faggots!"

In order to reach the holy of holies, you had to make your way through unimaginable piles of props, after which you went through the wide-open iron door of a soundstage. There, under the dim service light, the decorative remnants of something exotic, perhaps the eastern palace of a padishah, were still enjoying the last memories of a brief film career, the palm trees dusty and, in places, slumped over, and the vases made of pressed cardboard. In the corner, quite out of keeping with the atmosphere, there was a white piano with a darkened and peeling veneer—a pensioned-off member of a glittering revue—and beside it sat the piano player, very thin and gaunt, looking for all the world like an alcoholic, or someone who has recently recovered from a severe illness.

The young woman who had just entered, a stout French peasant, advanced shyly, looking around with both fear and confusion at this temple of celluloid illusion, with its rows of turned-off projectors disappearing into the upper darkness. Wrapped in tobacco smoke, the man with the cigar looked critically at the newcomer from head to toe. He poured himself a considerable quantity of brandy in a water glass, took a swig, set down the glass on the piano, and only then asked:

"What kind of work have you been doing up till now?"

"I'm from Colombes. I used to work in a bistro."

"You've come to the wrong address, little one. The laundry is just around the corner."

"But I can sing—"

The man nervously waved his hand. "Wonderful. You'll sing in the laundry. Next!"

The next was Hilde. She calmly approached; dusty soundstages were not news to her, no different, in fact, from the UFA studios, the only exception being that in France, which had raised up freedom as one of the three main pillars of society, the strict order not to smoke, fanatically observed in Babelsberg—despite the importance with which the big shots with cigars regarded themselves—was here just a cordial suggestion. Here, it wasn't only the studio chief but even the fireman on duty who under the "No Smoking" sign concealed a lit cigarette in his cupped hand.

Alain Conti—this was the name of the producer—gave her an indelicate once-over and what he saw obviously satisfied him completely. Nevertheless, he rudely asked:

"Do you also come from Colombes?"

"No, Berlin."

"Ah, well, then, a Boche. And you've probably played at the Komische Oper with Max Reinhardt."

She caught the sarcasm but calmly replied:

"If I was working for Reinhardt I wouldn't be in your lousy studio."

At that, Alain Conti whistled and exchanged a smiling glance with the pianist.

"Okay, hold your horses. Here every German immigrant tells tales about his glorious past, every Russian peasant was a count or a first cousin of Pushkin's, and it's us who're the bumpkins. Do you sing, do you do a bit of ballet?"

"Haven't tried."

"And I haven't tried to fly an airplane. Okay, it means no. Pull up your skirt. Higher. Higher. I said—higher!"

This time Hilde blew a fuse.

"You should have announced in the newspaper you were looking for whores, not extras."

She angrily grabbed her bag, but the man clutched her by the hand.

"Wait, where're you going? Move over there and come back!"

"Where?"

This time Conti in his turn screamed at her:

"I said 'over there'—are you deaf?"

"Listen, mister! I came here voluntarily and I don't intend to listen to the screams of hysterical faggots!"

The man put his cigar straight on top of the piano, with the lit end pointing outward, something he was probably in the habit of doing, because the spot was brown and burnt; then he patted the piano player:

"Hey, did you hear what side Alain Conti plays for? Well now, *mein gnädiges Fräulein,* we'll have to prove the contrary. Otherwise I don't see anything to condemn here—after all, faggots are human beings too. And now you, the Hungarian, what do you have to say about it?"

The pianist murmured something unintelligible and drew a finger along the keyboard from one end to the other.

Conti pulled the bag out of Hilde's hands and like a strict teacher issued commands:

"Okay, enough empty talk. Now, do you see that palm tree over there? Walk up to it and come back."

She hesitated, then followed the order.

"Okay. Are your papers in order? Do you have a valid visa?"

"Yes, at home."

"Work permit for France?"

"Of course," she lied.

"Fine. Leave your name with the secretary. Monday morning, eight sharp, no fooling around, don't be late. We're shooting a musical comedy and have to rehearse. Twenty-five francs a day, to start. So you're a Boche. What's your name?"

"Well, you just said it: Boche!" burst out Hilde.

"Calm down. You're probably new in this fucking town and don't know that here every German is Boche, every Russian—Ivan, and every American—Johnny."

"And every Frenchman?" she challenged him.

For the first time, in his inimitable Hungarian accent, the pianist spoke:

"Every Frenchman is a bastard."

"Exactly right," agreed Alain Conti. "A bastard and a fag."

# 18

IT WAS AN UNIMPORTANT musical comedy, the set a cute little square in the center of which had been erected a monument for war heroes. It had a fountain and gaily colored awnings over the cafes; naughty maids; and amorous, aging bonvivants. There, around the fountain and the monument, and under the glow of the projectors, the entire population was singing and dancing their heads off more or less in the style of those Austrian film operettas with Jan Kipura and Marika Rökk. This movie project seemed even more insignificant to those who knew that in the adjacent soundstage Jean Renoir was shooting *The Rules of the Game*, that artistic premonition of the rising world catastrophe.

And in fact, the sands from the hourglass of History were already measuring out the last days of peace in Europe, though here, under the cardboard plane trees, the merry, happy inhabitants of the village square were still singing and dancing their carefree carmagnole.

It was late at night when they finished shooting a joyous crowd scene, and Hilde, makeup removed, again dressed in her only suit, the one she'd arrived in from Germany, almost bumped into Alain Conti, commander in chief of the army of extras.

Embracing her by the waist, he drew her to himself, enveloping her in the smoke from his cigar.

"Listen. You're a magnificent kid who'll go far. What're you doing tonight?"

"First, take your hand off my ass."

"Sorry, it was unintentional. So, what are you doing?"

"In what sense?"

"I know a little place in the Porte de Lilas where you can get genuine calvados from Normandy. How about it?"

"I hate to disappoint you, boss, but what I'm doing tonight has nothing to do with what you're doing tonight in that little bistro in the Porte de Lilas."

"Don't forget. I have to prove to you I'm not a faggot."

"I'll take your word for it. And, frankly, you're not my type."

"Okay, kitten. No problem. Ciao!"

"Ciao, boss!"

And Hilde Braun dashed outside.

In the street young extras and bit players were merrily grabbing the arms of their waiting boyfriends while engines were revving up, headlights were turning on, and car doors were slamming shut.

The Paris night was coming to life.

Hilde had just taken a quiet side street toward the metro when, behind her back, she heard footsteps. She quickened her pace, but someone caught up with her and grabbed her by the elbow. Thinking this was Alain Conti again, she stopped and angrily shook her arm free.

But what she saw was a completely unfamiliar type, dark and mustached, possibly a Corsican or Algerian, who looked at her with a silent grin.

"I've fallen for you, you know," he said, finally. "I've been following you for three days."

"Don't you dare touch me!"

"So we're very untouchable, are we! But why, little one? I just wanted to invite you for some absinthe with my friends."

"This must be my lucky night for invitations! Well, you know where you can shove your absinthe, don't you?"

Hilde turned to go, but the stranger calmly took hold of her shoulder and swung her around. She was trying to extricate herself from his hands when, from the darkness of the entrance next door, someone stepped out and silently blocked her way.

Frightened, she looked around: on the opposite side of the street two more men, leaning against the wall, were calmly smoking and keeping an eye on the situation.

"So it's shove the absinthe, is it?" said the mustached man, laughing. "And now the dear blonde miss will learn once and for all who shoves what and where it goes!"

At this instant someone grabbed Hilde under her arm and dragged her forward. This was Alain Conti's pianist, who said calmly, with the same indescribable Hungarian accent, "Fuck off! The girl's with me."

"Where'd *he* come from?"

At this point, it looked as if an unequal struggle of two-against-one was inevitable. Under the gaslight in the street the blade of a Spanish jackknife flashed in the hands of the guy with the mustache.

One of the observers on the opposite side of the street said to his companion, "That's Conti's pianist, the Hungarian. Let's get lost—the police are coming."

There was a quiet whistle, and then, as if on orders, the strangers dispersed. The two policemen slowly approached. "Any problems?" one of them asked.

"Everything's fine, boys. Mademoiselle Boche . . . excuse me, I don't know your name, come with me, don't be afraid."

The policemen kept going till they reached the end of the street, then turned the corner, alongside the tall windowless building—probably a soundstage.

The man and the woman walked with rapid steps in order to get out of the dark street, and Hilde twice glanced furtively around to see if they were being trailed.

"Don't look; just walk. For them it's enough to know you're scared."

"I'm not the scared type."

The Hungarian coldly laughed.

"That's because you don't know what was in store for you. You're neither the first nor the last. These pimps were going to rape you, beat you, and stuff you with drugs until you softened up. Then when you forgot even your mother's name, they'd put you to work for them. But you don't have to worry. They're not going to bug you again, now that they know you're one of Conti's girls. He doesn't forgive—he'll pluck their pricks like meadow daisies."

This he pronounced with his usual wooden Hungarian accent. Most probably Attila the Hun, who was in all likelihood an ancestor of the Hungarian pianist, had spoken better French.

They stopped at the metro entrance. She was silent for a moment, then decisively offered her hand.

"Thank you. Good night."

"I'll see you home. It's early for me anyway."

"You look like a bright guy who gets things right away. If you're coming on to me, I hope you understand you'll only be wasting your time."

The Hun gave a laugh.

"A new friendship is never a waste of time. And so you won't have problems with your conscience, I insist on telling you that the other day you were close to the truth. Not completely but almost. It isn't Conti who plays for the other side, but me. My name the Hungarian way is Keleti Istvan, and the French way—Istvan Keleti. So with me everything is upside down. Does this reassure you a little? Come on, sister, I'll buy you a beer, because I've been sober much too long."

# 19

THUS BEGAN THE FRIENDSHIP between two souls lost in the big foreign city. Keleti Istvan or Istvan Keleti, called for convenience "The Hungarian" at the movie studio, had been in the recent past a pianist in a nightclub somewhere in Budapest. There he got mixed up in some shady affair with morphine, managed to get out in the nick of time, and tried to pass for a political refugee. In spite of suspicions on the part of the Paris police regarding Mr. Keleti's motives, the traditional liking of the French toward the *czardas* created a certain disposition in his favor, and he received a one-year work permit.

That had taken place the year before, and the metronome had not stopped ticking off the flow of time, for at least half of which he was soused, though this was not the business of the police.

The two of them were sitting in the cellar of a small bistro, almost empty at this late hour, and drinking the promised beer. In fact the third by now.

"And so, Boche, these idiots deny you an extension," said the Hungarian. "For me, well, okay, I get it—a dark guy from the Hungarian Puszta. A queer, a drunk, and a drug addict. But you, who could only improve the degenerating French nation!

And you say you're a Jew. A Jew who doesn't receive the right of asylum in the dear cradle of revolution and human rights!"

"The cute little letter I got from the cradle consisted of two lines: '*Regrettons beaucoup*, but if you please, collect your stuff and get lost!' At the American consulate they told me they understood my situation but that I have to have patience. Patience I've got, but what I don't have is time or money. Soon I won't even have a place to sleep. The little hotel where I'm staying is managing to swallow up the last of my savings."

The Hungarian nodded in sympathy, scratched the back of his head, and finally said:

"Well, sister, look at it this way. If you're not too hoity-toity, you can live at my place. It's nothing special, but still! Let's drink to the immigrants of Europe. And to Europe, which doesn't give a damn about immigrants."

He downed his beer, looked at Hilde, and caressed her hand.

"What matters most is not to lose heart—sometimes even the American dream comes true. And now, sister, shall we knock back something harder?"

They did as the Hungarian suggested. Hilde didn't remember whether the exercise with "something harder" repeated itself, because he dragged her with difficulty back to his small apartment somewhere close to Les Halles—a small box with a curtain hiding the sink. And with a common toilet between the floors, an old French invention, comparable in the suffering that it inflicted on the inhabitants every morning to that other emanation of the spirit of French inventiveness, the guillotine.

Homosexuals are often tender souls. She woke up in his bed while he was still sleeping, curled up into four parts within the sagging armchair he'd dragged home from some unknown garbage dump. Next to him sat an open metallic box similar to the ones in which our grandmothers once upon a time used to keep their snuff. This one, however, did not contain snuff, but rather a white powder.

He, the Hungarian, was the one who introduced her to that strange doctor, Hiroshi Okura. The Japanese man had graduated in medicine from Harvard and was now a specialist in the Paris hospital of the Jesuit order St. Anne. During his off-duty hours he had agreed to be a consultant at the movie studio, where the exiled German director Georg Pabst was wrapping up *Shanghai Drama*. There, in the secret studio buffets, and the sometimes endless night breaks to rearrange the lighting, the lonely Doctor Okura had become close to the Hungarian pianist.

He was an educated man, in the true sense of the word a Europeanized Japanese; from his Asian background what had survived were his delicacy and his exquisite, sometimes irritating politeness.

One time, when leaving the studio with her new Hungarian friend, Hilde discovered Okura waiting for her downstairs at the exit, where he presented her with an enormous bouquet of tea roses. "Won't this bankrupt you, this huge quantity of roses?" Hilde said, gasping.

"For me it's just a small pleasure."

"Imagine what large ones would be like! Thank you, Mr. . . ."

"Hiroshi. Doctor Hiroshi Okura. My friend—" The Hungarian hurried to introduce him.

"Thank you. You really are very kind, Doctor Okura."

The Japanese man, who was rather short, looked a little comic in his dignified top hat and white silk scarf, for which top hats and scarves his compatriots in general had a peculiar passion. The top hats most probably had the purpose of making their wearers taller or else seemed a demonstration of fashionable openness to the Western world. As to the Japanese attachment to white silk scarves, it could be explained only by the painful addiction of the Japanese to American films about drunken billionaires.

The Japanese man hesitated before saying:

"If I may be so bold, would you do me the honor of having dinner with me? Are you familiar with Japanese cuisine? Please, do not refuse me. Our mutual Hungarian friend, I hope, will accompany us."

"Absolutely not! I know this Japanese number of yours with the cold raw fish and the warm sake!" Istvan Keleti categorically objected. "Don't be offended, doctor, but only someone who has grown up with Hungarian cuisine can know the extent to which yours is foreign to me. And I also have an appointment with friends." But since Hilde was showing obvious signs of hesitation, he added, "Go on, say yes, girl. You have no idea how stubborn the Japanese are once they get an idea into their heads. Especially if it's war or dinner at a Japanese restaurant."

Finally Hilde surrendered herself to the insistent pleas of this small man with round thick glasses through which his eyes always looked a bit surprised.

# 20

FOR THE FIRST TIME in her life she found herself in a Japanese restaurant, where everything was surprising and new to her: the kneeling geisha, who offered hot fluffy hand towels, and another, also with her legs folded under, who poured tea and handed over the steaming cup with both hands, like a priestess at a sacred ritual. Then the sticks of red wood that Dr. Hiroshi Okura was teaching her how to use, and the ceremonial delicacy with which he poured warm sake from a miniature jug.

She drank, choking and laughing with teary eyes. Like a good student, she would look at the hands of the Japanese doctor and get upset when she dropped a piece of vegetable or fish from the two damned sticks whose tips always managed to miss each other.

In a separate space, a white, astonishingly immaculate box of lacquered wood and rice paper, with soft light flowing in from everywhere, they sat on silk pillows, with their stocking-feet hanging down into a deep niche under the table, probably an adjustment for Europeans unused to eating on their knees.

"You have never been to Japan?" he asked

She silently shook her head: no, she hadn't.

"Probably everything here is very foreign to you."

"I have the feeling that I'm in some made-up, non-existent world of light. Maybe it's the warm drink."

"Sake."

"Maybe, but I feel like I'm floating in a thin mist, carried by white winds. . . ."

"Good for you! You have embraced Japanese style!" enthusiastically exclaimed Hiroshi. "'Carried by white winds.' This is so Japanese!"

"Really? Say something in Japanese."

Hiroshi Okura looked at her with his nearsighted eyes through his thick round glasses. He thought for awhile, then he said something smooth, beautiful-sounding, but incomprehensible.

"What does that mean?"

The Japanese man took his eyes off Hilde and, looking intently at the cup of sake, spoke quietly, as if reading its bottom:

"Your hand was caressing me—like a white wind. This was a dream and it passed—like a white wind. . . . Lonely, weeping in the branches is—the white wind."

"It's very beautiful. Who's the author?"

Hiroshi shyly smiled. "I made it up just now."

"I've heard that doctors often become poets."

"Sad poets. But often poets are doctors. For ailing souls."

"Aren't you too timid and modest? You remind me of a village teacher. Tell me about yourself."

Doctor Okura shrugged his shoulders. "A village teacher? . . . Yes, perhaps. I am a wind from a distant sea. A Japanese who studied in America, practicing in Paris. Something like a fruitless tree, planted in a foreign soil. I have parents in Okinawa. My father is also a doctor, and he also studied here in France. I intend to work at his clinic. He is a remarkable man, my father—Professor Santoku Okura. He insisted that I specialize here in France, because he believes in Voltaire and Auguste Renoir, and not in military doctrines. And now it's your turn. I don't even know your name."

"Braun. Hilde Braun. I'm from Germany."

"And will you stay in Paris? Or are you going back to your country?"

"No, I'm not staying, and I'm not going back either."

"Then, you are on the road to . . . where?"

"To nowhere."

The Japanese looked at her, expecting her to continue. But she stubbornly remained silent. Finally he said:

"Well then—a traveler to nowhere. We might all be going in the same direction. And then?"

"That's it. The rest is just details in the landscape."

He raised the small porcelain cup of sake. "*Kampei*, Hilde-*san*. To your health!"

"*Kampei*, Hiroshi-*san*. To yours too."

# 21

THOUGH IMPRACTICAL BY NATURE and deeply engrossed in music, Theodore Weissberg was well aware of the enormous, virtually impossible task with which the German Jews had been saddled within the new borders of the Third Reich: the closer the world inched toward a military solution to its problems, the more difficult it was becoming to receive a visa for even a temporary sojourn in neighboring countries. Sensing the growing tragedy, many, mostly from the scientific, artistic, and political elites, managed to sneak out of Germany just in the nick of time, before the doors of foreign consulates, both Western and Soviet, slammed in their faces. But there were countless more of those naive souls who, until the drunken insanity of Krystallnacht, somehow thought that Nazism, with its unprecedented brutality, wouldn't last.

Even more complicated was the situation of those small existences that constituted the vast majority—ordinary people who from the outset had neither relatives abroad who could help nor the means or courage to break with their customary routine and take the fateful step of leaving everything behind. They fearfully abandoned themselves to the waves of chance, with the fragile hope that since the question concerned so many people, sooner or later a way out of the situation would be found.

Indeed, the way out was found, later, but it was hardly the one that people had been hoping for. The Nazis discovered it and called it "The Final Solution to the Jewish Problem." As yet it didn't mean holocaust, gas chambers, and crematoria. Far from it—the decision made at Wannsee for the physical extermination of the Jews in Europe was still in the bright future. For now the Gestapo was actually encouraging resettlement, and the international Jewish organizations even complained about it, since their funds for the support of an unlimited wave of refugees were rapidly running out. It became public knowledge that there were unofficial attempts to convince the French government to donate the island of Madagascar as a place to settle the German Jews. It was, however, the West that stood up against such an idea. There they were well informed about Stalin's failed efforts to create the artificial Jewish country Birobidjan in the Far East: a bunch of marshy territories along the banks of the Amur that, sooner or later, could be turned into the world's largest concentration camp for Jews.

Nor was it just the West that rejected such solutions. After unsuccessful attempts to sway Nazi circles in Germany itself, prominent Shanghai finance magnates from the world of the Jewish Baghdadi—Sir Elias Ezdra and Sir Victor Haim—exercised considerable influence over the Japanese authorities to limit and in the foreseeable future to block the flow of Jews from Europe to China, Manchuria, and Korea. They insistently let the Japanese believe that they would in no way oppose such restrictions—indeed, just the opposite: Tokyo would receive understanding and support for measures of this kind. Much later, when the world was apprised of the hidden meaning behind the geographical names Dachau, Mauthausen, Maidanek, Auschwitz, and Treblinka, certain people confusedly tried to purge their memories of this pressure that had been put on the Japanese authorities.

And so, when the saving necessity of leaving Nazi Germany at all costs and in the face of whatever risks became for everyone a deep realization as well as a goal for survival, it was already late.

Then a new joke went around:

Asked by foreign journalists about the ultimate end of his policy, Hitler declared that it was to expel all the Jews from Germany, as well as the Italian tenor from the Opera.

"Why the tenor?" asked the *Figaro* correspondent.

"It's just what I thought," Hitler sighed with relief, "the international public won't react at all to the expulsion of the Jews!"

This some of the sons of Israel were to feel on their own backs.

The case of the *Saint Louis* was not the only one, but it will do. With a nod of permission from the Nazi authorities, for whom the original version of the "Final Solution" simply meant the expulsion of all Jews from the borders of the Reich, and a good deal more only a little later on, when those borders were supposed to be commensurate with the borders of Europe itself, the ship raised its anchor in Hamburg and sailed off to Cuba, crammed with refugees, including the holds. The local Cuban authorities refused to allow it passage even into the harbor of Havana, and after two weeks of stubborn attempts the ship was forced to leave the territorial waters of the Caribbean island and to continue its journey to the United States. There, pressured by interested parties lobbying the Senate, President Roosevelt, to whom the refugees had addressed a desperate radiogram, for a long time remained deaf to their pleas. No small role was played in the making of his decision by messages sent on the part of several American-Jewish organizations, which drew the president's attention to the unfairness that would result should competition develop in certain traditional activities of theirs, particularly after the heavy trauma endured by the American economy during the Great Depression, which had only recently subsided. They warned him as well about the danger posed by the German Jews, many of whom held leftist beliefs, in the possible importation of the contagious disease of communism. Mr. Goldsmith, owner of a small clothing factory in Detroit, had nothing against his fellow tribesman, the clothing manufacturer Herr Goldschmidt from Cologne; he had even signed a petition for the defense of German Jews. But he had no desire to see them on American soil as competitors for his own business, for whose well-being three generations of Goldsmiths had sweated and toiled. The motives of the American embassy in Germany were no doubt quite similar, in that it unofficially and delicately suggested to the highest Nazi circles that it would be advisable to discourage those who, infected by immigrant fever, yearned to receive a small piece, even a crumb, of the American dream.

Thus there finally arrived at the ship Roosevelt's confused but decisive answer: a new wave of immigrants from Germany would not be allowed into the United States.

The *Saint Louis* then drifted down along the coasts of the New World, but Mexico, Chile, Argentina, and all the others to whom it had appealed also answered with a refusal, the official explanation being that the quota for foreign immigration had long ago been filled.

After several months of wandering along the littoral of humanism and solidarity, the captain of the *Saint Louis* finally turned his wheel back toward good old Europe. And there good old England and France didn't even respond to his pleas for entry into their harbors in either the continent or their colonies and dominions. In Italy the anti-Semitic laws were already in power, forbidding the acceptance of Jewish refugees. Switzerland was only issuing transit visas with no right of sojourn; Belgium and Holland politely replied that they were ready to accept up to . . . two hundred people. From Amsterdam came the strict refusal to give permission for asylum in Surinam, Curaçao, or any other Dutch colony.

A similarly strict refusal was also received from the Soviets. By the way, the refugees had no particular appetite for Soviet asylum; the last wave of the by now habitual show-trials and purges had recently ended, and in those regions of Ukraine and Byelorussia populated with Jews, the persecutions, both obvious and secret, that had subsided after the Revolution were now being revived with growing strength. The shooting of the Jewish Anti-Fascist Committee and of those implicated in the "Doctors' Plot" was still in the future, but already their distant roar filled the air.

At last the ghost-ship was forced back to Hamburg.

The final part of this fairy tale is recorded in the archives of Auschwitz and Treblinka.

These insane attempts to obtain asylum were discussed more than once at the home of the family Weissberg on Dante Alighieri Street, No. 3/5—a luxurious two-story Empire-style house in a prestigious, aristocratic neighborhood, with a spacious garden to which every spring a gardener would come to redesign the flowerbeds.

It would be painful to leave all this and to start running toward dark uncertainty.

And the name of this uncertainty was Shanghai—Shanghai the open city—with anxious questions about the future across distant and immensely foreign waters. But Elisabeth Müller-Weissberg, in contrast to her indecisive and easily hurt husband, had strong nerves, and a true female instinct for security and finding ways out of trouble.

Some of their acquaintances had already received letters from China. Those who had decided early on to make the move wrote with relief that they had managed to get out of the Nazi hell, but honestly warned that Shanghai was another kind of hell, unfamiliar and ruthless; that unemployment, economic crisis, and epidemic disease had caught the city in a steel vise. They also wrote that a desperate struggle for survival awaited those who had no means or relations abroad, especially in the States, ready to assist family members in need. But at the same time virtually all the letters sounded the alarm that hesitation and delay of any kind could prove fatal: rumors were already circulating around Shanghai that the city was overpopulated with refugees, and that local authorities, helpless to solve even the most elementary problems of logistics, and under pressure from foreign missions, were worried about their own safety and tranquility, and would soon tighten and probably bring to a complete stop all immigration from abroad. At that point the very last open city in the world would slam its doors against those seeking salvation.

From Trieste or Genoa to Shanghai only two small ships, under the Italian flag, offered regular passage, the *Conte Rosso* and the *Conte Verde*. The voyage took six weeks, through Port Said, Hong Kong, Singapore, Bombay, and Manila. Apart from the price of the tickets, passengers had to deposit with the shipping company four hundred dollars per person, a considerable sum for that time, to be returned to them when they set foot on Chinese soil. This insecure and rather doubtful guarantee, which was required by the Japanese authorities, made it virtually certain that the immigrants, especially in the first months, would have minimal means with which to establish themselves. It was doubtful as well because Jewish charitable organizations started raising and providing this four hundred dollars per person on the condition that three hundred of it be immediately sent back to Germany, by mysterious means, for the rescue of the next lot of refugees. This in part made the whole exercise useless; yet, accepting this condition remained the only way out of a desperate situation, since the German consular authorities, at least till the beginning of the war, which was already knocking at the gates of Europe, would issue exit visas only when presented with a ship ticket that was in turn tied to those infernal four hundred dollars. To this were added the problems of those immigrants who, encountering the inexorable realities of Shanghai and faced from the outset with the fear of remaining there without means, stubbornly refused to give back the three hundred dollars they had promised to return to the charitable organizations. This created internal tensions among the newcomers, unsolvable moral situations, intolerable enmities, and even physical clashes between refugees who had left behind loved ones in Germany themselves awaiting their turn.

By the late spring of 1939, seventeen thousand had managed to reach Shanghai, and up until a few months before the beginning of the Great War, to those who had paid the necessary amounts and were expecting a passenger berth on the *Conte Rosso* and the *Conte Verde*, another thirty thousand were added.

In August of that same year the Shanghai harbor authorities unexpectedly announced that they were placing serious restrictions on the reception of ships carrying immigrants from Europe, with exceptions being made only for those who already had relatives established in Shanghai. Under these circumstances, representatives in Germany of the shipping companies started returning the money deposited with them by prospective refugees. In spite of everything, however, there still remained difficult but feasible alternatives for saving lives, not so grand in scale, but possible—through Siberia, through India, and even through Japan itself.

Yet right at that moment the most insurmountable barrier came up: in the early morning of September 1, at 4:45 to be precise, fifty-seven divisions and five brigades of Hitler's Wehrmacht attacked Poland from the north, west, and south. Land routes, along with the trans-Siberian railroad, suddenly turned out to be closed. Before the eyes of those trying to escape by this route, the earth was already burning.

The flow of refugees from Europe to Shanghai drastically subsided, and later finally ceased altogether.

The violinist Theodore Weissberg and the mezzo-soprano Elisabeth Müller-Weissberg were among the lucky ones who managed to take one of the last voyages of the *Conte Rosso* before, on its way back from a distant run to the shores of China, where it had deposited six hundred and thirty-one passengers, it happened upon a mine, and sank to the bottom of the sea.

## 22

HILDE AND HIROSHI OKURA stood on the rocky shore. Seagulls circled above, screaming, and, below, the ocean stormed and foamed. It had been a sudden whim of the Japanese man to take off on this free Sunday for the northwest, toward the Dover Strait, in order to breathe its salty air. As always, the Hungarian had refused to accompany them, preferring Sunday's relaxed and lazy before-lunch immigrant gossip in the café across from the church of Saint Germaine des Prés. There he planned to knock back a couple of glasses and go home befuddled. "Active Sunday Rest" was what he called this and similar forms of wasting his days off.

Over the past few days now, this Dr. Hiroshi had become increasingly preoccupied and strange, responding reluctantly and evasively to Hilde's questions, promising her that later on he would tell her something of particular importance, but continually postponing it and revealing nothing. For the moment all she could do was just enjoy the ocean breeze, since she was beholding the Atlantic for the first time in her life. Or, if not its boundless expanse, at least that strip of it that separates the Continent from England.

The Japanese man took her hand to help her down the steep rocky pathway as the wind threw a salty spray against their faces.

She shivered in her thin summer clothes and he took off his coat to wrap her in it. At this moment they were very close to each other, face to face, and he became aware of the tender fragrance of "Mon Boudoir" mingled with the scents of sea and algae. Hiroshi was the one who turned away first. Inhaling the wind deeply into his chest, he took out a handkerchief, and, nonplussed, started wiping his glasses.

"How funny you look without glasses!" Hilde gaily laughed.

"I can't hear!" Hiroshi tried to outcry the waves, which were breaking against the rocks along the shore.

"I said you look funny without glasses!" But the wind carried her words away.

"I can't hear again!"

"I said you were the dearest character I've ever met!"

"This time I heard you!" Hiroshi outshouted the roar of the ocean.

"And what did I say?"

"That I look funny without glasses."

They had lunch at a small, very cozy, and rather expensive fish restaurant not far from the shore. Hiroshi was still deep in thought and closed within himself when Hilde finally decided to ask:

"What's going on with you? You promised to tell me later. Now it's later."

He stretched out his hand on the table.

"All right. Give me your hand, for courage. I am leaving, Hilde. This very night. In fact we are saying good-bye."

"Tonight? My God! For long?"

"Maybe forever. There is mobilization in Japan. I have been summoned to appear . . . as they say . . . under the flags."

Hilde was silent a long time, then she asked with a muffled voice, "But do you have to go? Is it inevitable?"

"I have to. It is inevitable. If it is mobilization. . . ."

"But you're in Paris. What's going on 'there' is far away. Why not just not go? Didn't you say that your father didn't believe in military doctrines?"

"Military doctrines are one thing, the motherland—another. I know it's hard to understand. But there is something, I do not know if it is a curse or a blessing, but we are different in the way that we are perhaps mystically connected with our 'tribe,' and the islands, like nobody else anywhere. This is not national discipline, or the attachment of the slave—but something deeper. An umbilical cord, a fateful interdependence, karma or call it what you will. So I must leave!"

"And when did you find out?"

"I was already expecting it when I gave you that first bouquet of roses. Hilde, Hilde-san, I thank destiny for that opening in the clouds that bestowed a little bit of light on me. You are a sunbeam, and I thank you. But I also worry about you. What are you going to do? What will be your next station?"

"There are no stations if there aren't any trains."

He kept silent, his thumb almost imperceptibly caressing her hand, which he was still holding on the table. Then he gently said:

"Could I leave you some money?"

Hilde sharply withdrew her hand.

"If you do, I'll leave right away!"

"I understand. I was expecting it. But give me a chance to thank you for the good turn you have done me by accepting my friendship."

"I don't remember doing you a good turn."

"You don't even understand how you opened a window to other horizons for me. How you gave me the gift that makes life worth living. Now I want you to accept this from me—with the most sincere admiration."

He reached into something between a doctor's bag and a student's satchel, which as an orderly and conscientious specialist at Saint-Anne's, the Carmelite hospital, he always brought with him, and took out a flat box of violet velvet. A thin metallic band with a golden gleam encircled the box, at whose center glistened a golden hieroglyph.

He drew a finger over the surface of the hieroglyph and quietly read:

"Peach-blossom."

Before her astonished eyes lay a necklace of Japanese rose pearls, which had probably cost a truly outrageous sum of money.

"You're crazy!" she barely whispered.

"Crazy is the world we live in. Please, accept this—as a token of my gratitude, only distant and modest. With the color of a blooming peach tree in the foothills of Fujyama. If you do not accept it, you will hurt me deeply! My train leaves tonight at ten from the Gare de Lyon. If you come to see me off, you will give me unearthly joy . . . like a white wind . . . ."

The last words he spoke in Japanese.

They stood in front of the sleeping-coach of the train to Marseilles exactly as she had stood two months before in front of the train to Berlin.

"Have a safe journey. I'm happy I met you," she said simply.

"In Japan they say that every meeting is the beginning of a farewell."

"In Germany they say that every separation is a small death. How many times can a person die a little bit, Hiroshi-san?"

He took off his glasses and blinked, as if specks of dust had come into his eyes.

"May I kiss you?" Hilde asked shyly.

"You are not obliged to, but you may."

She leaned over a little to kiss Hiroshi on the cheek.

This time the uncle was Japanese.

# 23

"SO, YOU'VE DECIDED TO ditch us?"

This is what Alain Conti asked, holding the cigar tightly between his teeth.

Hilde silently nodded.

"And if I raise your pay by fifteen francs per shooting day?"

"I'm embarrassed to tell you this, Alain, but I lied to you. Your secretaries believed my blue eyes and didn't even ask to see my work permit. I don't have one. They turned me down. Yesterday I stopped by my old hotel in Ivry, and there they made my day with the news that the cops have been looking for me and asking around for my new address. I've got to disappear."

Alain Conti scratched his nose.

"First, you didn't lie to me because I've known it for a long time. The Hungarian told me. And now someone has framed him. That's the game. But don't take it personally. It turns out you're not the only victim. The police action, it seems, is across-the-board. War is coming and the country is cleansing itself of troublemakers. The motherland, *la belle France*, is shaking out its rugs before one of our victorious legions passes beneath it. Get it?"

"No."

"It doesn't matter. Look, I could still cover for you, for the time being, while those nincompoops are searching the hotels in Ivry. Do they know you work for me? They don't. Then why should we do them any favors? And you are number one also in my personal program."

"Thank you, Alain, but I don't want to be a number in anyone's program. I'm fed up with all that."

Alain Conti poured himself half a glass of cognac and only after downing an enormous gulp remarked:

"Look here, my dear girl, we're all a number in someone's program. How many billions of us are on this fucking planet? I don't know, exactly, but that many billions are doing their number. And you know what the trick is? To be a passenger on the train and not someone seeing people off at the station. And if possible on the express train, first class. That's the magic trick—to be part of what's happening. I could tell about you from the very beginning: you're born for the train, your seat is reserved and I'll put you in it. You've got time to think it over, if in the meantime you don't come up with something better. But remember: the girls who come through our studios always remain our girls. You can always find me if you're down on your luck. You know where I drink my cognac."

Suddenly there rushed into the semi-dark soundstage, where the bent-over Oriental props were still gathering dust, a bald-headed, chubby fellow.

"I hope I'm not late, Mr. Conti!"

"It's all right, Claude. You are, but let it be the last time. Sit down, the sheet music is over there."

Alain Conti took Hilde under her arm and with polite insistence pushed her toward the other side of the space.

"Come on, your majesty. Sorry, but we're just getting down to work."

At the exit she turned around and cast a glance at the chubby man who had taken Istvan Keleti's place and was quietly running through a tune.

"What's happened to the Hungarian?" Hilde asked. "Last night he came home respectably drunk, and this morning he slipped out early, before I was even awake. When he sobers up I still don't understand."

"Now this, my girl, is the high professionalism of the real drunk! You ask where he is. Didn't I tell you the country is cleansing itself of troublemakers? A couple of things have happened with the police. Small stuff. If you want to see him, he's just across the way, in the bistro. And tell him not to come popping in here drunk so he can do something idiotic. I'll stop by during the lunch break. Now give us a kiss and scram."

Alain Conti, the commander in chief, hastily kissed her and then hollered at the assembled girls:

"Quiet there! This is not a bazaar! Next!"

# 24

HILDE ENTERED THE BISTRO across from the studio and looked around for the Hungarian. Sitting in a corner, next to a glass of cognac he'd long ago consumed, he was still bony and yellow, as if he'd just checked out of the morgue the day before.

"What happened, Istvan?" she asked worriedly, taking a seat at the round table. "Why aren't you at work? Conti told me something, but he didn't quite explain it."

"Would you like some coffee? Hey, *garçon*, a coffee for the lady! What happened, dear sister, is that someone framed me. This morning they came rushing in from the police and Conti had to pay a tremendous fine out of his own pocket because he'd hired a foreigner with an expired work permit." He stopped while the boy served the coffee, and only after that continued. "Here's the situation. And, to tell you honestly, people here are right: there are a million out-of-work Frenchmen and we're taking the bread out of their mouths. Now it's true that bright horizons are opening up for them and that unemployment among musicians is going to go down—someone will have to play when the firing starts, right? Poor Conti! He had to stuff the pockets of the inspectors so they wouldn't cancel my visa too. And you? Did you go to the American Embassy today?"

Hilde sighed heavily: was there any point in explaining in detail The Law of Universal Disgustingness? That morning, as soon as the American Embassy opened, she was there, standing in line with those who'd been hopelessly waiting since early dawn. But unlike the other supplicants, she'd been personally received by the consul. He'd been *so so* kind when announcing to her that her request for an immigrant visa had been rejected by Washington on the grounds of—insufficient grounds. But as he stealthily cast a glance up her long legs, the consul advised her not to lose hope. Nor did he fail to interject among other things a delicate invitation for a date that Hilde, again, *so so* delicately declined.

"And there you are. Well, it's like this, my dear," said the Hungarian. "America too, like all great democracies, likes to give advice and pat you on the back, but doesn't like it when you drop in uninvited for lunch. At least not if you aren't Einstein. She takes those whom she needs, but doesn't give a shit about the others, who need her."

For a long time—for a very long time—Hilde twisted the cup of coffee in her hands while silently turning over some idea that had dawned on her. Finally she said, "Will you buy me a vodka if I show you something?"

"I'll buy you two, but we'll split them like brothers."

Out of the bag in which she lugged around a thousand useless trifles all over Paris she took the flat box of violet velvet. Under the bistro's low-hanging globes, Dr. Hiroshi Okura's necklace gave off a matte pink luster. Hilde waited for the wide-eyed Hungarian to draw it between his fingers and only after that continued:

"It was given to me as a gift by our Japanese friend. I think it's real. I would like to keep it; I've never had such an expensive thing. But people who have to count their centimes for a single croissant don't have the right to such luxury. Besides, I don't have a dress for it. I know this is immoral, the bottom of degradation, but we've been at the bottom for a long time now. What do you think? If you sell it, will the money be enough for both of us? I mean that plan of yours—Saigon and so on."

"Shanghai," indifferently said the Hungarian.

"Let it be Shanghai. What's the difference?"

# PART TWO

# 25

THE MURMUROUS PRAYING OF a group of worshipers, most of them old men, filled the cold air with vapor, while above their covered heads flowed the clear baritone of Rabbi Leo Levin. He was reciting the sacred words in Hebrew with the pronunciation typical of German Jews:

"*Shema Yisrael Adonai Eloheinu Adonai Echad.* Hear O Israel: The Lord our God, The Lord is One."

It's doubtful whether on that Saturday morning the words uttered in a half-destroyed pagoda, temple of other gods, dwelling-place of other shades, could reach the Eternal and Only One.

This house of God had until recently been a small neighborhood temple in Hongku, that enormous poverty-stricken antheap, one of many in Shanghai marked by bleak desperation and misery. The roof, with its twisted-up corners under which peeked out angry dragons painted in red and gold, had almost been incinerated by Japanese bombs. The shock waves had carried away its eastern part and the fire had swallowed up as well thousands of wooden tiles hand-carved with Buddhist texts—antique printing molds used centuries before Gutenberg was struck by a similar idea. The half-burnt tiles were diligently arranged by the new inhabitants in a corner of the pagoda, the way bricks are laid out for future construction, because the newcomers also knew from their Book of Books that construction begins with the Word. And that those who had abandoned their temple and fled would return one day and again look for their prayers.

To turn a deserted pagoda into a synagogue—this was unheard of! The thought had occurred to the tireless rabbi of Düsseldorf, Leo Levin, a worldly, jovial guy, a teller of amazing stories, but also, considered from the strict perspective of Orthodox Jews, a heretic, inclined to opt for pragmatic earthly needs rather than divine commandments. He had listened with deep respect to remarks, uttered between clenched teeth, that the two partially burnt dragons and the huge statue of Buddha, with its scratched gilding, did not conform to Judaic tradition and its requirement that a house of divine worship not violate the inflexible and insurmountable prohibition against any depiction whatsoever of God, human beings, and animals. He had patiently explained, moreover, that although Buddha, with his legs crossed on top of the blooming lotus, might not have been, after all, an ordinary mortal, he was nevertheless far from being Yahweh either, that dragons were not real animals but mythological creatures, and that in the Talmud there was nothing mentioned with respect to the Chinese case. And that whatever isn't explicitly forbidden could be considered allowed, couldn't it? To a certain extent this calmed his congregation down, even though they never accepted at heart the marble beast with its teeth bared that looked like a lion and had paws and stood on a stone sphere at the entrance to the newly sanctified synagogue.

By day, in the Bird Market, Rabbi Leo, Leonhard Levin, M.S. in theology and Hebrew studies, sold rice rolls made by his wife Esther, a former teacher in one of the Düsseldorf high schools. In the afternoon, the rabbi was always selflessly helping the God-fearing souls thirsty for a cleansing prayer and a bit of spiritual light in the darkness of this strange, infinitely foreign and hostile city. Rabbi Leo was eternally ready to give advice, to do unpaid physical labor for the settling of those newly arrived from Europe, to circumcise a Jewish baby boy or to perform a marriage. On her shoulders, in turn, his wife Esther Levin had calmly taken on their new life in Shanghai, without the unnecessary drama to which were inclined not a few of her sisters-in-destiny, inhabitants of the thrice-cursed dortoirs. Stuffy, fetid, crammed to the ceiling with beds, people, and suitcases, these were communal dormitories on Shuqing Street for from forty to fifty people in several abandoned weaving and tailoring workshops hit by the bombings and turned by the Carmelite nuns into shelters for refugees in dire straits. In contrast to these unfortunates, the wealthier immigrants had already accommodated themselves one way or another across the river, in more prestigious quarters. For example, there was the jeweler Jo Bach from Nuremberg, who, rumor had it, had been smart enough to smuggle out, in the soles of his shoes, eight diamonds as big as hazelnuts. It's possible that their hazelnut proportions were exaggerated, but isn't that why rumor exists in the first place—to exaggerate the truth without affecting its core?! This Mr. Bach had already managed to irritate everyone as early as the voyage over with his obligatory joke that the only difference between himself and the composer of the same name was the fact of circumcision. At present, nevertheless, the circumcised Bach was living with his wife and two unmarried daughters in quite a decent family house on Fuzhou Road, and the nuns at least didn't have to worry about him and those who were similarly set up.

These Carmelites were Chinese, all of them, except for Antonia, their mother superior, who had come to Shanghai a long time ago, when she was very young, from somewhere in Alsace, which was why, apart from her native French, she could also speak good German. Chinese she had learned here and with its help she was able to pound her fist on the desks of various sleepy community-service bureaucrats in order to procure still greater supplies of ingredients for the free public soup kitchen, which offered impoverished immigrants a daily bowl or two of food. In her untamed and persistent way she was also able to solicit medicines necessary for the quickly improvised Jewish Refugee Hospital, led by Professor Sigmund Mandel, the former chief surgeon of the renowned Berlin hospital Charité. Mother Antonia was a generous and selfless servant of her order, always at her post: in the past, during days of famine and war, and the Great Typhus, and also now, when she had to help the wretched souls arriving in waves from the Nazi Reich.

The sisters from the order would meet the newcomers at the dock itself, supervising the children, giving special care to the old and the sick, and paying particular attention to those men and even more particularly those women whose hair was cut short—an almost infallible sign that they had passed through the camp at Dachau. Even before his relatives could recognize him, the nuns fell all over themselves helping the flautist with the short haircut, Simon Zinner, who was unable to carry his two suitcases on his own. His hands were wrapped in bandages covering the terrible wounds on the fingers Hansi Steinbrenner had smashed.

His musician colleagues who had arrived several months before were kissing him on his unshaven face:

"Sim, dear Sim! It's a real miracle you survived Dachau!"

"I forgot to die," gravely said the flautist, holding his bandaged arms high, as if he were surrendering.

Those who knew well the indomitable Simon Zinner understood that he never gave up, as he would prove later.

And so, the passengers kept coming down the ladder, while the Carmelites' brass band kept cheerfully playing Strauss waltzes under a banner with a welcome sign, in German: *Wilkommen!*

In this exotic picture of Chinese nuns blowing trombones and trumpets in order to serenade the blue Danube at the mouth of the brown and muddy Yangtse, there was something at once grotesque and endearing. Such an unexpected, festive welcome gave heart to the refugees, who were confused and exhausted from the long journey, and kindled that genetically embedded hope in the hunted tribe of Israel that things were not so immensely tragic and would eventually work out for the best—a tender hope that would soon be tested to the limit.

Endearing too was the friendship that spontaneously developed between the old mother superior, a strict Catholic, and the jovial rabbi Leo Levin, with whom, apart from shared problems and worries concerning the reception, accommodation, and support of the refugees, she was connected by a profound secret: he, unbeknownst to the nuns, was teaching her how to play poker, with black beans—in other words, chips costing one Shanghai cent each. It's not beside the point to add that in the game with the trusting nun, who was becoming increasingly addicted to gambling, the winner, as a rule, was the rabbi. This did not dishearten Mother Antonia, who, as she doggedly acquired the art of bluffing, accepted as a divine truth the rule of dedicated players that it's not the gain that matters but the game, and not the loss but the thrill. Not infrequently, though, when the old woman owed more than one Shanghai dollar, meaning a hundred beans, and could conceal neither her doubts about supreme justice nor her suspicion that the Jewish God was helping His rabbi, while His Son was turning away from His faithful servant, the rabbi would generously forgive the debt and reshuffle the cards for a new hand.

The rabbi's wife, Esther Levin, was pining for her beloved high school, which she had voluntarily left. This had happened on the day when the powers that be in Berlin demanded that the new German history, which she happened to teach, include the heroic episode of the Munich plot, when, in November 1923, Hitler and a group of fellow National Socialists attempted a coup d'état in the name of Germany's glorious future and had to spend a little time in the fortress of Landsberg. There, in his cell, the Führer dictated to his faithful associate Rudolf Hess the first part of his monumental work *Mein Kampf*, and the greatness of the thoughts and future plans contained therein history teachers were now obliged to explain. The high school principal, a decent enough fellow from the old generation, difficult to entice with German propaganda and faithful to traditional German virtues, accepted with relief Esther's voluntary resignation, since the firing of a Jew, a teacher of the Third's Reich's rising generation, however painful from a moral standpoint, was, in light of the existing situation, inevitable. Now the professor of the new history was frying rice rolls on a stove knocked together with Rabbi Leo's help out of old tin cans in the yard of the half-collapsed raw silk-weaving workshop. At first, this operation had been conducted under the guidance of a small, wrinkled, thousand-year-old, but very friendly Chinese neighbor who didn't speak a word of any foreign language, just as Esther didn't speak a word of Chinese. But the two of them managed somehow to understand each other and now, people were saying, the Jewish woman's rolls were no worse than the Chinese original.

Of course you had to work and make a living somehow in these conditions of heavy economic stagnation, to accept anything, even the most menial job, because no sooner had even the first ships started arriving than the rents for the small, uncomfortable living-spaces, which had neither pipes nor running water and were infested with bedbugs and rats, doubled and tripled. Early each morning, with the exception of Saturdays when he had to conduct the Sabbath service, Rabbi Leo Levin shouldered a bamboo pole with baskets dangling from either end, and, running to the rhythm of the twisting bamboo, headed directly to the Bird Market with his supply of fresh, still warm rice rolls. Comically bouncing along beside him and carrying a similar load was his partner and first assistant in the roll business, Markus Aronson the astrophysicist, skinny and tall as an electrical pole, passionate and unwavering disciple of the quantum theory. This was the same Markus, the once-upon-a-time assistant of Einstein's called Markusle Quantissimo, who to everyone's astonishment had refused to get out and go to the States with his great teacher. The road to truly major science, Markusle had thought, would run through Germany, which was why he'd rejected an immigrant's destiny. When he finally realized that his personal road in Germany was leading not to expanding galaxies but straight to the concentration camps, it was already too late: the barriers to America had gone up. Now the road to survival went right through the Bird Market.

It would be a serious delusion to think that there, at the market, they sold only chickens, ducks, and swamp woodcocks hanging upside down by their stretched necks, black eggs boiled in soy sauce, and swallows' nests. The main attraction, especially for foreigners from the West, were the live feathered creatures who sang and chirped in tenderly woven and painted cages. Neither was it a rarity to see grasshoppers hopping amid sticks of rice-straw—a type of pet unknown in the West. By the way, as far as pets go, dogs weren't for sale here. To the horror and disgust of the Europeans, they were offered on the meat market in the lower part of Nantao—alive, in bamboo cages, resigned, with weary eyes, next to pigs cut into pieces, buffalo guts, fish freshly caught or dried and salted, swarms of snakes that right there at the market, before the customers' eyes, were skinned alive, as well as lobsters, crabs, and gigantic abalone shells.

But people get used to whatever they have to, and the Europeans had to accommodate themselves to the idea that in these meridians man had included the dog in his food chain. This was the situation, even though you'd never see a westerner in the cheap joints offering dishes made from dogs. In the big restaurants for Europeans on the opposite bank, serving dogmeat was strictly prohibited and punishable by special ordinance.

The first person to benefit from this sentimental European attachment to the starving man's best friend was the pickpocket and petty thief Shlomo Finkelstein, a former prisoner in Dachau. Out of the gardens of the French and English quarters, as well as the tennis courts and golf clubs, domestic dogs started disappearing, from poodles to mighty German shepherds. With what means the diminutive, short-legged, bald, and chubby Finkelstein managed to lure these pets and carry out the complicated procedures for their kidnapping and transfer remained a secret, but probably the operation involved somebody's two-wheeled market hand-cart. The worried owners of the dogs who had disappeared were forced to look for them as soon as possible among the Chinese, Vietnamese, and Korean vendors at the meat market, and to pay for them as well according to the number of kilograms of living weight. After all, the market-stand owners had paid money for the merchandise, and "business is business, *masta-masta!* Okay?"

# 26

RABBI LEO LEVIN HAD to confess that after leaving his rice rolls this morning with his partner Markusle, he had run slapdash through the Saturday service, even the singing of the Kaddish. He loved those beautiful lyrics, which exuded a desert sadness, a plea for mercy, and a pledge of fidelity to the Almighty, and had been rendered with such perfection throughout the millennia as to have neither a single word too much nor a single word too little. Nevertheless, for an experienced rabbi and a first-class cantor, it was child's play to skip whole passages without being detected. Now, that's the honest truth, let's not kid ourselves, and if what he did was a crime, then the Only One would have forgiven it, because outside in the street, wet from the spring rain that had just fallen, who should be waiting for him in the name of some very serious business but the violinist Theodore Weissberg and the surgeon Professor Sigmund Mandel. The three of them had been selected for an important mission today from the steering committee of the Jewish Refugee Community of Shanghai. This was the official name of those who, since 1937, had been coming here from Germany and Austria and concentrating themselves mainly in Hongku, a huge district, really a separate city in itself. The name of this German-speaking group of Jews did not correspond precisely to the significantly more complicated reality of Shanghai, because the refugees from Nazism were just a part—true, the most destitute part—of the Jewish population of that city. Apart from the rich Baghdadi, long ago settled in the high-end part of the International Concession, there were, in the city, two more Jewish communities of modest Russian immigrants who could barely make ends meet, no more than four or five thousand Ashkenazim in all, who among themselves spoke Yiddish—a strange linguistic mixture of Medieval German and Old Hebrew, spiced with a Slavic word or two. One of these communities consisted of refugees from the Cossack pogroms set in motion by the waves of anti-Semitism that followed the Russian defeat in the Russo-Japanese war of 1905. The other consisted of those who had found asylum here after the October Revolution in 1917 and the civil war that followed, when both Red and White troops, after each military failure, would take out their anger on the Jewish neighborhoods of Berdichev, Odessa, or the Czernowitz region, every one of them with its small, defenseless Jewish townlet or hamlet, called a "shtetl" or "miastechko." These would periodically fall victim to the apparently "spontaneous" but quite often intentionally ignited anti-Jewish attacks, which resulted in enormous waves of refugees—to the Far West, and America, and to the Far East, through Siberia and Irkutsk, China and Korea. Here they belonged to the lower middle class of small owners and clerks who more or less earned their bread for themselves and their relatives.

Despite the myth of Jewish solidarity, these communities in Shanghai had almost no communication with each other; edgy and hostile, they treated every newcomer as if he were a competitor in the struggle for bread and a place in the sun. It is not irrelevant either that these immigrants came from drastically different cultural layers of Europe and the Near East, with a different history, tradition, and language, with almost no similarities between them, apart from a common religion and the memory of distant kinship.

The rabbi and his two companions were moving through the human masses of Hongku, this hubbub of people shouting, selling, buying, hawking, pulling pedestrians by the tails of their coats or ready at any minute to snatch someone's hat and dash through the labyrinth of meandering side streets; people with no arms, or no legs, no today, no tomorrow, and no hope, begging for a handout. Hovering above all of this was an indescribable din, split by the banging of wooden hammers on planks, dry as the rattle of distant machine guns—a method for attracting the attention of buyers.

The three of them were unaware that twenty or so meters behind them, shadowing them and rather rudely pushing aside the pedestrians standing in his way, was Shlomo Finkelstein—that pickpocket fellow and seller of live dogs. He had voluntarily taken upon himself the mission of bodyguard because he knew better than the others the hundred and one Shanghai ways of being robbed without noticing it. Moreover Shlomo, primitive and semi-literate, felt genuine respect for educated people, or those who stood above him in things of the spirit, a reverence he had exhibited at Dachau, where, revealing the one noble feature in what was otherwise the visage of a thieving crow, he had taken under his wing his helpless protégé Theodore Weissberg. They had arrived in Shanghai at different times, but as soon as he had caught sight of the Weissbergs at the dock, Shlomo Finkelstein had joyfully employed himself as the guardian of his old camp comrade and the latter's aristocratic wife.

It isn't easy to make your way through a crowd that hasn't figured out yet what sidewalks are for. Here and there, on rugs spread out directly on the road, vendors were offering vegetables, rice, and medicinal herbs and spices, completely deaf to the Japanese motor patrols that were passing only an inch away and desperately honking their horns to try to get through. And on the sidewalks themselves every Chinese family that possessed two crates for chairs and one taller crate for a table and had managed to acquire a small stove and three or four kitchen utensils was opening its family restaurant for two customers. The modest piece of meat and the small staring fish that hung under the fresh bamboo awning and were abundantly covered with street dust had to serve as bait.

The three representatives of the Jewish Refugee Community evaded the crowd only when they finally stepped onto the bridge that separates Hongku into two parts; moments later behind them there appeared Shlomo's bald head. Below them flowed the thick muddy waters of one of the tributaries of the Yangtse—the Soochow, a deep canal rather, on which floated rare junks and motor barges. At the two ends of the bridge, the entrance and the exit, Japanese soldiers warmed themselves at sinking fires made from wood scraps, lit in gasoline cylinders as early as the break of dawn, when, for the season, it was still quite cold. And no one knew or could know that soon this not-large but strictly guarded iron bridge, the only portal linking one world to another, would play a dramatic role in the life of Hongku.

The reason why the three of them, together with their volunteer bodyguard, would leave their everyday tasks and undertake today's movement into the world of those with full stomachs and power, was more than alarming. Already for the third time in the last month a large group of young Chinese Fascists, urged on by the anti-Semitic newspaper *Yudaia Kenku*, had mounted a pogrom against the Jewish communal dormitories, destroying and looting several Jewish shops and stands, and throwing a bottle of gasoline into the newly opened and very modest pastry shop named, with endearing nostalgia, "Vienna." The Japanese soldiers had remained indifferent to the incident, their task being the security of bridges and strategic crossroads, and not the maintenance of order in the streets. They had even observed with laughter and mirthful shouts how the Chinese nuns threw themselves into the fray to drag out from under the feet of the fighting men the aged, long-retired doctor Sybil Goldenberg, who, after her arrival in Shanghai, and as her strength permitted, would help Professor Mandel in the infirmary.

At first, the Chinese municipal authorities hadn't gotten involved, but when the former flautist of the Dresden Staatskapelle, the indomitable truth-lover Simon Zinner—he of the Seventh Correctional Unit and the smashed fingers—organized a resistance group and it all came to a head with physical violence, there quickly appeared twenty or so uniformed city police officers on horseback. A number of fellows had light wounds, and there was even one bleeding head; those affected weren't so much the offenders but the defenders. Simon Zinner was arrested for disturbing the peace and two hours later, after the matter had been investigated, released. The Chinese youths who had caused the ruckus had already evaporated and no one took the trouble of looking for them either.

*Yudaia Kenku* was published in Japanese and Chinese, but it was no secret that financially and ideologically it was directly supported by official German circles in Shanghai. In fact the newspaper was an almost literal translation of Nazi propaganda in the Reich, from which articles and cartoons were simply reprinted. After the umpteenth attempt had been made to replicate Krystallnacht also in a Far East translation, the leadership of the German-Jewish community in Hongku decided to lodge a formal protest with the high commissioners of the Shanghai administration against their scandalous passivity in the face of the hideous felonies of the Fascist gangs. Attention was drawn to the fact that the hooligans were acting undisturbed, in contradiction to the official policy, proclaimed by the authorities, of tolerance and neutrality vis-à-vis the conflict in Europe.

Proclamations are really just a lot of hot air, useful, evidently, for throwing smoke in the face of foreign countries, in this case the United States, with which Japan was currently engaged in intensive negotiations for a non-aggression pact. At any rate, the Japanese leader of the military occupation in Shanghai, General Hisataki Kikan, refused to receive the delegation. His prerogatives, so the answer went, were of a purely military nature and did not extend to civil problems. The puppet Chinese municipal authorities had already replied to insistent letters from the Jews newly arrived from Germany that legally they were German citizens, with valid passports and exit visas issued by official German institutions, and that, given the established international status of the city, it followed that their problems should be addressed by the local German officials. Those municipal authorities still didn't know that in Berlin they were discussing the question of stripping the German Jews of their citizenship and deporting them as "unwanted foreigners." So for the time being they remained citizens of the Reich, with the obligations, but hardly the rights, following thereof.

The most inaccessible turned out to be the French, who, having dug themselves into their "*Concession française*," had circled the wagons, as it were, and were indifferent to any problems that didn't relate directly to the interests of France. Their concerns were understandable: France was already yielding to the relentless advance of German tank divisions pushing ahead in waves from already-conquered Belgium, and nothing else now mattered. Even the French military commissioner, Major Lefèvre, raised his eyebrows in surprise: "What's all this got to do with us? We've got our own troubles, gentlemen. And they're hardly smaller than yours!"

And he was right, the military commissioner, since as early as April the Germans had swallowed up Denmark, Holland, Norway, Luxembourg, and Belgium in big fat gulps. Next on the list was France.

The hope that Guderian with his armored divisions would bump his nose against the Maginot line and start spinning his wheels collapsed like a sand tower, all talk about the line's impregnability and absolute unassailability having turned out to be empty illusion and foggy propaganda. The Nazi detachments didn't even waste their time with destroying its concrete forts; they were happy enough to use Belgium and the Ardennes as diversionary routes and sink into France like a hot knife through butter.

The distinguished representative of Albion, Lord Charles Washburn, with his slender and stately bearing, silver hair, and mighty upturned moustache, was the universally recognized chief of the International Concession. The former representative of the governor-general of Punjab, who had spent his youth in the gentlemen's clubs of London and on the hunting fields of India and Namib, now, with polite indifference, kept them standing in front of his desk while he informed them that the English administration in principle did not involve itself with the communal affairs of the Chinese. And that probably the whole matter was just an instance of youthful high-jinks to which no particular attention should be paid. Giving support to the Jewish communities might even harm them by drawing attention to existing antagonisms with the local population. Indeed, the influential Baghdadi were quite reserved toward their German kinsmen, whom they regarded to a certain extent as poor relations who had shown up uninvited at a family gathering. In the present delicate political situation in Shanghai, as he put it, it would be best to address directly Baron Ottomar von Dammbach. As the gentlemen well knew, England was at this very moment at war with Germany and for this reason the English here unfortunately did not maintain official ties to the representatives of the Reich. Lord Washburn looked at his pocket watch and cheerfully, almost joyfully, concluded the conversation with a charming, "It was a pleasure, gentlemen. I hope . . ." and so on.

This was not their first expedition to the peaks of local power. The Jewish community in Hongku had thousands of unsolved problems, about twenty thousand to be more precise, as many as there were newly settled refugees from National Socialism, and the present unsuccessful attempt to solve at least one of them was hardly the first defeat for the three parliamentarians. And so, from this Shanghai knot of intertwined authorities it turned out that complaints against the actions of the Nazis had to be addressed to none other than those very Nazis themselves.

So today, the three of them—a rabbi, a surgeon, and a violinist, guarded by a professional pickpocket—were on their way directly to the mouth of the wolf, Baron von Dammbach himself.

The small delegation walked along the riverbank boulevard, past the mirages of European shops and restaurants, offices and banks that they had long forgotten, while Sikh policemen, in white gloves and white turbans, regulated the stream of cars, bicycles, and rickshaws. A world a stone's throw away and as inaccessible as the moon.

At luxurious Nanking Boulevard, with its jewelry and perfume stores, hotels, fashionable beauty salons, Viennese pastry shop, Bavarian beer pubs, nightclubs, fancy store windows that did not lag behind those in London, red buses, and yellow cabs, the three of them had to stop and take a breath. Far behind, leaning against an electricity pole, Shlomo patiently waited for them.

With brisk strides an honorary Scottish troop marched by, blowing their bagpipes. They had probably just come from the harbor, where some big fish had been received or dispatched. In any case the tall dignified men in their plaid kilts, radiating self-confidence, convincingly symbolized Britain's vainglorious grandeur.

The three lit cigarettes and said nothing to each other, not even a single word. But each knew what the others were thinking —about that world beyond the river that they'd just gotten out of, like prisoners on a short home leave. A world built out of humiliating misery and suffering to which they already inseparably belonged and to which they must soon return, only to immerse themselves in its sticky stench.

The official representatives of the Third Reich were cozily set up not far from the Hippodrome, in the center of the German Concession. Their two-story cottage, located at the end of a well-maintained park, with two wings spread out as if for an embrace, and tall windows, was constructed in a French rather than the commonly accepted English colonial style, and blindingly white, as if made out of crystal sugar. In the middle of the mowed lawn, on a pillar, lazily waved the flag with the swastika. Exactly at the back of the residence, on Great Western Road, you could find the elite German school, for five years now completely inaccessible to Jewish children, including those whose parents could afford to pay the excessively high fees.

The air was cold, but clear and clean; it was monsoon season and after the fallen rain there wafted the scent of newly cut grass and blooming jasmine; apparently even nature on this side of the river was fresher and friendlier.

Before entering this little patch of Germany, guarded in front of the wrought iron gate by two uniformed German policemen —as if it were the mowed lawn in front of the Reichstag in Berlin, and not thousands of kilometers to the east—Theodore Weissberg suddenly noticed Shlomo calmly standing on the corner. The latter was startled when the violinist beckoned to him with his finger, and looked around to see if the matter concerned himself or someone else, then threw away the small stick on which he'd been chewing and submissively ran up, ready to fulfill any request.

The violinist softly scolded him:

"You're always on our tail, Shlomo. I asked you not to do it!"

The fat little man sniffled, kept silent for a while, stepping from one foot to the other, and at last said guiltily:

"I'm keeping watch."

"Over whom? From what?"

Shlomo reached into the inside pocket of his diminutive worn-out coat, too tight to cover his big belly, and still looking guilty, handed over a wallet.

"This is yours, Mr. Weissberg. You didn't notice how this guy with a squashed nose snatched it from you as early as Hongku. But he didn't realize I was right behind him."

Apparently in this case two schools of pickpocketing had clashed with each other—the Asian and the European. For now the score was in favor of the latter.

Rabbi Leo and the professor burst out laughing, and Theodore in confusion took back his wallet and sourly murmured something that must have sounded like an apology.

# 27

ON THIS PARTICULAR SATURDAY morning Theodore had more than one reason to be sour and dejected. Today Elisabeth had wanted to talk to him privately and so he hadn't gone out hunting for work, as he did every God-given day at the crack of dawn. In Shanghai this very rarely meant a job you'd actually want, but rather any kind of occasional and sporadic work that paid half a buck—washing a car, sweeping a sidewalk in front of a fancy shop in the Concession, hauling someone's luggage. Any kind of work would do—except the kind you could do with pleasure, the kind that matched your abilities. Especially if they, your abilities, were confined within the circle of classical music. And in this, since the beginning of the Japanese invasion, nobody was interested anymore; there was no one to pay for it. In "French Town," it was said, in the past there had been a rather decent chamber orchestra, but after the general mobilization in France, when many had been compelled to return to the motherland, the orchestra had fallen apart. For the last time, just before the bombings and the subsequent Japanese invasion, the Peking Philharmonic had toured here and, although only average in quality, it was still a worthy representative of the genre. Since the occupation, Shanghai had in general become a bar-dominated, unspiritual city that shelled out money only for entertainment. Clubs with an orchestra, mainly the elite ones in the big hotels with dance floors, had long been over-supplied with musicians, and for every occupied place in the orchestra, there were ten or so candidates for the same music stand who remained out in the street. The situation was complicated by the circumstance that the greater part of the unemployed musicians were Asian, and it was their labor that was preferred because they were paid considerably less. Theodore was a renowned virtuoso, no doubt, but the club owners, especially those that were Chinese, couldn't have cared less about what kind of a big fish you were in Europe. Moreover it would be difficult to say that he was endowed with the ability to adapt to this new environment—to play rumba over the din of forks and knives or amid the shouts of waiters and tipsy clients, to handle situations different from the familiar ones in which he had once worked and achieved success.

Even the idea, tossed out by his musican-colleagues, all of them scattered about in their almost hopeless struggle for bread—now car-washers, now porters or lowly servants—to get together in the evenings and play, seemed to him an immeasurably complicated task. This is why Simon Zinner took it upon himself to make it happen. His fingers, smashed in Dachau, had healed up all crooked, and he was terminally separated from his favorite flute, but Simon turned out to be a first-class organizer. During the day the former flautist worked as a busboy in the kitchen of one of the big hotels in the Concession, but every Tuesday and Thursday evening he managed to gather his colleagues together for the next rehearsal. This cost him a good deal of effort and persistence; people returned to Hongku too exhausted to work up the appetite to make music. But Zinner's stubborn insistence overcame their apathy and gradually the rehearsals turned into a ritual that created a little variety in their otherwise gray existence, taking the musicians back to forgotten joys and feelings. The first public concert in the steel construction factory's semi-destroyed hall was set up for the Jewish holiday Yom Kippur. People wept when Theodore Weissberg, his voice breaking with emotion, announced the formation of the "Shanghai Branch of the Dresden Philharmonic." At the very front, as distinguished guests, sat the nuns from the Carmelite Order, including the "colleagues" from the brass band. The sisters were led by Mother Antonia, proud and happy with this concert, which she considered an important sign that life among the desperate refugees was gaining strength again.

The conductor and first violin was, of course, Theodore Weissberg. The performance of Tchaikovsky's "Concert for Violin and Orchestra" was, as the newspapers would have put it, a "smashing success." Again there were tears and endless applause from the audience, which was released, at least for an hour, from its Shanghai woes. And to this point at least Theodore Weissberg's abilities could be extended to help overcome the unusual difficulties that life had heaped up every single day along the refugees' path.

This was not the situation with his wife Elisabeth.

She accepted with dignity and even—if this could be said of a woman—manliness the ordeals that destiny had dumped on her with particular lavishness. By the time she and Theodore had arrived in Shanghai, they were already almost completely without means of survival. The Nazi authorities allowed the taking out of up to ten Reichmarks per person, and those dollars from the Jewish aid organization, the "Joint," handed out by the shipping company when the ship disembarked, melted into thin air before people could even feel them. With his typical naiveté Theodore had accepted his wife's story about some burglary or other that had taken place at their house while he was still in Dachau, when all the family's precious possessions had disappeared. They hadn't managed to find a quick buyer for the house on Dante Alighieri Street, and they hadn't tried too hard to find one either, with their deep-seated conviction that sooner or later the day would come when they could return and would need a house to give them shelter. They didn't know, nor could they know, that even before the end of the war, their beloved Dresden, and with it their Empire-style home, would be nothing more than a pile of rubble.

The main worry was not lack of money, however, because Elisabeth, very soon and not without the help of the generous Mother Antonia, found a job as a teacher of piano and German in the family of Jonathan Bassat, one of the long-established Baghdadis. Mr. Bassat, short and stout but otherwise cheerful, from the family of the famous Alexandrian bankers Bassat, was the owner of a big export agency on Edward VII Avenue, and Elisabeth gave lessons to both of his children, a boy and a girl, every day.

No, it wasn't money that was the problem, even though the payment received from the Bassat family was barely enough to eke out a modest living, given the steep and constant rise in prices.

Even the young Chinese Fascists couldn't throw Elisabeth off balance. When they broke into their dortoir, the communal dormitory, crying "*Nagoni!*" and started breaking everything in sight with their short bamboo sticks, she didn't panic. *Nagoni* was a contemptuous name for foreigners, in this case Jews. Especially the newcomers from Germany. There were no men at this hour in the sleeping chamber and when the women and children started screaming as the thugs shouted and broke windows and beds, Elisabeth grabbed the first three-legged chair she could reach and waved it at the attackers.

"You dirty hoodlums, get out of here! I said, out, you damned vandals!"

She stormed like a fury and the result was quite unexpected: a command in Chinese was heard and the heroes quickly slipped out. The last one—possibly the leader—a young Chinese fellow with a Heidelberg student hat, threw a curious look at this tall, impressive woman who, with her copper hair and green eyes, had not become frightened. And they hadn't wanted to do more than just scare these female *Nagoni*.

"Do not insult the Vandals, Ma'am," he said in decent German. "They are a German tribe and not Jewish trash!"

She threw the chair at him, but the young Chinese guy had rushed laughing to slam the door behind him.

So the problem was not the Fascists who had stormed the dortoir. Far from it. The problem was the dortoir itself.

Elisabeth was not a spoiled doll but a tough and brave woman, ready for any ordeal. Or almost any. But what she couldn't take was life in these disgusting communal bedrooms—noise, snoring, people crying in their sleep, every moment someone coming and going, this one whispering to that one, a child choking on a cough, a hungry person crunching crackers in the middle of the night. The worst was that in the former silk-weaving workshop there was no plumbing, and during the time when it had still been in production, its industrial waste had flowed directly into the waters of the Soochow. Now, with refugees living in the space, every morning duty groups had to take out to the street the wooden buckets with their filth. And to wait there, in the heat and cold, in sun and rain, for the clumsy two-wheeled cart called the "shit wagon." Drawn by a buffalo, this was a huge wooden container into which an old Chinese man would empty the buckets so that later he could dump the load in the rice fields and swamps at the delta, in Pootung. You paid five cents per bucket.

Then again there was the waiting in the street to hear the clapper that announced the coming of the hot water man. Ten cents per gallon of boiled hot water, Ma'am. Spring water. Good water for drinking, Ma'am, very good. Ten cents. To use boiled water both for drinking and for abundant washing of vegetables was even more important than regular meals, because the water for the general population was disgusting. It smelled like the swamps and teemed with diseases—typhoid, dysentery, and every other known and unknown intestinal malady, right up to and including the sinister amoeba, unfamiliar in Europe, that nestles comfortably in the liver and slowly destroys it.

This was what Elisabeth couldn't bear—this life without a place of their own, without a toilet and running water. She, who didn't allow a speck of dust on the piano varnish, an unnecessary crease in the drapes, a dirty ashtray, a carelessly thrown magazine. She, who was in the habit of taking a shower twice a day!

Sitting on the bench at the muddy waterside street known as Soochow Creek and following the curves of the river, she burst into tears—for the first time. Looking helplessly around, Theodore took her cold hands and kissed them.

"I can't go on like this!" she cried. "We'll get work. I'm ready after the lessons at the Bassats' to do any kind of work. Anything. Cleaner, dishwasher. But I just can't take it anymore! I want my own room, a small room, whatever it is. A closet. A match-box. But I want to know when I close the door behind me that inside there's just you and me!"

And this time Theodore couldn't keep to himself his anguish over the fact that she had taken upon herself the whole burden of earning their keep. His contributions to the family budget occurred randomly and were more than pitiful—one more proof of his inability to handle the difficult reality of Shanghai. During the night he couldn't sleep because of worry and care for Elisabeth, the German who was now suffering because of him, the Jew! This tortured him, the thought itself causing him acute physical pain, like a blade that pierces the chest for an instant, a brief painful instant when it seemed to him that his heart stopped beating.

For the hundredth time he went back to the same theme:

"I am sorry, Elisabeth. My darling! I am sincerely sorry that I am the one who became the reason for all this. But I don't know, I really don't know how. . . ."

She nervously interrupted him:

"Stop talking nonsense! Stop right now or otherwise I'll lose respect for you! I'm your wife, understand? I'm asking you: Do you understand it? Your wife! You have neither forced me to accompany you, nor are you in any way to blame for the atrocities of those idiots in Germany. Stop it, do you hear me, you're driving me crazy! From you I want one thing, and one thing only! A place to live! A place of our own!"

It was easy enough to say, but available housing in half-burnt out and overpopulated Hongku was hardly cropping up all over the place, while outside the area, in the foreign concessions, rents, as well as hotel prices, were astronomical and completely out of reach for the barely surviving refugees. Exactly at that moment destiny sent Shlomo Finkelstein to put an end to this unpleasant conversation, which had been repeating itself periodically now for several months in more or less the same vein. The fat dwarf approached from the river, hugging an enormous bunch of blooming jasmine.

"For you, Mrs. Weissberg," respectfully said Shlomo.

Elisabeth tried to speak severely:

"Thank you, Shlomo. You're very kind, but tell me honestly, where did you pick them? And do try not to lie to me!"

"In the English garden," replied Shlomo, as innocent as a newborn.

"You understand, don't you, that this is theft?"

"But why, Ma'am? The garden is public. It doesn't belong to anyone."

"You'll find out to whom it belongs when they come and arrest you!"

"Don't worry, Ma'am. I paid the policeman who guards it twenty cents and he helped me pick them."

She laughed through her tears.

With insane hope in his voice, Theodore asked, "Shlomo, is there any news about places to live?"

Shlomo sighed and guiltily opened his short arms. "Nothing. Nothing at all, Mr. Weissberg. Available places in this destroyed and burnt-up neighborhood?! The Chinese too are jammed ten people to a room. I'd offer you my pantry, but it's a hole in which even a fox would suffocate."

Seeing the desperation appearing on the face of his protégé, Shlomo hurried to say:

"A little patience, Mr. Weissberg. Just a bit more. I've found out that many Chinese families will be going to their relatives in the South, toward the mountains. This happens every summer. Maybe then. . . ."

Truly this was so. As soon as the winter passed, during moonless nights, whole families secretly stole out of town, carrying their pitiful possessions to the villages in the South, to the mountains above Hanzhou, where the first rice harvest was drawing near and life was relatively easier. The Japanese authorities shut their eyes to these illegal nocturnal migrations toward territories under the control of the nationalists because it made it easier to handle the problems of everyday life in the city. And it also opened up living space for the Japanese immigrants, mainly those without property, villagers in the process of becoming proletarians, left without means of survival on islands choking with overpopulation. After the beginning of the Japanese invasion, in the northern part of Hongku, seventy thousand Japanese had settled in waves that spontaneously formed a community, a kind of small Japanese ghetto called Little Tokyo.

# 28

AT THE ENTRANCE TO the residence they were met by the baron's personal secretary, a real beauty whose typical Nordic good looks immediately caught the eye.

With reserved politeness, the blond secretary invited them to come in, and made an excuse that his eminence the baron would be a bit late because at the moment he was receiving a Japanese business delegation. Today was full of surprises: for the first time they were being received not uneasily, as annoying intruders, but benevolently, with emphatic although rather cold courtesy. And not just anywhere, but at the official legation of Nazi Germany itself—the same one about whose actions they had come to complain!

"Tea? Something cold to drink?"

The Chinese servant in traditional black silk attire poured the tea, bowed, and, silent as a shadow, disappeared. Rabbi Leo took a sip of green aromatic tea and with unconcealed, almost childish curiosity, looked at the cup, which was made of bone porcelain, its matte black coating decorated with golden dragons. With dragons he was lucky. It's said that they keep trouble away, a belief that up to now hadn't quite proved its truth, since these fire-spewing creatures had perhaps the selective ability to guard only Chinese people. Enigmatic and indecipherable as a complicated Chinese ideogram are the subtleties of Far East mysticism! He threw a quick look at the secretary and met hers, which was full of concentrated attention. Though she was riffling through some papers, from time to time she would pensively lift her eyes to the three of them, as if she were trying to penetrate their minds. What was it that was stirring up the imagination of this German woman so strongly? wondered Rabbi Leo. Maybe she had never met a rabbi in traditional clothing. It was certainly possible, because in Shanghai rabbis were rarer than the white Amur tiger in the zoo. Or was it that she had never seen German Jews? This could have happened too, especially if, according to Nazi anthropology, she had grown up in a racially "pure," Aryan environment.

Professor Mandel was far from sharing the same feeling. A typical neurotic with a high pale forehead bisected by a tense vertical vein—as if at the moment the surgeon were trying to lift a really heavy weight—between his fingers he was nervously twisting a piece of paper into a little ball. He also threw a hidden look, full of tense mistrust, at the secretary. Wasn't she also one of those SS bitches, polished for the world but not infrequently behaving with considerably more fanaticism and cruelty than the men?

She was the first to break the silence:

"How do you feel here, Mr. Levin? Excuse me, I don't know how to address a rabbi."

The rabbi raised his eyes from the cup. "It doesn't matter, Miss. I am, as it's customary to say, just a servant of God. In this case it's important how the servant addresses his employer, especially ours. After all, the Lord is a rather severe and angry old man!" Then he added merrily, "Otherwise we feel wonderful. Especially recently since the price of dried grasshoppers went down."

Professor Mandel somberly interfered. "Don't take him seriously. We live badly. It couldn't be worse!"

"Oh yes it could." Rabbi Leo repeated the old Jewish quip with unfaltering optimism.

The secretary laughed, but her smile immediately vanished. "I know. I know that you live badly. Have you been in Shanghai a long time?"

"For different times, Miss," replied the rabbi. "Professor Mandel and I were among the first, since last summer. Mr. Theodore Weissberg has been here for . . . it seems to me, five months. . . . Or have I got it wrong?"

"Seven," said Theodore.

"Theodore Weissberg? The violinist?" the woman exclaimed with amazement.

Theodore nodded in confusion. "Excuse me . . . do we know each other?"

"Oh, no. But I know you. I attended a concert of yours once in Potsdam."

"Incredible! To meet at the other end of the world someone who once heard you in Potsdam."

"You were brilliant!"she said sincerely. "Especially in the *Solo Caprices* of Paganini!"

"Thank you. It's very nice of you to say so."

He kept silent before adding with quiet sadness:

"Potsdam, yes. . . . The parks of Sans Souci, the blooming apple trees. Like infinite white clouds along the banks of the Werder. Now it all seems to me as if it never existed. That I dreamed it. . . . Solo caprices!"

"You didn't dream it, Mr. Weissberg. It existed and I'm ready to testify . . . I'm sorry that circumstances developed not to your benefit, but let's hope. . . ."

"Hope for what?" Professor Mandel asked a bit aggressively. "Did you leave us something that we could hope for?"

She seemed somewhat offended by the professor's sharp tone, because she added more drily:

"Let's hope that the war will soon be over. That's what I wanted to say. The news we're getting from Europe is wonderful. Extremely encouraging. After the lightning-like breakthrough of our tank columns in the rear of the French, our armored divisions have started a mass offensive. According to last night's communiqué from Supreme Headquarters, the withdrawal of the enemy is massive and Paris will fall in a matter of days."

"My God," involuntarily uttered the rabbi.

"You didn't know about it?" she asked evenly.

"Of course not. Over there, in Hongku, we don't have a radio."

Why did Theodore Weissberg have the distinct feeling that the secretary had announced the news only apparently by chance, and only apparently disinterestedly, but rather with the particular desire to inform them about the progress of the war? At least that's how it seemed to him. Such was her look, which, fixing itself directly on him, expressed something more, something unspoken. A warning against a danger lying in wait for them? Or some new trouble that was dangling above their heads? The blonde secretary didn't appear to be stupid, and she couldn't have not known that for the hounded Jews the news could hardly have been, as she put it, "wonderful" and "extremely encouraging." Or maybe he was just deluding himself with wishful thinking, and her dispassionate tone was meant simply to underscore the winner's triumph, the Valkyrie's having set her foot on the defeated enemy's breast?

Over them hung a tense silence, which at last the rabbi bravely interrupted:

"Excuse me if this is too impertinent. But over there in Hongku we're completely isolated from news about events in Europe. And very few of us can afford the luxury of buying newspapers from the Concession. We've learned that since the beginning of the war you've been publishing a newsletter. Could we have access to it?"

"Of course. It isn't confidential. We're even interested in having the public here be well informed. Especially now when the signing of a tripartite pact between Rome, Berlin, and Tokyo is about to take place and will change a lot of things here in Shanghai. It's even quite possible that it will change them radically."

Again the same intense look in Theodore Weissberg's direction, again the same feeling that she was in fact warning the violin player about something menacing that was floating in the air. . . .

The three of them silently looked at each other, but said nothing. A tripartite pact! Didn't this mean that the war in Europe and the war in the Far East, so distant and so different from each other, with such incommensurable goals, were uniting in a common system that would grip the planet as in a pair of pliers?

The secretary didn't wait to observe their reaction, but carelessly added, "But these are, so to speak, future plans and possibilities. If anything new comes up, I'm ready to let you know about it. In general, in case you need to you can easily call me on the phone. They know the number at the central post office."

"Thank you, you're very kind. Quite frankly, we had gotten out of the habit of . . . how to put it. . . ."

She smiled warmly. "You don't have to say it. It's understood. After all, we're all from the same land, aren't we?"

"After all . . . yes. Partially," Professor Mandel somberly interjected. Apparently he wasn't the kind of person inclined to compromise for the sake of dialogue.

Rabbi Leo, on the contrary, was one of the amiable and flexible representatives of humankind.

"How can we find you? Your name, if you don't mind?" he asked.

"Braun. Ask for Miss Hilde Braun. They'll connect you."

# 29

WHEN FRANCE AND ENGLAND simultaneously declared war on Germany, Hilde and the Hungarian happened to be on their way to Toulon.

In the big harbor city people were seized with patriotic euphoria; blue, white, and red flags waved from the windows, as if it were the eve of July 14th, the Republic's national holiday, and not the beginning of a new war. As yet no one suspected that on that not so distant day, on which the fall of the Bastille was traditionally celebrated, the flag that would flutter above the Eiffel Tower would not be the French Tricolor but Hitler's swastika. On the Champs-Élysées, instead of France's vain equine praetorian guard with its glittering shields, a German armored tank column would pass by—muddy, dusty, not so hearty, but for that very reason victorious. Because exactly a month before the holiday, as early as June 14th, Paris would be in the hands of the Nazis, and seven days after the fall of the capital France would sign a humiliating capitulation in a certain railway car at Compiègne—the very same railway car in which the kaiser's Germany had signed its capitulation little more than two decades before!

But none of this had happened yet, and few were those who believed that it would happen. For the time being people rang out with "*Le jour de gloire est arrivé. . . .*"

The military cycle was stirring up its whirlwind again: humankind had achieved amazing success in the development of new arms, but not of new ideas that would forbid their use.

Mobilized reservists marched buoyantly in the streets; the people, gazing in rapture at tank divisions, saw in them the proud and unquestionable superiority of France. She was, by the way, superior to the Germans in all kinds of other arms—from heavy artillery to combat planes—and this was an indisputable axiom. The proprietors of bistros offered soldiers free wine and cigarettes; from the radio and over the squares came a ceaseless cascade of enthusiastic marches. And it never occurred to anyone that at the same time the lazy and nearsighted French command was just now starting to ponder the strategy and tactics of the war—as if it were an impending event and not an already burning reality. And that what had to happen was already happening.

At the harbor the chaos was complete: they were loading military units, horses, and matériel to reinforce the contingents in North Africa and unloading English troops from the Middle East, while Polish volunteers and Amsterdam Jews persistently searched for places on ships to England. It wasn't clear who was going where, or why, and to believe that in this swarm one could find a free space on one of the overstuffed vessels was more than a naive hope. But perhaps in acknowledging the absurdity of the situation lay the key to overcoming it: the two of them looked for a solution to their problem not there, where all the others were looking for it, on the central piers, but a little off the beaten track, on the fishermen's quay. Istvan Keleti's matchless French, and Hilde's charming, ever-promising smile, bolstered by some American dollars, roused compassion and a feeling of solidarity. And thus they were taken on a fishing trawler to Bizerta, on the opposite shore, without having to show their passports—with long-expired visas. At the moment, by the way, those among the border police who were interested in such problems were few.

The route from Tunisia to Egypt turned out to be not that much more complicated than taking the Paris metro at rush hour: on the northern shore of Africa there circulated countless contraband ships, as well as fishing boats that followed schools of sardines and readily accepted, for a paltry sum, one or two passengers without being interested in annoying details like documents and nationality. The heads of the English and the French colonial authorities there also burned with other cares quite different from the obligation to prevent the comings and goings of deserters or duty-free traffic in Algerian cigarettes and Moroccan arak.

In the nightclubs of Alexandria the two of them were received as a rich couple that excited looks of surprise from the English officers and their girls, who could only with difficulty see the connection between this angular and always slightly tipsy cavalier and his gorgeous companion. "The living Nefertiti with the mummy of Akhenaton!" commented Xavier da Silva, captain of the ocean liner *Asunción II*, under the flag of Panama. When the captain, who had the looks of a finely aged bonvivant, slithered up to them with a bottle of gin and with great courtesy asked to sit down at their table, Hilde still had no suspicion that her lucky star was rising again. But after the first friendly glass it became clear that the little ball in the wheel of fortune had stopped exactly at her number: in two days, the *Asunción II* would raise its anchor and through the Suez Canal, the Red Sea, and the Persian Gulf make its way toward the Far East, and then through Macao, Singapore, and Manila straight to the open city of dreams—Shanghai!

For the time being they were, we could say, if not exactly rich, at least relatively well provided for: Dr. Hiroshi's necklace of pink Japanese pearls, sold at a solid Paris jeweler's on the Rue de Rivoli, allowed them to pay for two first-class cabins—worthy of one living Nefertiti and the mummy of the pharaoh Akhenaton. Indeed, in light of the black uncertainty that was awaiting them, this was a frivolous waste of money, but the two of them had estimated that in the eyes of their new acquaintance, Captain Da Silva, they shouldn't look like destitute refugees. The big Egyptian harbor even without them was jammed with hunted, often destitute, weatherbeaten adventurers, international crooks, fugitives from the French Foreign Legion, or simply wretched unfortunates.

The captain reached into the deep secret reserve he maintained of cabins for "fire escape" needs, especially after he found out that the two new passengers were neither newlyweds on a honeymoon nor lovers, but rich idlers looking to get as far away as possible from embattled Europe. He never found out that the lady was a Jew and her cavalier someone who had absconded from the Hungarian police because of a morphine deal. The two of them had sensibly decided that it wasn't necessary for ship captains to know more about their passengers than was required.

The border authorities in Alexandria carried out a rather superficial and careless inspection of the passengers on the *Asunción II*, inasmuch as it was coming from Stockholm and had stopped in transit at the port of Alexandria. The English major looked with suspicion at Hilde's German passport with its colorful French visas, but her explanation that she was a fugitive from Nazism who was coming from France on the way to Shanghai seemed convincing enough. This by the way was the truth itself, even though truth quite often is the most unconvincing part of the mystery called life. The war was still young and inexperienced; the Germans still allowed people who carried British passports to sneak out of the occupied countries of Europe; the British did not impede the movement of German diplomats; Soviet emissaries were zigzagging the planet left and right without problems. The time had not yet come for the suspicious scrutinizing of every stranger, for putting foreigners, especially subjects from the enemy camp, under special surveillance. The witch and spy hunt, as well as the repression of citizens on both sides, would happen, and not without reason either, sometime later—quite a bit later, when the sky over London, Nuremberg, or Leningrad was torn by nighttime aerial sirens and people realized that it was no longer about a brief and banal military conflict, but a bloody life-and-death clash that had no equal in human history.

# 30

THE ENGINES IN THE holds roared distantly and monotonously, causing a light vibration in each atom of the ship. Hilde was absentmindedly looking through the open porthole, since there was hardly a difference between whatever had happened an hour ago or was going to happen an hour from now—apart from the red African sun, which was expanding by dimensions unseen by her and rolling toward the horizon like a big bloody disk.

The *Asunción II* was still crawling south along the Suez Canal between the shores of Africa and Asia; on either side of the ship there passed and sank into the drowsy summer dusk cheerless semi-desert landscapes, rare date groves, tired fellahin, camels walking to their mud-hut villages, goats, and long-horned, hunch-backed oxen.

She was startled by the ringing of the doorbell and the delicate knock that followed. In came a dark-skinned, dark-haired man in a summer uniform with golden aiguillettes worthy at least of an admiral. The dark man, with a thin Mexican mustache and moist, rather protruding eyes, handed her an envelope and performed a ritual bow as if in front of him indeed stood the true and divine Nefertiti.

"At your service, Miss Braun, and Mr. Keleti. At the behest of Captain Da Silva. . . . If you need something you can always find me through the valet. I am the Chief Mate; my name is Paco Ramirez and I am at your disposal round-the-clock. Excuse me for disturbing you."

With his damp gaze he ate up the blond passenger, bowed again, and disappeared, this chief mate, who looked more like a pimp or a drug dealer.

The envelope, with a heraldic sign and the name of the ship in the upper left corner, contained an invitation, handwritten in a beautiful calligraphic style and informing them in a tortuous linguistic baroque that Captain Da Silva would consider it a very high honor if the two of them would agree to dine with him at the captain's table. *Allow me to express my most sincere . . .* and so on. Apparently the captain, as a real Latin American and caballero, had not been deprived of a weakness, typical of those geographic latitudes, for elegant formalities. Hilde smiled at the convoluted and archaic but otherwise endearing French from the time of Rabelais without giving the invitation any special importance. She didn't know that this hoity-toity navy blue envelope, with something like a king's heraldic coat of arms on it, was going to play a crucial role in her near future.

The Jewish girl with a German name and a German passport had just received a ticket with a reserved seat in the train of which Alain Conti—the commander in chief of starlets—had spoken.

The dining room for first-class passengers was on the upper deck. Through the wide-open square portholes a small breeze wafted from the desert and rustled the satin drapes. Two rows of fans on the ceiling offered some slight relief against the heavy heat of the tropical night without overcoming it.

A small female string orchestra was playing and despite the early hour the tables were already occupied to the last seat: one of the sure signs on every ship embarked on a cruise to faraway places that the epidemic of that most difficult-to-cure sea sickness —boredom—had already spread.

When Hilde and the Hungarian entered, escorted by Paco Ramirez, the first to jump to his feet and walk to meet them was Captain Da Silva, who performed gloriously the ceremony of introducing the new passengers. At the table were already seated one Finnish couple, who were on their way to their country's commercial delegation in Victoria, a British colony that the Chinese called Hong Kong, and two Swedish engineers traveling to Shanghai, whence they would have to transfer to the regular ships to Kobe. They did not conceal the information that they were representatives of the Swedish arms factories Beaufort, which were developing new kinds of howitzers easily transportable in mountainous conditions. To the innocent observer it might have seemed strange that neutral Sweden was taking part in the production of new weapons for warring countries, but during the war that had just broken out and hadn't even turned yet into a global affair, there would happen many and even far stranger things.

Minutes later there arrived at the table, accompanied by the generous chief mate Ramirez, a plump middle-aged woman, powdered and smiling, with merry dimples in her cheeks. There was something open and unpretentious about her conducive to easy, unconventional conversation. Apparently she was already an old acquaintance and the center of the small society around the captain's table because all those who had been invited stood up to meet her.

Captain Da Silva presented to her the new dining companions: Hilde and the Hungarian.

"Your fellow countrywoman, Miss Hilde Braun. And maestro Keleti—a Hungarian pianist."

"The maestro," just now crowned with this title, bowed and kissed the hand of the newcomer, something that in his Paris environment he would never have done. But as the French say, noblesse oblige!

Captain Da Silva continued the ceremony with the mutual introductions, announcing with solemn ardor:

". . . and our dear friend Baroness Gertrude von Dammbach!"

She behaved with utter naturalness, this von Dammbach, smiling at Hilde in a kindly and friendly way: a fluffy baroness, sweet as a homemade doughnut.

And that's how it all started.

Vodka and Russian caviar, champagne with French goose liver and truffles, ice cold Chardonnay and Scandinavian smoked salmon—everything was worthy even of the most exquisite Paris restaurant. And every element in the ritual, down to the smallest detail, was overseen by the chief mate Ramirez, who was standing up behind his boss and performing the functions of a sort of master of ceremonies for the evening.

No one paid attention to the brief looks exchanged several times between Paco Ramirez and the Hungarian; people were busy with themselves and with the chicken in Madeira sauce. Neither did anyone notice the furious looks that Hilde threw at the Hungarian while he guzzled alcohol at a tempo unsuitable for this kind of society.

The baroness was an amiable and genuine woman who from the very first moment liked Hilde. She even caused a bit of commotion at the table by managing to get everyone to change places so that the two of them could sit together.

"I'm happy to meet a fellow countrywoman. . . . From which part of Germany are you, dear?"

"Berlin. But I used to work in Babelsberg. *UFA*."

"Oh, *UFA*! An actress?"

"Not exactly. . . ."

"Then exactly what?"

"How shall I put it? I was assisting the director Riefenstahl," stated Hilde and was surprised herself by her lie, which possessed a very distant relation to reality.

The baroness looked at her with sincere admiration.

"To Leni Riefenstahl herself? Amazing! Dear, why does it seem to me that I've seen you somewhere before?"

"It's hardly possible," replied Hilde.

"No, no! When someone makes an impression on me, I remember it all my life. Where have I seen you? Where, where? . . . In any case I envy you!" She leaned toward Hilde's ear as if to an old intimate friend and whispered, "In the twenties I was a dancer at the Friedrichstadtpalace music hall. That's just between us, all right, dear? Since we never know what trouble will come our way. I was dreaming of becoming a film actress and instead I became a baroness!"

And she burst out into her contagious, ringing laughter. Then the laughter suddenly stopped.

"I remember! I've seen your photographs in *Der Stürmer*! Right?"

"My God," thought Hilde, "so it means after all that the great Werner Gauke twisted those idiots around his finger and got them to publish the photographs!" In fact why not? It was their five hundred Reichsmarks that constituted the main capital with which she had started this whole adventure!

"It was a little like this," she said reluctantly. "I suppose they took some photos of me, but I've never seen them personally."

"Of course. I remember them well. . . . In Paris! Exactly right—in Paris, wasn't it? Amazing. And to meet you where? On some ship! Life, dear child, is fantastic with its whims. An assistant of Leni Riefenstahl herself! Unbelievable!"

For the baroness, one vodka as an aperitif, two glasses of champagne, and a modest quantity of Chardonnay, not counting a sip of old Bordeaux, were more than sufficient and she spontaneously kissed Hilde on the cheek.

When they parted, the tropical night was already pitch-dark and starless. The ship lights were reflected in the water like wet, immovable black asphalt and only the vibrations of the body of the ship and the gurgling of the invisible foaming water suggested that the *Asunción II* was moving.

Having taken a shower and put on her bathrobe, Hilde decided to visit the Hungarian. To drop in on him just like that, an old habit from the time when they'd shared a home in Paris in the small apartment by Les Halles, but also from the need to have a chat with him about everything that had happened during the evening. Because the adventurer, the dreamer, the architect of this whole insane journey was he. And she also had to cajole him a little after having probably offended him with her fierce looks all throughout dinner. Her worry at the time turned out to be futile; despite the considerable quantity of alcohol he had imbibed, he had behaved as decently as a Hungarian maestro worthy of his title.

Hilde was just opening her door when through the aperture she saw how, across the way, chief mate Paco Ramirez was stealthily slipping into the Hungarian's cabin. Seconds after that the lock on the inside clicked.

She smiled, went back to her cabin, and quietly closed the door behind her. A sly fox, this Ramirez! Early in the evening he had cast an ardent look at her with his protruding, moist eyes, but this had turned out to be a roundabout and deceptive maneuver! She never understood how these fellows—the homosexuals—sniffed each other out. In fact she wasn't trying to understand it; the problem didn't concern her.

A little later the inevitable happened that she had long ago sensed with her mysterious female instincts: there was a quiet knock on her door and Captain Da Silva entered her cabin with a bottle of champagne.

"May I?"

In desperation she shook her head and lied with inimitable genuineness:

"You're very kind, Captain. And surprising me with this unexpected and fantastic idea, but I just now threw up everything I drank and ate this memorable evening. In reverse order."

"A glass or two of champagne will tame the seasickness, you adorable thing, I assure you."

"A glass or two? If I drink one, I will throw up one. If I drink two, I will throw up . . . how many, in your opinion? And besides, dear captain, it isn't really a matter of seasickness. I'm pregnant."

She herself had always been surprised at the spontaneous lies that fell out of her mouth before she could even realize it. She lied impulsively and naturally, lies just welled up from within, and there wasn't a thing she could do to prevent them, just as you can't stop hiccups or your eyes from tearing.

An inconsolable sadness appeared on Captain Da Silva's face; he clicked his heels and, bowing modestly, walked out backward, the way you walk away from an audience with a queen.

This Captain Da Silva was a true caballero!

After a second, at just the moment when she was about to lock the door, there was another knock. Again it was Da Silva, who entered with a ballet step, excused himself, and quickly took his champagne. The night was only just beginning.

# 31

TIMELESSNESS FLOWED ALONGSIDE THE ship—monotonous and boring.

It was early afternoon and the two of them were lying next to each other on the chaise longues. Around them spread out an endless expanse of water, water and nothing but water.

The baroness, under a lace sun hat that almost hid her kind and fluffy face, turning it into a tangle of light and shadow, suddenly remembered something:

"Dear, we've been together so many days now. I keep asking you and you never give me a clear answer. I still can't understand the purpose of your journey. Singapore? Manila? Or is it a secret?"

"It's not a secret. Let's just say: the end of the world."

"And more precisely?"

Hilde tried to remember the name of the end of the world but couldn't come up with it this time either. She stretched out her arm and patted the back of the Hungarian, who had fallen into an afternoon nap. She suspected that in this drowsiness of his a role was played by the mysterious white powder that he concealed in a snuff box. Hilde never asked about this, knowing that every person is wrapped in a thin veil of his own secret weaknesses and vices.

"Istvan, where's the end of the world?"

Startled, the Hungarian didn't understand the question and turned to the dedicated, at-your-service chief mate, Ramirez.

"Paco, where's the end of the world?"

The latter looked briefly around; such an intimate and revealing form of address was inappropriate for shipboard society. But nothing happened, no one paid attention, and the chief mate announced with an official tone, staring at the endless horizon, "According to the latest research, sir, the earth has recently been round. Therefore, the beginning and end of the world is in each one of us, sir."

The baroness applauded:

"Bravo, bravo, a true philosopher! Do you know, you're not stupid at all, *mon cher*!"

"Not to sound immodest, but I have the same impression, Baroness," replied the chief mate with dignity, and without taking his eyes off the horizon.

"But I still don't understand your ultimate destination. Confess it to me finally, dear child! We're friends now, aren't we?" said the baroness, mildly but insistently.

Hilde tried to squeeze her memory:

"Yes . . . what's it called? Saigon! It's Saigon, isn't it, Istvan?"

"Shanghai," the Hungarian corrected her, nodding off again.

"My God, then we're traveling in the same direction!" exclaimed the baroness. "And you're calling this 'the end of the world'? Listen: Shanghai is the beginning of hell, dear! The first of the nine circles! Believe me—I've lived there a whole eternity. And what do you intend to do in that cursed place, if it isn't a secret?"

"I don't know. I really don't know. It's very intimate and complicated . . ." whispered Hilde, with sincere desperation. She couldn't reveal the real reason—the Jewish reason—for this journey to the "first circle of hell." "I don't really have definite plans."

The baroness sank into thought; then with kind sympathy caressed her hand and recited something that could be an excerpt from a novel for housewives:

"I understand. Personal drama, a big crush, a desire to run away from yourself. . . . Clear as day. But don't tell me, my child. Don't stir up the memories! And if, as I suppose, you're not a millionaire, what are you going to live on in that crazy and confused city?"

"I'll look for work. Any kind of work."

"Jesus, Maria! In Shanghai, where for a long time there's been no work at all? Where every second person is unemployed? No, no, don't tell me! You, dear, were not born for 'any kind of work.' And don't tell me otherwise!"

The baroness thought for a moment, and, since Hilde showed no desire to tell her otherwise, continued a little more calmly:

"What have you studied?"

"Language and literature at Humboldt University."

She didn't find it necessary to point out that she had started in this field but hadn't finished in it.

"I've got it! So, do you see?!"

Hilde didn't understand what she needed to see, which hardly prevented the baroness from triumphantly continuing:

"In Shanghai I know a dear old man, otherwise a complete nincompoop, who would find you a suitable job. I swear to you! He's fond of beautiful women, but don't worry—he's completely harmless. He'll court you, he'll mount fierce campaigns to conquer you, but these are just ritualistic jousts. At the end he'll prefer to drink a beer and won't lay a finger on you."

"Sigmund Freud, virtual sexology. And who is this love shaman?"

"Who, you ask? Why Ottomar! My husband, dear child. Baron Ottomar von Dammbach!"

And the baroness again flooded the distant horizon with her ringing laughter.

The Hungarian, without opening his eyes, raised his arm and waved his fingers:

"Paco, are you here?"

"Of course, sir."

"Could you bring me a vodka? Double, please. With ice and just a hint of lemon juice."

"I'm sorry, sir. The buffet is closed."

"How fed up I am with everything here. My God, is there no end to this journey?"

"Every journey that has a beginning also has an end, sir."

"And exactly at what time do we arrive at this damned Shanghai of yours?"

"Exactly at midnight, sir."

"And what time is it now?"

The chief mate looked at his wristwatch. "Four thirty in the afternoon, sir."

"God, as late as midnight!"

"I'm sorry, but I can't change the timetable. The *Asunción II* will reach Shanghai exactly at midnight in nine days, sir."

# 32

HILDE USHERED IN THE three delegates of the Jewish Refugee Community of Shanghai to the diplomatic representative of the Third Reich. A Jewish delegation, at an official visit with the supreme emissary of Hitler's Germany! This fact in itself was remarkable and constituted one more proof of the perversions and paradoxes possible only in the open city of Shanghai.

Baron Ottomar von Dammbach was a tall, slightly stooping man not in his first youth, with light blue, almost colorless eyes and with straight, fading, combed-back hair that had once-upon-a-time most probably been straw-blond. Even the most zealous observer of racial purity could hardly have doubted the Celtic or Viking blood running in his veins.

What all three of them immediately noticed was the round badge with the swastika on the baron's lapel, signifying that its bearer was a member of the National Socialist party. Such a badge sometimes caused horror, especially among those belonging to the tribe of Israel, but to others who were familiar with the situation, it was often not such a disturbing and unusual sign, since it was known that everyone who occupied a responsible post in the government hierarchy had to be a member of the party, which had merged with the German state itself, its policy and future. Moreover, the three of them couldn't have known that the baron himself had a dismissive attitude toward his own badge, being a cadre diplomat from the old school. He had resigned himself with chagrin to the new party postulates just on the threshold of his impending retirement pension, which motivated his principal dreams not so much toward the forthcoming titanic, thousand-year Reich predicted by the Führer, but rather toward nearer days of rest among his children and grandchildren on the small family estate of Dammbach in Thuringia.

The baron left his seat behind the desk by the gilded bust of the Führer and with a generous gesture pointed to the armchairs just now vacated by the Japanese visitors.

"Please, gentlemen, be seated!"

Hugging the file folder, Hilde remained standing at the tall window.

"Am I free, Mr. Baron?" she asked.

"No, stay. I want you to take dictation. I am listening to you, gentlemen."

Professor Mandel described the situation with those Fascist youths who periodically terrorized the German Jews in Hongku. By nature incapable of diplomacy, he expressed his suspicion in exceedingly sharp and unmeasured words that the German diplomatic legation in Shanghai was behind these outrages.

Rabbi Leo tried to mitigate the professor's tone after he observed the baron raising his eyebrows in surprise. "We don't mean you personally, of course, Mr. Baron. But without doubt someone is financing and encouraging both the newspaper and these anti-Semitic crimes. Judging by the . . . how to put it . . . the style, these are hardly Chinese or Japanese circles. . . ."

"Japanese, certainly not," said von Dammbach, pressing his lips into a twisted smile.

Apparently he had something against the Japanese but didn't say what it was. It wasn't a secret that despite officially proclaimed cordial relations, the ties between Hitler's Germany and Hirohito's Japan were not particularly marked by collegial tenderness. The two sides jealously and stingily shared their secret plans with each other, while addressing with the utmost suspicion the declared intentions of the other side, which too often differed from those in reality. Probably it was not the object of a particularly closely guarded secret that in the shorthand record of a dialogue between Hitler and Colonel-General Yodl, the head of the Supreme Headquarters of the Wehrmacht, the Führer qualified his Japanese friends as "liars" and "crooks." On the other hand, "the Jewish problem," about which Hitler's elite was taking with pathological obsession ever more radical measures, was, to insular Japan, not a problem at all, in that the Jewish presence there was hardly visible. As far as the conquered parts of the continent were concerned, despite a certain degree of social discomfort related to the presence of Russian and German Jews, the Japanese were fruitfully cooperating with those five to six hundred Baghdadi families, which possessed strong international links, especially to the States. It was not surprising that business circles in Tokyo flirted with this rich community, seeing in it a useful ally in their efforts to overcome traditional Japanese isolationism.

The baron lit a long Egyptian cigarette, but did not offer one to his visitors. Pensively, and with great interest, he looked at the burning fire from all sides and finally said, "Look, gentlemen, I'm not God. I understand you, but apart from the diplomatic legation, the commercial, political, and propaganda structures here are directly subordinate to their central offices in Berlin. Without a doubt, nominally I am the head of the German community in Shanghai, but . . . nominally, if you get what I'm thinking—" And while failing to find a suitable word for his helplessness, he nervously added, "After all, I'm not the one who stuffed you in this hole! You yourselves boiled your porridge, now you have to eat it!"

"You know well the circumstances that pushed us to this step," quietly said Theodore Weissberg. "We would never have left Germany if—"

"Let's leave those 'ifs' aside, gentlemen. I am not inclined to discuss with you the official policy of the German government!" the baron nervously interrupted.

"Excuse me," said the violinist, still quietly. "We did not intend to discuss the actions that became possible because of the indifference of some and the silence of others. They do not depend on your will, and even less on ours. We only wanted your interference—"

"All right, all right, I understand what you want. I will try to do what is within my power. I don't believe that as of tomorrow they will start inviting you to balls. But I hope those kids around *Yudaia Kenku* will stop bothering you. Still, I also want from you a reciprocal gesture of loyalty. I must insist that you compile detailed and precise lists of your fellow citizens who have arrived in Shanghai from Germany and Austria since 1937. May I count on you to do this?"

The three of them looked at each other. Why exactly 1937 was clear: this was the year of the invasion; since then Shanghai had been under Japanese jurisdiction. But to whom and why were those lists necessary?

Theodore Weissberg threw an involuntary look at the secretary standing by the window and holding the file folder tightly to her breast. It seemed to him that, almost imperceptibly, she was shaking her head no.

Full of deep suspicion, he asked, with a hollow voice, "Why do you need these lists?"

It wasn't out of the question that the baron himself was insufficiently informed, because he tried to give his voice a certain nonchalance:

"They want them in Berlin. Maybe for compiling national statistics or something like that. . . .With the greatest possible detail concerning sex, age, health, and so on."

Theodore again cast a glance at the secretary and again noticed her barely perceptible shake of the head.

The three of them were silent in confusion.

"For us this would hardly be a doable task," finally said the rabbi. "You've probably never set foot there, so you don't know what a thronging chaos there is in Hongku. And we're not talking about a hundred or so, but thousands upon thousands of German immigrants dispersed throughout the city—every one struggling for bread. I suppose you know that we don't have an administration. We don't have even a typewriter or a telephone. And I don't believe it would be possible to find so many people and put them on lists. After all, Mr. Baron, this is the population of an average-size German town."

"An average-size Jewish town!" the baron viciously corrected him.

"Then why don't you ask the Japanese authorities for such information?" asked Professor Mandel, letting the remark go. "We were not dropped here by parachute, Mr. Baron! We all came by sea, completely legally and with regular papers, didn't we? I don't mean some Czech or Latvian Jews who came by the Trans-Siberian Railway. The Japanese authorities at the port itself were doing the most pedantic inspections, weren't they? All newcomers were recorded in the border registers; from us they were practically asking for the maiden names of our grandmothers. Why don't you look there?"

The baron again gave a twisted smile.

"I didn't ask you for the name of your grandmother! I know that if it wasn't Rebecca, it was Sarah. As far as the Japanese authorities are concerned, if I ask them for information about the temperature in Tokyo at the moment, they will hide even that! No, no, gentlemen, I'm relying on you. Personally. And I require it with explicit firmness, as of German citizens."

"For the time being . . ." bitterly inserted Professor Mandel.

"While you still are!" The baron, no longer so obliging, stood up.

With this the audience was over.

# 33

THE INFORMATION POSSESSED BY Ottomar von Dammbach's personal secretary turned out to be authentic: exactly one week before Mussolini attacked Greece, the Tripartite Pact between Italy, Germany, and Japan was signed in Berlin by the foreign ministers of Germany and Italy, von Ribbentrop and Count Ciano, respectively, and on the Japanese side by the ambassador to Rome, Saburo Kuruso. Despite differing goals and secret rivalries, the three sides at this stage had common strategic interests and first among these were the zones of powerful English influence and military presence in Europe, Africa, and the Far East.

The news spread quickly from one ear to another among the immigrants in Hongku. People were anxiously asking each other if the Nazis were now going to exert pressure on their new Japanese allies similar to the pressure being put on the small German satellites Hungary, Croatia, Romania, and Bulgaria, or on the puppet authorities in occupied Europe from whom Hitler's emissaries constantly and with the stubbornness of raging bulls required clear, aggressive, and uncompromising support of their anti-Semitic policy.

What direction this pressure would take here in Shanghai, thousands of miles away from Europe, no one knew for the time being, but Rabbi Leo Levin took into consideration Theodore Weissberg's impression that the baron's secretary had given a negative signal. The violinist was not one of those people who quickly and easily get their bearings in unforeseen situations, much less those in which doubtful and inexplicable movements of the head are concerned, but in any case the rabbi judiciously asked his wife to burn the modest register of the synagogue. In it he had been recording births and funerals, donations for the mutual-aid fund, circumcisions, weddings, and bar mitzvahs.

But joy is the sister of sorrow: this notion, or something in a similar vein, the thousand-year-old Chinese woman who was Esther Levin's teacher of rice-roll cooking tried to express when she saw her neighbor pensively tearing pages out of the thick notebook and throwing them into the fire. The old woman believed in that doubtful but ever vital maxim, and if it couldn't be applied to all cases, at least this disturbing news coincided with a happy event for the Weissbergs: Shlomo Finkelstein had finally found, at an acceptable price, the housing they'd been yearning for.

It was a small mud dwelling not far from the steel factory, leased by relatives of local residents who had long ago escaped to the mountains, with two rooms and a low additional building for storage. After the occupation in '37, a family of Japanese cooks had settled there who had now found work in a fancy Japanese restaurant on the other side of the river, in the International Concession. So there were two magnificent small rooms, the pair of "matchboxes" of which Elisabeth had been dreaming for months, and in the additional building Shlomo crafted an almost real shower out of a gasoline tank salvaged from a truck burned during the bombings. In comparison to the general conditions in Hongku, which was sunk in ruin, stench, and misery, this was a miniature oasis, a little house clean in the Japanese way, with flowered curtains on the windows, where the happy family of departing cooks, saying goodbye with countless ritual bows, had even left some furniture.

Elisabeth's dream of a secluded corner of their own was thus fulfilled, though, on the other hand, it threatened the family budget, which had been getting thinner and thinner, with complete collapse. The communal bedrooms, it was true, with their provincial train-station waiting-room atmosphere, were repulsive and nasty, but they were free; Mother Antonia's nuns took care of that. Now a payment had to be made on the first of every month, and people were already saying that at prices that were very modest compared to those in Europe, even so rents had gone up several times.

This compelled Elisabeth to overcome her pride and complexes when Simha Bassat, the wife of Jonathan, came to her with a request to find a suitable Jew for an assistant gardener. It had recently become the fashion, dictated sometimes by sincere sympathy, but not infrequently by vanity and ostentatiousness, for rich Jewish families, long settled here, to take one or two servants from the circles of the newly arrived German Jews in dire straits. It was a form of support offered instead of handouts, since Chinese labor in many cases was more effective, as well as less pretentious, and also considerably cheaper. In return, you could talk to the servants in German, a sign of high social and cultural status long established among the Shanghai Jewish elite, comparable to the pride of Jewish middle-class families in what had once been Austria-Hungary, who would hire Swiss governesses for their children.

Elisabeth without hesitation offered her husband for the vacant job. To the question about his profession she mumbled something indefinite, like "clerk." She didn't mention that Theodore was a famous violinist, in order not to create moral dilemmas on the other side; after all the Bassat family didn't need someone to perform Sarasate, but an assistant gardener! In this way the member of the Prussian Academy of Art and the soul of the Dresden Philharmonic, the virtuoso Theodore Weissberg, became an assistant to the old gardener, the virtuoso in the growing of flowers and vegetables, Wu Laozian.

The red buses of the city municipal company went as far as the Bund and then circled around for a return trip. They went no further, beyond the river, where the population of Hongku had neither the habit of using public transportation nor the means for it. For Elisabeth and Theodore, rickshaws were too expensive and taxis absolutely out of the question. For this reason early every morning the Weissbergs walked the five kilometers from the neighborhood of the steel factory in Hongku across the bridge above the muddy Soochow, then along Garden Bridge above the Yangtse by the English Garden, in order to arrive on time at the house at 342 Cardinal Mercier Boulevard.

There both of them plunged into their work: Elisabeth with German and piano lessons for the children, and Theodore with hauling manure, digging flowerbeds, or weeding.

This morning Simha Bassat, leaning reflectively on the parapet of the veranda, was observing the work of the old gardener and his assistant.

"Mr. Weissberg, do you have a minute?"she called out in German.

Regardless of the region and the main language surrounding them, educated Jews before the Second World War as a rule spoke German, more or less, this at that time "most Jewish" of foreign languages. Mrs. Bassat spoke it decently even though she had never been to Germany. The most distant and exciting journey for her had been the visit to Jerusalem, in the English protectorate of Palestine, the land of her distant forefathers.

It was not customary to address a man from the service personnel with "Mister," even in German—especially in these latitudes, where the division between masters and servants, rich and poor, Asians and Europeans, carried the smell of a slavery that hadn't ended so very long ago. But in this case you could sense the respect that Mrs. Bassat felt for this modest, shy, but without a doubt highly educated European. Just like most "Germans," as here they called the newly settled Jews—intellectuals or not—he also had to accept any kind of work in order to survive. Mrs. Bassat appreciated that, with extreme effort and without affectations of any kind, he was doing menial labor, albeit sometimes clumsily, as an assistant to Wu Laozian, this stately old gardener with his thin little beard like that of a medieval mandarin. Laozian was the son and grandson of the Wu gardeners, who had been working, since the time of the Empress Tsu-hi, and even earlier, before the Opium War, for the fathers and grandfathers of the Bassat dynasty. He had worked for them since his adolescence when old Menachem Bassat, and his father, Jeroham, too, were still alive, and this is why the old man was considered part of the household just like a piece of family furniture passed down from one generation to the next.

Theodore propped his shovel against a tree and approached, respectfully doffing his shabby straw hat.

"Yes, Mrs. Bassat!"

"I was looking at you and thinking," she said, "that with your wife, who is as gorgeous as she is learned, you probably had a different life in Germany. . . . Probably more meaningful."

"Oh, yes. . . . Definitely different and more meaningful, Ma'am."

"And this, to tell you the truth, disturbs me a bit. Because you deserve a different fate."

"You shouldn't worry, Mrs. Bassat. On the contrary, I am grateful to you. . . . You know that it isn't easy to find permanent work in Shanghai."

"Yes, yes, it's not easy," she said gravely, though it was obvious that her thoughts were somewhere else. And without further ado she suddenly asked, "What do you do on the Sabbath? I mean—do you celebrate it as do all decent Jews?"

Theodore was nonplussed: What did it mean according to Mrs. Bassat to be a "decent Jew"? He remembered his earliest childhood when sometimes on Friday evenings he would go with his parents to visit his grandmother in the Dalem quarter in Berlin; he recalled the trembling hand with which she lit the candles, the round bread that his father would break, solemnly giving a piece to everyone. He even remembered the silver chalice with the gilded interior and the shiver from the one gulp of thick red wine that he was allowed regardless of his age. "Shabbat shalom." Yes, this is how it was: Shabbat shalom. Saturday Peace. But since then so much water had flowed under the Spree, and with it decades, and the Saturday peace too! "Decent Jews"! What on earth did she mean by that?

"It would be a pleasure for us," continued Mrs. Bassat, "if this Friday you would have dinner with us. It's our son's birthday. Unfortunately we cannot invite the old Laozian. After all he is Chinese and not of our faith, you understand?"

Theodore swallowed the truth that Elisabeth was also not of "our" faith. And was he, he himself, a Jew through his mother and father, of "our" faith, though he never, or in any case only too rarely, and for reasons other than religious, set foot in the gleaming synagogue on Oranienburgerstrasse?

"And later we will have guests. You know, on these meridians worldly life starts late, after ten in the evening. I hope it will be enjoyable."

"Thank you, Mrs. Bassat, this is very kind, but. . . ."

She caught his look: Theodore was in worn-out duck trousers —for a long time now he had had no others—with braided sandals on bare feet and a shabby blue shirt.

She waved her hand.

"That doesn't matter. Jonathan, my husband, has more clothes than he needs. True, he is short and chubby, and you. . . . But we can always think of something!"

# 34

ELISABETH, WHO HAD PERFORMED on the great stages of Europe and all the way to Carnegie Hall in Manhattan, who had attended haughty palace receptions and countless official ceremonies, accepted this invitation with unexpected excitement, like a student before her senior prom. In the midst of dark and joyless Hongku, it seemed to her that even for a brief moment, for just an hour or two, she would re-read a page of something distant and irrevocably gone—just as one browses through a book read long ago in order to remember favorite lines.

She didn't trouble herself about her clothes: in the big suitcase something could always be found. Mrs. Bassat put together an outfit for Theodore, even though it didn't exactly fit. This the Weissbergs weren't worried about either, but rather how, on the little money they had, they were to find a gift for the small birthday boy. To give a ball to a boy or a doll to a girl seemed banal to them; they had to think up a present that would be at the same time both modest and dignified.

Finally, with the help of Rabbi Leo Levin, they came across an old Chinese merchant who displayed his wares on a threadbare rug laid out right on the asphalt not far from the pagoda-synagogue. To the interested buyers the merchant offered a rich and more than colorful assortment, from glasses with one lens missing to a broken alarm clock, false teeth, a set of keys from unknown doors, springs of undefined purpose, and used car lights. But among the carefully arranged goods, what caught the eye was a small smiling Buddha made out of nephrite, a fish between his hands, hanging on a string with a red bead at the end—probably a charm worn out by long twisting and turning in hands and pockets. And since the fish is a symbol of Jerusalem, and the synagogue in Hongku was in any case a hybrid between a Jewish temple and a Buddhist pagoda, the figure of Buddha hugging Jerusalem seemed to them a fun and meaningful present.

There, during the purchase of this charm, Theodore and Elisabeth received their first lesson in mutually beneficial Far Eastern trade. The rabbi personally took upon himself the task of bargaining, since in the rice-roll business he had acquired some of the principles and rituals of interpersonal trade relations in Hongku. The old seller for openers asked for one Shanghai dollar and made it clear that he wouldn't budge from that price. The rabbi thought for a while and then with the decisiveness of a suicidal man offered one cent. Theodore fretted about the huge difference, but Rabbi Leo asked him to keep to the side and not interfere in an area unfamiliar to him, and then repeated his offer: yes, yes, one cent! Then the seller showed mercy and generously reduced the price by half—50 cents. The negotiations were carried out with fingers, with everyone speaking his own language and drawing numbers in the air. Finally, Rabbi Leo, after a long dispute between the deaf and the mute, generously raised his offer to two cents. The old man shook his head: no, *masta-masta*, no: last thirty cents! But after the rabbi angrily waved his hand and left, the seller ran after him, finally offering a reasonable compromise—twenty cents. The deal was concluded, both seller and buyer shaking hands for a long time. Rabbi Leo was satisfied that he had indeed put his trading skills to use, buying at a price five times lower than the original, and the seller too was happy, having managed to raise by twenty times the price offered by the client. Everyone was happy and even more than happy about the course the commercial operation had taken.

The Weissbergs afterward laughed for a long time, and the rabbi explained to them in a mentoring tone the principles of the mutually beneficial deal that had just been concluded, "If I'd immediately paid him the original price of one dollar, the old man would've gone home crushed and feeling as if he'd been robbed, I assure you. And with the deep conviction that he'd had the misfortune of coming across a mentally retarded nitwit. The day for him would've been wasted because I would've denied him the supreme pleasure of the game. Here even the children know that the originally quoted price is always excessively high and the one offered by the buyer excessively low. This is good commercial form. Because trade without the rituals of haggling, sulking, and conning each other, which sometimes lasts for hours, is as sad, monotonous, and boring as a rainy November day, no matter who wins or loses. It's just the same in poker. Ask Mother Antonia, who finally understands the rule that the game is more important than the profit. The Jews, who are famous as merchants, can only be apprentices to this old man!"

Thus spoke Rabbi Leo Levin as he entered his peculiar synagogue with the fire-breathing dragons and the snarling, lion-like beast, its paws on the stone globe at the entrance.

The maid brought in the rice for Laozian, with his favorite stewed vegetables, respectfully laying the tray before him on the wooden table and bowing.

"Enjoy, Bo Laozian!" she said and returned to the kitchen.

"Bo" means uncle, and the old man was flattered that both the masters and the entire household staff addressed him in this way.

Across the way, in the big house, despite the early hour, the windows were radiant with light. Friday evening was sacred for the masters; this was long ago known to the servants. Their dinner starts early, as is customary with the Jews; this too was known. The lights are put on before sunset because tomorrow, until early Saturday night, it is forbidden with them to light a fire or to touch matches, burn coal, or even flick an electrical switch. It is also a sin to ask your servants to do this for you. Don't ask why: that's the way it is with the Jews, it's always been like that with the young masters, and with the old ones too.

The gardener ate his rice, sipped his tea, leaned on his pillow, and with delight lit up his long clay pipe, looking at the garden—the fruit of his labor and skills.

Here, in this corner of his little white house, his sons had been born; here his wife had died. He had always dreamed of making remarkable gardeners of his two sons, worthy of the name of their Wu ancestors. But they wanted to become soldiers and one night, influenced by a friend, they secretly left town, joining the army of General Chiang Djunjang in Chunking. Since then the old man had only once received from them, through people who had slipped into town, a respectful letter for the Lunar New Year, with wishes for good health and long life and a round metallic box with foreign pipe tobacco. He had smoked the tobacco—a fragrant English kind—a long time ago, but kept the box as a precious family relic and sometimes, when he was overcome with heartache for his sons, Bo Laozian tenderly contemplated it for a long time in its small niche in the wall. There had stood as well for a long time now the porcelain statue of old Shu-Sinh, the god of long life, propped against his curved stick with a little gourd on his belt, for it's known that the road of the young to old age is extremely short, while the road of the old through death is very, very long and it's necessary to carry a gourd for water!

Some old men measure the passage of time by the mild sound of the bone beads on their chaplets; Laozian measured it by the divine, rhythmical breathing of nature. First, when people hadn't even realized that winter had passed, the magnolias would bloom and immediately after them the blossoming plums and sour cherries would impatiently run toward the sun, followed by the flourishing peach and almond tree—tenderly pink as the fruit of lychee. Then the heads of the narcissi would pop out and the jasmine would whiten; then in the lake the lotus and the lily would open their cups, followed by vain and abundant clusters of overflowing flowers: yellow acacia, mimosa, red and white oleander, and the blood-red colors of the pomegranate, brought all the way to China from the distant shores of the Euphrates. Finally, white and yellow Japanese chrysanthemums, big as cabbages, stepped forward, with dignity, to complete the procession. And bounding up from spring to late fall all around them were the most cheerful, attentive, and obedient children of the flower garden—those dear coquettes the roses, which everywhere spread their lavish charm and laughter. Then late autumn would come, announced below the veranda by the yellowing aspens, which would profusely sprinkle the grass around them with golden coins while telling the end of the story. So then the whole thing would repeat itself from the very beginning and again from the beginning, since people and gods alike can never have enough of listening a thousand times to the good fairy tales.

Yes, this is how it's been arranged from time immemorial—everything in its natural order, just as the child becomes an old man, and life naturally passes into death in order to make way for new life. This is the way it's always been; this is the way it will always be. When the old Jeroham became so feeble that his mind started wandering hither and thither, he broke into a guttural tongue that no one could understand. The young master said that this was the tongue that people spoke in the Land between the Rivers. But did anyone know where it was? Soon after that Jeroham quietly died lying under the blooming jasmine, and perhaps his soul flew off to that Land between the Rivers, if this is what the Bassat masters call the place where the souls of their ancestors roam. Guests and rabbis came from distant places and the grandfather of Laozian prepared himself for the funeral by dressing himself in white and lighting a stack of aromatic sandalwood sticks in the pagoda, even though this wasn't a part of Jewish tradition. The smoke rose straight up, which meant that the soul of the old Jeroham was satisfied. And on his deathbed Laozian's grandfather paid three Buddhist monks in yellow clothes to pray not only for his soul but for the soul of his master. It mattered not at all that he was from a different faith; one prayer more doesn't hurt anyone, if it's good and comes from the heart! Once this was done, at peace with himself, he followed Jeroham into the celestial paths.

And the father of Laozian had followed his master, the father of Jonathan, but not before forty-nine days after the latter's death had passed, oh, not before that! Because even fools know that in every person seven earthly spirits live that hold him as an anchor, and his soul cannot fly to the heavenly abodes until he frees himself from them. This is why prayers are needed, the burning of aromatic charcoal and the evaporation of celestial steam with which you obtain their mercy so that they'll let you go in peace. Foreigners believe that this happens on the fourteenth day, but it isn't so: every spirit is held in the body for seven days, and seven by seven makes forty-nine, and not a day less! Jews don't believe in this; well, it's their own business to believe in whatever they want, but Laozian's father took care to do everything necessary to release his master's soul from the earthly spirits so that it could go light and clean to its life beyond. Only after that could Laozian's father, old Wu, prepare himself for the long journey. And this is how the world is arranged: the servant to follow his master—grandfather with grandfather, father with father!

It was a real misfortune that Laozian was already becoming a man when Jonathan was born. It would mean that this time the gardener would be going to the beyond well before him. But there was nothing to be done; can you hold onto life by force if it doesn't want to stick with you anymore? On the other hand, it was consoling that Laozian was at least going to dig the celestial garden and arrange it in such a way as to make the old Jonathan Bassat happy when he too sank down into death.

# 35

MRS. BASSAT LIT THE candles in the silver candelabra on time, this being the obligation of the mother. Mr. Bassat pronounced the sacred *Baruch ata Adonai Elohenu* . . . then broke the bread in pieces—the obligation of the father.

The small family celebration went magnificently. Two Chinese maids presented the Jewish dishes cooked personally by Mrs. Bassat—delicious, exotic in an Arabian way and completely unfamiliar. The hostess assured the guests that everything was kosher, according to tradition, and that none of the dishes was unclean, but neither Theodore, much less Elisabeth, paid attention to Jewish notions of "clean" and "unclean."

Then Theodore gave the ten-year-old birthday boy the small nephrite Buddha with the fish, Elisabeth played the piano, and everyone sang "Happy Birthday." There was a cake with candles and everything was done according to custom.

While they were talking around the table, the guests naturally touched on the topic of Young Fascists raids in Hongku, and the recently signed Tripartite Pact. But the conversation on this topic somehow never got off the ground: Mr. Bassat completely shared the opinion of the English governor, Lord Washburn, that these stories about teenagers didn't deserve attention, and as to Nazism, and its alliance with Japanese militarism, it was clear that the host accorded it no special significance at all: they were political deals, as he put it, that don't concern us as Jews. No one asked us, we are words from a different song, and we should remain apart from all that.

Jonathan Bassat was an hereditary merchant, the descendant of Baghdad Jews, who, after the fall of the Abbassids, joined up with the caravans of their good Arab neighbors and partners, and took off for the Silk Road; politics didn't interest him particularly. Mrs. Bassat didn't take part in the conversation at all, finding it dull. Europe, as well as the drama that was happening there, were too, too far from here. Anti-Semitism, with its roots in the European Crusades, its militant intolerance of Jews and their faith, as well as its primitive religious superstitions, paraphrases, vignettes, and fantasies, which had been developed throughout the ages—this type of anti-Semitism was foreign and unknown to them. The Bassats, of course, were well enough informed about events in Europe, it was in the center of world news, but they addressed it with approximately the same curiosity and interest with which you look at the weekly movie news about the next coup in Uruguay, without being completely aware of who in fact has revolted against whom and what it's really all about. It couldn't be said that Simha and Jonathan Bassat were indifferent to the fate of their fellow Jews, not at all, but for them it was on the same order of events as if a distant and muffled roar were fading away somewhere beyond the horizon—accidental attacks of banal racism that come and go like chickenpox, perpetrated by ignorant souls. Especially in Germany.

"My God," exclaimed Simha, "would anyone question the place of the German spirit in the avant-garde of world civilization? Do let's talk about something more pleasant. Did you see the latest film with Fred Astaire? Do you know that his real name is Austerlitz and that he's a Jew, that genius Fred Astaire?"

No, they hadn't seen the film: there's no cinema in Hongku.

To sum it up, the new and rather unusual closeness around the Sabbath table between the rich Baghdadis, the Bassats, and the Berlin family of the poor teacher Elisabeth and the assistant gardener Theodore Weissberg had started humanly and naturally. The tone was set by Mrs. Bassat herself, who even sat by the keyboard next to her children's teacher, so that they could play duets. There was no hint that the good beginning was destined for a very different conclusion, very soon.

The senior maid, a fat Chinese woman, joyfully rushed into the sitting room, leaned into the ear of the hostess, and whispered something. Simha Bassat beamed and jumped up. "Finally, Jonny, the ship has arrived!"

While Jonathan ran outside, the hostess excitedly explained:

"An old business partner of my husband's. He's just arrived through Kobe from Germany. A really, really very pleasant man. You'll like him, I'm sure. Really, I don't doubt it."

When Mr. Bassat ushered in a smiling general from the Wehrmacht with a swastika on his sleeve, Simha jumped up spontaneously to greet him:

"What's this I see, Manfred? You've become an officer! My God, our Manfred—an officer!"

The general clicked his heels and raised his hand in a Hitler salute, as was the official custom, then opened his arms, and embraced and kissed the hostess on both cheeks.

"Not just an officer, but a general! But ranks like these are acquired, unfortunately, not on the battlefield but behind a desk. What can one do, my friend: we, the bureaucrats, are also destined to take part in the war in our own way! And it changes many things—not just national borders, but also clothes. Otherwise how do you find me? Does it suit me?"

Imitating the coquettishness of a fashion model, he turned himself around, and she laughed and said:

"War fits you perfectly! How are our friends? Good news?"

"The best. We've opened a branch in Paris. I was there last month—a wonderful, admirable city, where one feels right at home! Here—this perfume, it comes from there. And it's for you."

With a gallant and joking click of his heels he presented her with a beautifully wrapped package:

"*Voilà!*"

Then came the banal mutual introductions, the pleasant surprise that Mrs. and Mr. Weissberg had come from royal Dresden. Judging by the family name, German Jews, right? It doesn't matter; I have many Jewish friends there too! Maybe you know the Zimmermans? No? They turned out to be Jews too! A big joke, but in Germany I've met very decent people who've suddenly discovered that they have Jewish blood, without ever suspecting it! Some of them take it hard, but what can you do—blood is blood! Don't be offended, I have nothing against you, on the contrary—I even admire you. But you have to confess that you've turned out to be very clever—now you're building roads, while our boys are dying at the front. Later in connection with this I'll tell you a terrific Jewish joke!

The guest didn't even show the slightest curiosity about what these German Jews were doing in Shanghai; more important was the second piece of good news, namely, that the general had come from Kobe with a proposal for Mr. Bassat's company concerning a considerable increase in deliveries, provided that the Jewish banks in Shanghai opened a new line of credit. War, gentlemen, is war! And war is fed on tin, chrome, and raw rubber, to say nothing of gasoline, right?

This seemed witty to him and he laughed.

"War is fed with people," quietly inserted Theodore.

"Oh, this is dark symbolism. German Jews have this tendency. Let them be philosophers and let them complain about the existing order. I don't mean you, but most of your kind in Germany are social democrats and even communists! Am I right? While here the Jews are different, oh, quite different! Really, it's nothing personal, I have millions of friends and partners among your people. Right, Jonny?"

Jonathan Bassat silently shrugged his shoulders; he apparently didn't like the direction the conversation was taking. The general immediately realized that he had to withdraw his troops from this slippery terrain and merrily concluded:

"It's a prosaic truth that war needs strategic raw materials just as now I need a good stiff cognac! Ah, it's so good after all this craziness in Europe to meet old friends again in a peaceful and friendly corner!"

He smarmily kissed Mrs. Bassat's hand. There was something natural, but also stupidly noisy in this importer—overdressed in his general's uniform—of things that fed the war.

Then the guests came rushing in—worldly life, as the hostess had said, did indeed start late in the evening. Most of them were representatives of big German companies with their wives; there were also two Chinese bankers from Singapore and one high Japanese officer.

What followed afterward stayed in Theodore's memory as a collection of torn and mixed pages—an unclear and chaotic recollection of words, smiles, jokes, local gossip about engagements and adulterous affairs, and isolated phrases.

The Japanese officer didn't get the jokes at all and after they were explained to him, he sat there for a long time smiling and nodding. He was most probably doing it out of politeness, because the Japanese notion of what's funny and ridiculous in life was as distant from the European as was the German general's sensitivity toward issues that deeply and painfully touched Jewish nerves.

Theodore felt as if he were sitting on thorns; twice he wanted to go, but Elisabeth pressed his hand: it's not polite, my dear! And Simha Bassat herself, perhaps swayed by the desire to smooth out the impression left by some of the general's crude remarks, didn't permit a word to be said about leaving:

"How come, my dear, when White Lily is just bringing in the punch! She's been working on it since morning and you will offend her mortally. The fun is yet to begin, right?"

White Lily was the fat maid, and the dear guest from Berlin agreed after the third cognac to sit at the piano on his own, for a little night music. And he didn't play badly, for a supplier of tin, thought Elisabeth.

"Play us something more modern, General," said one of the guests. "Since fashion only crawls to our godforsaken end of the world after a two-year delay!"

"And we'll dance!" merrily added the hostess.

Unfortunately, the general was seized by the vain desire to be the center of attention in this small society. By a diabolical accident, what he came up with was not one of the latest hits in Europe that had just been requested, but rather, as he accompanied himself, this song, which he sentimentally sang:

*In einer kleinen Konditorei*
*Da saßen wir zwei*
*Und traümten vom Glück. . . .*

Yes, yes, that was it exactly—that three-times accursed "little pastry shop"! The same tune to which those clever fellows building bridges instead of fighting were marching off to their daily labor! Under whose rhythm they smashed the fingers of Simon Zinner, the flautist of genius!

Theodore didn't feel the crystal glass slipping from the small plate, splashing the punch all over his clothes, and crashing onto the tiles. . . .

The piano went silent; the general turned to see what was going on.

The hostess jumped up with a napkin in her hand.

"It's all right, Mr. Weissberg! It's nothing; it will wash out. It doesn't leave stains."

"It does," said Theodore with a face as white as the napkin.

Theodore rarely drank and this perhaps is why the alcohol had gone so quickly to his head. He grabbed his wife by the hand, dragged her fiercely outside, looking a little comic in the too-short trousers and sleeves of the borrowed suit.

With the best intention the general said:

"Don't worry; I can give you a miraculous paste for all kinds of spots!"

"But, Mr. General, can you lick my ass?!"

This is what the delicate, shy Theodore Weissberg, member of the Prussian Academy of Art, said before leaving the hospitable house. He had heard it in Dachau from the trade union miners.

The hostess stood there with her mouth open; the guests looked at each other: now what was that all about?

# 36

HE HAD BEEN WALKING behind Hilde for almost an hour already trying to remain unnoticed. This, by the way, wasn't difficult—to hide and remain unnoticed in the colorful crowd that nearly around the clock flooded the brightly illuminated streets of the International Concession's commercial and business center. Hilde had apparently already finished the workday because she wasn't hurrying anywhere, but rather window-shopping and rummaging through outside displays of clothes and trinkets without buying anything. She entered a perfumery and hesitated a long time before choosing a lipstick. Then she wandered a bit around the French bookstore, opened and skimmed through a volume, then another one, paid for a fashion magazine, and walked out again.

Nankin Road is a terribly long and tiresome boulevard; after hesitating, she finally entered a small Viennese pastry shop in order to sit and have a bite to eat. It's hard to believe but there one could order an almost real Sacher torte or a warm fruit strudel no worse than those that had been served on Kärtnerstrasse during the good years.

He stayed outside where young prostitutes tried to attract foreign sailors by grabbing their shirts:

"Sailor, sailor-man! Short time two dollars, long time five dollars! Sailor!"

"Sailor" was the accepted term for addressing foreign sailors, and, judging by the official exchange rate, nailed at six Shanghai dollars to one American, the offer was more than attractive: for a "short" encounter, two Shanghai dollars, for a full assortment of services—five. Afterward, when the deal had been struck, the action was transferred to the courtyards behind the solid stone buildings of the boulevard. There you would find the houses of the Chinese who serviced the huge city. The courtyards, surrounded by two-story residential buildings, most of them wooden, and some of them also burned in the Japanese bombings, swarmed with children. Old women would cook on the wooden terraces and an intolerable smell of fried onions and burnt peanut oil floated under the lines of laundry hung out to dry. There were also dens of vice where one could get a pipe of opium, cheap contraband alcohol, or love for a "short" or "long" time. These dark and stinking bordellos were officially prohibited and hounded by the police, but one could often encounter as clients or partners in this forbidden business these very same keepers of the law.

The young man who was following Hilde by secretly looking through shop windows in order not to lose sight of her was familiar to her. In fact an old acquaintance. She had once known him as Vladek. At least that's how, under this obviously invented name, he had introduced himself in Paris, which now seemed as long ago and far away as a dream. He had been in Shanghai three months already and during this time he had been torn by contradictory feelings: on the one hand to look for her and find out the whole truth about her; on the other to slap her twice in the face, turn around, and disappear from her life forever. He knew that both ideas were unrealizable and absurd, and that likewise any action of this kind forbidden to him. Just as it was also completely forbidden to him, impermissible and punishable, to get involved in any kind of public disorder or scandal.

In fact a great many things here were forbidden to him. And he had to beware of a great many things. The most important of all, the most critical, was the disclosure of his identity. Here he had a Swiss passport under the family name of Vincent. This is how he was registered with the Japanese command: the freelance journalist Jean-Loup Vincent. So long, Vladek!

He discovered the presence of Miss Hilde Braun in Shanghai from the society columns of the newspapers, which were often taken up with this charming blond Valkyrie who appeared either at cocktail parties or charitable receptions with her friend Baroness von Dammbach, or in her role as personal secretary to the baroness's husband, the official representative of the Third Reich, Baron Ottomar von Dammbach. In the gossipy pages of the local press it wasn't rare to come across transparent hints about an intimate relation between her and the baron. To annoying and insinuating questions on the part of the excessively curious scandalmongers for the tabloids, which were abundant in Shanghai, the baroness replied with ringing laughter. No answer—just laughter, which only fed the suspicions that, it seemed, didn't disturb the baroness one bit. She apparently had more authentic information about the case.

For three months now this Swiss Jean-Loup had been knocking about Shanghai in the guise of a freelance correspondent for European newspapers; he often, you could say even daily, stopped by the Agfa shop on North Sichuan Road. There he would develop his photo reports before sending them to unknown destinations. And he was often in the company until very late of a certain Alfred Kleinbauer, known in all the local pubs for his preference for Russian vodka.

During all this time one question kept gnawing at him: had Hilde Braun been an undercover Gestapo agent in Paris? Had she given his address to the police, as a result of which there had followed such adventures as his arrest, interrogation, and deportation? What was her hidden purpose? Why was she trying to pass as a Jew, a refugee from Nazi Germany, if now she was working in the diplomatic mission of that same Germany? Indeed the very same, but at fifteen thousand or so kilometers to the east, where most probably she had started a new game, on a clean page, with a new legend and a changed biography. Jewish women couldn't be employees of the official German legation, that much was clear, but an undercover agent—why not?! Especially knowing that the diplomatic representatives themselves were often under the surveillance of their officially subordinate staff, sometimes even chauffeurs or low-ranking officers. This was standard practice in almost all secret services.

He followed Hilde when she left the pastry shop and walked down toward the river. But exactly there, at the intersection, where the broad and always gay Waterside Boulevard sprawled along the right bank of the Yangtse, and the ships cut through the waters of the great river, and the strings of barges and the countless junks scurried off in all directions, she had to stop. Far behind her this Jean-Loup—this strange Swiss man with the open, rustic Mediterranean face—also stopped.

The passersby also slowed their steps, and those behind them, still not understanding the situation, pushed against them, to see what was going on. In front of them, from the riverside, a thick wall of people was approaching—a human mass, swaying under cloth placards and simple cardboard posters inscribed with Chinese characters.

Few of the Europeans who'd been out on the boulevard were able to read what they said, but the English signs that cropped up here and there suggested the nature of the event: "Japanese Out, China Is Not a Colony!" "Stop the Plundering of China!" "Jobs and Security!" "Down with the War!"

The demonstrators were a mix of university students and workers, people in decent city clothes and the duck outfits of metal workers and weavers, young and old, even mothers with children. In front of them marched an imposing group of distinguished old men—scholars from the local university, renowned intellectuals, and bearded Buddhist philosophers. The latter, with their whole appearance and traditional clothing, resembled the porcelain miniatures from an old family prayer alcove, that is, they resembled them but only up to a point, for those here, unlike the wise celestial grandfathers, were marching under very earthly political slogans.

From the opposite side of Waterside Boulevard, from the English Garden, came deafening police whistles, the clatter of horses' hoofs, and warning shots. A second later mounted Chinese police from the municipal security department, created and maintained by the Japanese military administration, cut into the crowd and started beating people at random with leather whips.

Hilde didn't understand how she happened to find herself dragged into this human windstorm, this chaos of shouting, running, fighting people, amid the clatter of horses' hooves, police whistles, and smoking gunshots. The chain of horsemen was trying to push back the demonstrators, and policemen on foot, armed with bamboo sticks, started striking out blindly at the crowd until some police chief or other attempted to outshout the general noise by hoarsely issuing brief, threatening commands in Chinese.

Two cops were dragging a young woman who was attempting to pull away from them and shouting, while a little girl crying with terror clung to her skirt. One of the policemen angrily shoved the child, who fell over onto the asphalt. Out of the blue Hilde rushed to the child and snatched her away almost from under the horse of a mounted policeman, who leaned over his saddle, pulling at Hilde and tearing the sleeve of her dress while she resolutely defended herself and the child with slaps and selected curses from almost every European language she knew.

Another horseman grabbed her by the hair and dragged her away. Then the man who had up until now been following her, this same Swiss fellow Jean-Loup, seized his arm, wrenching him forward and down from the saddle. The policeman flopped heavily to the ground, but immediately jumped to his feet and raised his pole, which required Hilde's unexpected defender to knock him down again with a right uppercut.

Hilde, hugging the crying child, literally became numb with surprise; in front of her, all tattered and panting, stood that young man from Paris: in the flesh!

"Vladek, is that you?" she barely whispered.

He was unable to answer the meaningless question because the policeman, who was short and scared, had risen to his feet again and was reaching for the pistol in his holster. For this reason the exercise with the uppercut had to be repeated.

# 37

THE WHITE SPACE, WITH a single barred window, was jammed with demonstrators who had been arrested. About fifty of them, both men and women, were sitting on hard benches or right on the floor and whispering quietly. When Hilde and Vladek were pushed inside, rather harshly, people became silent, even though the two Europeans could hardly comprehend a word of their vigorous murmurings. There was no room on the benches; Vladek looked around and sat down in the corner without showing the slightest interest in his companion. She hesitated and then submissively sat down beside him on the dirty cement floor, strewn with cigarette butts and roasted peanut skins. The tension between them was palpable; several times she gave him an expectant look in the hope that he would speak, but each time, sullen, on edge, he turned his head away.

Again she cast a brief glance at him: no, he hadn't changed, at least visibly, but he was hardly the high-spirited, friendly guy from Paris who had generously given her the gift of Notre Dame cathedral. Hilde could guess the reason for his hostile behavior, but this was neither the time nor the place to clarify absurd situations. And hers was more than absurd, illogical, implausible: war was weaving its paradoxes and designs, and Hilde's fate was just a modest thread in its complicated pattern.

"You didn't answer me about what you're doing here," she said finally.

"And you?" he replied somberly, without looking at her. "What are you doing?"

"Not what you're thinking."

"What, in your opinion, am I thinking?" For the first time he turned to her and rudely asked: "Did you give the police the address of my apartment in Paris? It was you, wasn't it?! No one except you knew where I was living. No one! Even my comrades from Spain."

She looked at him in astonishment, opened her mouth but didn't utter a sound. The suspicion was so absurd and so insulting that Hilde couldn't immediately find words to reject it. This time it was her turn to feel like slapping him twice across the face, even here, in this room packed with those who'd been arrested.

At this moment a low-ranking policeman entered, looked around, and calmly said, pointing at the pair of Europeans sitting on the floor:

"You two. Come."

Smoke hung everywhere in the small office. The man in charge, a captain from the municipal police force, was making sure of that. Under the square spot on the wall where someone's portrait had probably once hung, replaced now by a smaller color print of the Forbidden City in Peking, he thirstily sucked on his cigarette, his fingers yellowed by cigarettes, emitting thin plumes of smoke through his teeth and suspiciously leafing through the arrested man's Swiss passport, scrutinizing in particular the pages filled with gaily colored border stamps. A tense silence hung in the air. Hilde and Vladek were sitting on wooden chairs across from the captain's desk, awaiting their fate.

The telephone rang, the captain lifted the receiver and listened, then said something in Chinese and put the receiver down. Only then did he raise his eyes from the passport and say in almost flawless English:

"Miss, your official mission has confirmed that you are their employee. Good. This clarifies your identity. But it does not acquit you of your actions. Do you have anything to add in your defense?"

"I have no reason for a defense. For the hundredth time now I'll repeat what I've already said: your police behaved disgustingly, Mr. . . . Policeman."

"Captain." He made it easy for her.

"Yes, all right, captain. This was a peaceful demonstration. There were children there! I told you and I repeat: I will not leave things this way and I will inform Baron von Dammbach about everything that's happened, right down to the smallest and nastiest detail!"

"That is your right. And it is our right to keep you under arrest for up to three days. During that time we will make an effort to find the person who snatched away your purse. Even though, if I have to be honest, I have no particular hope that it will be found. The theft of personal property is a private matter, and the fact that you are a German citizen does not release you from responsibility. Up to three days! . . . Unless the Magistrate's Office gets involved—something I would not recommend to you."

With the stubbornness of a punished schoolgirl she insisted:

"All right then, I'll stay for three days! I'll even stay with great pleasure, to shame the idiots on your police force!"

The captain raised his heavy eyelids, fixed his glance on Hilde, and finally said with indifference:

"For indecent and insulting behavior you can receive three more."

"Altogether six. And then?"

"Then," interfered Vladek in French, "I'll wait for you outside and teach you a lesson that you'll never forget! Don't piss this guy off; we've got to get out of here as soon as possible."

"You get out then if you don't find it humiliating to toady to them!"

"Why just look at her, a national heroine! Joan of Arc! Or where you come from, who was it? Brunhilde?"

"Don't talk between yourselves and waste my time!" the captain interrupted, leafing through the passport again. "Jean-Loup—"

"It's pronounced without the final p."

"I know how it is pronounced, Mr. . . . Ven Sian. . . . Have I got it right?"

"Exactly right. Ven Sian. You pronounce it like someone born on Lake Geneva."

"And where were you born?"

"In Lausanne, as it's written."

"And where is this lake?"

"In the same place. You may not believe it, but Lake Geneva is in Geneva. In Switzerland, for the time being."

The captain took this statement on faith and pushed a sheet of paper toward him finely inscribed with Chinese characters.

"Sign here, Mr. Ven Sian."

"The writing is in Chinese. I don't have the honor of understanding your characters."

"With this you are confessing," patiently explained the captain, "that you assaulted an officer. Sign here."

Vladek hesitated whether to dip the pen in the ink. Then he scratched the back of his head and peacefully said:

"Now look, magistrate. What happened, happened; there's no need to go over it again. But here it's only just us; in a way, we're almost friends. Let's settle the matter like good neighbors, okay? You know very well what sympathy we have in Switzerland for the Shanghai police! Will that do?"

From the pocket of his tattered, semi-military shirt, Vladek took out and pushed toward the captain a banknote of fifty Shanghai dollars. The latter, with a professional gesture, put it in his drawer.

"Here you quickly remembered half of the characters! And the other half?"

Scrambling through his pockets, Vladek helplessly turned to Hilde in French:

"Can I borrow the rest of the Chinese dictionary from you?"

"I'm sorry, but in the chaos, as you heard, they snatched my purse. And frankly this problem doesn't concern me. I'll stick out the three days under arrest!"

"Six," Vladek corrected.

"Let it be six. So that the world will learn what's going on in Shanghai!"

"Don't worry, the world will learn nothing. Including anything about the heroic deed of Brunhilde, who lay for a week under arrest with the lice-ridden petty thieves and prostitutes, sick with scabies." This seemed insufficient to him and he enthusiastically added, "And syphilis! . . . And leprosy!"

Hilde, itching all over, suddenly lost her bravado.

"That's enough. I get it. But what shall we do?"

Vladek turned to the policeman and said with the most accommodating tone:

"My dear magistrate, let's agree, as civilized people, to the following. You have my honest word that tomorrow I will bring you fifty dollars."

"For you, Mr. . . ." he looked at the passport, "Mr. Ven Sian, your honest word is priceless, but in any case, your passport stays with me."

"The passport, boss? Over my dead body!"

"Oh, why dead bodies? We are civilized people, you said it yourself. But your passport has to be retained in any case. That's how it's done. You will receive it in due course. What kind of pen do you have?"

Vladek beamed. He hadn't though of that.

"A Montblanc. With a gold nib, eighteen carat. Here, I give it to you as a precious souvenir of friendship. If you refuse, you'll disappoint me!"

The captain took the pen, unscrewed the top, and after casting a skeptical look at the nib to see where the carats were marked, jotted a few lines on a white sheet of paper.

Vladek triumphantly said, "You see—it writes!"

"All right, I believe you when you say that tomorrow you will bring the money. And I hope, Miss, that this incident won't be repeated. Send my regards to the honorable baron."

Hilde silently and somewhat confusedly nodded, while the policeman again leafed through the Swiss passport.

Vladek judged this interest wrongly and reached out his hand to take it back—after he had added to the tokens of sincere friendship the eighteen-carat Montblanc pen. But the captain laid his hand over the passport.

"And the passport?" Vladek said despondently.

"I told you: you'll get it in due course. Meanwhile you're free to go, Mr. . . ."

"Ven Sian!" Vladek shouted, jumping up from his seat and angrily heading for the door.

"Hey, wait a minute. Are you leaving me here?" shouted a frightened Hilde, who only a minute ago had been insisting on staying for six heroic days under arrest by the Shanghai police.

Visibly annoyed, he walked back, caught her by the hand and roughly dragged her along.

While waiting for the car from the German diplomatic mission, the two of them sat right out on the sidewalk in front of the police station. She remained silent while Vladek smoked angrily:

"Are you going to tell me now who you really are?" he asked finally.

"The same person I was in Paris. The same, I swear. But it's complicated, very complicated, Vladek. This was my only chance for survival. Do you understand?"

"No. I'm not even going to try. So you're being fed at the hands of the Gestapo?"

"My God, what nonsense!"

"So how's it possible for a Jewish woman, as you claimed to be, to be trusted by those Nazi gangsters?"

"If you mean the baron, far from being a gangster, he's just a nice old man who's done a million favors for me."

"In exchange for . . . what?"

"The Chinese climate isn't good for you, stop talking nonsense! It's just that from my passport it isn't clear that my parents are Jews with changed names. I've told you how from Braunfeld we became Braun. And how through a mix-up I was able to get out of Germany. . . . So that I could get myself into this adventure here! Or have you forgotten?"

"I haven't forgotten anything. And then what?"

"Are you telling me you don't know how well they can judge a person's identity by his passport?! You, the Swiss?! I happened to have some luck, but how long will that hold out? But this has got to stay just between us, Vladek. If they find out, it's all over with me!"

He was silent for a long time, before asking with suspicion, "And you didn't give the police my Paris address?"

"My God, what absurdity! No! No, no, and no! Believe me!"

"It's too early to believe you. Before I find out who you are in reality."

"And who are you in reality?"

"I'm also the same person I was in Paris. If you remember."

"I remember. A polyglot who disappeared suddenly without a trace and without calling anymore. From all this mystery with the police and everything, all I know is that you were mixed up in something illegal."

"I'm curious to find out how you came to this conclusion, since everything I've done has always been strictly within the law."

"Oh sure. Tell it to my hat. Czech, Polish, Portuguese. Now it turns out you were born in Lausanne. I'm proud to know an upright Swiss guy who has everything in legal order. You're probably a modest producer of cheese! You weren't doing anything illegal, right! And I, the fool, was dragging myself after you like a lovesick kitten!"

Vladek was silent for a long time, before somberly and angrily pointing his finger at her, as if he were going to pronounce a verdict. He finally said:

"If you want to know, I'd fallen pretty hard for you too! In fact very hard!"

He spit in the street dust and pensively rubbed the gob of phlegm with his heavy military boots.

"Well, maybe not that hard, but still . . . I kept thinking of you after I'd left Paris."

"And where were you?"

"Somewhere. It doesn't matter. But I couldn't call you; there was no way. And I didn't know where the hell you were living."

"Now you know. But you don't seem to me the same guy who used to toss shoes over the Paris bridges."

"And you're not that desperate girl who didn't even have money for a baguette with ham. Are you going to tell me what happened with . . . your Jewish problems? With the refusal of those idiots to give you asylum? How is it you find yourself here? How come you're a secretary to a Nazi?"

"I don't respond to more than three questions at a time. Not now. And not here. You can always find me by telephone. I can't get rid of the feeling that you know the number well."

"Yes, it's true, I've reached for the receiver a hundred times and then given up. I'll call you; I have to know. But don't forget you owe me: today you wasted half my workday. And fifty dollars."

"A hundred, if I understood correctly."

"You'll pay the other fifty."

"Whoever offers a bribe pays for it. I'm not taking part in the corruption of the Empire of the Sun. For the six days of arrest that you saved me from, I'll chip in one dollar. Shanghai. And not one cent more!"

"Is that so?! You got me involved in this mess. In your place I'd cough up the whole hundred dollars—in the name of the Third Reich."

"No, you go and pay it—that's what I'm saying, get it? If you have the money, of course. Otherwise I can lend it to you.

In fact, what kind of work are you doing in Shanghai? On the level."

He kept silent for a moment in his attempt to formulate his response more convincingly.

"I'm freelancing now."

"You say it like you were a member of the Senate in Paris. How long have you been here . . . freelancing?"

"Three months. And I already know five Chinese words."

"A real polyglot."

She thought pensively for a while, hesitated, and finally said:

"Do you know what the porter asked me—you know, the fat one, you remember her, when they arrested you? She asked if you were a German spy."

"No, absolutely not."

"As far as the German spy part goes, I believe you one hundred percent, all the way. I'm sure of it. But I also know you've never told me the truth, not even once. Now, when you finish with your Swiss period, don't try to persuade me that you're a Senegalese freelancer. By the way, I've always said that Swiss cheesemakers, before leaving their dairy farms, have to take a course in good manners. You could, for example, offer me a cigarette."

Vladek fumbled in his short pocket and took out a crumpled pack. Hilde was surprised to see the soft, almost empty cigarette, then with a start pulled back from the huge smoky flame that burst from the gasoline lighter.

"A formidable lighter! In a war it could serve as a flamethrower."

"Is that so?" he said absently, and then suddenly, out of the blue, he asked, "What kind of guy is this baron of yours?"

"Why? Have you been reading that nonsense in the papers?"

"I'm not asking you about your love relations. They don't interest me. I'm asking something else: Does he share his views with you about, for example, this person Adolf Schiklgruber, more popularly known as Hitler? Does he talk about such things with you?"

"I'm not so sure he's obliged to do so with his secretary. Why? You want to tell me something about the baron? I think I know everything about him."

"Is that what you think?" he said, while his thoughts flew in some other direction. He mechanically waved his hand. "No matter. Let it be."

She stood up.

"Here's the car! Sorry about the mess, Ven Sian. Despite everything, you have no idea how happy I am that I saw you again. You'll call me sometime, won't you? Please, call me!"

She tried to kiss him on the cheek, unshaven for several days, but he pulled himself back.

A black Opel with a Nazi flag on the right fender stopped in front of them—the personal vehicle of His Excellency Baron von Dammbach.

Biting his cigarette and squinting his eye from the hot smoke, Vladek gazed after the black limousine for a long time, until it blended into the stream of rickshaws, bicycles, and buses.

The guard at the entrance of the police station grinned and said:

"That was a beautiful—very beautiful lady. Yes-yes!"

# 38

LORD WASHBURN'S SECRETARY THREW a significant look at her wristwatch and with unconcealed surprise scrutinized the man standing in front of her, his soldier's shirt unbuttoned and his military boots as big as boats.

"*Mister* Vincent, it's none of my business, but may I allow myself to draw your attention to the fact that Lord Washburn is not accustomed to a lack of punctuality on the part of his subordinates."

Mr. Vincent was surprised in turn:

"Subordinates, did you say? Oh, subordinates! Look now, young lady, I'm not a subordinate of the lord's for three reasons. At least three! First, because I'm not a soldier in Her Majesty's colonial army, but a freelance journalist. Second, I'm not an English subject, but through a lucky coincidence Swiss. And third, as a rule I subordinate myself to nothing and no one apart from the laws of my canton. They have their own state laws, in case you haven't heard."

This barrage of words to some extent confused the secretary, though she didn't lose heart. "Please, don't sit on my desk! Lord Washburn insisted that—"

"He asked most politely, you mean—"

"If that's how you like it!"

"I like you, young lady. But I'm not a skirt-chaser and I grant you your freedom. And so, what did Lord Washburn ask?"

"He ordered you to appear before him immediately! This, I hope, doesn't violate the laws of your canton. And please keep it short, because he has another meeting." And the secretary, in order to be convincing, looked at her watch again before ushering him into the office of the lord.

The room was large, somber, and modestly furnished. There was something military about it, though at least the stone Buddha in the corner, next to the British flag and under the modest portraits of Their Majesties, suggested that the barracks was located in the Far East. A fan rotated on the ceiling, and almost the whole wall to the left of the desk was taken up by an enormous map of Shanghai with its shorelines.

The lord was standing in the middle of the office—perhaps to prevent his visitor from advancing further than the door.

The man who had just come in introduced himself cheerfully. "Jean-Loup Vincent, sir. At your service!"

With the self-assurance of a general who doesn't shake hands with lowly privates just like that, Lord Washburn declined the proffered hand. His own hands crossed behind his back, he looked with curiosity at the ragged Swiss with the unbuttoned shirt and rolled-up sleeves, stopping with surprise at the latter's enormous, thick-soled boots.

Vladek followed his eyes and bent over to admire in turn his boots for a moment.

"Ah, my boots. Great, aren't they? From the Spanish Republican Army. For two years I marched as a correspondent with them from Gibraltar to the Pyrenees and in spite of everything they're still like new! You'll die laughing but during the bombing of Madrid—"

The lord interrupted him. "I have not invited you to tell me the story of your boots!"

"Oh, really? Then how can I be of use to you?"

Only now did it become clear why the lord was keeping his hands behind his back: in them he held the Swiss passport of Jean-Loup Vincent.

"Try first, Mr. Vincent, to be useful to yourself. The Shanghai police have lodged a formal complaint against you for violating the statute concerning foreign journalists who take part in public disorder. You have assaulted a peaceful policeman."

"He wasn't so peaceful, I assure you. They were the ones doing the hitting!"

"I advise you not to interfere in their way of life. If I understand correctly, you have come from Spain."

"You could say that. . . ."

"Have you come from there or not? Yes or no."

"You could say that I've come from there. But first I stopped in France—to visit the Louvre—Mona Lisa and so on. And then, since I was there, to see one thing or another on Place Pigalle, if you know what I mean. Then I stopped in Switzerland to visit my mother. I was there three months."

"It makes me boundlessly happy that you visited your mother. But perhaps you've noticed that here it isn't Spain, where everyone gets involved in things as if they were in their own kitchen."

"I like the comparison with the kitchen. Honestly, I'm not flattering you! Especially knowing what a mess they've cooked up there. And if it hasn't turned into Spain here yet, it will, believe me."

The lord tilted his head with surprise, looked intently at his visitor, and finally said, "I don't follow your complicated thought."

"It was the same with my teachers, who were always throwing me out of class. And then, just for laughs, it would turn out that I was right. What I mean is that Spain was a way for European militarism to test its capacities, just like Shanghai is, for the Japanese. In Europe the rehearsal finished with complete success: the Spanish Republican Army was defeated. While England and France, in case you've heard, pretended to be absentminded under the motto of 'Non-intervention' and 'Better Fascists than Communists.'"

"My view even now!" said a convinced Lord Washburn.

"I don't doubt it. You're a true-blue British gentleman! So here's what I want to say: I wrote reports about the English volunteers for the International Brigades. Brave boys; England can be proud of them. At Teruel many of them fell, but not for Spain or communism; they were defending democracy, milord. And they lost the battle. The dress rehearsal of fascism ended with complete success, and now, on the European scene, its solemn opening night is taking place. The destruction of Guernica was the apotheosis of Spanish flamenco, but now the dance is continuing in a German interpretation. Soon also British towns will be leveled to the ground, I assure you."

"What laughable nonsense!"

"Yes, quite right—and you can die from laughter. Especially when the performance will touch you a good deal, and painfully too. Want to bet?"

But the lord seemed unwilling to gamble. Vladek sniffled, looked around, and shyly asked:

"May I light a cigarette?"

"No."

"I thought so. But we were talking about something else. Listen, sir, to what a modest freelance journalist has to tell you: Shanghai is the Spain of the Far East. And here after the dress rehearsal there will be a premiere on a much vaster scale. That's what's going to happen, if you don't give the Japanese right now the opportunity to learn that at the first attempt on their part to expand the invasion, you'll stuff them up a dog's ass."

"Hm!"

The lord's confusion was not without cause, because just then at the door stood Baroness von Dammbach, beaming.

"I do hope I'm not disturbing you. I'm always as punctual as your Big Ben, milord!"

Lord Washburn bowed slightly.

"You can never disturb me, Baroness." And turning to Vladek, he handed him his passport. "Take it and evaporate. We will have an occasion to speak further about the rehearsals."

"Yes, yes, with the greatest pleasure. Frankly, judging by your stern secretary, I was expecting to meet a much haughtier lord."

And Vladek patted him on the back in a friendly manner, at which the lord literally choked.

As he left, the Swiss citizen Jean-Loup Vincent threw a look full of curiosity at the baroness. She in turn took a good look at the shabby man with a sweat-stained soldier's shirt and clodhoppers like boats.

Only after he closed the door after himself did she ask:

"Who's that character?"

Lord Washburn twirled his finger against his temple.

"And so, milord, I came to speak to you about the snipe. Knowing what a first-rate shot you are, I don't doubt that on Sunday they'll be falling like rain from the sky."

"My eyes, my eyes, my dear, are not the same anymore. If you had only seen me when I was young, in the hunting fields of Namib!"

"Oh, I'm sure the lions you shot rained down from the sky!"

He laughed, took her two hands, and kissed them.

At the meeting with the Jewish Refugee Community of Hongku, the lord hadn't lied when he'd said that because of the war between England and Germany he no longer maintained official relations with the representatives of the Third Reich in Shanghai. This was the truth itself. But the unofficial links continued; people here had become friends over the years, their children had mutual respect for each other, and today the baroness was coming to make arrangements for a picnic-cum-snipe hunt. At least this is what had been announced to the secretary.

Additional proof that war can also bring people on both sides of the front closer together.

Especially when it's far away from them, at the other end of the world.

# 39

ISTVAN KELETI, CALLED "THE Hungarian" for the sake of convenience, raised himself up into a sitting position on the dirty tattered rug. He drew a hand over his face, looked around with red, sleepy eyes, and slowly realized where he was. He glanced at his oversized wristwatch with its protective grid, bought on the black market from the Royal Marines: it was Sunday, December 7, six p.m. Time to take off for that damned sailor's tavern, The Blue Mountain, on Nansha Road, not far from the harbor. Not that there was a mountain there, only the dirty, heavy brown waters of the Yangtse, with junks flecked with cormorant droppings, and Japanese police scooters swaying on the fishermen's dock every time a larger ship passed by.

Through the spiders' webs hanging down from the two small windows streamed the dim light of the fading winter day, as if it were driving and mixing the layers of bluish smoke that floated under the ceiling. It was chilly; the low, dingy space hadn't been heated for a century. On rugs by the walls, blissfully intoxicated or quietly and pensively smoking their long bamboo pipes, lay threadbare coolies who, during the night, with their rickshaws, had made a dollar or two and were letting their last chance for a decent meal go to waste here; petty Chinese merchants who would only open their popcorn, roasted pea, and multicolored syrup stands late in the evening when the crowds began rambling along the streets; despondent Russian immigrants in Cossack uniforms; and one European pale as death: from her looks, probably a Scandinavian.

This was a cheap smoking room for people with modest means. Here they offered the kind of opium called "second smoke"—already used once in the expensive, luxurious, and almost inaccessible opium dens for the elite. Ecstasy now came from burnt poppy resin with its heavy secondary tars, which went right to your head, making you quickly and deeply dizzy before hitting you like a hammer blow at the base of your skull. While you dozed, sunk in ecstatic forgetfulness, you could tolerate it; your soul was filled with a sweet and dreamy languor. The consequences, however, were an insurmountable disgust with food of any kind and a whopper of a hangover, from which you could escape only by flying off again to paradise on the wings of the next pipe.

The Hungarian's mouth was dry and bitter, his tongue scratchy, as if strewn with wood shavings, and every time he swallowed it hurt. It's always this way when you wake up from second smoke, and now he was yearning for a large, an enormous, in fact a whole bucket of rice beer—that disgusting yellow liquid without hops and foam, which nevertheless quenches thirst far better than two-liter bottles of boiled water with its foul stink of the swamps. "The cheapest headache remedy in the world!" was how the Hungarian ranked this yellowish Chinese piss, provisionally called "beer," in the beverage chain of Homo sapiens—a two-legged being punished by evolution with the largest brain so that his headache could be the largest too.

He painfully stood up and stepped across the bodies lying on the floor. On his way he yanked down the skirts of the woman, sunk deep in the contemplation of oblivion, in order to cover her bare thighs.

"Good-bye, dear Ilona! Or are you Ingmar? Or Jeanette? Love and kisses to Europe, which you're dreaming about now with your eyes open. Our dear nasty Europe! I hope you find a way out of here—with all my heart I do."

Speaking in Hungarian, and looking with compassion at the young woman who was sleeping with her mouth half-open, her unseeing eyes fixed on the ceiling, he sighed and waved his hand: no matter what, she wasn't getting out; that, at least, was clear! Second smoke holds you fast, like a rusty wolf trap, or an old prisoner's chain nailed to the wall, or a stone anchor dropped in the impenetrable depths of the soul.

In the small vestibule he splashed some water on his face from a basin. With a ceremonial bow foreign to this lice-ridden den, an old woman, her teeth black from an unknown lacquer that made her mouth look like a dark abyss, offered him a towel of dubious hygiene and the Hungarian disgustedly waved it aside. You can bet with the highest degree of probability that this ancient priestess in one of Shanghai's countless Temples of Second Smoke didn't understand Hungarian, but Istvan Keleti insisted on speaking to her anyway in his mother tongue.

"Thank you, Countess Maritza, thank you, yellow-faced mimosa. Here's your moolah. And a tip, till next time!"

He poured ten or so small copper coins into her gnarled hand, and started down the squeaky plank staircase.

It was humid outside, cold and nasty. The heavy skies, the flashing multicolored billboards, and the illuminated shop windows on the unusually empty streets created the strange and tense impression that there was trouble of some kind hanging over the city. As the rickshaw conducted him to the harbor, it dawned on him that during his opium idyll of non-existence, something must have happened, something unusual. On the corners and the roofs of hotels and tall buildings, Japanese soldiers stood guard, while here and there armed vehicles and small Italian-made tanks blocked intersections, their gun barrels pointing at an unknown enemy. Suspense enveloped everything: the rare pedestrians were hurrying home, while above their heads, quick as wasps, flew small Japanese fighter planes that you could hear rather than see as the Shanghai evening fell.

The Hungarian lightly tapped his foot against the back of the coolie, who slowed his steps and turned his head without stopping:

"What's happening, *masta-masta*?" asked the passenger in English.

The thin coolie was probably convinced that his reply was also in English, and to be respectfully addressed as *masta-masta* flattered him, because as he ran he poured out, gasping and panting, a tirade of which the Hungarian understood nothing.

Except for the word "Nippon."

All the same, it seemed as if it were the most important, indeed *the* crucial word about what was going on.

A little later he again lightly tapped the coolie with the tip of his shoe.

"Stop, Your Excellency! Stop!"

The gaunt man nailed himself to the spot, submissive as an old cow.

The Hungarian ran to the cigarette shop in the shadow of the Palace Hotel. Smiling, the seller bowed three times before showing the buyer a pack of cigarettes made from dark Algerian tobacco.

The Hungarian shook his head. "No, not cigarettes. What's been going on is what I want to know. Brrrrr . . . *Avion! Nippon. Realiz? Verstehen? Understanding?* What's been happening with the *Nippons*?"

A friendly smile again beamed from the vendor's face; he started nodding with understanding. "Yes-yes, sir!"

And he changed the cigarettes for a pack with a Japanese label.

The pianist waved his hand, grabbed the pack, paid, and went out to the accompaniment of three new bows.

And so *Nippon* means Japan.

Well, that much is clear. But now what?

The news had spread across the city like lightning: world radio stations had announced in tongue-twisters, one on top of the other, that early this morning, the Japanese air force had mounted a sudden and devastating attack on the American naval base at Pearl Harbor on the island of Oahu in the Hawaiian archipelago. The attack was more than unexpected, considering that at that time intense American-Japanese mutual non-aggression negotiations had been taking place and that it was only a matter of time before a pact was to have been concluded.

The air strike had been so overwhelming that in the resulting apocalypse the Japanese had in a very short time managed to take out eight battleships, six cruisers, and one torpedo boat. The number of planes destroyed on the ground and in the air was 272, the number of dead Americans 2,476.

Sunday, December 7: this was the day when the sinking of the Arizona, one of the symbols of U.S. military presence in the Pacific, put an end to a peaceful America. Henceforth the American dream put on a military uniform. But everything has a price and Japan had to pay hers, the most painful so far: despite the chaos that reigned at Pearl Harbor, the Americans succeeded in shooting down the plane with Admiral Yamamoto, the genius military strategist who had been managing the whole operation from the air.

The wind rose had suddenly changed its direction and the two continental wars—the European and the Far Eastern—turned literally in minutes into the Second World War.

This was also the beginning of Japanese expansion. One day after Pearl Harbor, the Japanese army took over Malaysia, and after it the Philippines. One after another, the British colonies of Singapore and Victoria, also known as Hong Kong, followed by Burma, New Guinea, and the Dutch East Indies, raised the white flag. Next on the list were the distant horizons of New Zealand and Australia. The island Empire of the Rising Sun was soon to not only rule over the Great, or the Pacific Ocean, but to take over almost the whole global production of rubber, tin, quinine, and rice.

All of these developments still lay ahead. For the time being this all-encompassing and victorious Japanese expansion, comparable in speed and scale to the uncontrollable march of Hitler's army in Europe and North Africa, was still ripening in the womb of time. It was only in the tavern not far from the docks, where every night till early dawn he had to dream up on the wretched piano his improvisations to popular American film melodies, that the Hungarian immigrant Istvan Keleti would learn the location of this geographic and strategic military notion "Pearl Harbor," unfamiliar to him until that moment.

The tavern, located beneath a one-story hotel with only a few rooms, was a somber, damp place with bare brick walls and a cement dance floor where the sailors could dance with their girls. It was lower than the pavement, this Blue Mountain; you had to go down a dozen steps to get to it, the maximum depth permitted in Shanghai, which had been built on pilings driven into the marshes. Cellars only half a meter lower were constantly filled with water and that's why this huge city had no bomb shelters. It was also one of the acceptable explanations given during the time of the Japanese bombings about the excessive number of civilian victims.

Hilde had gone down only once to this dive, when she was looking for her friend from Paris. But there were so many sailors hungry for a woman's caress who stared at the blond beauty, and so many whistles and catcalls, that the Hungarian had hurried to take her out.

Now they'd been sitting for awhile at the Viennese pastry shop. Istvan was picking with disgust at his cake, even making several touching efforts to swallow a bite or two.

Propping her face on her fists, Hilde was silently observing her friend. The skin of his face, dry as paper and stretched between his cheekbones, gave away the distant Asian origin of his ancestors, and had acquired a blue-brown color with reddish tints—a sure sign in his case of the interference of poppy derivatives.

He was the first to break the silence:

"So, how's it going for the girl from Les Halles in Paris?"

"Like this," Hilde said, shrugging her shoulders. "I'm getting by, somehow. How's it going for you?"

"It's a shitty job. Believe it or not, but I miss even the crummiest Budapest bars. With the mellow drunks, the red wine, and the sentimental Gypsy tunes. The Hungarians don't have a sea, apart from that puddle Lake Balaton. I don't know if you've ever heard of it. And thank God for that, because I'm sick of sailors now. I've even started to miss Alain Conti. A manly man."

"He's probably fighting somewhere in Africa."

"That means you don't know him. He's from the human race that doesn't let itself get screwed. Alain Conti fighting? Hell no. You really don't know him! Right now he's probably drinking cognac beside a white piano and not giving a damn about which shithead will rule over France."

The Hungarian had no idea how far he was from the truth. Much, much later, only after the end of the war, would he learn that Alain Conti, the movie man with the pipe, the general in charge of the Conti film girls, had been shot before dawn on February 4, 1944, by the Paris Gestapo for having hidden English paratroopers.

The two of them chatted a bit more—in that Vienna pastry shop at the end of the world.

Then it became obvious that their paths had irreversibly diverged: she couldn't come to the tavern and he didn't want to hear about that white German mansion with the flag flying its swastika over the lawn. Hilde tried to lure him again to Nankin Road, to the pastry shop or the French bookshop, but from the look of disgust on his face she understood that this was a hopeless effort; he was attracted by other types of occupations far removed from pastry shops and bookstores. Istvan guiltily mumbled that when he found some "free" time he would look for her so he could pay back his share of the money they'd received from the sale of the pink pearl necklace.

Hilde was not such a fool as to believe him.

By the way, in the same tavern, from nine in the evening till midnight, a singer, someone called Elisabeth Müller-Weissberg, an attractive woman with green eyes and copper hair, would entertain, and sometimes bring even to the point of rapture the sailors from the German military and merchant ships. She successfully performed the repertoire of Zara Leander, one of the shining stars of the Third Reich. For an experienced pianist like the Hungarian who accompanied her, it was clear that this singer, with her high professional and academic background, had probably sung in her former European life in front of other kinds of audiences no doubt different from those in The Blue Mountain. Doutbtless she was sincerely trying hard in this genre that was so foreign to her, though it had to be admitted that Zara Leander, with her husky voice and passionately drawn-out lyrics, remained an inimitable model. Nevertheless she elicited raucous and warm reactions from the English, French, and German sailors, some of them accompanied by sneering shouts and others by ecstatic applause. Shanghai was still a hospitable port, open to all ships, and the sailors were collegially and benevolently disposed toward one another despite the war burning in Europe. But if at the time they had heard the rumor that Zara Leander, the Führer's favorite, who was much loved by the Nazi elite, was working for English counterintelligence—a rumor, by the way, that was neither confirmed nor denied—the whistles and warm responses accompanying Elisabeth Müller-Weissberg's numbers would perhaps have been reversed.

No one here knew what winds had brought her to the Far East. She was uncommunicative, and she always managed to keep the sailors at a respectable distance. The singer would delicately make them understand that they were only going to waste their time with her, while the tavern was always full of accessible girls of all races and for every taste; the steep stairway at the back led straight to the pink abodes of Chinese Eros. She didn't drink and she refused all offers of drinks and all attempts at intimacy. This also included Istvan Keleti, who never managed to overcome the cold, invisible wall that the singer had raised between herself and others. Perhaps the one thing they had just slightly in common was German, the only foreign language of which the Hungarian had a decent command—an inherited memory of the once-upon-a-time glory of the Austro-Hungarian empire.

Late at night a tall, skeletal man would come to pick her up, wearing the worn-out clothes of a common worker or hotel carwasher, and the two of them would hire a rickshaw to take them home. As far as the Hungarian could understand, this was her husband, probably a Jew fallen on hard times with whom she was living somewhere on the opposite shore. The tavern proprietor, the fat Yen Qingvey, always elegant, his hair always slick with brilliantine, paid too little, and this odd, mixed couple —the more or less elegant singer and her shabby husband—couldn't afford anything beyond the stinking slum of Hongku. Istvan Keleti had better luck: *Mister* Yen had given the Hungarian a storeroom under the roof of his hotel for which he deducted one third of his pay.

# 40

AS A RULE, MEN in government have faith in neither bad dreams nor bad news, preferring to leave themselves lovingly and trustingly in the hands of their pleasant delusions, which are as comfortable as house slippers. This is sharply sensed by the sycophants who crowd around the throne and hum the dreamy melodies His Majesty yearns to hear. Once upon a time, they say, in the distant past, the sultan cut off the head of the messenger who had ruined his lunch with unpleasant tidings. Lord Washburn, of course, was far from thinking about cutting off the head of his good old friend Baroness von Dammbach when she invented for the ears of various secretaries and every other kind of gossipmonger the idea of a picnic with a snipe hunt. It was more than obvious that her husband, the baron himself, as the representative of a country at war, couldn't show up willy-nilly at the English governor's official residence without its being noticed by an alien or ill-intentioned eye. It would have been a gross violation of accepted diplomatic protocol, after England had declared war on Germany. But his wife could do it and her arrangements would make everything look like a remnant of the good old romantic days in the International Concession.

The issue was hardly the snipe—in fact, far from it.

Baron von Dammbach, it's already been said, felt toward the Japanese military elite both deep antipathy and distrust, which he wasn't always able to conceal behind diplomatic smiles. And when he received a coded and strictly confidential order from Department B4 of the Headquarters for Reich Security in Berlin to commandeer a guarded residence, a hotel, and apartments for two hundred SS and Gestapo officers in connection with the upcoming turnaround in Japanese-American relations, the old diplomatic fox Dammbach could almost smell what would follow. As far as Japanese-American relations were concerned, at least in front of the world, things were heading toward the concluding of a non-aggression pact, so that "turnaround" couldn't mean anything other than in fact a heating up of hostilities. The baron couldn't predict exactly what Japan would do next, but as a supporter, with very grave reservations, of the new masters in Berlin and despite the swastika on his lapel, he considered it his duty as a friend to inform Lord Washburn discreetly about these developments through his wife. He left it to the conscience of the English governor to pass the information on in whatever ways he thought best.

The baron possessed reliable evidence that in Shanghai there was a well organized and efficient group of American agents, led by Major Robert Smedley, who officially passed himself off as a sort of military attaché. Some time ago, at the end of the twenties and until the beginning of the Japanese occupation, there had been an American journalist about town, Agnes Smedley, a close friend of Dr. Richard Sorge and quite probably a secret Russian agent. Whether this coincidence of names was an accident no one ever found out, but if a connection between the two Smedleys did exist, didn't it also imply a convenient exchange of unofficial information between American and Soviet intelligence, at least on a number of questions pertaining to the Japanese? Certainly as a possibility it made sense, insofar as both America and Russia were equally interested in knowing Japan's intentions and secret plans. This is why Baron von Dammbach was scratching his head, without being able to find an answer to the question of how American intelligence, usually well and punctually informed, could have possibly slept both here and in Tokyo through so dramatic a decision on the part of the Japanese government as to change the direction of Japanese-American relations.

One way or another, the baron had no wish to go further than Lord Washburn; it was only toward him, his old and discreet partner in poker and hunting, that he was willing to stretch the boundaries of his personal security. By the way, this wasn't the first time that they'd exchanged such confidential information, convinced supporters as they were of the principle that the shared secret is the foundation of mutual trust and good friendship. Moreover, the baron didn't hide his reverence for mighty Albion, nor Lord Washburn his sympathies toward the new Nazi rulers of Germany, often the subject of heated debates. The paradox in this case was that it wasn't the official representative of Nazi Germany but the British governor who favored Hitler's efforts to secure living space for the German nation for the next thousand years—of course, if under "living space" you understood the endless territories east of the Reich, in Soviet Russia.

At first the Englishman had burst out laughing:

"My dear, dear old friend! How can such dark thoughts cross your mind? No later than a month from now the non-aggression pact will be signed. I have it from a very reliable source."

The baroness persisted:

"I don't believe it, I don't believe it, and I still don't believe it! Your source may be reliable, but two hundred responsible representatives of the Gestapo and the like don't show up in Shanghai just like that on somebody's whim. And in relation to some impending change in Japanese-American relations at that! In any case, it was our duty—mine and Ottomar's—to let you know. The rest is up to you."

In the end Lord Washburn promised to ponder the situation despite the laughable suspicions of his German friends. He could take advantage of the opportunity provided by the traditional gathering every Monday for a glass of sherry at the Gentlemen's Club on Bubbling Well Road. There he could eventually whisper a thing or two to Major Smedley. Yes, maybe it would be worth it!

It was Thursday, before noon, almost five days until Monday morning—enough time to think it over. The Lord, following a confirmed English tradition, preferred not to act in haste but to contemplate each of his steps calmly, sometimes even overdoing it with his cautiousness, and perhaps this is why he had always remained a bachelor. But between Thursday and Monday, there was a day off, Sunday, December 7, when the world found out about the events at Pearl Harbor on the paradisal island of Oahu, which was transformed in a matter of minutes into the gates of hell.

For the consolation of poor Lord Washburn, shocked by both the terrible news and the sense of personal guilt that he hadn't immediately sought out the American major, it would perhaps have been sufficient to tell him the secret that the one radio center that had by chance survived in the otherwise completely leveled navy headquarters at Pearl Harbor had received, four long hours after the total destruction of the base, an alarming cryptogram from Washington firmly commanding that measures of the first order be taken in imminent anticipation of a massive Japanese attack. It was only natural to respond to this order, stuck somewhere in the jammed channels of coordination between the armed services, with a resounding sailor's curse and a polite, "Thanks a lot, it's already happened. Almost 2,500 of our boys killed!"

The aforementioned developments evoked the thought that American intelligence in Tokyo, as well as in Shanghai, had done a good job, sniffing out the Japanese attack in time, but, as has been said, the sultan doesn't like to have his lunch ruined with unpleasant and unwanted news.

At least this is how it appeared at first glance.

# 41

TO BELIEVE THAT IT was only Washington that had the bad habit of rejecting every piece of information contrary to its preconceptions about the world is more than naive. French nonchalance, which almost bordered on treason despite precise information gathered by agents about Hitler's real plans, proves the point as well. No one's lunch in Paris was spoiled even when reports started flowing in that suddenly thousands of German tourists were pouring into Luxembourg and spreading tents all along the French border. No one bothered to talk to even one of these German nature lovers and to inquire a bit further about what they were doing there and why they preferred border landscapes to all others. And what about sleepyhead Moscow, carelessly ignoring intelligence from the Ramsay group, which, together with other reliable sources in Europe, kept issuing warnings about impending German aggression against the Soviet Union? On this dramatic issue, alarming coded messages were sent three times to the Center and doubled up for extra measure by the Agfa studio on North Sichuan Road in the Shusan corner. Both Japanese and German counterintelligence intercepted these coded messages, broadcast to an unknown address by an obviously highly experienced radio operator and always too brief and too fast for their source to be identified.

On May 15, 1941, at 2 a.m. local time, Vladivostok caught a weak signal and immediately passed it on. Decoded at the Center, it warned:

> Germany will attack the Soviet Union on June 20 or 22. Ramsay; on May 21, at almost the same time: Germany has amassed at the Soviet border 9 armies, 150 divisions. Ramsay; and four days later, on May 25, at 5 a.m.: Attack will follow June 22 at early dawn, along a wide front.
>
> Ramsay.

But the Kremlin masters had their own views on the matter, preferring to contemplate their navels rather than listen to unpleasant news. They neither believed the warnings nor took the necessary measures, appeased as they were by the recently concluded and amicable non-aggression pact with Hitler. The accumulation of German divisions on the Soviet border was explained to the Russians by the emissaries from Berlin with a cunning wink: you do understand, boys, that this is just to distract England? And the guys in the Kremlin, who got the point, winked back: keep going, *druzya, bonne chance*! But when the Germans invaded exactly on the previously announced "June 22 at early dawn," the Russians, those same fellows who'd been winking from the Kremlin, were caught with their pants down. In those days the Soviets resembled a virgin warned multiple times by family and friends not to go around in the company of bad boys because a certain something might happen to her. And when it did happen, she desperately wrung her hands and cried out, "My dear God, how did it happen like that, out of the blue?!"

Then, at the beginning of the German invasion, when there was bloody fighting for the Brest fortress, Alfred Kleinbauer, owner of the Agfa studio, and his friend, the journalist Cheng Suzhin, would get drunk with sorrow that the warnings had been ignored. They explained it to each other with reference, among other things, to vague and long-delayed rumors about the shooting of leading Soviet functionaries, including Yan Berzine, "the Boss," who, with his erudition and experience as the teacher of a whole generation of Soviet agents, was irreplaceable. What these shootings in Moscow were all about just as the country was being put to the test no one here could comprehend, but the Agfa people were completely engulfed with tasks, and they put aside their doubts for another time. The wide network of Suzhin's Shanghai informers had fallen into a funk, though it wasn't because of Berzine or even the shootings of an impressive cohort of high Soviet military leaders. Far from it. They didn't even believe the newspaper headlines, taking them for banal anti-Soviet propaganda; what had them really worried were the initial, inexplicable, and serious defeats of the Red Army. This network—a metropolis in itself—consisted of well-intended pacifists and friends of Russia, mostly from scientific circles, public figures and businessmen with broad connections to the Japanese as well as a number of figures from the military and business elite who functioned in the big Far East city. Cheng Suzhin strictly followed the prohibition against any form of contact with the deeply subversive Chinese communists; he was also forbidden contact with White Russian immigrants. Despite unsettled personal accounts with the Soviets, feelings of solidarity with Russia, which was now in a tough situation, were beginning to run high in those circles, in the midst of which there functioned both silently and successfully a Soviet intelligence network concealed behind some "Union for the Return to the Motherland" that fell, by default, under Japanese observation. This is why, even at the Russian baths, Cheng Suzhin preferred to keep his distance from the regular Russian visitors.

On December 6, 1941, on the very eve of the Japanese assault on Pearl Harbor, the Agfa studio had every reason to rejoice: world agencies that day were unanimous in announcing the news that in Moscow, which was facing a deadly threat, the Red Army had launched a decisive and powerful counterattack against thirty-eight elite German divisions—the backbone of the Nazi operation "Typhoon," whose initial target was the immediate takeover of Moscow before the beginning of the heavy Russian winter. The blow was so hard, the agencies claimed, and the German losses so significant that for sober observers it meant if not the beginning of the end, at least the end of the initial, easily won German victories. Even the military specialists in Hitler's headquarters painfully realized that it was a question now of strategic defeat and that from now on the war in the East could be prolonged but no longer won. It was also why the sin of Vladek, who had unconscionably allowed himself to become embroiled in a street scuffle, could be magnanimously forgiven. A decisive role was played by Cheng Suzhin, who, as a good student of Dr. Sorge, always thought that bold, complex-free behavior, rather than the overly cautious kind, like that of a girl in a convent, was the best defense against potential suspicion. That same night Vladek indulged himself in what he otherwise never did: for the sake of reconciliation he downed, with Kleinbauer, a whole glass of Russian vodka. Then he threw up, vowing repentantly to himself never again to follow his boss blindly in anything, since the latter always found a reason to get drunk—one time over good news, the next over bad. Today the news was both good and bad—good from Moscow, and bad, very bad from Tokyo.

For the people at the Agfa studio, unpleasant, or, to put it bluntly, alarming news severely dampened, in fact threw a bucket of ice water over, their enthusiasm for the salvation of Moscow. Even though in this business he was just a technical assistant, a taker-down of shorthand and a cryptographer, Vladek was bursting with pride over his modest contribution two months earlier, when he had personally encoded in German a certain message he had received through a courier from Tokyo. The Japanese group was apparently feeling that the noose around its neck was getting tighter and that its transmissions were being intercepted, and that it therefore had to become extremely cautious. This is why it had preferred to take the roundabout route for the two-line text encoded at the Agfa studio through letters and numbers from the pages of the *Annual Statistics Report of the German Reich for 1935*, which would enter the history of Russian intelligence during World War II, but for now, dressed in its worn-out cover, lay haphazardly about in the studio among other old newspapers and magazines—just a little book by means of which for many years the Ramsay group, both in Shanghai and Tokyo, had been keeping in touch with the Center. The fateful message, transmitted through the 39th shortwave sector by Kleinbauer, who was at one and the same time a mediocre photo-colorist, genius radio operator, and unwavering fan of vodka, sounded like this: "*Der sowjetische Ferne Osten kann als sicher vor einem Angriff Japans erachtet werden.*"

Or, freely translated: the Soviet Far East can be certain that it will not be attacked by Japan.

This time the Kremlin trusted the information from Ramsay and released mighty army divisions that were quickly transferred from the shores of the Amur and the Ussuri to the Moscow front. The first to feel the influx of these fresh troops as yet unexhausted by battle was the German army, up to its neck in Russian mud and snow. Later they would once again experience a dramatic face-to-face encounter with the people of Russia's Far East in Stalingrad, where the parameters of the German defeat would finally be drawn.

But this was the triumphant side of the matter. The other was considerably less joyful—indeed, deeply troubling. Soon after the message was sent, the head of the Ramsay group in Tokyo, that merry cynic, salon lion, and family friend of the German ambassador Major-General Eugen Ott and his Japanese wife Hanako Ishii, the one person above suspicion, otherwise known as Dr. Richard Sorge, was arrested—never to learn the consequences of his stellar radiogram. The failure in Tokyo, which happened with the help of German specialists in radio interception, was an utter catastrophe. Sentenced and shot much later with Sorge, on the exact date of the twenty-seventh anniversary of the October revolution, was the journalist from *Asahi Shimbun*, Dr. Hotsumi Ozaki, a soulmate of the prince's son and foreign policy advisor to the cabinet of Kinkazu Sayonji. Arrested and tortured by the Kempeitai secret police and given heavy sentences were, in addition, the European collaborators Max Christiansen-Clausen and Branko Vukelic, as well as sixteen renowned Japanese scientists, writers, and public figures, at the head of which were Yoshinobo Koshiri and Shige Midzuno. No less terrible was the arrest of Hisataki Haieda from the South Manchuria Railroad Company, the person who'd been the first to observe the movement of a considerable number of Japanese army divisions to the Soviet border.

The Japanese elite were radiant, as was evident in the Tokyo press, while at the other end of the world, in Berlin, the Nazi bosses Heinrich Himmler, Heinrich Muller, and Joachim von Ribbentrop fumed at how they had allowed this genial jokester, in whom they had placed their trust, to lead them by the nose for so many years.

But the Tokyo brouhaha, which by the way cost the German ambassador Eugen Ott his career, was weakly covered in the West, where the press was occupied with something else, namely, closely following and commenting on the first resounding Nazi defeat of World War II. No one at that time ever suspected the link between this event and certain people who were being tortured at that moment in Tokyo in the underground chambers of the Kempeitai. There, in one of those chambers, on December 15, one week after the attack on Pearl Harbor, the technical specialist and courier of the Ramsay group Yoshio Kawamura was tortured to his last breath. His arrest in Shanghai had forced the Agfa studio to take down its radio transmitter, rapidly disassemble its parts, and terminate any contact between the members of the group. But the worry that his arrest would lead to a collapse of the Shanghai network turned out to be baseless: Kawamura, in spite of cross-examination under inhuman torment, personally observed by the minister of internal affairs Admiral Suetzugu, did not betray a single person or give away a single name or address.

In those days a rumor started spreading that Joseph Stalin had made a special personal contribution to this turnaround at the Russian front. It's possible. But it's too superficial to attribute all victories and defeats comfortably to a particular person, even though rumor, as well as history, is fond of simplifying and personifying things, so that they can be digested more easily. It was hardly just the message coded by the Swiss journalist Jean-Loup Vincent that played the decisive role in that dramatic Moscow saga. To attribute the conquest of Troy, after a fruitless ten-year ambush, to a hollow wooden horse, the collapse of invincible Jericho to a blast of trumpets, or the saving of doomed Rome to a gaggle of geese is an attractive literary idea, but it hardly constitutes the whole complex and most often bloody historic truth. Moreover, historic truth itself is a very conditional notion —something like a suitcase with a double bottom, where at customs certain things are revealed, while others under them remain hidden. Examples of similar customs frauds are numerous, among them, as it would turn out, the case of Pearl Harbor.

But one way or another, for Shanghai these dramatic days did not lack consequences: not a month had passed before two passenger Junkers aircraft unloaded the first group of Gestapo and SS functionaries at the airport in Lunghoa. Because of the apparent risks of flying through the strictly guarded sky above the front lines and Siberia, the airplanes arrived in three days using a roundabout route with layovers in East Turkey and Bangkok. The message on their arrival gave Baron von Dammbach heartburn, in spite of which he went to the airport accompanied by his personal secretary, Miss Hilde Braun, to greet the esteemed guests from Berlin.

The same day, before the new arrivals had even unpacked their bags, the first joint meeting took place at Bridge House, the Shanghai department of Kempeitai. Owing to the baron's rank as supreme representative of the Reich, his presence was required at the meeting, where it fell to his personal secretary to type up the German version of the shorthand record of the meeting and prepare it to be sent by courier to Berlin.

# 42

THE RUSSIAN BATH, SITUATED at the end of Guanzhou Street, at just the spot where it runs into noisy Chunking Boulevard, was a public facility frequented not just by Russians. One could even say that here Russian was almost drowned out in the motley chatter of other foreign languages. Often through the multiple spaces of the extensive bathhouse, amid the clouds of hot steam, there flowed large, boisterous groups of naked Chinese merchants, towels around their waists, in addition to Europeans of all nationalities, and even Japanese military men. The air resonated with the Babel of tongues, the clinking of water bowls, and the spouting of water in the tubs. On the heated wooden benches various rituals were performed at length, with an Asian or perhaps Roman indulgence. Lovers of this method of wasting time were attracted to the place by its cleanliness and good service, by the clusters of fresh birch branches they found so exotic and with which the bathers would beat their bodies until they turned red, by the ice-cold Russian kvass, which was immediately turned into streams of sweat, by the fat Tatar masseurs who would pound your body till you dropped. And last but not least, by the direct access, right after the cool rooms for relaxation, to the Russian restaurant adjacent to the bath, with its inimitable "ukha" fish soup and Siberian pelmeni, accompanied, of course, by authentic Russian vodka. Waiters in boots and baggy tucked-in trousers and Russian linen shirts, endearingly reminiscent of pages out of Gogol or Dostoevsky, would carry around steaming Russian samovars and pour tea into glasses with nickel holders. The Russian Bath and restaurant had long ago turned into something like a public focal point for meetings, gossip, business deals, or just passing the time. Unlike the elite restaurants and clubs on Nankin Road, here the Chinese were not denied access, which made it an even more attractive establishment for middle-class people who maintained both business and social relations with their local partners.

After making sure that tomorrow's edition of the newspaper was set to the last announcement concerning Miss Y's engagement to Mr. X, the political observer Cheng Suzhin was in the habit of coming here with his colleagues from the *China Daily Post.* On this particular Wednesday evening, however, Suzhin broke with his regular routine and came alone, to relax, as people say, after a strenuous night spent with Alfred Kleinbauer from the Agfa photo studio and his young Swiss colleague Jean-Loup Vincent. There'd been good reason for the night's fervor: military news from the depths of the Pacific kept flowing in like water from the bath's bronze faucets and in the Center they were thirsty for fresh information.

Dead-tired and utterly mellow from his session in the sweating-room, a hybrid between a Finnish sauna and a Chinese laundry, he heard beside him a thick, mild voice:

"I'm glad to see you, Mr. Cheng!"

Startled out of his lazy, rambling thoughts, the journalist peered intently through the thick vapor to discover that he was seated not far from Major Smedley of the American mission. They had at one time often met at press conferences and banal diplomatic cocktail parties given for or without an occasion; Cheng Suzhin had interviewed him several times. According to rumors making the rounds of the Shanghai papers, Major Smedley really oughtn't to have been here anymore. After Pearl Harbor and the outbreak of war, the Japanese authorities had declared the continued presence of official American diplomatic and trade representatives undesirable. On this list, as a persona non grata, their military representative in Shanghai was naturally included too, and it was suggested that by the end of a ten-day period he should go to hell. Concerned about rumors of possibly imminent repression, confiscation, and exile, ordinary American citizens—and there were many of them here—quickly closed or transferred their property and businesses to friends and relatives.

"You startled me, Major! I thought that by now you'd be far from here, beyond the visible horizon," said Suzhin, moving closer to the American.

"And you guessed right, with a few hours difference. Because tomorrow in fact I'm off for home in a New Zealand cargo rickshaw called *Tuatapere*. You've never seen a more wretched crate, but what can be done—if there were nothing better I'd leave for the States in a canoe."

"Yes, it's true, the war has scared off the shipping companies and they've hidden themselves in the shade of the harbors. I do hope all the same that you will successfully reach your destination. . . ."

"Hope and religion are the crutches of the man on his way to Eternity. I'm not religious, so what else do I have but the hope that we'll crawl at least to a port with a regular connection to the States. If the Japanese submarines don't pierce our belly in the meantime."

And the major burst out laughing as if he were telling a joke.

"You can rest assured, at least as far as the submarines are concerned," said the Chinese man. "Events you expect usually don't happen. I'm not just saying this to be polite, but we'll miss you—a long time ago you became part of our life here."

"Thank you. And please, don't be offended—this is your country—but I'm not going to miss Shanghai. Not at all! Honestly speaking, I've had it with everything here."

"I understand what you mean. This city is not the coziest and safest place in the world."

"I'm afraid there aren't any cozy and safe places left anymore. You saw what happened to that earthly paradise Pearl Harbor."

"And what exactly *did* happen there?" asked the Chinese man with the utmost sincerity, and almost childish curiosity. "I don't mean what was announced in the communiqués, but what was concealed."

Major Smedley poured a dipperful of hot water over himself, shook his dark blond hair, issued a moan of pleasure, and only after that said:

"Is this a journalistic question or are you just asking?"

"Take it as a simple question. And if you tell me what you think, I will not quote you. Scout's honor!"

"Okay, but tit for tat. The first move is yours, Mr. Cheng. And you'll tell me what in your circles they've already sniffed out about the case. America, as you know, is not indifferent to world opinion."

"Yes . . . sometimes," Suzhin reluctantly agreed.

Cheng Suzhin knew very well who Major Smedley was; only a simpleton could believe that he was just an American relay officer. Without a doubt, before boarding that *Tuatapere*, which was probably a freighter, one of those weatherbeaten tubs that roamed up and down the islands, he'd made sure to secure a solid network of informers. This was standard operating procedure, part of the rules of the game: when departing, you never leave the estate behind without faithful servants to water the flowers.

By the way, Major Smedley had his doubts about Cheng Suzhin. His professional intuition told him that the Chinese journalist's reports about the political aspects of rice production and the black market were hardly his only occupation. Here was the chance to confirm or deny his suspicions, at least to the extent that he could do so in a bathhouse.

They were separated by the ministrations of the masseurs, though not for long.

In the restaurant, while savoring Russian blinis with Iranian caviar, a required part of the ceremony with the Russian soup (crowning glory of the sturgeon, which had dipped itself in chicken bouillon), the American asked:

"And so, Mr. Cheng, I'm waiting for the rest of the story."

Suzhin did not get it immediately.

"Ah, yes, the rest of the story! We were talking about . . ."

"Pearl Harbor."

"Yes, yes, Pearl Harbor." Hesitating a bit, Suzhin toyed with his spoon, looked intently at the concentric circles in the soup, and finally raised his head. "Major, they are saying that in certain Washington circles, the unexpected Japanese circus act in Hawaii was hardly a surprise. That they had anticipated it and waited for it with bated breath."

"Oh, with bated breath! And why is that, in your opinion?"

"Now it's your turn to tell me. That is what we agreed on, did we not?"

"The agreement stands. But we said—step by step, one after the other. For the time being I would add a conditional 'getting warmer.' Just like that, for courage. Each of us has already taken a step. What's your next?"

"The next is the rumor that in the days before the strike your high command quietly withdrew your topnotch military units from the island of Oahu, leaving as a target some scrap metal from the First World War. And that the drama about your irreversibly damaged ships was exaggerated, since, they say, in a month or so, most of them will be back on the water again. That's what they say. . . .They also say that the damage suffered has been highly exaggerated for internal consumption and to stir up patriotic zeal in the average Yankee."

The American looked intently with his clear blue eyes at the Chinese journalist and asked with mild insistence:

"Who says? I haven't come across such a statement in either the press or official commentaries."

"It can't be possible that you haven't heard of the secret report of Otto Skorzeni to Hitler."

That same instant—no, in that fraction of an instant—Suzhin froze: he had just made an irreparable blunder!

The Skorzeni report, which hadn't yet been published anywhere, was accessible only to a very limited circle of those closest to the Führer. The Chinese man knew its general outlines, which had been received in a coded radio message from the Center in Moscow. But Suzhin couldn't know the source of this information, because the source itself was also deeply secret. Much later, after an entire geological era, when a portion of the Soviet secret archives saw the light of day, it would become known that the content of Skorzeni's report had been transmitted to Moscow letter by letter from Manfred von Brauchisch, a famous

Nazi sports enthusiast, one of the organizers of the Berlin Olympiad and a deeply undercover Soviet agent. A sufficient proof of the fact that the world is full of paradoxes is that this Olympic activist was the son of field marshal Walter von Brauchisch, one of the chief architects of the "Barbarossa Plan" for the blitzkrieg against the USSR and a member of Hitler's secret military-political council. His son had free access to his father's office with its sacred secrets, which were regularly leaked to the Kremlin, even when the father's armies were making their way through the Russian steppes in the same direction. The brief coded message about the Skorzeni report was received at the Agfa photo studio and decoded by Jean-Loup Vincent. It was accompanied by an insistent demand for the swiftest possible information about Pearl Harbor and the data that had been leaked to Japanese military circles. And did they know over there whether the strike on the American naval base, touted by the official press in Tokyo as a triumph of Japanese military strategy, had in fact turned into something like a trap? A quite expensive trap as far as the United States was concerned, since the affected ships could be repaired, but the boys who'd been killed and sent home in tin coffins covered with the Stars and Stripes could hardly be returned alive to their mothers. In any case, preliminary information about the strike then being prepared by the Japanese had been received in enough time for the taking of preventive measures, but somewhere in the celestial spheres of Washington, following complicated and far-reaching strategic considerations, it was decided that this alarming piece of information would be silently passed over, and kept secret from even those *bonzi* closest to the Oval Office. The war was scarcely over when it would become known that even the British secret services had done their job well, but that Churchill had both immediate and farseeing reasons for withholding information about the impending Japanese attack. Had the guys in Tokyo figured out with whom they'd in fact found themselves in a corner with their pants down? This is what they wanted to know in the Center.

At that time the Ramsay group in Tokyo had already been destroyed, and the hope of ferreting out a possible change in Japanese orientation had been delegated to the network of Shanghai informers.

"And so, Mr. Cheng, I'm burning with curiosity. Where has Otto Skorzeni's report been published?! Or do you have a personal correspondence with Canaris?"

Admiral Wilhelm Canaris was the head of Hitler's intelligence and Skorzeni's immediate boss. Cheng Suzhin realized that by demonstrating how highly informed he was, he was sinking deeper and deeper into a swamp from which there was no getting out. This is why he mumbled vaguely:

"Apart from Canaris one can learn a thing or two from other sources . . . I'm a journalist, this is part of the job and . . . how do you put it . . . ?"

Major Smedley's eyes sparkled devilishly; he understood his Chinese friend's difficulties. For some time he kept silent, playing cat-and-mouse with the Chinese, and at last mercifully helped him to escape:

"Okay, okay. Everybody keeps tight about his sources. Now it's my turn. Provided that you'll forget who told it to you. With the strike on Pearl Harbor, regardless of how painful a sacrifice it's been for America, and it's been truly painful, especially as far as its cost in lives goes, the Japanese, without wanting or suspecting it, have saved England."

"England? I don't get the connection."

"It's a direct connection and you're smart enough to figure it out. If you follow the American press, before the attack on Pearl Harbor, eighty-two percent of the American people were categorically against America's entry into the war. The figures are about the same for the Senate, which furiously opposed Roosevelt's desire to participate in an anti-Hitler coalition, which would be the only way to save the doomed British Isles. At the moment, eighty-seven percent of the population north of Mexico want vengeance and insist on immediate retaliatory strikes on all fronts. Our Atlantic fleet has already been posted to provide American help for London and Murmansk. Our marine infantry divisions and our air contingents, warmly supported by the whole American public, have already begun direct military action. The end is still far away—very far—but our old uncle Winston Churchill will from now on be able to take a quiet nap in the afternoon. And the price of his afternoon nap is Pearl Harbor. We couldn't prevent the Japanese aggression, nor its first considerable victories. They were unavoidable—America was still unprepared for war in the Pacific. But Roosevelt could at least draw a benefit from the first Japanese strike. And this was actually a strategic move on his part. Now do you get the connection?"

And the major again laughed boisterously—a jolly fellow, this Smedley!

"Does this mean that President Roosevelt knew about it, but kept silent about the attack being prepared on Pearl Harbor? Even with the risk of sacrificing so many people? From the point of view of England and the long-term interests of the States, it makes sense, but looking at it from the side of the mothers of the dead. . . ."

"Here we come to the end of our game. In war there are things relating to the feelings of mothers that even the gods don't discuss among themselves. Cheers, my friend Cheng. Bottoms up!"

Cheng Suzhin didn't realize in time that the American was getting him drunk. Major Smedley was pouring glass after glass, deliberately, as if he were conducting a medical experiment: these Chinks sure get drunk easily on hard liquor, like cats on valerian! Glass after glass of vodka and the restaurant started spinning around Suzhin. Major Smedley himself was hardly falling behind; he was draining the Russian shot glasses in one breath, but his eyes remained clear and slightly ironic. He poured again:

"Bottoms up, for friendship and a common victory. And this time, really common!"

"In . . . wha . . . s-s-s-sense?"

The restaurant was wheeling slowly around its axis like a planet, the Russian waiters were coming in pairs from somewhere above and sinking in the vague, distorted space. Two times Suzhin dropped his glass and vodka spilled over the white tablecloth. And still, in his muddled mind, the question continued to spin: In what sense a "common" victory? What does China have to do with all this Anglo-American mutual flirtation? What does the American want to say? What's he driving at?

Major Smedley, as if sensing his question, explained with a smile:

"We're allies now against the common enemy, aren't we? I mean you personally. Look, this is what the newspapers are writing."

And he took out from his jacket pocket a folded issue of the Russian *Krasnaya Zvezda* or *Red Star.* He put the editorial in front of Cheng's face, without ceasing to look at him intently.

Suzhin took the paper with uncertain fingers, cast a surprised look at the text, and stuttered:

"Th-th-this . . . is in a . . . f-f-f-foreign language. . . ."

"What do you mean 'foreign'! It's Russian! You surprise me, my dear Cheng. Don't you speak Russian?"

"Dirty bastard" flashed through Cheng's mind. "Ah, you dirty bastard!"

But he just said almost guiltily:

"N-n-n-o. . . . What does it s-s-s-say?"

The American looked at him with admiration:

"You win, Cheng Suzhin! One to zero for you. In this case I'll pay the bill."

Suzhin wasn't faking it; he was really quite drunk. But when he threw himself on the seat of the rickshaw, he smiled dreamily.

"The Yankees have no equals in drinking, it's true. But I'm a dirty bastard myself; I myself have no equal. Otherwise the number with the 'Red Star' was perfect. I'll remember it!"

He stretched out with pleasure and almost immediately fell asleep with a contented half-smile on his lips, while with a rhythmic slap-slap of his bare feet, the coolie took him to the Park Hotel.

# 43

HILDE PAID FOR AND let go of the rickshaw at the bridge above the Soochow, the entrance to the south side of Hongku. The sun was setting behind the low heavy clouds, huge and fiery like the red disk on the flag that swung above the wooden observation tower. The Japanese soldiers down below, at the big iron bridge, looked with curiosity at the tall blond beauty who obviously didn't belong to the world into which she was shyly stepping.

Minutes after that she plunged herself into the hullaballoo of Hongku, this human ant colony with its unfathomable mix of Asians and Europeans. A piercing wet wind blew from the sea, while through the air floated playful ice crystals that immediately turned into black mud. Beyond the river, in the Concession, last night's snow nestled shyly in sparse white spots on the mowed grass of the parks, to the joy of children who rarely saw the white miracle falling from the sky. But that was way over there—not here, where white snow, transparent rain, and fresh breezes with the scent of jasmine came to a dead end. Everything clean stopped here. And Hongku began.

Hilde made her way with difficulty through the street, which was stuffed with pedestrians, and jammed with hand-pushed two-wheel carts loaded with vegetables, deafening and constantly ringing bicycles, and vendors of everything that could be bought and sold sitting directly on the rug-strewn pavement. She was holding her purse tight, with all her valuables left behind smartly in advance, for during that anti-Japanese demonstration she had already lost an item, enough to teach her a lesson. With almost threatening insistence vendors offered her trinkets made out of wood, bone, and clay, about whose purpose she hadn't the slightest idea, while crippled beggars pulled at her skirt and reached out their arms to her. She hadn't forgotten the instructions Baroness von Dammbach had given her upon their arrival in Shanghai. "Never, my dear child, never give alms to a beggar. Before you know it you'll be surrounded in an instant by hundreds of tramps from everywhere, as if they've crawled out from the bowels of the earth, and what an aggressive bunch they are too, with their stretched-out arms. They'll pull you by your clothes, they'll push you, you may even see the flash of a knife blade. It's happened that certain overly sentimental and compassionate guests have had to be saved by the police with their bamboo sticks. Don't forget this, dear!"

A diminutive woman, with a very dark, almost black face, but with slanting Asian eyes, in outer appearance an island woman from the depths of the Pacific, started passionately pulling her in some direction for something the point of which Hilde hadn't the faintest idea. Unable to speak a common language with her, she shrugged her shoulders, guiltily gave her a pleasant smile, and with a certain rough insistence detached herself from the woman's small hands. She was clearly aware of the dangers awaiting her here in the enormous, overpopulated neighborhood, a source of dark tales about sailors who had disappeared and curious tourists who had sunk into it never to be found again—as if they'd been lost in the dark chasms of the sea. People said that the criminal world in Hongku lived in tolerable coexistence with the population, which for its part regarded both the Chinese and Japanese security forces with wariness and hostility. "I don't know, I didn't hear, I didn't see"—most police investigations here ended with these uncooperative answers. Once, they say, the police and the administration of the big hotels beyond the river issued a warning to foreigners to stay away from exotic visits to Hongku, but since the large neighborhood had been settled first by a huge wave of Japanese and later by numberless immigrants from Europe, which made it an even more chaotic and unmanageable place, the authorities had helplessly washed their hands of the obligation to protect overly curious foreigners.

Here and there Hilde would stop pedestrians with European-looking faces, most often dressed in the worn-out duck clothing of common workers, without doubt German Jews, because all of them would respond to her questions in flawless German, always pointing in the same direction—to the southern part of the swirling human galaxy called Hongku.

Finally she discovered the place she'd been looking for. It was a small square and at its end stood the pagoda that had been turned into a synagogue.

Hilde walked diffidently in the cool semi-darkness of the temple, the floor covered with large red tiles made of baked clay. Uneven and worn by the feet of worshiping multitudes throughout the lengths of Chinese time, it had also absorbed the sandalwood aroma of Buddhism, and the memory of the monotonous prayers recited by generations who had come here to kneel before resuming their journey to eternity. The scarce beams of the sun that would now appear and then disappear behind the heavy clouds streamed through the gaping crevices in smoky, flaming, and dying spills—as if the Chinese gods were curiously peeping from the depths of the universe at this strange pagoda, which had given shelter to prayers in a strange language to a strange, distant, and incomprehensible god. At the end, on something like a small platform, calm and mysteriously smiling, with legs crossed on his enormous lotus, sat the huge chipped Buddha, looking intently at the crudely wrought iron menorah set up before him. And hardly anyone could decipher the meaning of that barely perceptible smile—ironic, conceited, or maybe sympathetic.

"Are you looking for someone?" a voice shouted from above.

Hilde searched for a long time until she discovered Rabbi Leo Levin, sitting on a beam, with a hammer in his hands.

"Yes, I'm looking for you, Mr. Levin. I am Hilde Braun, from the German embassy."

"My God, Miss Braun! Just a minute, Miss, I'm coming right now!"anxiously said the rabbi, who disappeared into the dark space between the beams.

Somewhere behind the Buddha the wooden steps squeaked and momentarily, panting, in front of Hilde stood Leo Levin, his dusty worker's clothes covered in cobwebs, his face begrimed here and there by something black, most probably the charred beams. He didn't extend his hand to the visitor, but just guiltily opened his dirty palms.

"I'm glad to see you, Miss . . ." he paused expectantly, not even trying to hide his uneasiness with her visit.

She too, it seemed, was no less uneasy, because she hesitated a bit and said, "May I look around?"

Hilde took a few steps, fixed her eyes on the statue of the Buddha and the hundreds of wooden tiles with engraved prayers arranged in the corner. She took one of them, studied it with curiosity from all sides and then again carefully put it back in its place. She walked around the pagoda slowly and her high heels made an echo when they clicked in the silence.

"So this is where you pray?" she finally asked.

"Yes, there was no place else."

"Doesn't it bother your people that the temple isn't Jewish?"

"What difference does it make? In the olden times people used to pray to trees or rocks. No matter where—they always needed to pray. Probably more important than the temple are the prayer and the hope that it will be heard."

"Trees and rocks, you say. . . . But I remember from school, from religion classes, something like this: 'I am your God. And there shall be no other gods before me.' This is approximately what it said, isn't it?"

"It was written by people."

"So he isn't the only one, your God?"

The rabbi thought for a while and then, not immediately and with some sadness, responded:

"To tell the truth, I don't know any more. But how are the Chinese worse than us? Or, let's say the Hindus, or the Polynesians? Why should their gods be false, untrue, and our own the real one and the only one? With you at least he's not so lonely, he has a son. People feel the need to believe. Let's leave them to do it as they wish, to believe in whomever they wish to believe in. And if this soothes their sufferings, why should we deprive them of this last refuge of hope?"

"Regardless of which faith?"

"Regardless of what it's called and in which temple it's professed. People have too many hardships to burden them with one more, probably the most difficult to bear: doubt in the authenticity of their gods. True, sometimes even the gods are powerless to help, or they confuse our already confused lives. But let's not forget that they also have problems owing to their great age—we need to learn to understand them and to forgive them."

And the rabbi laughed soundlessly at his own thought.

"You're a good man. I'm weak in theology, but unlike you, religions are not so generous and well-intended toward one another. I remember some time ago when you visited us you said you were a servant of God. To which God, if gods can be so many and so different. To which one?"

Leo Levin opened his arms.

"To mine. Each to his own. If God is truth, and justice and love between people, then I am His servant."

"And what if He doesn't exist at all?"

"Then people can rely directly on me without addressing the heavenly authorities for help. Does this sound too heretical for a rabbi?"

Hilde didn't respond to the question, while Leo Levin continued to wipe his hands mechanically on the shabby cloth, expecting the visitor to finally state the purpose of her visit. After all, she had hardly made the effort to come to this cursed neighborhood only to see this paradoxical temple and to nibble at theological themes already long worn out by nibbling. Finally he couldn't bear the protracted silence and carefully asked:

"And so, Miss Braun . . . to what do I owe the honor?"

She had become sunk in thought and seemed startled:

"Ah, yes! Do you regularly receive our newsletter?"

"Of course. And we're very grateful to you, for us it's a window on the events in Europe. True, it's quite a . . . how to say . . ."

"Nazi window?"

"Something like that. . . ."

"You should expect this. It isn't published by an educational organization."

"I understand," agreed the rabbi. "Nevertheless, we appreciate your gesture."

Again a tense silence hung over them. She looked around, took a deep breath, and finally decided to speak directly:

"Mr. Levin, you can probably tell that I haven't come because of the newsletter. Even though if any of your people have seen me and recognized me, I would ask you to explain my visit to them this way . . . I'm sorry, but I've come with bad news. And I'd like you to be the first to know. After that you'll make your own judgment about how to proceed. I can't give you advice."

The rabbi looked at her intently and anxiously, but because she did not continue, he said quietly and encouragingly:

"I'm listening to you."

"If you remember, they asked you to hand over lists of all your people in Shanghai. You didn't give them, and this is your right. But in the very near future you will find out why they wanted them. On account of the insistence of our . . . I mean to say German authorities, who continue to treat you as their former citizens, the Japanese will turn part of Hongku into a ghetto. This affects you directly, you who have come from Austria and Germany."

Leo Levin didn't react at first; he didn't even quite comprehend the meaning of her words.

"This . . . what does it mean?" he asked.

"You don't know what a ghetto means?"

"Unfortunately, I know it only too well. But I don't understand—how come we, here, in Hongku. . . .This is impossible—if you knew this neighborhood!"

"Anything is possible. I don't know Hongku, but I know the people who have made this decision. They will have no doubts about implementing it. I can't tell you exactly when and how. Soon you'll find out everything."

The rabbi was looking at her speechlessly, and she continued, impartially and evenly, as if she were reporting a message from her boss von Dammbach at a press briefing:

"You will be placed under strict orders. That is, your movements out of the ghetto will be severely limited. This means that all of your people will have to come back within the borders defined by the authorities. Your whole crowd. This will probably burden you with new and unexpected suffering . . . or call them hardships, if you wish."

Leo Levin swallowed.

"This is impossible and monstrous. A ghetto! Oh, my God, a ghetto—in the middle of the twentieth century. . . ."

"In Europe, in the middle of the twentieth century, some even more horrible things are happening."

"But in a city with an international statute that guarantees—"

"The world, rabbi, is at war and no one can guarantee anything to anyone anymore!" Interrupting him coldly, she opened her mouth to say something further on the topic of the violation of international guarantees and statutes, but with a wave of her hand gave up.

The rabbi said with conviction:

"The English authorities will not allow it! This they will not!"

"Don't be so sure. Because soon there won't be any English authorities here. Or have you forgotten that England and Japan are already at war?"

Hilde again cast a long look at the Buddha, as if expecting him to express his point of view too. But he was contemplating the case, still smiling mysteriously. She kept silent for a while and then said:

"Well, this was it, Mr. Levin. I can't help you, but I wanted you to know about it. So that it doesn't come to you as a bolt from the blue. I'm sorry."

The rabbi thought for a while, suddenly struck by the stupid hope that it wasn't true, that it couldn't be true. . . . Maybe it was some kind of game of endurance?

"Tell me honestly: this business with the ghetto, isn't it the invention of those kids from *Yudaia Kenku*? You know—to scare us?"

"Unfortunately not. I'm really very sorry, but it isn't."

He looked at her sharply, while something a bit cunning and playful and yet distrustful—in a Jewish sort of way—came into his eyes:

"And why are you telling me this? No, really—why? Or do you really mean something else? After all, you're von Dammbach's secretary!"

Hilde just shrugged her shoulders.

"Everyone looks for his own way to . . . well, let's say—come to the temple. Even though it sounds a bit too exalted. Honestly speaking, I don't believe in such clichés about temples and celestial truths that we need in order to shelter our earthly sins. Anyway, it doesn't matter. I told you so that you'll know. And please give my warmest regards to Mr. Weissberg, he truly is a great musician! I read somewhere that he's even organized symphony concerts here. In your situation I find this to be more than strange."

"Why? A concert could also be an expression of the obstinate Jewish will to survive."

"That's probably true. I'm sorry I couldn't make it. I would like to listen to some decent music in this dull city! In any case, give him my regards. And tell him that Potsdam and the blooming apple trees along the banks of the Werder do exist, he didn't dream them up. And not to lose hope that he'll see them again. Now I have to go, don't see me off. I will ask you to keep to yourself the source of this information. I'm doing something that . . . you understand yourself—isn't right, to say the least."

She didn't even shake hands with him, but departed at once, leaving the rabbi standing in the middle of the pagoda. In comparison with the enormous Buddha behind his back, Leo Levin was a small man with disheveled hair, covered in cobwebs, with black traces of charred wood on his face.

At the exit, Hilde stopped for a short moment and pensively looked at the two dragons scorched under the twisted corners of the roof and at the leonine beast stepping with one paw on the stone globe in front of the gates. She caressed the twisting curls on his head and again sank into noisy teeming Hongku.

# 44

CAPTAIN MASAAKI SANEIOSHI, CHIEF of the Shanghai Kempeitai, doesn't understand the Germans. He just doesn't get them, and that's it! The captain has to honestly admit this to himself even though in front of his superiors he passes for a man who knows Germany and its language in detail, as well as the inhabitants of this distant land. Regardless of how he looks at the issue, from whatever side, these are strange people whose reasoning is unfathomable!

Saneioshi-san has a law degree from Leipzig, and a diploma from the highest police academy in Berlin; the supreme head of the SS and Gestapo Heinrich Himmler personally decorated him with an honorary medal. He supported the idea about closer military and political ties with Hitler's Germany in the common struggle against the English-American and the Bolshevik demons. So far so good, friendship is friendship, but everything needs to have a foundation in logic and to bring real benefits to the cause. The captain is a pragmatic fellow.

And what benefit is there in stuffing thousands and thousands of people into this hole called South Hongku, a whole army of tramps and lowlifes, an uprooted, frightened mob—just because they're Jews? Not that he likes them in any way, or feels something like, let's say, sympathy: Captain Saneioshi knows nothing of the human weakness called sympathy; he considers himself a cruel and tough warrior, the descendant of samurai. He is boundlessly faithful to his motherland, ready to follow whither she calls, even to die for her glory and the honor of the emperor. True, this has never prevented him from keeping his own personal accounts and private sources of income; he's no moralist, life makes its own demands, and police salaries in Japan aren't so high, to speak frankly. But these are other, personal issues. As far as the job is concerned, the captain has more than once been a direct and unfaltering participant in mass police operations and the cruel treatment of demonstrators, but all that's been reasonable and useful, while today's action on the part of his German friends neither brings a benefit nor shows common sense. Pure insanity is what Saneioshi-san thinks about it, paranoia and nothing else! What else could this senseless idea result in besides overburdening the Japanese military units, the Chinese community police, and a whole army of clerks—all of them in insufficient numbers—with out-of-the-ordinary obligations in addition to the usual work of guarding strategic sites and keeping order in Shanghai? Shall we add to it the Shanghai Kempeitai, which he heads, and which has labored mightily with problems connected to illegal anti-Japanese, anti-military, anti-communist, nationalist, and students' organizations? They keep growing like poisonous mushrooms—step on one here, three more sprout over there.

To speak directly, this is a stupid idea, a useless waste of time—of energy and time! We're creating one more dangerous tinderbox of tensions, epidemics, and problems, we're turning the local Chinese population against us, we're creating worries and dumping them on our own heads about things that don't concern us at all. This is the situation; they should know about it in Tokyo and think about it carefully well in advance before offering to his Excellency Minister Nobumasa Suetsugu for his signature that slippery-tongued order number K-013/42: For the good-faith and cordial facilitation of our German allies with respect to their plans related to persons of Jewish origin, former citizens of theirs, residing at this time in Shanghai.

This administrative order is the legal basis for the proclamation on the part of the Imperial government in Tokyo for the formation of a Shanghai ghetto.

And all of this in the name of a fragile union against the enemy. Yet in military terms an enemy is measured by its navy's tonnage, the number of airplanes, the quantity and quality of its army's materiel, its military preparedness and potential, and the covering of its rear. And in political terms, is there anyone in Shanghai who knows more than Captain Saneioshi about the structures and methods of subversive organizations? No, there's no one. But what do these shabby German, Austrian, and God knows what other types of Jews here in Hongku have to do with the problem? Teutonic metaphysics!

Saneioshi-san does not and will never understand his German friends' fanatic, almost mysterious obsession. And why exactly now, when their armies are fighting for their life at countless fronts around Europe and Africa, have they, so it seems, undertaken this stupid thing as if the rice harvest—as our fathers would say—depended on it!

The instincts of an experienced police chief, which have always helped him penetrate deeper than the visible and often deceptive surfaces of things, tell him that the Germans won't stop here and that this stupid transfer of people is just the beginning of worse things to come. Possibly this operation, which seems to him so devoid of common sense, has secret dimensions and further plans that by long habit the Germans are hiding from their Japanese allies. It was his duty to follow the order and he was following it. He wearily recalled the German phrase *Abwarten und Tee trinken* . . . let's wait and see and drink some tea.

Outside a repellent drizzle falls, its small lines cross-hatching the beams of the automobile headlights so that the view out the front window looks like a roll of film ruined by overuse. The car has stopped at the corner of the bridge; the engine runs quietly; with the back of his hand, the driver, from the low ranks of the Japanese police force, from time to time wipes the window, which instantly fogs up again. Captain Saneioshi is sitting next to the driver, while behind him two Germans in SS uniforms are silently smoking and observing the Jewish exodus. Speaking of uniforms, Captain Saneioshi as a rule prefers, except on formal occasions, to wear his civilian clothes. Following the signing of the Tripartite Pact, Nankin Road has lately been flooded by German experts, advisors, and representatives of all kinds of military, police, and administrative officers who proudly strut in their uniforms around the bars, teahouses, and restaurants, as if the Germans, and not the Japanese, have taken over Shanghai—the great city at the mouth of a great river.

At some point one of the men in the back seat, probably Stockmann, yes, this is his name—Hauptsturmführer Willy Stockmann—jumps outside, spreads his legs, and opens his officer's raincoat. The wind blows the stream to the left, dispersing it, and from here—from the car—you can only see his back and the sparkling sprinkles. He shakes himself carefully, gets back into the car, lights a cigarette again. Silence. There's nothing to talk about. Everything has already been said.

Saneioshi-san closes his eyes; he's sleepy. Let's just get it over with!

The chaos that happened that rainy night was unimaginable: the Japanese authorities had given seventy-two hours, three days and nights, for the process of resettlement—a very nasty deadline that would run out at midnight. According to the order pasted on the walls and written in Chinese, German, and English, this was the deadline given to the Jews who had arrived in Shanghai after '37, that is, after the city was placed under Japanese jurisdiction, regardless of where they were settled—in the suburbs or the upscale neighborhoods beyond the river—to transfer themselves without any conditions and exceptions to the south side of Hongku, also called the "Inner City," anyway, in this neighborhood choking with overpopulation. Those affected by this order, predominantly destitute German immigrants, had to move their pitiful belongings from their widely dispersed rented abodes or communal bedrooms around the suburbs of Hongku to the Inner City beyond the Soochow, marked on the map accompanying the order and called "The Zone." What "zone"? Why "zone"? Or was this a newer and more understandable way to signify for the local people the European idea of the "ghetto," which was otherwise unfamiliar in the Far East? Not just a Jewish neighborhood—such neighborhoods formed on ethnic grounds exist everywhere around the world, of all types, but a ghetto with its medieval, religious, and bigoted connotation. Why a ghetto here, thousands of kilometers away from Catholic Europe? There is no other reasonable explanation than the excessively zealous, idiotic, formal implementation of someone's vague intentions. This was neither a deportation nor a mere prohibition against inhabiting the central and luxurious areas, the usual practice in occupied Europe, since Hongku, already inhabited by Jewish immigrants, formed a chaotic periphery to the big city, another area filled with its poor. To move people from one of its ends to another was pure and simple harassment—bureaucratic, senseless, and malicious.

This is what Professor Sigmund Mandel was thinking, without even suspecting in what harmonic synchrony was his own mood with that of Captain Saneioshi from the terrible Kempeitai. The former chief surgeon of the Berlin hospital Charité, fired because of "incompatibility of the position with the non-Aryan origin of the person," had left Europe quite some time before certain momentous decisions were made on January 20, 1942, in Berlin, in a villa by a lovely lake, just outside the town, at the address Am Grosse Wannsee 56/58. Otherwise he, the professor, would have learned the meaning of the Nazi term "overcrowding" as a prelude to that other term: "Final Solution."

Expelled from Eden—this is how Professor Mandel, with his characteristic ironic bitterness, described the crowd that on that rainy night was streaming from different parts of Hongku to congest that corner squeezed between the Yangtse River and its Soochow tributary. In the opposite direction streamed a thinner, reverse flow of Chinese people who, judging from their meager possessions, were hardly better off than the Jews. They passed each other on the iron bridge without saying a word; indeed, it was impossible that they should even speak. The Chinese, unpretentious and friendly by nature, would throw such looks that if the Jews who were moving in the opposite direction could translate them into a comprehensible language, they would probably feel to what extent the crowd going in the opposite direction had come to hate them. And it had reason to hate them: because of them—the visitors who had inserted themselves here uninvited and unwanted, instead of staying in their distant Europe—they, the Chinese, were now required to drag by two-wheeled carts, bicycles, or on their backs all their household belongings, children, and paralyzed old men.

The professor said sourly:

"What do you think of this, Rabbi? You should know about these things. Is this what in your opinion God's punishments look like? For sins that from a judicial and moral point of view have been unproven. . . ."

They were standing and smoking under the eaves of a small pagoda while the crowd surged into the square. Frightened, in complete disarray, it continued the panic-stricken and not very tolerant struggle that had begun the day before for shelter or at least a dry warm corner in the mandated new living-space. Two representatives of The Jewish Refugee Community of Shanghai, protected from the rain under a canvas tent, were sitting behind a long counter probably taken out of some ruined tailoring loft. They were lit by a blinding kerosene lamp that made people's faces look deathly pale—a congregation of the living dead grouped in front of lists and cards with addresses and an open map of the neighborhood. The clan chieftains themselves, sleep-deprived and helpless, were trying to establish order and fairness in the distribution of the communal dwellings, frighteningly few in comparison to what was needed. And every one of those in need had his own convincing reasons to push the others or to ask for an exception: a sick wife, an old mother, small children.

Rabbi Levin looked intently at the crowd, inhaled, and choked on the hot smoke of his cigarette.

"What can I say, Professor? I don't know if it's a punishment. Maybe it's an Exodus. Not just any exodus, but a biblical one. If you've read the second book of Moses. God's intention, incomprehensible to us mortals. The old man up there has something in mind, but does anyone know what it is? Of course, this is surely not the exodus from Egypt to the coveted Promised Land, but rather a transition from Egyptian slavery to the Babylonian. But it is said: 'Is there shadow without light, night without day, and evil without good?' Even slavery is not without meaning and lessons. Otherwise how would people learn the price of freedom? I am not Moses and the Soochow River is not the Red Sea. But South Hongku may turn out to be something like a new Sinai. That's what I think. Through it we will wander again, with God's help, until a dispersed community acquires the belief that it is not a mob of slaves but a small part of a great nation with a common destiny. The deep meaning of the forty biblical years, if you remember."

"A fine way of looking at it, isn't it? Forty years!"

"Take it as a biblical symbol. It might not be forty, but four or four hundred. But don't think that they don't have a meaning of their own, or that they have nothing to do with God's intentions. I don't say this because of my love for paradox, but the Nazis in the twentieth century with their madness will fulfill one historic and supreme assignment: they will again make a nation out of the Jews dispersed around the world, Jews speaking different languages, Jews thinking different thoughts. The initiative taken by the Zionist Theodor Herzl will be completed by Hitler."

This is what Rabbi Levin said looking at the chaotically bustling crowd and choking again from the cough caused by cheap Chinese cigarettes. Then he stepped on the cigarette butt and went back to the synagogue full of old men.

It was Friday, the night of the holy Sabbath, and people were expecting from him soothing words and an appeal to the Only One for help.

"*Shema Israel . . .*"

Along the adjoining streets, delineated by spirals of barbed wire and a thin cordon of Chinese policemen, through the streams of light pouring from a shifting military projector, thousands of people moved like phantoms, carrying bundles and suitcases, pushing two-wheeled carts or wretched, ancient children's prams, stuffed with odds-and-ends.

They went in one direction, the same direction, across the iron bridge over the Soochow toward the Zone. And the Chinese crowd went in the opposite direction, from the Zone to the murky abodes of their own hopelessness.

The wind from the sea whirled up gusts of drizzling rain. The headlights of a black car that had stopped at the corner by the bridge lit up the opening in the barbed wire through which the refugees had to pass in order to enter their new place of residence. No one here knew Saneioshi-san and the two Germans in the car nor could see them in the darkness, but if anyone had looked closely, he would have noticed the burning tips of their cigarettes.

The Chinese policemen, positioned in a line along the whole length of Soochow Creek—the riverbank street at the bridge, separating Hongku from the rest of the huge neighborhood, not far from the mouth of the river where the Soochow entered the muddy waters of the Yangtse—were freezing in their rain-soaked cotton jackets. They felt neither hatred nor sympathy for this crowd, not even knowing what exactly was meant by a "Jew." Maybe something else, something different, but weren't all Europeans, no matter what you called them, different from themselves, speaking a different language, dressing differently, their food and even their laughter different? And why exactly these pitiful and desperate human beings had to be relocated from one part of the damned neighborhood to another, while so many Chinese families had to leave their anthills in order to inhabit new ones—well, it was none of their business; it was not the concern of the man in uniform to know the reasoning of his bosses. These policemen were predominantly peasants, illiterate, obedient and patient, longing for their own lands, houses, and children. And mostly for the fields they had lost in the war. After all, what is a peasant without a field? A hut without a roof, a pot without a bottom, a dried-out spring. Time was, they had once owned land, good, fertile, blessed land, but now it was gone. Everything had been taken from them, by their own people and by intruders. This is why they were here—because of those sixty Shanghai dollars per month, equal to ten American dollars, in addition to some free rice, a uniform, and a secure bunk bed in the barracks. This wasn't very much, but it wasn't very little either in this crisis, when a whole multitude of old men, women, and children at the village were waiting for your help. And maybe the rain would at least stop, since there was no one to offer you even a bowl of hot tea!

This is what they were thinking this rainy night: a Japanese captain who considered himself the descendant of samurai, the once chief surgeon of the Charité hospital in Berlin, the former chief rabbi of Dusseldorf, and the chain of freezing policemen—recently arrived Chinese peasants.

# 45

MOTHER ANTONIA AND HER Carmelites were as always endearingly assiduous in their ministrations. They, together with a large group of men, had already managed to put into some kind of order three communal hostels—those infamous dortoirs—in long-abandoned and dilapidated warehouses. But the half-dark spaces, lit only by a row of tall, barred windows, were extremely inadequate as shelter even for the oldest, weakest, and most urgently in need. In one of the warehouses, there lingered a pleasant smell of anise and other unfamiliar herbs; probably at one time spices had been stored here, and many old Jewish women insisted that the Mother Superior settle them exactly in the "aroma bedroom," in that very one and no other! It wasn't easy for Mother Antonia to hold her anger, to swallow undeserved insults on religious themes from the capricious old women, but in the end, with a little firmness, she introduced fairness and order. But it wasn't like this everywhere. Huge crowds of refugees, having lost patience with the elders' notions about the order of settlement, had virtually taken by storm the offices, even the hangars and the stairway landings of the semi-destroyed steel factory. Those who possessed some material means and had left the richer parts of the city, like Bach—the circumcised one—with the two daughters and the eight diamonds, though now perhaps it was seven or even six—had managed to rent, at unbearably high prices, several houses vacated by the Chinese. Two to three families would settle in the miniature houses, the rooms like grasshopper cages—without water and sewage, without any domestic conveniences whatsoever. The owners required advance payment for many months ahead, because they themselves, required as they were to leave the Zone, didn't know when or how they would come back. Yet settling in houses that had been vacated—this is what the order said—would be punished very severely. This order concerned not just the Jews but the remaining Chinese in the neighborhood, since whole labyrinths of small streets in South Hongku remained unaffected by these measures, the local residents, for reasons unknown, not being subject to exile. In this way, quite naturally, Chinese and Jewish streets were formed, even complete little neighborhoods. As for restrictions specifically concerning the Jews with respect to movement outside the Zone, every policeman on the bridge, even the last fool, could easily tell the difference between a Chinese and a Jew—even without documents!

And still, in the background of the crowd's midnight madness, an act of collective solidarity deeply moved Professor Mandel, by nature a bitter skeptic: the fantastic speed with which, even before finding shelter for their own families, men and women organized by the former flute player Simon Zinner managed to transfer the Jewish Refugee Hospital, together with those patients unable to move on their own, to the Zone. The classrooms of the local elementary school on Chaofung Road had been turned into a hospital—a long one-story building resembling a warehouse, with a floor of stomped-on clay, abandoned during the "Japanese war." The school roof had been ruined in places by the bombings, but a number of rusty iron sheets that were lying around, as well as the canvas that Mother Antonia had begged from Portuguese missionaries passing through Shanghai before continuing on to Macao, provided a dry corner just to start with for the most seriously ill. In the small teachers' room where a torn 1937 calendar still hung and a shabby stuffed heron was gathering dust, Professor Mandel had set up his operating room.

That night for the first time Elisabeth did not go to sing at the Blue Mountain. During the day she had asked Shlomo Finkelstein to run to the harbor and tell the owner of the establishment, Yen Qingvey, about the resettlement then under way, to ask him to excuse her for the time being and to assure him that as of tomorrow and the future. . . . But what tomorrow? Were there going to be a today and a tomorrow and a future in South Hongku, turned into a ghetto, a concentration camp, a hell?

Aloof from the roar and fury filling the enormous industrial interior of the steel factory, she sat on her big leather suitcase, from which she had once been so inseparable during her bygone musical tours. Above her, heavy hooks swayed threateningly on their chains, people were crowding the multistory iron landings, and one family had even claimed a space way up high, at the dispatchers' cabin—a metal cell with dim, broken windows.

Elisabeth, benumbed, watched it all, though it made little impression on her. Perhaps she didn't even see it or realize its utter absurdity. The romantic period in the small house, tidy and clean in a Japanese way, with flower-print cotton curtains on the windows, and the gasoline tank turned into a shower by the always obliging Shlomo—all this had lasted for much too short a time and remained there, beyond the iron bridge over Soochow, beyond life.

Theodore Weissberg had disappeared somewhere and should have been back by now. In fact Elisabeth knew, or rather could guess, where he might have gotten lost, even though Theodore hadn't shared his intentions with her. That first morning, when all the Jews from the neighborhood had bumped their noses against the resettlement order that had been pasted on walls and telegraph poles, nothing had troubled him more than the dead look on his wife's face.

Then he'd worriedly said, as if the woes that had run over them were his fault:

"By Wednesday evening we will have to leave our home, Elisabeth. This is the deadline."

"Yes," she'd said, indifferently, "if we have to."

"I'm so sorry. The Zone starts only three streets away from here, but nothing could be done. Really nothing."

"Yes, I understand. . . ."

"Do you want me to help you get your things?"

"No, I can manage myself."

He looked at his wife with alarm.

"Are you all right, Elisabeth?"

She didn't respond, but just shifted her gaze to the tip of her shoes.

In such cases you either develop uncontrollable hysteria or are seized by complete, dull indifference. The latter, the indifference with which his wife took the news, was what concerned him most.

Then, like a drowning man clutching a straw, he was suddenly seized by the idea of going to the Bassats to apologize for his unseemly, scandalous behavior that time, and to ask for forgiveness. Maybe it was time now to spill the beans about Elisabeth's not being a Jew, but a pure-blooded German. This would make it easy to find a solution—after all their small home, rented and furnished with so much effort, wasn't in the Concession, somewhere on glamorous Nankin Road, but in Hongku, three steps away from the new Zone!

He was walking in the direction of Cardinal Mercier Boulevard, with the clear consciousness that this would be a humiliating encounter with former employers who had exhibited, you had to admit, a tolerance rare in this part of the world toward a servant and his wife, a poor teacher. That the Bassats maintained relations with that strutting peacock, the general, as well as with other Nazis, was none of his, Theodore Weissberg's, business and he'd had no right to get so flustered about it! Clearly, the alcohol was to blame, though of course this couldn't be a justification. In this embarrassing story Elisabeth had shown silent and calm solidarity with her husband even though his obstinate unwillingness to go back to work had pained her. She knew Theodore very well: he was a delicate and sensitive man, but on the other hand a donkey who could never admit a mistake.

Theodore had another reason for worrying. After they had failed for a long time to show up at the Bassats', one morning a rickshaw stopped in front of their small house in Hongku. This was a big event for the little street; people here didn't visit each other with rickshaws, nor had they the means for such luxury, and this is why they stuck their heads out the windows and doors with curiosity. The rickshaw listed quite considerably when White Lily—the really fat servant—stepped down from it. Even though it was after ten, Elisabeth was still in her nightgown. She would sleep late after coming home from work long after midnight, and never saw her husband, who, at early dawn, after preparing her breakfast, would steal out of the house.

White Lily beamed when she saw her at the entrance. The two of them fell into each other's arms and kissed. The Chinese woman said in her inimitable English that "mistress say you and he come back work, and forget about it, as nothing happened, yes-yes?"

During that visit Theodore was not at home, having left long before, as early as six. He was delivering suitcases and packages, running small errands, or washing cars at "The Imperial"—a middling-size hotel for foreigners, not far from the official German delegation, with nothing imperial about it except its name. His job had for a long time belonged to the librarian of the University of Munich, Karl Rosenbusch, a melancholic loner, but he had fallen gravely ill with beriberi. Through bloody expectorations and fallen teeth he had asked Theodore to replace him temporarily, so that the job wouldn't be lost. Probably both of them had known that this "temporarily" wouldn't go so fast, but both had pretended to be well-intentioned, naive optimists. The owner of the hotel, a Dutchman, immediately and unhesitatingly hired the sick employee's substitute, because most of his clientele consisted of German merchants either staying there or passing through on their way to Japan who always had problems with both the Chinese staff and their own lack of languages other than their mother tongue.

Her German origin had proven a lifesaver for Elisabeth too. In a Shanghai gripped by unemployment, the two spouses had had the incredible luck of finding work almost at once, thanks again to Shlomo Finkelstein, who had brought a crumpled and greasy German newspaper he'd picked up somewhere, the *Shanghaier Nachrichtenblatt*, with an ad from some bar called the Blue Mountain: four lines, heavily framed, which made clear that because of the character of its clientele—all sailors—this mountain, the blue one, was looking for a singer, European, who had to have not only an English but also a German repertoire.

Through White Lily, Elisabeth sent her thanks to the kind lady Mrs. Simha Bassat, promising that at the first chance she got she would stop by. But such a chance never came up; the Blue Mountain was open seven days a week. And Elisabeth's heart shrank at the memory of that birthday party for the little Bassat and the events that had taken place. She postponed her visit time after time, until finally she just never went.

Theodore approached the house with the tall iron fence at Cardinal Mercier 342. It seemed to him unusually quiet, with curtains drawn and windows closed tight. He climbed the three stone steps and rang, hearing the echoing sound deep inside, but no one opened the door. He rang again, waited for some time, and finally decided to go around the house through the garden.

After the third knock on the wide iron gates through which every autumn there entered teams of buffalo hauling manure and earth, he finally heard the trembling voice of Wu Laozian.

Their meeting was tender but also more than despairing: three weeks ago the Bassats had left Shanghai. Like most of the Baghdadis, they were British citizens who according to military orders were supposed to have been relocated to Japanese territories deep inside the country or else somewhere in Korea. But the master, Jonathan Bassat, had approached several high German officials he knew, as well as his broad connections with the Japanese administration, and finally managed to receive permission for his family to leave town with the big English steamship to Bombay—the same one on which the official British mission was leaving, headed by the governor Lord Washburn.

Old Laozian had been at the harbor together with all the servants to see off their employers. The women cried—not surprisingly—at one time laughing without restraint for no particular reason, at another bursting into tears. Mrs. Bassat gave everyone a gift as a souvenir: to Laozian she gave a good deal of money to maintain the house, in which he would remain behind as a good garden elf, as well as a piece of paper with the address of the Japanese commercial delegation to which he could go in case of need. She gave him as well an English pipe carved from the root of a rosebush and new glasses with horn rims. Now that the old man was alone, he guarded and took care of the big empty house, continuing to live as always in the small one at the end of the garden where his sons had come into this world and where he had sent their mother to the rice paddies in the beyond.

Theodore refused the old man's polite offer to come in for a cup of tea, bade him farewell, and walked brokenhearted the five kilometers from Frenchtown back to Hongku.

# 46

IN THE MIDST OF the panic caused by the three-day deadline, which was rapidly running out, the places where people hastily sought shelter were really very different from each other, from more or less normal albeit as a rule non-hygienic dwellings, to scores of utterly wretched places, brothels unfit to live in, communal dormitories, warehouses, and abandoned shacks that before the war had accommodated factory workers. Still, Rabbi Leo Levin stubbornly tried to calm the desperate new residents: "Slowly but surely, my brothers, with a little help from God and a little brainpower, everything will work out. It's not us, the Jews, who need to be taught how to adapt ourselves to a refugee community! Or did the first of the first wanderers, our ancestor Abraham, live in a villa with five bedrooms, with a sitting-room and a kitchen and did his goats graze not just on desert thorns, but jasmine and pansies?!"

By the way, from the very beginning, there was no lack of examples in support of the jovial, curly haired rabbi: the most entrepreneurial were already getting settled one way or another; the first modest grocery shops were already in operation. Several packing cases from a number of large machines were connected and turned into something like a wooden hut, comfortably appointed with broken furniture taken from God knows where, cotton drapes instead of a door and even a Chinese paper lantern in front—the first beauty parlor in the Zone. And the little sweet shop, Vienna, was resettled in a burned-out bus without wheels, its motor stolen long ago.

Some people from the rabbi's congregation disapproved of the idea of moving the hospital right into the abandoned school, since the children had to catch up on their education at least a little. But Rabbi Levin quickly found a solution to satisfy this need too by opening his own Yeshiva for the youngest, a synagogue school at the pagoda. There his wife Esther, without leaving her spring roll pursuits, again enthusiastically took up her profession as teacher, without Nazi educational authorities over her head to dictate to her what and how to teach.

These were thus the first ventures in following the Creator's six-day efforts to establish order within the universal chaos. Ideas in this realm were many: it's well known that the Jews, as well as their God, always have more ideas than they can put into practice, and give more instructions and advice than anyone is able to follow. But one way or another, life was beginning to assume its usual rhythm. And it appeared that one of the most amazing ideas for adapting to the new environment was the deployment of the water tower in the western part of the factory yard. A big hole made by a piece of shrapnel in the middle of the tower, which looked like a huge chimney that thinned upward, revealed ribs, as bare as a skeleton's, made of reinforced concrete; climbing these interior iron stairs, which were broken and twisted in places, all the way up to the wide landing at the top, required the perilous skills of a mountaineer. Two people had decided to attempt this heroic deed—the flautist Simon Zinner and Markus Aronson, that angular fellow, tall as a pylon, who had been Einstein's assistant. The ring-like space at the summit, which had a cistern in the center that had been drained a long time ago, a row of small gothic windows, and two miniature balconies, was turned into the extravagant residence of one former musician renowned in the past in the prestigious concert halls of Dresden, and one astrophysicist who had dedicated his brains and talent to the quantum theory, and, after arriving in Shanghai, to the spring rolls produced by the history teacher Esther Levin.

Go Yang fixed his eyes upward toward the top of the water tower, where two figures, who owing to the distance appeared to be quite small, stood on the little balcony. Then he looked at the multitude, which had become silent. This Go apparently took himself very seriously, because the tense silence continued for a long time. He had raised himself microphone in hand to the top of a wooden crate, and the yard, the heaps of ashes lying around, the piles of beams, the mountains of scrap iron, the flat roofs of the administrative offices and the foundries had all become black with thousands upon thousands of refugees. They were comprised of not the entire population of the Zone, which was too numerous to fit inside even this enormous factory yard, but for the most part young people, heads of households, people without jobs, and those who had come out of simple curiosity to hear what the representative from the authorities had to say.

And, as was obvious from his self-important look, he did have things to tell them.

"I am your commissioner Go!" suddenly fired off the short man, who was as stout as a wrestler and sported a faded black suit, seemingly never ironed and shiny from wear, his powerful neck squeezed tight by his tie. He spoke those words in German, which immediately created an approving stir among the people.

"You will address me as 'Mr. Go' and I will be ready to listen to you if you don't talk nonsense. You are in South Hongku. There is no shittier and nastier hole in the world. You should be aware of that and live your life accordingly. You are threatened by malaria, beriberi, plague, cholera, typhoid, dysentery, scabies, countless intestinal ailments, amoebas, and another hundred and one diseases, the easiest of all to cure being infectious hepatitis. Boil your clothes to kill the lice. Protect the children from rats. Wash your clothes often, soak the vegetables in plenty of boiled water, do not eat soft fruit, do not drink water from the tap. Pour chloride of lime into your toilets; they will give it to you for free in the commandant's office. If you have the chance to get the hell out of here and back to your Europe with its stink of bad cooking, do it right away. In all other cases you will obey me without question. Here I am the King of the Jews. Get it?"

The people were silent with expectation.

The King of the Jews took this general dead silence as a sign of complete agreement. He also kept silent for awhile, casting a triumphant look at the dense crowd, then again raising his eyes toward the water tower, apparently preoccupied with the thought of how those two idiots had managed to climb so high. Mr. Go was a high school teacher of German language and literature in Osaka, the Hansin province, and had translated and published in the local provincial newspapers various excerpts from *Mein Kampf*. From this book he had found out about the existence of Jews, a people against whom he would fight to the last breath, even though it wasn't quite clear whether there were any of them nearby in Japan. But on the very day that Shanghai passed into the hands of the imperial army and the flag with the rising sun started to wave above the town, he slipped out west, to the continent, and immediately put himself at the service of the Japanese authorities. Go Yang, after having read and even partially translated this fundamental work of Hitler's, had already identified himself as an expert on Jewish issues and perhaps this was the reason why he was appointed commissioner of the Zone. That its command had been delegated to neither a military nor a police officer, but to a former Japanese teacher, might have prompted those more intimately familiar with the Far East to discern certain subtle messages, signs, and codes that the Japanese authorities, on the one hand, were attentively and correctly assisting their German partners in their not quite clear intentions with regard to the Jews, or, on the other, and especially in front of the world, that official Japan was not becoming engaged with a problem that didn't concern her directly and only caused headaches.

"And now listen to what will henceforth be the regulations in the Zone," continued commissar Go. "I hereby declare a curfew from midnight to six in the morning. During that time the guarded bridge over the Soochow will be closed to Jews. During the day it will be available only to those of you who are able to show me a written document that they have jobs on the other side: I want to know exactly what and where. I will be the one issuing the permits. They will be green, yellow, and red. For one day, one week, and one month. No exceptions! Those who are busy with night work will ask me for additional permission to violate the curfew. Let's be clear: we are waging war against Jewish England and Jewish America. Our German allies are also fighting Jewish Russia. This is why for me you are prisoners of war under a mild regime—until I decide to harden it. This depends on you and on the respect you will give me. Enough for today. Now beat it!"

## 47

EVEN BEFORE OPENING HIS eyes, Vladek, as was his habit, reached his hand over to the pillow next to him and groped it as if blindfolded, but the bed was empty. Lazily rousing himself, he discovered the deserter. Hilde was sitting half-nude beside the window, smoking and looking out at the wide river with its crawling ships and junks. Muffled by distance, the ships' sirens, alarmingly broken up, reached their ears, as did the put-put of motorboats, and the horns of automobiles in the traffic down below on Waterside Boulevard. The light streaming in from outside diffused itself around the contours of Hilde's lovely body, so that it seemed as if she herself were softly emitting the radiance of the dawn.

"Come here," he said.

Lost in thought, she was startled by his voice.

"Come here," he said again.

"Knock it off. I have to leave. I'm late."

"You're not late for anywhere. It's Sunday."

"Please get it into your head that every Sunday, at eleven o'clock, Shanghai high society likes to take a stroll around the English Garden. Except when stones are falling from the sky. And Baroness Gertrude von Dammbach insists that her favorite plaything, namely me, be there, always, and stick with her forever."

"I also insist that you be here with me, always, and stick with me forever. Every Sunday, at 11 o'clock! And to do you-know-what. So how are you going to waste your time there?"

"You want a precise report? After the walk, we drink Viennese *café mélangé* with warm apricot strudel and whipped cream. At Frau Shnitzler's pastry shop on Kung Ping. Satisfied?"

"Typical German Sunday habits!"

"Just like us typical Germans."

"Middle-class bourgeois with aristocratic pretensions."

"You left something out—Fascists!"

"Exactly. But I forgive you. Come here!"

"No!"

"Or are you keeping your strength for His Excellency, the Baron?"

She threw the pack of cigarettes at him. There was a knock at the door, and a woman's voice was heard:

"Good morning, Mr. Vincent. Breakfast."

Vladek was renting a room at the hostel of May Dulac, a decent Annamite, the widow of the merchant Georges Dulac, one of the French colonialists who, after the First World War and the economic crisis that followed, had exchanged the mouth of the Mekong river for the mouth of the Yangtse. Whenever Hilde visited Vladek's room, Madame May, who was petite like most Vietnamese, would delicately knock and leave the tray with breakfast for two in front of the door.

Barefoot, Vladek dragged in the big breakfast tray, took a large gulp of tea, burning himself, and immediately disappeared into the bathroom.

Hilde again cast a pensive look at the river.

From the bathroom there came the sound of the shower and Vladek's not very successful attempts to perform the Mephisto aria.

Three months ago he had looked her up—something she'd been waiting for impatiently every day, with each ring of her telephone at the office. He tried to be nonchalant and a bit surly, but still he asked to see her. When finally Hilde caught sight of him at the French bookstore, where she'd agreed to meet him, she kissed him spontaneously. And he responded in the same way—without pretense, as if they were still in his attic apartment in Paris and nothing had happened and nothing had changed.

From that day on they met whenever possible, since Hilde had to deal with an endless work day, innumerable duties in the German embassy, and the constant shadow of her boss, the Baron, and Vladek frequently had reasons for his own mysterious disappearances. She eventually learned not to ask, or in any case to ask less, and he firmly followed the habit of answering with a joke and never telling the truth about who in fact he was, what he did, and for whom. Hilde was neither foolish nor naive enough to believe that his main occupation was to write exotic essays about the Far East for the Swiss papers. Initially she just suspected; now she knew—though no more than Vladek was ready to share with her.

While drinking her tea, she looked at him secretively above the cup: he was, if not exactly handsome, charming in a boyish way, with still wet, very curly, tar-black hair above his high, frowning forehead, his face rather rough and open in a rustic sort of way. That he was strong and broad-shouldered could be seen even through his shabby, cheap bathrobe. She had been planning to buy him a new one for a long time, but was nervous about his ironic reactions on the topic of "posh pretensions." She loved him as he was, loved him with an anxious, gasping, panicky love—with the feeling that at any moment again something might happen that would tear them apart. Strange to say, it was always the police that separated them. The first time it had been the Paris police, and the second time the Shanghai police, which Vladek had foolishly underestimated. Some people believe that destiny counts to three.

"Do you know what I want now?"

"If it's the same thing I want, come to bed."

"Cynic! I want you to take me one day to your motherland."

"The drama, darling, is that that's what I want myself. Except that I'm not wanted there. Just like you're not wanted in yours."

"Mine is Germany. What's the name of that motherland of yours that so lightheartedly renounces her children? Especially such smart beautiful guys like you?"

He gave her a long look in which you could read his desperation with her persistent questioning, but Hilde hastened to calm him down:

"Okay, okay, I get it. Switzerland. . . . You didn't tell me this time if I did a good job with the lighter," Hilde started, but swallowed the rest when Vladek immediately put a finger to his lips.

He had more than once warned her not to speak about these things in a closed space, even forbidding her to think about them, regardless of where they were, but she considered this effort at caution unnecessary, even ostentatious.

Vladek never shared even the smallest thing with her. When one time she tried to learn from him some insignificant technical detail related to the origin of the lighter, and was ready to get upset with the display of his petty distrust of her, he plugged her mouth with a kiss: "The less you know, the healthier it is for you. I hope you'll never have to understand this one day!"

He had warned her honestly that the business with which she was getting involved was not a joke or a romantic adventure, that it concealed deadly risks. But without the slightest exaggeration, Hilde agreed to collaborate. She didn't insist on knowing exactly who was interested in the information she could provide, or exactly how it would be provided. She wasn't interested in politics: this at least is what she thought, without realizing that she had already sunk herself in politics up to her neck. She was ready to work for the Russians, for the Americans, for the English, for the devil himself. For her only one thing was important: whom the activity was directed against. "And if by this I can accelerate by even one second, one single second, the end of Hitler and his gang, you can count on me!" This is what she'd said very seriously, and with real conviction, when she received the lighter.

It was a very ordinary gas lighter, which would burn with a huge, smoky flame. Nothing special, only slightly larger than usual, and decorated on one side with a miniature, barely visible glass pearl. In one part of the lighter, behind the pearl, there was a microfilm, which could store a hundred photographs. One hundred—this is no small thing! Up until now Hilde had been dropping into Vladek's pocket, whenever they met at pastry shops, cinemas, or just like that on the boulevards, ten very tiny rolls of film, each smaller than a soybean, wrapped in black paper. Ten rolls—well, this added up to one thousand pages of the top-secret archives of Baron von Dammbach. At the photo studio

Agfa, Alfred Kleinbauer, he who colored family photographs, would develop the films, and Cheng Suzhin would immediately send them by courier to Mukden. The further job of transporting them was undertaken by others situated across the border.

A simple business, simpler even than a soybean!

# 48

LIFE, AS RABBI LEVIN had predicted, gradually resumed its usual routine; the orchestra rehearsals, although with great effort, started up again. The musicians—they were rarely assembled all together—would meet, dead tired after the day's hard work, in the pagoda-synagogue generously granted them by Rabbi Levin. They formed an unimaginable mix of porters who hadn't shaved for a month, streetcleaners, and general laborers who either came straight from the weaving workshops in their worn-out duck clothes or quickly changed into their shabby, patched-up suits whose wrinkles still smelled of Germany. Theodore Weissberg was the conductor, tightly holding his favorite violin under his armpit. At the sound of the first notes, the players were transformed: they lit up with inner radiance or perhaps freshly inspired dedication to music, or the painful memory of another life, forever lost, on the concert stage—a life dedicated to the cherished muse, but also, in its way, haughty, with the exhilaration of the silent hall under the dimming lights, and a basket of flowers at the end from the president of this or that institution, followed by a gulp of champagne in the foyer. . . . Memories, sweetly vain, that for an instant seize you by the throat.

Life resumed its usual routine, no doubt about it, but at the lowest level of human existence: most people were literally starving. The free kitchen of Mother Antonia could scarcely provide even one serving of modest rice porridge to those most desperately in need. Relatively better, but still in the same situation, were those who had work, any kind of work, outside the Zone. Following the initiative of the flautist Simon Zinner, who apart from being a strict and uncompromising organizer of rehearsals was also, as always, the soul of social initiatives, all those who had any income at all, even the most miserable, had to put aside ten to twenty percent for the mutual-aid cash box. For some, this to a certain extent mitigated despair, though an indisputable sign of the extreme insufficiency of this fund was the constant growth of diseases caused by malnutrition, especially among children.

Yet the children, in spite of everything, started to play again. The youngest made mudpies and sold them for pebbles, the older ones kicked a ball made out of cloth, and the oldest were already learning the first lessons in how to fall in love.

Professor Mandel and his voluntary assistants fought day and night for people's lives in any way they could, but with an almost complete lack of medicines they were helpless to deal with so many patients. There were several especially severe cases and on a number of occasions they had to take the sick person to the city hospital, the Central Hospital of Shanghai, but this cost an immense sum in bribes, starting from the very greedy "King of the Jews," Mr. Go, all the way to the communal administration—expenses that ate up a considerable part of the meager mutual-aid funds.

The situation in the infirmary became even further complicated by a scandalous incident that cast a shadow over the fragile myth—so often put on trial—of Jewish solidarity: in the turmoil of the relocation, Professor Mandel's briefcase, made of topnotch black leather and holding three layers of extremely indispensable surgical instruments, was stolen. He had brought it with him from Berlin and cherished it as the virtuoso player cherishes his Stradivarius, because such a masterpiece from Solingen, such an example of fine German precision instruments, was impossible to find here, even if you had money. Rumors about this abominable theft spread through the Zone, though all hypotheses about who, when, and where the briefcase had been snatched were just a pretext for gossip among the talkative old men in front of the synagogue—Jewish gossip, just to pass the time.

The only one who could know anything about the case was Shlomo Finkelstein, the petty thief. He and no one else: this is what the old men thought and said. And when the rumor reached Shlomo that suspicion had fallen precisely on him or at least that he knew what had happened but was hiding the heroes of this affair, he wept with the insult. Elisabeth tried to comfort him, telling him that for her he was above suspicion, that he was a good and helpful man and that his "dog" business didn't concern the Zone and its residents. But these reassurances were futile; the groundless suspicions deeply scarred the soul of the rotund little man.

One morning, for a bribe of ten Shanghai dollars, Shlomo provided himself with a one-day pass from Mr. Go, something he did quite often. This time, however, Shlomo didn't head toward his usual partners at the meat market in Nantao, but descended toward the docks in the harbor. There, behind the warehouses and the fish market, amid mountains of crates and piles of stuff, was the market for stolen goods. The police knew about it, the place was a public secret, but the law-and-order institutions tried to avoid any business with the thieves' syndicate, which knew how to defend its people and interests. This Chinese syndicate was powerful and cruel; the darkest and most criminal elements in Shanghai belonged to it, so the police, for a modest monthly payment, preferred to stay away from these shadowy places.

In his eternally worn-out and overly long coat, his hands stuck deep in his pockets to indicate his benign intentions, Shlomo calmly strolled around the flea market of stolen goods, where all kinds of trophies were being offered: women's hats and bags, watches, military binoculars, firearms and knives, empty wallets of expensive leather, gold jewelry, sailors' passports, and everything else that could be snatched by the pickpockets and lugged here for sale. And there it was, on top of a wooden crate, exhibited as a rare display: Professor Mandel's briefcase, opened to reveal all three of its layers, so that one could see and appreciate the expensive chrome instruments, which sparkled in the sunshine like new!

Shlomo asked indifferently the price of the merchandise.

From the very beginning the transaction didn't go well: the seller asked for a thousand Shanghai dollars and not one cent less, apparently aware that the real price of the briefcase together with its contents was at least five times higher. The Asian game of bargaining and gradually arriving at a deal went nowhere; the price remained terribly high. One thousand Shanghai dollars, why that was an entire fortune! Shlomo didn't have that kind of money, he didn't even have a tenth of it, but he started looking carefully at the knives, scissors, small forceps, and all those other complicated instruments of obscure use, and to appraise them with a professional eye, at the end even checking if the locks were in order. And when the seller was diverted by some noisy quarrel to the side, and momentarily lost his concentration, Shlomo grabbed the heavy briefcase and ran away.

People shouted and started running up and down, but the fat, short-legged thief disappeared in the labyrinth of crates and piles. For a long time afterward the thieves who'd been robbed kept on shouting and whistling to each other, searching where even a mouse couldn't get in, but all for nothing—Shlomo had evaporated!

Beaming and panting, his chest wheezing, he brought the briefcase and handed it over to Professor Sigmund Mandel, who couldn't believe his eyes that his priceless treasure had been found. The professor in fact was so excited that he started running around the hospital to share his joy with his assistants, even forgetting to say thank you. Shlomo wasn't offended; with this act he, the expert in petty-theft from the open-air markets of Berlin and of pet-stealing in Shanghai, thought that he was completely rehabilitated in the eyes of the Hongku Jews.

Or rather, this is what he thought, although he was soon to hear different.

Many people read his act in their own way: he had participated in the theft but, scared of being found out, had returned the briefcase. A thief is a thief, or, as they say, "There's no straight road for the twisted wheel!"

So short, fat Shlomo walked up and down the streets, comical in his long, worn-out coat, looking like someone with the plague, rejected by everyone, meeting only mean or mocking eyes. As far as everyone was concerned he was a hardened criminal—a criminal and nothing else. An unworthy Jew—may God forgive me—who didn't even deserve to be let into the synagogue!

That's what they thought.

Elisabeth didn't understand why this time Shlomo said goodbye so theatrically. After all, it wasn't the first time he was going to town on his dog business. But now he was sad and somehow solemn, even kissing her hand, to her astonishment, and asking her for forgiveness if he had offended her by anything. Then he went down toward the river.

In the morning they found the body of Shlomo Finkelstein in the slippery muck on the banks of the Soochow, his back pierced with a knife in sixteen places and his throat cut.

# 49

A MONTH AFTER THESE tragic events, which for a long time embittered the already gloomy Professor Mandel, one particular Saturday turned out to be quite unusual, and charged with new and unexpected hope. Mr. Go, the commissioner, asked to see the members of the Refugee Committee and ceremoniously announced the news to them: the factory for automobiles and rubber goods in Qingpu, thirty kilometers southwest of Shanghai, was looking for a thousand workers.

Work for a thousand people—this wasn't news, this was a sensation!

Trying to contain the joy in his almost bursting heart, Rabbi Levin said with seeming indifference:

"I'm sorry, Mr. Go, but what are our people going to do there? Among them there are hardly specialists in this, how do you put it—field of rubber. And what are they going to be paid?"

"You don't think I'm also a specialist in rubber, do you? I'm a specialist in German culture and not a producer of hoses!" indignantly replied the former German teacher. "But they told me they have qualified Japanese masters there and that operating the presses, furnaces, and lathes is easy to learn. And to load, unload, and carry on production, I hope, is not a big philosophy. Or is it?"

He kept silent for some time, by long habit looking at people one by one, as if they were students who were expected to recite last Wednesday's lesson, and then continued.

"The average wage is twelve Shanghai dollars per day. There are no days off; it's wartime. Everyone will give me two dollars a day. Which is fair. It's compensation for my efforts to find work for you, so you can have grub to feast on. And so, gentlemen Jews?"

The "gentlemen Jews" asked for time till tomorrow, Sunday, to discuss the proposition with the community. Including the problem with the two dollars—fair remuneration for Mr. Go's efforts.

The news spread around the Zone with the speed of light: permanent work for two American dollars a day, against a bribe of two Shanghai dollars: it wasn't much, but who else would give it to you?! Hardly an hour passed before the orchestra had to stop its rehearsal because the little synagogue was about to explode with men who excitedly wanted to know when they were going to travel, and how, by what means. Exactly what kind of work would it be? Was there work for women? And children? Rabbi Levin, standing next to the gilded Buddha, was helpless to answer all the questions; he simply didn't know the answers himself. In any case he passed along the decision of the Refugee Committee and it was this: only one person per family. Only one so that more people could benefit! One thousand men who would provide for one thousand families. Everyone was required to put aside from his wages, apart from the two Shanghai dollars for Mr. Go, another twenty percent for the mutual-aid fund.

There was a grumble of dissatisfaction: well then, what would be left over for us? The rabbi meekly yielded the floor to Simon Zinner.

"This is our decision! And let's make it clear: there will be no cheating on the twenty percent for the sick, the disabled, and the unemployed. We will insist on it firmly. Is that clear? All right, that's final. Prepare and give Rabbi Leo a list of names; we want it by tonight. First you will enter the names of heads of families with many children. If the father is sick or too weak—the oldest son. And be careful. If you forget someone in serious need, you will make me very angry, not to mention Buddha here behind my back. And so, brothers, on Monday, at six in the morning sharp, everyone from the list be at the square!"

The rabbi concluded this unusual evening service with:

"A thousand people! Blessed be this Shabbat day! *Baruch ata Adonai Elohenu. . . . Amen!*"

Monday, even before the crack of dawn, from all sides of South Hongku, men were already streaming down toward the small square in front of the pagoda-synagogue, many of them with Chinese paper lanterns in hand because there were no streetlights in the Zone. During the long nights only the vicious meowing of the wild and still uneaten cats filled the thick darkness from which the day now painfully rid itself. As the sky in the east glowed pink, the two dragons above erupted in red flames, fiercely annoyed at being awakened so early. People were gathering in groups in which they excitedly and noisily commented on the unusual event, which presaged new and maybe better days to come. They carried food in bundles or wrapped in newspaper, because they didn't know if they'd get food there or not. This fundamental question was being examined from all sides—the way only Jews can examine a question, with the firm conviction prevailing that they would be provided with food there, at the factory. Especially if the factory turned out to be state-owned.

Among them, silent and closed up in himself as always, was Theodore Weissberg. Despite his fear of losing one job if he took another, he had resolved to go. He was fed up with the meaningless, monotonous, and depressing life of a servant, the humiliating running around like a boy for everything in that hotel. True, there were tips, that was so, and he was ashamed to admit it but he accepted them, even though with disgust. But now the Japanese were offering work, and no matter how heavy it might be, still, it was normal, dignified factory work! He knew what he was risking: the Dutchman wouldn't forgive him for even one day if he didn't show up, and would start looking immediately for a replacement. So to hell with his "Imperial" and his German businessmen!

Theodore had not discussed his decision with Elisabeth—if she was going to approve of it or not. Since they had settled themselves under a stairway in the administration area of the steel factory, she had become less and less interested in the surrounding environment; she was absent from real life, the way one is absent from school or from morning mass. She just wasn't *there*. She would go to the Blue Mountain and sing her German songs and come back, but she was living somehow by habit. Perhaps it was because she didn't know how not to live. She had no desires, no hopes; she didn't even know that this was called *survival*.

Led by the sleepy Mr. Go, who, still wearing his black suit and tie, growled at them for every little thing, the disorderly crowd started to drag itself across the bridge over the Soochow, guarded by Japanese soldiers. This was the border of the Zone. Beyond the bridge about fifteen Japanese military trucks were roaring and filling up the whole neighborhood with bluish diesel smoke.

# 50

THE BIG OPEN TRUCKS, bursting with people, were making their way with difficulty along the torn-up road to Qingpu, which hadn't been maintained in ages and over whose endless potholes they somehow managed to bounce. Green hills sprawled everywhere, with endless rice terraces that pressed up against each other, and, here and there, small stone pagodas—chapels possibly, or maybe the graves of ancestors. Early-rising peasants, up to their knees in water, their backs wet with sweat, shouted at their black, obedient buffalo, which, with their stretched necks, were dragging the plows, combing the thick swampy bottom. You could hear brief shouts and the song of the flat wooden bells hanging below the buffalo's necks, and you could see, on the surface of the water, the reflections of morning suns joyfully running alongside the trucks, each rice field with its own sun. Villages were nowhere visible, but you could feel the breath of rural life beyond the hills, with distant roosters and children's cries. Even the gray dust raised by the column of vehicles wasn't so annoying to the people, because it smelled of villages and dry grass, far from Shanghai's stink of gasoline and swamps. Everyone felt at once light and heavy-hearted—from this unusual day, from the fresh greenery, the hills, the distant violet mountains, the herons in the rice fields. Here, amid these vast spaces, it seemed to them that the sky with its white cranes had never been *this* blue, and, with a quiet sadness, they realized still more painfully the absence of the world they'd lost.

The trip wasn't long, that is, not very long.

Because when the rice paddies turned into barren, uneven fields and smoking factory chimneys, and big white buildings—silos, probably—started to loom in the distance, most likely the industrial suburbs of Qingpu, the trucks slowed down and finally came to a stop in the middle of a field.

Far ahead a big crowd of people—hundreds of men, women, and children—were blocking the road. A Japanese officer jumped out of the first truck cabin and ran in that direction. A roar, broken by the distance, reached all the way to the trucks. People were shouting in Chinese; the Japanese officer was shouting in his mother tongue. Just what was going on wasn't clear, but for a long time the column of vehicles didn't budge from its place.

Stuffed inside the trucks, people impatiently craned their necks, trying to look beyond the drivers' cabins and find out what was going on. In any case, despite the considerable distance, it was obvious now that the crowd consisted of Europeans—the men dressed almost the same in blue duck clothes.

Then the most unexpected thing happened: from that faraway point, amplified by a loudspeaker, there sounded a clear male voice that said in Russian:

"You there! Is there anyone among you who can speak Yiddish or Hebrew? You understand me, right? Yiddish! Hebrew!"

The people in the trucks looked as if they'd been struck by lightning. What?! Yiddish, Hebrew—in Quingpu? What kind of a crazy mixed-up place *is* this China?!

Rabbi Leo briskly jumped down from a truck and started walking toward the crowd, which stood about three hundred feet away. He passed by the first truck and caught a glimpse of the frightened face of Commissioner Go. Apparently the King of the Jews was also taken aback by what was going on.

"I speak Yiddish and Hebrew," said the rabbi.

A giant stepped out in the same blue duck clothes, a short bamboo stick in hand. He spoke somberly in Yiddish:

"We understand that you are German and Austrian Jews."

"Yes, most of us are," answered the rabbi, still bewildered.

"We're Russian Jews and we've been working at the rubber factory for a long time. Go with God back to where you came from. Because we're on strike."

"You're on strike? No one told us."

"Well, I'm telling you. Go away."

The rabbi looked around in confusion. Behind him Jews from the Zone who had jumped out of the trucks were approaching. They'd sensed that something was wrong and were running toward their rabbi.

One of them shouted out, in Yiddish:

"Listen you, clear out of the road. We're looking for work!"

"Look somewhere else. We're the ones who are already here," calmly said the giant.

"But our children are starving!"

"So are ours."

Simon Zinner, Theodore Weissberg, and the rabbi tried in vain to hold back their people, when with a spontaneous battle cry they surged forward to break through the wall of bodies and make way for the trucks. The Russian Jews took out bamboo sticks; children screamed. Blows poured down left and right. Bloodshed was inevitable. The Japanese officer raised a gun and shot a full clip into the air.

This had a sobering effect. People withdrew backward, and a gap opened between the two groups again, like an insurmountable abyss, like a trench at the front. The two sides, panting, looked at each other in silence, and with wild hatred.

The officer turned in the direction of the trucks and spoke in Japanese—something with shrieks and many words. Then everything became quiet.

In the uncomfortable silence that reigned, the flautist Simon Zinner said in Russian:

"Excuse us, we didn't know."

After which he turned to his people, switching to German:

"Get in, we're going back to the Zone!"

The officer returned his gun to its holster; from Zinner's expression it was clear that he felt bad that he and his colleagues had been used for some dirty deal.

"We're not producing automobile tires, we're producing war!" he thought, and walked back toward the trucks.

# 51

VLADEK GAVE A FRIENDLY nod to the two security policemen and crossed the evenly cut lawn in front of the German mission. The small white pebbles of the alley rustled under his Spanish military boots, which were living through their second, and, as it seemed, last youth. He stopped for a moment and gazed with curiosity at the pole with the half-lowered flag, the sign of national mourning. The wind made the swastika twist and wiggle in its folds as if it were broken with sadness itself. From the roof of the residence, on both sides of the obtruding semicircular official entrance, framed with columns, long black flags were swaying too like black tongues licking the facade. This is what the Führer himself had ordered: for the shocked world to sink in grief for the heroes of Stalingrad, who had fallen in the titanic battle against bolshevism. The forty-eight divisions and three brigades defeated by the Red Army, as well as the capture of General-Fieldmarshal Paulus, together with the whole staff of the German Sixth Army, was really a very heavy blow for Germany, worthy of proud national sorrow. This is how the Vikings used to die—unvanquished and proud. The Romanian, Hungarian, and Italian divisions, who had melted together with the snows along the Volga, had no one to mourn them. In any case not Hitler, who had judged them cowards and traitors.

One of the guards waited for Vladek to go further ahead and only then lazily dragged his feet toward the police booth and rang someone up.

It wasn't the first time Vladek had come here; he'd already interviewed in person Baron von Dammbach, a pleasant old man who had even offered him some French cognac. It was Hilde who'd made the connection. The baron liked this Swiss journalist, a jovial, amiable young man who didn't touch on sensitive issues, as if he could guess that on some aspects of the war von Dammbach had particular opinions quite different from the official line. He also liked the fact that, unlike most of the inhabitants of Switzerland, with their horrible dialect, so difficult to understand, this one spoke a university German, with a slightly harsh Bavarian accent in fact. One time Hilde introduced him to Baroness von Dammbach too, though the encounter at the residence was accidental. The baroness, her eyes red with tears, had just returned from the harbor where she'd gone to see off her old friend Lord Washburn on his way to Bombay.

His Excellency Ottomar von Dammbach was not in a good mood today, and despite the preliminary agreement to give an interview, he asked his secretary, Miss Braun, to receive the guest, to offer whatever she found necessary, but to excuse the baron: national mourning, you understand . . . Miss Braun had experience; she knew how to spare her boss from unwanted visitors.

The baron lit a cigar, and inhaled once, but immediately and disgustedly almost smashed the lit end in the ashtray. He didn't feel like smoking; he didn't feel like living. He tried to read his secretary's daily report about the incoming post from Berlin but angrily closed the file. The day hadn't started well; he couldn't stand these flags of black Chinese crepe that the wind would now and again blow in front of his windows, like a constant reminder that today he was obliged to grieve deeply and proudly, while what he was really suffering from was hemorrhoids, which made him feel very far indeed from a Viking, much less an unconquerable descendant of the noble Celts.

He was a tired, aging diplomat and he really *was* grieving, but for something completely different. He realized that he belonged to the old moderate days, the time long gone, that carried within its thick dark waters the memory of Verdun, of the national humiliation in Compiègne, and the Weimar Republic too. But still, whatever you say about political sins and wrong moves, it *had* been a more decent time, more human. Perhaps this was simply a nostalgic delusion: perhaps Germany was still the same, unchanging and unchangeable. Perhaps. But the baron wanted to be left in peace. He preferred a Germany with those old values and delusions, because Hitler couldn't offer anything in exchange, except for his crazy and lethal ideas for world domination. In any case that time had been more reasonable than this one, which was now like a malignant tumor consuming the heart of the Fatherland. Germany was doomed, doomed, doomed! No doubt about it. True, the German Reich was still intact, and hadn't yet lost any land; even after Stalingrad it remained distant and untouched. But it was losing something more important—hope. Hope itself is space, and it was shrinking, shrinking—this space of hope—like shagreen. National ideals were turning into spiritual disaster, trodden in the mud of the lost war, blown with the winds. Today Germany was eating itself, like a trapped scorpion. But this would not be *its* end; it would be *ours*.

The baron went to the tall French windows, which rose almost from the floor, and looked outside toward the mowed lawn. Just below, the flag of mourning swayed in the wind, reminding him to grieve.

He was grieving anyway.

Dieter had put his legs up on the table. He was smoking and listening to the radio, on which the German station would endlessly broadcast German music. Today there was no advertising for Chinese restaurants and bars, no inspiring, heartbreaking stories about the motherland from German travelers who had just lately been flooding Shanghai after each "Junkers" landed. Today was a day to weep.

The space for the radio connection was just under the roof, an iron door with a sign in German, "Entrance Strictly Forbidden," which barred the way to unwanted visitors. Here one could feel isolated from the world and completely secure—just the way Dieter himself felt during that period of time when, after driving the baron during the morning, he had nothing to do before lunch but kill time.

Dieter was a chauffeur, the personal chauffeur of Baron Ottomar von Dammbach. Owing to the policy of strict economy, he also had the job of radio operator—an easy enough position if you bear in mind the baron's infrequent radio connections with Berlin or the embassy in Tokyo. Coded contacts were extremely rare, considering the danger of interception by the Americans, the English, or the Russians, whose agents were thickly sown throughout the Far East.

Diligent and conscientious to an almost pedantic degree, and always reserved, Dieter never allowed himself to behave in an informal way with the baron and his wife. He had a precise understanding of his place, the limits of permissible familiarity, and his duties. If he allowed himself to act somewhat more freely with Miss Hilde Braun, the secretary, it was because she stood on approximately the same step as he did in the institutional staircase of this German diplomatic mission stuck up the horse's ass of China.

Stalingrad had affected him deeply; he admired and was proud of the heroism of the German soldier who, inadequately clothed and unprepared for the dog's cold of that climate, when even the chains of the tanks had frozen and broken apart, had fought a dignified though doomed battle. At the same time he thanked fortune that the war had found him so situated that he was released from having to take part personally in this valiant ordeal. Say what you will, driving a car around the dirty streets of Shanghai, chaotic and stuffed with people, rickshaws, and bicycles, may have been too tiresome for words, but it was certainly better than crawling hungry and frozen around the endless white death of Russia!

When the policeman at the entrance of the mission phoned him, as previously agreed upon, to alert him to the arrival of the Swiss guy, Dieter quickly removed his legs from the table. His duty, about which even the esteemed baron didn't know, was to observe the contacts of the staff with outside people, especially if they weren't German. The security of the Reich demanded no less. Not that he had any special suspicion toward this Swiss journalist, but it was hardly a secret that the fellow was involved in rather close relations with Miss Braun. This wasn't forbidden, but it wasn't desirable either, if you remember that the baron's secretary was often present at confidential conversations and had access to more than one state secret. Dieter had no reason to suspect Miss Braun herself—nothing wrong about having a boyfriend, as long as he wasn't Jewish. And this young journalist was pleasant to talk to, amusing and natural—

he'd immediately moved to the informal "you"—and Dieter had come to think of him as an old acquaintance since that now distant day when, on the baron's orders, he had taken the car to pick up the baron's secretary, who'd been arrested, from the sidewalk in front of the Shanghai police station.

Visitors, especially those who weren't immediately dispatched again to fulfill various tasks, were invited to the reception room, a small, semicircular salon above the entrance colonnade furnished with expensive Chinese furniture in the style of the Ming dynasty—red lacquered wood and silk brocade. The walls were hung, however, not with antique Chinese pictures but copies of the works of Lucas Cranach, created approximately at the same time but on the other side of Eurasia—not a bad idea by the German architect who, in the 'twenties, when the residence was furnished, had wanted to work with the idea of harmony between the two worlds and cultures. Here, some time ago, the delegation from the Jewish community had waited to be received by the baron; here the Chinese servant, quiet as a shadow, served guests tea and coffee. Dieter knew this well, and after unlocking the small iron door in the wall behind the portrait of the Führer, took out headphones from the niche, and found the right electric cord. Initially something in his ears hissed and crackled, but everything was in order. From here he could listen to what was being said in every more important room of the building, including the office of the baron himself. That is, he could hear but he couldn't see—television was still taking baby steps.

Hilde flew into the small reception room and quickly kissed the Swiss visitor on the cheek. Then she told him that the baron was sorry but that today's interview could not take place: "'In relation to Stalingrad,' the baron said, and asked to be excused. . . ."

While talking she pointed with her finger toward the crystal chandelier. He nodded.

The Chinese servant entered with a quiet bow and brought tea. They started talking about the latest news from the front. Vladek got a bit carried away in his praise of the heroes of Stalingrad, and to tell the truth he was saying it with sincere empathy, no doubt about it. No doubt too the eavesdropping chauffeur was happy to hear it from the mouth of a foreigner. With this difference, however, that the heroes Dieter was thinking about were totally different from those the Swiss journalist had in mind. But these are, as Hilde loved to say, merely details of the landscape.

Hilde too, and not just the baron, had reasons today for being in a lousy, indeed even sour mood. The reason was again the driver, Dieter. Last night, long after ten, she had stayed at the office so that she could put in order the Berlin courier post just received from the airport in Lunghua. The residence had sunk into darkness and silence, the only illumination coming from a green light above the secretary's desk that threw a circle of light on the documents that she was photographing through the small glass eye of the lighter, page after page. Then everything had to be returned to the envelopes, which had been sealed, until broken open, with red wax. She had the exclusive right to unseal such envelopes, before preparing them for a report to the baron.

She was startled by someone's attempt to open the door, but it was locked. There was a knock; still, Hilde took her time putting everything in decent order. Then she unlocked the door.

It was Dieter, who threw a suspicious look at the office.

"I saw the light," he said. "Why do you lock yourself in?"

"Shall I explain to you why a lady sometimes needs to lock herself in?"

"Your period?"

"Jerk!"

He looked at the office again, took a few steps and most impudently looked inside the bathroom, then said, apparently satisfied:

"Excuse me, I just wanted to see why the light was on. If you don't have that much work I could take you to the movies. They're showing a film with Paul Wegener."

"Thank you, Dieter," she said, responding to his peacemaking gesture. "I still have a lot to do. Everything in these piles has to be described, and then, tomorrow at nine, on the baron's desk. Paul Wegener can wait a bit."

It was hard to know what was eating the driver, but he stayed for another moment and looked at the room again, before saying distractedly:

"Well then. Good night."

Hilde had to hand over a new roll to Vladek—all of yesterday's mail. She said:

"Do you want to go to the theater together?"

"Theater? What theater is there in Shanghai?"

"Qinxi."

"Translated into an intelligible language?"

"Again Qinxi. A medieval theatrical genre. A kind of opera from Peking."

He frowned. "My God, opera. And in Chinese!"

"You'd hardly understand it more if it were in Italian. The cheese makers in your Alpine village probably don't know what opera means. It'll be fun—let's go for the sake of our general education—I mean yours."

It really was fun—for the first thirty minutes. At one time, deafened by cymbals and drums, he whispered in desperation:

"And how long is this torture for the sake of our general education going to last?"

She laughed quietly:

"Well, this is the short version—only eight hours. Don't shoot yourself, we're leaving."

The reason for her very great amiability was not the boredom with which Vladek was watching this exotic performance but a certain man, sitting exactly behind them, a blond European who, it seemed to her, was trying to listen to their whispers.

# 52

THE NIGHT OUTSIDE WAS cool, though the wind carried a hint of spring. Hilde looked around carefully; the blond man was not behind them. To keep him from suspecting her of paranoia, she said nothing about it to Vladek.

"It's true that according to our notions it's a little boring," she went on, guiltily, as if she had personally invented the Qinxi genre. "But this is a specific style of stage language that we, as Europeans, simply don't understand. Otherwise it would be good if everything in life were like a Chinese opera, clear and unambiguous: the face of the honest character on stage is always painted red; the bad guy, white; the brave one, yellow; and the gods—theirs are always gold."

"And what about mine?"

"Gold, of course!"

She again cast a glance behind her and saw nothing suspicious. Reaching inside the pocket of his raincoat, she found his hand and thrust her fingers in his palm. It was warm and moist.

Then, right there, into his palm, he felt her releasing the small roll of film. That night Kleinbauer would develop it; tomorrow Cheng Suzhin would get it to the courier on the ship sailing to Inko in the Laodun Bay. From there the film would be transferred to Shenyang, also known as Mukden.

After Mukden, all traces of it would be lost—temporarily—since the Berlin department B-4 at the Reich's Security Headquarters had sent a coded message saying that from some German diplomatic mission or other, most probably in the Far East, there was a serious leak of confidential information in the direction of the special Russian intelligence services. Apparently in Moscow, on the other hand, there was a German spy ring in operation that had sniffed out the situation. In Shanghai, this message had been received not by Baron von Dammbach—far from it—but by his personal driver, who was busy with not only official activities but also a number of other parallel concerns related to the interests of this same department B-4.

The rickshaw for two took them toward Rue Lafayette, in the French section, and stopped in front of the renowned Chinese restaurant Celestial Peace, familiar to every coolie in Shanghai. The owner, a Chinese man with decent French, led them up the steep stairway, which was dimly lit by barely flickering red lanterns with dangling silk tassels. The ascent was endless, as if they were climbing up to the very firmament of tranquility. From every stairway landing there issued a corridor, still dimly red, with heavy curtains in front of the spaces reserved for discreet or family dinners. He offered them a small private room, separated by a carved partition. The meal they ordered contained countless fish and meat dishes, and raw or slightly steamed vegetables, but the portions were miniscule, though very tasty, opening to the Europeans whole new and unknown gastronomic galaxies. Young girls in antique national costumes took small plates in silence from the rotating disk on the table in order to replace them with others.

For a long time Hilde hadn't had problems with chopsticks, which had given her such a hard time in the Japanese restaurant in Paris when she was having dinner with Dr. Hiroshi Okura. Every time she used them she remembered with a certain sense of guilt the shy Japanese man who had given her a necklace of pink pearls before disappearing forever from her life.

At least she thought it was forever.

Here, in the labyrinths of the restaurant, no one could eavesdrop on them. The Celestial Peace was seething with foreigners and local people and the Chinese music tenderly and unobtrusively filled up the space with its woven silk, heavy tassels, and red light, which covered everything like a thick crimson sauce.

She took a piece of meat with her chopsticks, regarded it pensively, but did not bring it to her lips, apparently seized by a thought quite distant from Far East culinary practices.

"You look worried," he said.

"We're eating like the children of the Chinese emperor. But I can't help thinking of the Jews in Hongku and the hunger waiting for them. Experts in Berlin have warned the baron about an impending economic catastrophe in Shanghai. Did I tell you that the Japanese have literally cheated them? I mean the Jews. It turns out they were counting on them to work as scabs."

"So I've heard. All the newspapers wrote about the strike. But probably in Hongku they don't get newspapers. Now listen to me: I'm asking you one more time not to go there again and not to meet the rabbi! You should take the hint; you understand the situation. And do *not* rely on your bulletins, which are nothing but naive fables—and so on. Remember, you heard it from me: the First Commandment is Do Not Treat Your Enemy Like a Fool. Always believe that he's at least as intelligent and perspicacious as you. If you consider your behavior from the point of view of this hypothesis, you have every advantage over him. A very important lesson for young lady novices."

"Thanks a lot," she said, rather put out. "But I didn't go to the rabbi. He came to me."

This was in fact the truth. Rabbi Leo Levin had managed to beg a one-day pass from Commissioner Go. The commissioner had initially frowned; moreover, the suppliant hadn't indicated that he was prepared to toss in at least a tenner. But when the rabbi just casually happened to mention that he was on his way to see His Excellency the Baron von Dammbach, Mr. Go, with sudden respect, immediately issued the pass. This was a green tin token about the size of a large button, with the letter "J" stamped on the metal. This meant that the person bearing it was a "Jude," that is, a Jew, and had the right to cross the border bridge over the Soochow. At night, before the curfew, the token had to be returned to the office of the Zone. Every delay was punished most severely, and the violator lost forever his right to pass across that bridge, unless he went "with both legs forward," as the King of the Jews used to say, to the Jewish cemetery lying beyond the bridge, in a small muddy field by the river where people would throw their garbage.

The reason why the rabbi had come to Hilde for help was a complicated and delicate case: the racially pure German Elisabeth Müller-Weissberg, a famous singer in the past, married to a celebrated Jewish violin virtuoso, was in a severe depression because of their living conditions, which she found unbearable. Couldn't His Excellency Baron von Dammbach intercede for her and her family to remain in Hongku, but outside this thrice-damned Zone?

Hilde without a doubt went in to see the baron but came out quite dejected: the law for mixed marriages is strict and unambiguous, said the baron. Unless the German woman divorced the Jew, there were no legal grounds whatsoever for separating her family from the others. "They should think about whom they get themselves married to and bear the consequences!" von Dammbach declared, refusing to discuss the matter further.

Having lost this particular small battle, Rabbi Leo Levin gloomily walked the road back to Hongku, but said nothing about the visit to Theodore Weissberg, who, after all, had his pride, which the rabbi didn't want to wound by putting him in the humiliating position of a beggar who's been denied charity.

"Is that what's bothering you—the singer's situation?"

"Well, yes, that too, of course. What's more, I know her husband, the violinist. But what's really bothering me is Dieter, the boss's driver. I get the feeling that he's following me. He keeps looking at me in this very strange way. If I'm not imagining things. . . . Late last night he showed up at my office. He's never done that before when the baron's been at the residence."

"Open your eyes, pussycat."

"I've told you a hundred times not to call me pussycat!"

"Okay, sorry, kitten. Keep your eyes open, but don't start suffering from excessive paranoia. Because this blocks the mind too. Often things are simpler than they seem. He may be flirting with you. Taking an example from his boss von Dammbach."

"Stop talking nonsense!"

"That's my forte, as my aunt used to say. By the way, where do you keep the gas lighter? When you're not there, is there any chance he could snoop around a bit?"

"Let him snoop as much as he wants. The lighter's in a cardboard chocolate box, along with rubber bands, paperclips and other office supplies. In the steel safe. Only von Dammbach and I have keys to it. Or should I carry it with me?"

"No, absolutely not. In Shanghai, every lady's purse could be declared stolen in advance on the day it's manufactured."

Hilde kept silent for a moment, picked at the fried vegetables with her chopsticks for awhile, and finally, following some thought that was plaguing her mind, diffidently asked:

"Vladek, does all this make sense?"

"All what?"

"What you're doing . . . you, your people. If you can't—if you don't even have the right to intervene in anything, to help out someone in trouble, like, for example, those miserable people in Hongku. . . ."

"Those are the rules of the game. To clench your teeth and not to interfere even if your heart is bleeding. To remain an outside observer in any and all circumstances. This is the Second Commandment in our . . . well, let's call it profession. I interfered one time in order to defend a certain foolish woman who was trying to start a fistfight with the entire Shanghai police force because of some kid. And they almost plucked me like a chicken!"

"That foolish woman was me, thank you very much. But in this case, even if any interference is forbidden you, can't you somehow do something to change the world? Make it better?"

"I don't know. For now there's just one goal: to keep Hitler from changing it. Because he'll make it worse. But in any case I think this does change us, because it's not from the weekly newsreel or the newspapers that we're learning the truth. We aren't observers from a distance, where the details get blurred, but right here on enemy territory. And the world, observed from this territory, looks different."

"In what sense?"

"In the sense that looking from the outside, everything about the Nazis is known, or let's say, the major thing is known: their insane barbarism, the mass shootings, the camps, the Jews, the Polish. . . . Clear and unambiguous as a propaganda poster. But when you're on the inside, you don't just see their army as a bunch of mere arrows on the strategy map; you start to make out within it individual people and individual destinies, conceited or desperate generals, confused soldiers, all turned into killers. Or killers who are already thinking about how to sneak away from impending retribution. You start telling phonies from victims. You notice, for example, in some ditch somewhere, five German soldiers in thin military coats who with blue fingers are cutting meat from the hip of the frozen artillery horse, then roasting it on the fire and nibbling at it half-raw. Or you start feeling sympathy for a fifteen-year old German boy who hasn't yet lived or loved, and from the ruins of Stalingrad is writing a letter to his mother in Saxony that she'll never receive. This is what things look like when you're inside them. This changes your knowledge of the enemy and who in fact is who. Without prejudice and curses. Your retina starts perceiving nuances, so you can understand the drama of others. And ours? Do you know where our drama is? In the fact that powerful guys everywhere, literally everywhere, insist that the data we hand over to them with so many risks and sacrifices correspond to their notion of the enemy—as determined in advance as your Qinxi opera. That's why those services which are delicately called 'special' are so often in conflict with the powers they serve. Because they question its convenient schemes, they destroy the sand towers of its illusions. Or, let's say. . . ."

Vladek felt that she was withdrawing.

"Are you here?" he asked. "Are you trying to understand what I'm saying? This too is for the sake of general education."

She stretched her arm across the table and caressed his hand.

"I love you."

"Again?"

"For a long time already."

# 53

THIS EVENING ELISABETH ARRIVED earlier than usual at the Blue Mountain; she just couldn't stand another day in the teeming chaos of the factory. She was irritated by the people who constantly stomped on the stairway under which Theodore had improvised a triangular dwelling partitioned by plywood. As usual he was not at home—if you could call this hole under the stairs a home. To his surprise the Dutchman from the Imperial Hotel hadn't yet found a replacement for him and had taken him on again, though a bit sourly and begrudgingly, it's true.

The children who would run all the time up and down above her head were driving her crazy, and so were the bored old men who would pick over political problems in front of her thin wall. People excitedly exchanged information about what had happened in Stalingrad, often spiced with tall tales whispered by an unknown science fictionist that there had been a military coup in Berlin, and that Hitler had committed suicide. But even this didn't engage her interest; she was too irritated by her surroundings.

Here in the Blue Mountain at least she had the relative quiet of the dressing room, its only opening to the world a small barred window for ventilation, and long periods when she could be alone, while down below the Hungarian would take apart Gershwin or Strauss and put it back together again.

This evening had started a bit strangely: on the table by the mirror the owner Yen Qingvey had left a white rose, a small nephrite bottle with some fragrance, and a note: "Happy Birthday!" He knew that today was her birthday, knew it from her passport. Qingvey held to the tradition of most of the Chinese employers of holding on to the documents of their employees while the latter were working for them; it was a kind of guarantee of honesty. And the rose and the nephrite bottle were an expression of attentiveness to the singer, who was bringing him new clients from the multiplying German ships, both military and commercial, at the expense of the English and American ones, which had suddenly disappeared.

Yen Qingvey didn't know that there was nothing anymore that could give joy to the imitator of Zara Leander. She was sick at heart. On the other hand, she was herself surprised that with her growing disgust with everything around her, with Shanghai, Hongku, this sailors' pub, with everything Chinese, with the Jews, even with her husband, she didn't feel the slightest nostalgia for Germany. She just didn't feel anything, except a deep weariness, and craved nothing at all except silence, after the maddeningly noisy living conditions of the steel factory. She no longer dwelled in the real world; she only wanted to lie down in the silence, to cover herself with it and to sleep long, a whole eternity.

Elisabeth sat in front of the mirror in her slip, lacking strength to put on the gown that she would perform in and that, with its golden shimmer, would cling to her body as it descended to the floor. Down below in the pub, the first rare visitors were already getting drunk, and the distant sounds of the piano reached up to her as if coming from deep underground. *An American in Paris*.

A German—a German woman—in Shanghai.

She looked at herself in the peeling yellow mirror, and touched the thin web of wrinkles around her eyes: she was thirty-eight! This was it: life had passed and what had been would never come again—neither the good nor the bad. The wheel of fortune doesn't go in reverse; that's just the way things are. Had her coming here been a mistake, or would it have been a mistake if she had stayed in Dresden and abandoned Theodore? It was all the same: life has no variant other than what's happened. A one-way street, without a u-turn, a leap into the unknown without the right to a second chance.

There was a quiet knock, the door opened halfway, and Mr. Qingvey stole a glance inside the dressing room.

"May I?" he asked delicately; without receiving an answer, he came in. "I'm not in the way, am I? I just wanted to congratulate you on the occasion of your birthday. And to wish you happiness and more success."

She looked at him in the mirror, threw the long silk shawl with fringes over her bare shoulders, wearily rose, and then sat down by the side of the table.

"Thank you for the rose and the perfume, Mr. Qingvey. I had even forgotten that I was born. I appreciate it. You are the only one who remembered."

"Well, how could I not? After all, you're my star. Wonderful and irreplaceable!"

"It's a pleasure to hear it," she said indifferently, and without even realizing it she was suddenly in his arms. She smelled the strong, thick aroma of Indian patchouli mixed with his whisky breath.

"Many happy returns of the day. . . . Do you allow a kiss?" he said, panting and stripping the shawl from her body.

She saw from very close the large pores of his red face, his widely spaced teeth, which bit her lower lip, and breathed again the smell of whiskey. Mr. Yen had started very early today!

Elisabeth pushed him away from her with disgust, but he attacked her again. She had no room to pull away; behind her stood the table with the mirror. So she slapped him with the back of her hand.

"Get out of here, you swine. Get out of this room, you stinking, fat, disgusting pig!"

Yen Qingvey, who had slept with half the bar girls and was used to their quiet, servile obedience, suddenly froze with surprise. She saw how his look changed, his eyes slowly filling with wild, uncontrollable anger.

He said quietly, very quietly:

"This is not the way you talk to the Master! Do you hear me, you German whore? No one has ever dared to talk like this to Yen Qingvey."

And he gave her a loud slap on the face that literally threw her head back. Then he left, slamming the door behind him.

Elisabeth sank in the chair, drew her palm over her cheek, which was burning with the slap, and stayed like this for a long time, in mute forgetfulness. Then, seized by sudden anger, she threw the nephrite bottle of perfume at her reflection. The mirror broke and divided her tired face into big, displaced triangles down which dripped the thick yellowish liquid with the same heavy smell of pachouli.

"Broken mirror," she said out loud. "Seven years unhappy love. Another seven years!"

The Hungarian downstairs in the bar switched to German and Austrian tunes—her cue.

She stood up painfully, took off the simple city shoes with which she would walk around Hongku, and tried to put on her soft slippers. Then from her left slipper a frightened rat jumped out, brushed at her leg, and with a shriek disappeared under the furniture.

Elisabeth screamed with horror and disgust. And only then she started to cry.

She cried uncontrollably, leaning her head against the white wall.

Half an hour later, the Hungarian, having lost patience, went upstairs. The dressing room door turned out to be locked. He knocked but no one responded inside. He knocked again and again. Silence.

When they broke in, they found Elisabeth—the mezzo-soprano Elisabeth Müller-Weissberg, once a star at Carnegie Hall—hanging from her long silk shawl, the one with the fringes. She had twisted it and tied it to the bars of the high window.

# 54

JUST AFTER MIDNIGHT THEODORE Weissberg came on foot to take his wife home as usual by rickshaw. The bar was full and smoky, the clients were flirting with the girls, the bartender could barely keep up with the orders. But Qingvey himself, leaning on the bar next to a full glass of whisky, was in a state of utter dejection. The drunken Chinese man immediately jumped from his seat, took Theodore aside, and, stuttering, with difficulty searched for words with which to announce to him as delicately as possible what had happened.

On the other side of the pub the Hungarian for a moment removed his hands from the piano, cast a look full of sympathy at the still uncomprehending Theodore, and immediately, as if scared that he might be suspected of complicity in the affair, turned his head and reapplied his fingers to the keys. The singer's drama had deeply shaken him, but in particularly delicate cases he always exhibited amazing clumsiness, withdrawing into himself, unable to express his feelings. In such moments too he would make awkward, involuntary gaffes, which was why he preferred to stay out of the way.

White as the wall of the dressing room, Theodore looked at Elisabeth's body as it lay on the sturdy Chinese couch, still not understanding that she was dead. Now and forever; no U-turn; one way only. It seemed to him as if she had fainted, that she had just felt sick, and that at any moment now she would get up again. The Hungarian silently handed him a cigarette. He took it, lit it, yet in no way realized that he was smoking.

You really couldn't say that Yen Qingvey was a bad man; he had just behaved the way masters customarily treated their subordinates, no better, no worse. Suddenly sobered up, he was troubled not only by the case and not only because he felt a certain sense of guilt and implication, but most of all because he wanted nothing whatsoever to do with the police. There wasn't a single owner of such an establishment, with its trade in girls, drugs, black market cigarettes, and whisky, and its clientele of sailors forever dragging contraband goods around in their bags, who didn't fear public scandal.

This is why he bargained for a very long time with the coolie of a double rickshaw, one of those who doze in front of the pub in expectation of late night clients. Qingvey raised the amount, then doubled it. Finally he managed to overcome the poor barefoot man's fear of getting involved in an affair like this—the secret transportation of a corpse.

Then into the pocket of the unsuspecting Theodore, Qingvey inserted the deceased's passport, between whose pages he had inserted five bank notes of a hundred Shanghai dollars each.

"The rickshaw has been paid for, don't worry. And the money, if you allow me, is for the funeral. We thought very highly of her; she was an extraordinary singer. But it's in our common interest that there be no police report, you understand?"

Theodore nodded, even though he didn't understand anything.

The Hungarian helped Yen Qingvey take the dead woman out through the backyard and arrange her in the double rickshaw. Once they had also helped Theodore climb aboard, the rickshaw then took off to the rhythm of the coolie's wide, even strides through the back streets, sunk in sleep, of Shanghai.

At one corner, the dead woman tilted and laid her head on Theodore's shoulder.

It had been a long, long time since she had done that.

There was no need for the green piece of tin. The Japanese soldiers, guarding the bridge over the Soochow, already knew the couple—the elegant woman and her shabby husband, who would come back in a rickshaw during the late hours from the other side of the river.

At three a.m. neighbors from the landing woke up the rabbi. He ran upstairs, got to work, and helped transfer the body to the synagogue. They laid it down on the raised wooden shelf with the menorah, behind which sat the Buddha, still so mysteriously smiling.

Theodore spoke:

"Please, go. I want to stay with her. Please."

The rabbi silently pressed his shoulder, and was the last to leave the little synagogue, quietly closing the door behind him.

Theodore sat on a wooden crate and for hours did not take his eyes from the dead woman, illuminated by the flame of a lonely candle.

At one point he sensed steps behind him, looked around, and saw Shlomo. The fat short-legged thief drew up an armchair in Empire style and sat on the other side of the dead woman. There had been such an armchair—just exactly the same kind—in their home in Dresden, on 3/5 Dante Alighieri Street; Elisabeth liked to sit in it when she read. Shlomo remained silent for a long time, looking with sadness at the woman to whom he had been so faithful. There was a bloody wound gaping at his throat, and his voice, simmering and bubbling, came straight from his Adam's apple.

"I'm sorry, Mr. Weissberg, it isn't my business to interfere, but it's all your fault. You and no one else. She should never have come here. Why did you take her with you? Didn't you know that nothing good ever happens to the Jews?"

Theodore said nothing in his own defense. He knew that Shlomo was right.

He woke up with the first sun rays that pierced through the slits of the broken roof. The candle had burnt down, and across from the dead woman there was no armchair in the Empire style. Shlomo had probably taken it away with him.

Mr. Go, King of the Jews, refused to give a pass to leave the Zone to anyone but Theodore and the rabbi. The case didn't interest him; Professor Mandel had issued a death certificate in which it was written in black and white that Elisabeth Müller-Weissberg, German, born in Dresden on April 17, 1905, had died from acute peritonitis. For Mr. Go, this was sufficient. It was neither the first nor the last case in Hongku.

She was buried in the German cemetery by the Evangelical church. The minister indifferently uttered a routine burial speech; Mother Antonia, a Catholic, sang "*Ave Maria gratia plena . . .*" and the nuns from the brass band performed something from Handel.

The Hungarian came to the funeral, but from the very beginning he fixed his gaze on one spot and didn't take his eyes off it until the end. His unblinking pupils were dilated, which is what usually happens after the use of different types of white powder.

Most unexpectedly from the flower shop at Nankin Road they brought in a big bouquet of white roses. Thirty eight white roses.

On the black mourning strip, there was a text written in Chinese characters. Only Mother Theresa out of all the Europeans was able to read it.

*To the heavenly singer, with a plea for forgiveness.*

*Yen Qingvey.*

# 55

HAUPTSTURMFÜHRER WILLY STOCKMANN HADN'T come to Shanghai to waste his time on this bunch of Jews. They were an extraneous botheration; there were people who supposedly specialized in the "Final Solution." If the big shots in Berlin insisted on applying the laws of the Reich to the ex-German yids who had snuck off to China, then let them send some of those people here who knew how to deal with shitty situations like this in a foreign country. After all Shanghai wasn't a German territory, but rather much like to such allies as Hungary, Bulgaria, and Romania, where there were Jews also whom it wasn't the job of the Germans but of the local authorities to deal with officially. And this required diplomatic skills that Willy Stockmann just didn't have. His main concern was the security of the Reich. And nothing else. This was a task considerably larger than the fate of some Moishe or other. It was the reason why he'd been sent here to head a group of specialists from the SS and the Gestapo who had to keep the rear end of the Fatherland safe from this side of the world.

He went to the harbor to meet, with satisfaction and hope, the regular arrival of the ship from Kobe, on which the team that intercepted subversive radio transmitters was being brought from Japan. There it had done an excellent job, proving once again the superiority of German electronics to the worn-out contraptions of the Japanese. The new invention known as the "Pelengator" had faultlessly intercepted the secret radio transmitter and, despite the claims of those loudmouth Japanese, had in actuality liquidated the "Ramsay" group in Tokyo—that nest of spies run by the Baku-born, half-German Dr. Richard Sorge. The rest of the job, the technical part, had been completed by local security forces; of course this can't be denied. Now Shanghai was next on the agenda, with its chaos of coded transmissions that had woven a thick cobweb in the air with threads from American, Soviet, English, French, and God knows what other secret transmitters.

The men arriving from Tokyo managed to squeeze themselves and all their equipment into nothing more than a not very big white van sporting the large engraved logo of Bushido, the Japanese company for oil paints, drawing, and art supplies. All four members of the group were specialists in radio interception, sent some time ago by Berlin. The driver, a German corporal from the signal corps, wasn't one of them. The metal ring mounted on top of the van sometimes puzzled passersby, but most of them looked at it with indifference—it wasn't the first time the Japanese had displayed peculiar advertisements! And the van itself would crawl out of the garage of the Shanghai police only in the evening, always discreetly parking at some distance from the center on dark and narrow streets, and never at the same place, so actually you scarcely noticed the metal ring's rare, almost imperceptible turn.

In the last ten days the people from the van had focused their attention on a circle casually drawn on the map of the city with a thick red pencil in the vicinity of Shusan Street, at the corner of North Sichuan Road. There, inside the circle, there were intersecting straight lines precisely drawn within the 32nd short wave sector whenever the clicking of Morse code was detected. From somewhere or other out there would come extremely short and fast signals, after which the area sank into silence. Though the white van shrewdly remained far from this area, the men inside went personally to check out the neighborhood. The buildings thereabouts had many floors, and were full of apartments, offices, restaurants, dressmaking studios, tearooms, and shops. It was from somewhere out there, from that swarm, that the short Morse signals were coming!

But from exactly where—this was the job of Captain Masaaki Saneioshi to figure out. His people, always in plain clothes, always very polite with the residents of the buildings, would walk around looking for made-up people, asking the doormen about made-up companies, assembling an exact registry of the residents and employees in the neighborhood. Everyone was described, everything was discreetly checked ten times, but so far they had failed to arrive at an acceptable hypothesis.

As usually happens in such operations, the answer came by accident. It wasn't the big specialists in interception who ran into it, but a beginner technician busy with servicing the receptor in the Bushido van. His name was Walter, Walter Haberle, a graduate of the naval academy in Bremen, who'd specialized in marine radio equipment.

When in the late hours the van started to move unperceived toward streets closer to the signals, the young man happened to notice a strange pattern: a minute before the coded transmission began, the three Chinese characters of the neon sign at the Agfa photo studio would switch off. Almost immediately after the transmission ended, the neon started blinking again as it always did day and night. Until the next transmission. Not wanting to be an object of ridicule, Walter Haberle didn't dare announce his discovery immediately. Moreover, on the list of the hundreds of sites to be investigated in the neighborhood, across from the address of the Agfa studio in the small Chinese house squeezed between blocks of flats, the Kempeitai people had noted: "A. Kleinbauer. German. Reliable. Beyond suspicion."

Walter Haberle nevertheless continued his observations and when he started estimating to the split-second when the transmission would begin and the moment when the three Chinese characters were going to light up again, he decided to announce his discovery. He also shared his supposition that the metal scaffolding with the steel net stretched between its bars, where the characters were mounted, was nothing but a radio antenna. An ingenious antenna that was, however, able to function flawlessly, without electromagnetic interference, only during the minutes when the neon symbols were switched off.

The naval academy in Bremen could take pride in its student!

At two fifteen a.m., when the three characters switched off, and in the van they started getting the quick, dry tap-tap-tapping of the Morse code, the Kempeitei people attacked from all sides.

The operation was observed from the dark side street where Captain Saneioshi's black Opel had stopped with its lights turned off.

As on that rainy night of the Jewish exodus to South Hongku, in the back seat sat Hauptsturmführer Willy Stockmann, chain-smoking.

"At the moment inside there are at least three people," said Saneioshi-san, turning to the German. "I ordered my people to start shooting only as a last resort. I want them alive. The way we got them all in Tokyo."

"Correct. The living say more than the dead."

When they broke in and stormed the studio, two men in plain clothes, without losing a single second, ran up the narrow staircase. But after the very first couple of steps they had to stop and plaster themselves against the wall, because Kleinbauer started firing from upstairs with his nine-millimeter "Walter," while Cheng Suzhin was destroying every possible clue. There wasn't enough time though and Kleinbauer shouted between shots, "Burn it! Set it all on fire immediately!"

Cheng Suzhin hesitated, threw a quick look at Vladek, who was breaking the bars in front of the vaulted window, then at the giant blocking the way from the staircase to the laboratory with his huge body.

"No. Run first!" cried Cheng Suzhin.

But Kleinbauer, hit again and again, felt his shirt, looked at his enormous blood-covered palm and howled as the shots flew by:

"Do you hear me?! Burn it all, I'm telling you, you Chinese monkey! Set it on fire and get the hell out of here!"

Captain Saneioshi's men finally managed to climb the stairs, but the upper floor of the studio and the roof above it—the one covered with green enameled tiles, the corners twisted in the Chinese way—were already seized by flames. In the black poisonous smoke of burning celluloid, they bumped into a sprawling body: the family photo colorist and passionate admirer of Russian vodka, the German beyond suspicion, Alfred Gottfried Kleinbauer, had shot himself in the forehead.

The police failed to find anyone else in the studio, apart from bloody traces leading to the broken vaulted window with its view of the dark Chinese yards below.

When the firemen who had flown to the scene extinguished the fire, they discovered only one microfilm that had survived the flames. Dipped in the almost completely evaporated solution in the developing tank, it was in the form of a roll hardly bigger than a soybean.

# 56

THE DOOR OPENED ABRUPTLY and after Willy Stockmann, two German civilians came barging in, their pistols drawn as if they were facing a whole machine gun contingent instead of just von Dammbach's secretary, startled and scared.

Standing up, Hilde tried to speak with calm indifference but her voice trembled:

"Can I help you?"

"You'll find out later!" barked Stockmann. "I need the baron."

"I will report—"

"Not necessary. We already spoke on the phone."

And he unceremoniously rushed into von Dammbach's office. Before closing the door behind him, he said to the other two:

"Don't let this one leave!"

Standing behind the desk, Hilde felt the blood draining out of her head as a wave of cold shivered up her spine and seized the whole back of her neck, gripping it with icy pliers. She felt a devouring fear that paralyzed her brain and her will. Where was Vladek now to tell her what to do? Had something bad happened to him too? Did these men from the Gestapo know anything or were they just feeling around in the dark?

The front door opened, the driver Dieter popped his head in, cast a glance at Hilde, grinned, and closed the door again.

The civilian agents were standing on the two sides of the door—silent, expressionless, and unperturbed.

Not much time had passed before the baron and Stockmann came out of the office. The old diplomat, who usually had control over himself, was now white-lipped, his chin trembling with emotion.

"Miss Braun, this is most probably about some unfortunate misunderstanding, but please stand aside. I have given permission for a search."

"May I ask—" started Hilde, but the Hauptsturmführer abruptly interrupted her:

"*We* do the asking. Shut up!"

He nodded to his people and then it all started: the drawers, behind the armchairs, under the desk and the windowsills: everything was checked, carefully, precisely, without disturbing files and objects. Apparently these fellows, the civilians, were not from the political services but experienced cops from Kripo, the German criminal police, which customarily worked very carefully.

"Hand over the key to the safe!"ordered Stockmann.

Hilde looked at the baron with fear and a question at the same time. He nodded: "Give it to him."

From her neck she removed the chain where the quite solid key was hanging, hidden until now under her blouse. She handed it over hesitantly, as if relinquishing to them a gun with which they were going to shoot her. Her last hope was that they had no proof; the documents could have been photographed early on, from an airplane, or at the airport, or by anyone who'd had access to the residence. In this key—this key to the safe—her doom lay in wait!

With the same precision, the file folders were taken out of the safe, leafed through, and again meticulously returned to their place. Then they came to the chocolate box, stuck somewhere in the back.

Pale, with his chin slightly jutting out, Baron von Dammbach remained standing by the wide open door to his office in the haughty posture of a noble unjustly suspected of a low deed.

*The end! This is the end!* Hilde didn't even dare imagine what was going to happen next. Many times she had wondered what a failure would look like; she was not such a fool to think it could never happen. But failure, even though it differs from death in being avoidable, has something in common with it: you know that it's always ominously hanging over your head, but in your mind you reject it. This is only human.

The agent emptied the contents of the box on the top of the desk: paperclips, erasers, rubber bands, pins, a bottle of glue. Office supplies and nothing else. Hilde was astounded: yesterday the lighter had still been there, she had no doubt about it, because she had personally loaded it with new microfilm.

"Where is the device?" asked Stockmann.

"What device?"

"Don't play dumb now! The camera!"

"I don't know what you're talking about. . . ."

"You'll soon find out. Very soon! Take her!" Then he turned to von Dammbach: "Excuse us for the disturbance, Mr. Baron. You didn't want to believe it. Now you'll be convinced!"

Absently, almost imperceptibly, the baron nodded.

Dieter stopped the car in front of the English Garden. It was protected by a tall cast-iron fence; its big gate, adorned at the top with the gilded symbols of the British crown, was wide open.

Only at nightfall would it be locked to keep the thieves, drunks, and bums from this carefully tended place for rendezvous and relaxation, which would proudly stand comparison with the royal parks in Europe. Early every evening, after finishing work, and if there were no other, more attractive engagements, Baron von Dammbach and his wife would follow family tradition and walk there for an hour—that quiet hour before dinner.

"Thank you, Dieter. In an hour, as always—here."

"Understood, Mr. Baron."

The garden was really magnificent, with the hanging branches of exotic trees, and evergreen bushes and eternally well-kept lawns. In the quiet lake, amid the rocks hauled here from the Chinese wilderness and wondrously lapped by the water, there was the reflection of a small exquisite pagoda.

The two walked quietly along the pathway, which was covered with red pebbles, and from time to time politely nodded to acquaintances from the Shanghai elite—lately becoming rather thinned out, since friends from the American and British missions had been driven out of the country.

At one point Baroness Gertrude von Dammbach, looking intently at the points of her shoes, with which she was dallying with the pebbles under her feet, whispered:

"I can't stop thinking about her. . . . Poor soul! Do you think she'll make it out of there?"

"Hardly. Those fellows have the bite of a bulldog."

"Probably now her friend, the Swiss fellow, will be affected too."

"If he hasn't been already."

"But why did she do it? Why?"

The baron kept silent for a long time before he answered:

"She probably had her reasons. Insofar as I got to know her, she isn't someone with an empty head; neither would she be tempted by money. She must have had reasons that we're hardly likely to find out. . . . Maybe love . . . if that young Swiss man was also . . . or. . . . No, I don't know, I simply don't know. I don't want to guess."

"Can't you help her?"

"I'm afraid not."

They were standing on the Garden Bridge, famous in Shanghai for promenades.

Leaning on the parapet, the baroness didn't take her eyes off the thick water that was floating beneath them in its endless journey to the ocean.

"Poor soul," she whispered again.

The baron, with his unlit cigarette between his lips, looked around, carelessly reached into the pocket of his English trench-coat, and took out the lighter. As he clicked it, a gas flame flared up. He lit the cigarette, inhaling deeply. Switching off the lighter, he twisted it in his fingers, pensively looked at the small glass eye on the side, and threw it in the water.

The bridge was too high for anyone to hear how it splashed and was forever lost in the muddy brown depths below.

# 57

SEVERAL HOURS BEFORE DAWN there was a quiet knock on the iron gates leading to the garden of the Bassat family at 342 Boulevard Cardinal Mercier. And then came another knock, and another, in the cul-de-sac alley between the Bassats' and the thick brick wall bordering the neighboring property; through this passage, in other times, the suppliers of vegetables, bread, and meat would enter every morning with their two-wheeled carts straight into the yard, by the entrance to the kitchen.

Finally, through the cracks in the door, a gas lamp shone, and the aged voice of the gardener Wu Laozian was heard.

"Who's that knocking?"

"Bo, it's me, Chin Lankao, do you remember me? The son of the carpenter Wang . . . Chin Wang, who made altars for family gods."

On the other side the old man was silent and it wasn't clear whether he was trying to remember or didn't believe what he heard.

"You say you're Lankao? . . . Lankao went far away a long time ago."

"Here I am, back again.

"Lankao the Crazy?"

"The same, Bo Laozian. With the scar on my cheek. The friend of your sons."

"O Lord!" cried the old man, excitedly pulling the iron bolt.

It was after the Japanese war when Lankao and the sons of Laozian, instead of staying in Shanghai to follow their fathers' professions, decided one night to leave town and become soldiers. When had that been—five, six, seven years ago? Old age merges the days together and you confuse what happened yesterday with what happened seven moons ago and seven times seven too. That's what old age is like—you forget what happened yesterday and you remember what happened ages ago, which seem, in their turn, like yesterday! Wu Laozian remembered well the day when a Japanese bomb fell on the carpenter's house and killed Chin Wang and his wife, the mother of Lankao. Then the gardener Laozian, with the permission of his mistress, Mrs. Bassat, took the young boy to raise him together with his sons. He was a bit crazy, Chin Lankao; he would often get into fights with the neighborhood kids and in one such bout of foolishness someone had cut his cheek with a knife. Wu Laozian angrily muttered under his breath about these hijinks, but most diligently healed the wounded boy—the old gardener knew about these things.

The mischief-making didn't last long, because the day the Japanese military ships disembarked and the enemy army entered town, the three youths decided to escape and join the fighting. Wu Laozian never forgave his foster child this new folly of his. He knew that it wasn't his sons who had dreamed up this midnight run; it was without doubt the whim of Lankao and no one else! And here he was now, after so many years!

Wu Laozian didn't see well anymore, it had been a long time since he'd had good vision, and even his glasses, the new ones with their horn-rimmed frames, didn't help much. This is why he put the lamp close to Lankao's face, and looked at him intently. He'd grown up, he'd become a young man who, you could say, would have been handsome if the scar on his cheek hadn't been so conspicuous—a deep furrow reaching almost from his eyes to his lips. The old man looked over the young man's shoulder; not far from where he was standing there was a covered rickshaw with a half-naked, shabby coolie, and in the darkness of the rickshaw, it seemed to him, there was a passenger.

"You are not alone?" asked the old man.

"I have someone with me, Bo Laozian. Can the rickshaw come in? I'll explain later."

"Let it come in. If it's with you."

On the wooden bed, and covered with just a rug, lay the passenger from the rickshaw: Cheng Suzhin, the journalist from the *China Daily Post*, badly wounded in the hip and with a twisted, and possibly even broken foot, which had turned into a big, swollen, bluish-red lump. Laozian carefully washed the garden knife with rice brandy, then with its edge made two cuts in the form of a cross, and took out the bullet. He squeezed out the pus and washed the infected wound, and then sprinkled it with some yellowish-green powder made of grass and dried mushrooms. The old gardener knew what to put on an open and infected wound—and how!

"And who shot you? The flesh is torn and decayed to the bone, badly decayed. And I don't like the look of the foot at all either!" The old man, who had started tightly bandaging the lump with a piece of cloth, raised his head and alarm could be heard in his voice: "Have you done something illegal? A robbery or something?! I know, you're one of the crazy ones!"

Drops of sweat had appeared on the wounded man's forehead. Maybe from pain, because he was pressing his lips in order not to scream. Looking at him, Lankao said worriedly:

"Not me, Bo. For a long time now I haven't been one of the crazies. Only the name remained. But you can't get rid of a label, just like you can't get rid of a scar. . . . He was wounded by the Japanese police."

"Japanese? Why? And when?"

"About two weeks ago."

"Two weeks?! You're out of your mind—two weeks! And it's only now that you're getting him fixed up?"

"We wanted to take him out of town, but it didn't work out. They've tightened security from all sides and we had to turn back. It's not so easy to sneak away when you're carrying a stretcher on your shoulder. So, we took off, but then we came back. I'll tell you about it some other time," said Lankao, unconsciously throwing a quick look at the gaunt coolie who was sitting quietly in the corner.

The old gardener looked at him too. Here, in the light, one could see the difference between him and any other coolie from Nankin Road: the eyes! The difference was in the eyes. Usually the eyes of most coolies were submissive and expressionless, or indifferent, or wearily shrewd, with the cunning of a hungry, regularly beaten dog who tries to filch a bone behind the owner's back. This fellow's eyes were alive and sparkling, glancing thoughtfully from person to person, with something elusive about them hinting that he was perhaps a man of the brush, ink, and letters, perhaps a teacher, perhaps something else, but without doubt an educated man from a family different in all respects from the hereditary clan of coolies.

"This is not a coolie," the old man reflected. "In no way. And on the whole this business doesn't seem right!" This is what he was thinking, but instead he asked aloud, as if afraid of the answer:

"And how are my sons? Are they alive? Have you seen them?"

"One of them. I've seen one of them, he's well and sends you his regards. The older one, Tsuan. He sends his regards and asked me to look for you, in case of need. . . .That's what he said: if you need anything, go to my father, give him my regards and tell him. He will not refuse you, I know my old man."

The gardener gave him an undoubtedly cross look:

"Is this what he told you? And what did the other one say, the younger one?"

Lankao was silent for awhile, then murmured awkwardly:

"We don't see each other. He's in another army. With Chiang Kai-shek."

Old Laozian trembled:

"If I understand you correctly, does this mean that Tsuan is with Mao?"

"That's right. With Mao."

"How is this possible? That one of my sons is with Chiang, and the other with Mao! The two armies are fighting each other!"

"What's true—is true: they *are* fighting each other. That's what's going on in China, Bo Laozian—it's brother against brother. And the Japanese against the two. That's the story, no matter what we say."

He looked at his wristwatch, then at the silent coolie again and said:

"We have to get going before daylight."

"How are you going to do that; the wounded fellow can't walk!"

"No, he can't walk. But I thought maybe he could stay with you—for awhile."

The old man didn't expect this.

"Stay with me?! A stranger, wounded by the Japanese? For how long?"

"Well . . . until he gets better. Till then."

"That's a long time!"

For the first time Lankao, Lankao the Crazy, smiled, and because of the deep scar his face became strangely contorted:

"It means a short time, Bo. Just a little while. Because soon the war will be over. Then we'll take him to a hospital. The big state hospital. Thank you for accepting—"

"What do you mean 'accepting'?" angrily said Laozian. "You didn't even ask!"

"Look now: Are you going to just leave a wounded person in the street? A good man, an honest man. . . . Are you going to leave him in the hands of the Japanese? I'm asking you: you tell me."

The old man kept silent for a while, thought a bit, scratched his gray hair, then, drawing his closed hand along his long, thin, medieval mandarin-looking beard, angrily said:

"All right, all right! You come uninvited and you make yourself right at home! All right, I don't say anything. Now I'll boil him some tea for the pain so he can sleep. I have certain herbs. . . . And you, when you see my son Tsuan, give him my regards. And tell him not to shoot my son Luan. Tell him this is what I said!"

# 58

THE COVERED RICKSHAW STOPPED at the dock, where hundreds of junks swayed so tightly against each other that it seemed as if they were huddling together to keep warm during the wet nights by the river. A neighborhood of junks rocking to the breathing of the water, as if they formed the back of a floating monster, one of the multitude of such neighborhoods that floated beside the big city, in which people were being born, growing up, falling in love, and dying, without expecting any more from life than what their fathers and ancestors had gotten.

Early-rising housewives were pouring dirty water in the river from the washing; others were squatting by small burning stoves and boiling the first rice; somewhere someone yawned noisily, a baby cried. God's new day, for the simple, the poor, and the illiterate, was beginning.

Lankao the Crazy got out of the rickshaw, looked around, and quietly whistled. Then, from under the shadows of a pile of fish baskets, emerged Vladek.

The coolie, or more precisely the man playing the role of the coolie, led them across the wooden bridge, from junk to junk, farther and farther toward the open, foaming, lapping water. There, moored and rolling with the anxious tide, was a big fishing boat—the kind that goes out into the open sea to chase schools of tuna.

Lankao and the coolie moved aside, whispered to each other for a long time, and finally said good-bye. Lankao gave a sign with his head and was the first to jump aboard. Vladek then followed.

A minute after that the motor was purring, the coolie gave a short wave, and began walking away from the junks in a business-like manner without waiting for the boat to leave.

With its small wooden cabin at the front, the boat had but one person to operate it, a silent, barefoot fisherman, who looked Korean. It was only when they entered open water that he put up the big black sail with his strong and skillful hands. It looked like the open, many-jointed wings of a bat, like a butterfly, like a woman's huge fan. And it mingled now with hundreds of similar fans—black, gray, red—that seemed suddenly to have been set free from the big cramped city and were making their way in all directions from the mouth of the river to the endless horizon. Just like the junks, the brown waters of the Yangtse were crawling toward the sea to meet and mingle with the clean aquamarine of the ocean.

It was early morning, time for fishing.

The two banks of the river were getting farther and farther away from each other; from the West, the mighty silhouette of Shanghai became smaller and smaller, until it eventually melted into the early morning mist.

Beyond, the water was incredibly quiet, with glinting accents like the iridescence of an open abalone shell: the blue of the sea tenderly and gracefully merging with the pink reflections of the waking day and the floating white clouds.

Vladek was sitting at the back of the boat on top of a dirty folded rug stinking of rotten fish and dead seaweed; he was smoking and silent and somber. The sense of failure was overwhelming, crushing. Coming after the smashing of Ramsay in Tokyo, this debacle, in Shanghai, was a real catastrophe! Kleinbauer had committed suicide—the poor, lazy, alcoholic Saxon had shot himself in order to save the others—Cheng Suzhin would be out of commission for a long time to come, and Vladek himself was on the lam. If there was one thing different in this situation from that in Tokyo, it was that apart from the defeat of the Agfa studio, the police couldn't arrest anyone. Which meant there'd be no one talking, either. Because people weren't made out of steel. This was something you always had to keep in mind; it hadn't been only one or two who, finding themselves in the hands of the Kempeitai, had broken and given names, links, and addresses.

He couldn't even call Hilde; to do so would be to violate the rules of elementary safety: without a doubt the police were listening in on the telephones to catch the tail end of the broken thread.

Hilde! It hurt to think of her, and he was seized by a vague alarm as well: Would she be able to duck down and hide, to destroy all those clues? About ten days had passed, sufficient time to realize that something had happened and that mortal danger was hanging over her. He only hoped she wouldn't look for him! But maybe he was worrying in vain. Most probably the baron had already been informed about what had happened and this could only mean that Hilde knew it too.

Damn it, after Paris, here he was disappearing for the second time without being able to call her! And if the police took an interest in finding out where he'd disappeared to, it would without doubt lead them to her. True, neither in the Gestapo nor in the Kempeitai did they know that he was in the studio that night, but any disappearance of his couldn't pass unnoticed. How much did they know? What could they learn? In any case, if trouble was going to land on her, it would be his fault. His and his only! He was the one who'd involved her in this dangerous playing with fire! On the other hand, the world, the whole world, was fighting a life-and-death battle with Nazism. And as with any battle, there were cherished ones among the victims. Whose fault was that? In this inhuman battle, was it only a question of the evildoers and the righteous?

Futile questions without an answer. Or with a thousand different answers. But, he hoped, maybe Hilde would be able to stay on the sidelines; maybe she would be spared this bitter cup!

So that's what Vladek was thinking, leaving the mouth of the great Yangtse. Though the horizons were distant, one day he would find again the path to his lost motherland.

But he would never see Shanghai again.

# 59

WHILE THE KOREAN'S BOAT was carrying the passengers ever farther away from the shore, about a mile away from it the big ship *Kawasaki Maru*, under the Japanese flag, issued three deafening salutes upon entering the mouth of the Yangtse. On board, among the curious early passengers, and leaning on the rails in impatient expectation of his first glimpse of Shanghai, stood a short Japanese officer with thick round glasses—the colonel from the sanitary authorities, Doctor Hiroshi Okura.

One hour later the colonel was already on shore, where he hired a rickshaw to Bridge House, the Shanghai department of the Kempeitai.

These were good days for the Kempeitai, successful days, in the judgment of Captain Masaaki Saneioshi. It was a most estimable proof of the fruitful cooperation with those friends from the Gestapo and the SS. Saneioshi-san was in fact satisfied with the work that had been done, while Hauptsturmführer Stockmann was in a rage. In Germany you could arrest and deport twenty thousand people in one night without the neighbors ever finding out about it, while here, on the very next day, the press had noisily gossiped about the Agfa studio case, garnished with the most incredible hypothesis about the place and role of the arrested Miss Hilde Braun, the new "Mata Hari," as the sensation-hungry newspapers put it. Here, for a hundred U.S. dollars, every rag could get hold of confidential information from any police chief it wanted—and the Japanese called such wholesale corruption order and discipline! As a result of the brouhaha in the newspapers, most of the coded radio transmitters had taken in their antennae like snails their little horns, and were keeping silent. The Germans say, *Einmal ist keinmal*, which means that once doesn't count, while the Japanese count to one and are happy with their success, without making the effort to think what it would look like if they were able to keep their mouths shut! It's true, three more stations had been intercepted, but this was like going on a lion hunt and killing a cat, since one transmitter that had been exposed was involved in coded messages all right—in principle forbidden—but in this case received by commercial companies in Tokyo interested in company secrets about the price of rice and copper or trends in the Shanghai stock exchange. The other two were amateurs, students from the Polytechnic who had been transmitting to each other; they were arrested, slapped twice across the face and likely to get, in the worst case, some kind of symbolic sentence.

The other day, though, the drowsing Bushido caravan, which resembled a patient but disheartened fisherman whose bait hasn't moved in ages, had unexpectedly come across a short searching signal that received an immediate response and restored Hauptsturmführer Stockmann's good mood. The people in the caravan excitedly jumped up and started drawing new lines on the map, delineating the parameters of the running radio dialogue. In the late hours, a coded transmission was intercepted again from the same source, intriguing and curious in every respect. First, because the intercepted transmitter hadn't, like the others, gone silent out of fear. The reasons could be different: those working with the transmitter either hadn't been informed about failures that had recently occurred, or, like wild roosters, had become deaf from their own love song. Second—and most incredible—was that the signal wasn't localized somewhere around the central Shanghai neighborhoods, but in Hongku, this wretched quarter where people didn't even listen to the radio—some because they didn't have one, others because they simply didn't know what the word meant.

Early in the morning of April 4th, just as dawn was starting to break and the steel factory was still sunk in sleepy silence, a number of the old men who despite pleas, prohibitions, and curses nevertheless continued to go out in the early mornings and pee right inside the factory yard, happened to notice in the semi-darkness a white caravan that had quietly inserted itself between the administration building and the hall. A few minutes after that about a hundred uniformed men rushed into the yard—the old men couldn't tell the police from the army, nor the Chinese from the Japanese, but for them it was clear that something bad was about to happen.

There was a brief command and then those who had just entered the yard ran and surrounded the water tower.

The attempts of several brave Japanese men to climb the broken, twisted, and, in places, virtually unusable iron stairs were met from above by revolver fire. Apparently the tower couldn't be taken by storm; its defenses were impenetrable.

Suddenly, though, the story was over in less than half an hour—even more quickly than Hauptsturmführer Stockmann, who had very little trust in the Japanese, could imagine. Not far from the factory, near the bridge to the Inner City, there was an installation of Japanese anti-aircraft artillery. It got the job done right away. One of the cannons, dragged near the factory, fired off three shells that exploded and turned into a heap of rubble the platform at the top of the water tower where those crazy men had been living—the flute player Simon Zinner and the astrophysicist Markus Aronson, seller of rice rolls. True, the ideal goal of every police chief to take the criminals alive wasn't reached, but the transmitter, no matter whom it had been serving, had been silenced forever.

Commissioner Go, who had shown up quite late, running and panting with the excessive effort of putting himself at the service of the Kempeitai, was the one who gave the most precise information about the people who had petitioned to inhabit the round space with the vaulted windows and the two miniature balconies on the side. He was hoping to receive a certain portion of the glory by declaring that he'd always had his suspicions about those two! But both the Germans and the Japanese were too preoccupied with their own worries and there was no one to pay attention to the King of the Jews, who, in addition to being the greatest expert in Japan on the Jewish question, had personally translated *Mein Kampf.*

The only one who had any idea what it was all about was lying with a high temperature in the small white hut of the gardener Wu Laozian, for as early as the Russian Bath, Cheng Suzhin had predicted that Major Smedley, from the American embassy, wouldn't leave Shanghai before depositing his property with reliable people who would remember to water the plants. . . .

# 60

CAPTAIN MASAAKI SANEIOSHI WAS more than a little surprised when it was reported to him that a colonel from the imperial sanitary forces wanted to visit him. His astonishment grew by leaps and bounds when the colonel, visibly discomfited, announced to him the purpose of his unexpected visit: an audience with the prisoner Hilde Braun.

Saneioshi-san politely invited the short, bespectacled Hiroshi Okura to sit down, and offered him a cigarette.

"Excuse me, colonel, but how do you happen to have information that this lady has been arrested? And that she's here with us?"

"It's been in all the newspapers. I read about it in Korea, where I'm the chief doctor at the military hospital in Kwangju. Miss Braun is an old acquaintance of mine, very old and dear. I would be grateful to you if you would allow me a visit with her."

Pensively folding a piece of paper into a roll, Captain Saneioshi twice gave a curious look at this shy colonel, and finally said:

"First, the investigation is still in progress, and any contacts with the outside world are most unwelcome. You yourself understand why. And second, you do realize, don't you, that an irregular meeting like this with such a person constitutes a danger to your own career and your honor as an officer? A Japanese officer who maintains relations with a spy from an enemy country!"

"Yes, I read all about it. Mata Hari. I have no reason to worry, Saneioshi-san. The meeting I am requesting is personal . . . very personal."

Saneioshi smiled with his eyes.

"A little love intermezzo?"

"That, if you'll pardon me, is none of your business. It really isn't. . . ."

"Everything is my business. Every little thing. Even the brand name of her lipstick. Even the person with whom she went to the Celestial Peace restaurant and what they had for dinner. By the way, do you know that she has a lover? Some journalist who has lately disappeared, who was passing as a Swiss."

A dull pain hit Doctor Okura for part of a second—an unpleasant feeling of emptiness in the gut. He realized that to feel jealousy over a free woman with the right to make her own choices was more than stupid; between them really there was nothing more than a lovely acquaintance, and they had parted early on in Paris as good friends. Yet this feeling was uncontrollable, an illogical sense of violated rights, a primal, forbidden feeling! He never thought that she would have stayed behind in Paris like a Japanese widow, sunk in mourning for him! This, at least, was what Hiroshi Okura knew, but the mind doesn't always hold sway over the heart. He said carefully:

"I'm sorry if I'm intruding upon strictly—how to put it—confidential matters relevant to the investigation. But was Miss Braun really acting on behalf of a foreign secret service?"

"For the time being she hasn't confessed to anything; the only evidence we have is indirect. More I can't say."

"I'm ready to vouch for her. If the word of a Japanese colonel has any weight. Whatever you think, whatever you suspect her of, she is an extremely wonderful person incapable of committing a crime."

"Certainly, as far as you're concerned, you could see it this way; I'm not arguing with you. But everything, colonel, is a question of perspective. And there are different criteria for what is or isn't a crime. I respect your feelings but I'm afraid I cannot help you."

Then the shy Okura did something that in other circumstances he would never have dared. He did it before thinking about it, spontaneously, at the first impulse. He reached inside the inner pocket of his officer's jacket, took out his wallet, and on the desk of the captain counted out one thousand American dollars.

"Please. For a short while. Just five minutes!"

Captain Saneioshi looked at him with sad surprise. This Doctor Okura had to have fallen completely head over heels for this woman, no doubt about it, if he was offering an amount like this for just a short visit! He wearily and unhurriedly counted the money in a businesslike manner, put it away, and only then said with a sigh:

"All right, but I hope you won't regret it, colonel. You're a doctor, you've seen many things. I hope you won't regret it. Please, leave your weapon here."

The cells were in the basement, accessible through the backyard. They went down the brick steps, with a senior guard walking in front of them who opened door after door through the endless vaulted corridor, lit up by the dim light of bare bulbs. After the captain and the colonel had gone through the passage, the guard with the utmost diligence locked the barred doors behind him. Doctor Hiroshi Okura, who had grown up in the care of his rich parents, and had wasted time and money in fancy schools in New England and Paris, had never seen anything so terrible—another world, dark, underground, and unknown. In the large cells they were sitting directly on the wet stone floor, leaning against the walls, with hands on the back of their heads, tens of dozens of people arrested for who-knows-what crimes, in any case probably not for stealing, because the Kempeitai were the political police. Japanese guards were lazily walking around the corridor, peeping in the cells and ominously knocking the keys against the bars if anyone dropped his arms.

Her cell was at the very end—single, with light coming from the corridor. She was sitting on top of the bulky stone tiles, almost imperceptibly swaying her body, and, as it seemed to Doctor Okura, silently humming some song.

The eyes of the doctor, who was in any case suffering from poor vision, became adjusted to the semi-darkness with difficulty. And this was all right because the horror of what he saw only gradually swam up from the shadows until it finally took on sharpness and reality.

Hilde saw them, tried to arouse her memory, smiled. The right side of her face had turned into a gigantic blue swelling; her eye was completely closed, and when she smiled, he could see, on one side of her mouth, a gaping black void: her teeth had been knocked out. Her matted hair was pulled out in patches and in some places there were wounds left—uneven circles of broken skin.

"What have you done to her?" Okura whispered, terrified.

"I warned you that the sight wouldn't be pleasant. But everything we do, we do for Japan!" coldly responded the captain.

Hilde, still swaying, looked at the two uniformed Japanese men with her remaining open eye.

"Do you recognize me, Miss Braun?" the doctor asked with a shrinking heart.

She nodded silently, but expressed neither joy nor some shift in mood possibly brought about by this encounter. It seemed that she was indifferent to everything.

"Can I be of any help to you? I will bring you warm clothes and medicine. I hope they will not refuse me. . . . Do you need anything?"

She shook her head no.

Then she mumbled something in French:

"Hiroshi-san . . . I'm already being carried on the white winds. Don't worry about me."

Captain Saneioshi abruptly interrupted her:

"Speak German or English!"

But she paid no attention to him, as if she didn't hear him.

"If you want to do something for me . . . excuse me, I'm speaking with difficulty. I hope you understand me?"

The captain shouted again:

"If you don't stop speaking French, I will cancel the visit!"

She just waved her hand contemptuously and only then did the doctor notice that the tips of her dirty fingers were covered with blood—and that the nails were missing.

"Hiroshi-san, please go to Hongku. . . . Do you understand what I'm saying?"

"I understand, Hongku," he answered quietly.

"Find the rabbi. There's a rabbi there. Tell him that I am a Jew and that I ask to be buried in the Jewish cemetery. If they want me there."

"Stop! Enough! The End!" Captain Saneioshi began to shriek.

She tried to smile and mumbled in German:

"I've already put in The End, you beast!"

The colonel from the imperial sanitary services, Hiroshi Okura, was quietly crying and was not ashamed of his tears.

Five days later Doctor Okura had to lay another thousand dollars on the desk of Captain Saneioshi in order to receive the earthly remains of Hilde Braun.

It happened as she had requested before her death: Rabbi Leo Levin recited the prayer for the dead according to tradition and the body was laid to rest in the muddy soil of the Jewish cemetery by the river, in Hongku. Apart from the Japanese colonel and the rabbi and the three dedicated old men from the synagogue whose duty it was to wash the dead and wrap her in a shroud, no one saw and no one found out what the Kempeitai had done to her. With Jews the coffin is closed and the living have no right to look death in the eye. "While they really ought to," the rabbi thought as he mechanically pronounced the words of the Mourners' Kaddish. "Sometimes they really should. So that people will know and remember!"

No one knew her Jewish name; it wasn't registered anywhere. They didn't even know the date of her birth, or where she'd been born; her documents had stayed with the Kempeitai. This is why on the white marble headstone that Okura ordered, he insisted that under the Star of David the stonecutter write only this:

HILDE BRAUN

*A white wind from distant lands*

# 61

THE ECONOMIC CATASTROPHE ABOUT which Baron von Dammbach had been given a timely warning by the German experts became a fact. The collapse of the dollar was just an outward expression of the crisis: within less than a month, what had been a fixed rate of six Shanghai dollars to one U.S. dollar jumped to a thousand to one. You could see it in the price of an egg: one thousand dollars and not a penny less.

Although the China of Chiang Kai-shek had a separate, relatively independent economy, countless invisible veins connected Chunking with Shanghai, and you could hardly say who had influenced whom more in this invisible economic collapse. The nationalists had begun collecting "patriotic" gold from the population, sending it to Taiwan, and issuing paper notes against it—"gold yuan." As a result of this draining of the gold reserves, in those territories controlled by Chiang Kai-shek one U.S. dollar was now exchanged for twenty million "gold yuan."

If in Shanghai you could speak of an economic crisis, then in South Hongku it had turned into a general humanitarian tragedy. It was harder and harder to find work; Mother Antonia was overwhelmed; and, day by day, the chances of keeping her kitchen for the poor in operation were rapidly diminishing. The most wretched and pitiful means of survival came only from those couple of hundred people—living skeletons, really—who were busy repairing the dilapidated road to Lunghoa. You have to admit that many of them did this with skill; the time they had served in apprenticeship at Dachau was obvious.

For Professor Sigmund Mandel, who from fatigue and malnutrition had started to look like a hunched shadow, what discouraged him most was the morning it turned out that the hospital had no medicines—not even so much as a bandage or a drop of iodine.

There was complete desperation in the Inner City.

In reality, distant echoes came all the way from both the European and the Pacific fronts, but they had no perceptible influence on the Zone's hopeless situation, and even unverified news about the capitulation of Italy, and the unstoppable advance of the Red Army toward the borders of the German Reich, or about the conquest of the Marshall Islands, the Philippines, and Okinawa by the Anglo-American allies, was received with skepticism as only the old men's latest fantasies.

Yet as paradoxical as it may sound, it was exactly during the days and months of general desperation and futility that Theodore Weissberg's "Philharmonic" flourished. The violinist, who had lost everything irreversibly—starting with Elisabeth to his last hope for survival—threw himself with all his heart into the saving world of music. The organizer and the soul of the orchestra, the former flautist Simon Zinner, was no more. The torn bodies of the two men from the water tower had been taken down by Japanese military mountaineers. But by this time there was no real need to make special efforts to organize the orchestra: most of the players were jobless anyway and would ask each other when they would meet again at the synagogue-pagoda for the next rehearsal.

They would rehearse famished; sometimes Mother Antonia barely managed to offer them some rice porridge or a bowl of pea soup.

But sometimes, when everything looks as hopeless as can be, and there's no way out of the situation, things take an unexpected turn. On this nice, sunny day, the orchestra had undertaken a somewhat strange, or rather even frivolous piece, one quite removed from the academic notion of a philharmonic. Theodore Weissberg was conducting "The Blue Danube" in the yard of the steel factory, but his orchestra had merged with the nuns' brass band. You couldn't say that the results were perfect, but who bothered about such details! Hundreds of couples were dancing the waltz on the trodden earth, in the yard of the steel factory, as if this were the Vienna Opera's spring ball.

It was the 9th of May, the year was 1945, the end of the war in Europe.

Time was, the Chinese Carmelites would welcome those who had just arrived in Shanghai with "The Blue Danube," and now here they were getting ready to see them off to their distant journey home.

People were genuinely happy. For the first time in a very long time, they were fondled by the hope for an end—a final, irreversible end to this world disaster. Young and old floated merrily by in the dance, children too, happy to be feeling the imminence of return.

And then the tragedy enfolded them in what all remembered as the most terrible day of their lives. The sky suddenly darkened with countless airplanes, which started to lay down a carpet of bombs over Shanghai.

"The Japanese!" shouted someone. "Take cover!"

A panicky, chaotic flight ensued. One and the same thought struck people as they ran: whereas in the West, in Europe, Germany was capitulating, over here Japan was still insisting on demonstrating that it was master of the situation. But why was it exactly Shanghai that they were bombing? After all, the city was in their hands.

Those fleeing were bitterly mistaken: the airplanes were not Japanese.

They were American Flying Fortresses, which were taking off from their base on just-conquered Okinawa, and, in wave after wave, systematically destroying Shanghai.

Along its whole length, Nankin Road was cut in half, as by a knife. Their facades destroyed, buildings collapsed one after another, revealing, as if on the stage of a theater, bedrooms, kitchens, restaurant interiors, and hotel lobbies. Crazed with fear, people ran through the thick smoke, amid flames and buckling walls, under the maddening roar of the bombers. And they kept coming and coming, wave after wave—systematically, calmly, undisturbed by Japanese anti-aircraft, which had been completely silenced.

It was unclear whether something had aroused the fury of the American pilots or it was just some blundering commander who'd given them the wrong coordinates, but their last load of bombs fell on Hongku, right in the center of the Zone, in the Inner City!

The densely populated neighborhood literally boiled with explosions. Wood and mud houses flew in all directions. The air was filled with smoke, dust, screams, and children's cries, while above all reigned the constant, powerful, menacing roar of the airplanes, which were flying low—sometimes so low that you could see their identification marks. Only then did the people, who had only a minute ago been dancing to "The Blue Danube," realize the whole paradoxical, meaningless, absurd truth: America was killing the people who'd been waiting for her with so much hope!

Rabbi Leo Levin climbed on the roof of his improvised synagogue, which had already been burned once during the time of the Japanese bombing, and shouted out to the sky:

"Bastards! Crazy idiots! Don't you see where your bombs are falling?! Do you hear me, you shitheads?"

Well, the shitheads didn't hear a thing. Up there in the sky, hardly anyone could notice the small rumpled man, waving his fists from the roof of a pagoda.

Those killed numbered in the dozens. Professor Mandel, completely covered with blood, his sleeves rolled up, fought for the lives of the injured. He was helped, as much as possible, by volunteer women, Jewish and the nuns. Sheets and shirts were torn, because there was no gauze, and no bandages for dressing the wounds. Rice brandy flowed from small shops that had been destroyed, and wounds were washed with beer, because there was nothing for disinfection, not even boiled water.

At one point the colonel from the imperial sanitary forces, Doctor Okura, imperceptibly came up and stood by the professor:

"I've come to help," he said simply, taking off his colonel's coat.

"Yes, thank you. But how can you help in this hell where we have no disinfectant, iodine, gauze, bandages, syringes, ether, adrenaline. Nothing!" said Professor Mandel, in desperation.

"I know," said the Japanese man. "Your rabbi told me. But you will have."

Only a little time passed before an ambulance with red crosses and a sign in Japanese and English reading "Shanghai Military Hospital" pulled up in front of an elementary school in Hongku that had indeed been turned into that facility. Two Japanese orderlies began to unload trucks filled with medical supplies, including actual medicines, in quantities the professor hadn't dreamed of in years.

Then came dead silence. For a long time now the sun of this 9th day of May had gone down in the West, blurred by the smoke of burning Shanghai. But two men—one a professor, fired in Germany because of his Jewish origin, and the other a Japanese colonel, who had run to Hongku because of his human origin—both of them covered in blood to the elbows, were continuing the struggle to save people's lives.

## *Finale to the Symphony No. 45 (The "Farewell" Symphony) by Joseph Haydn*

### Adagio

Since that day in May, months had passed. Shanghai was again rising from her ruins.

This time the nuns weren't playing waltzes at the harbor; the bombings had thrown half their instruments in the air. Now new musical scores had landed and were chirping on telegraph wires and trees by the riverside, or pecking crumbs at the feet of people climbing up gangways to the ships. And even if the instruments had been in one piece, they wouldn't have worked. At least this is what Mother Antonia said as she exclaimed angrily, "You try blowing on a trombone while you're crying!"

She herself was crying and hugging the rabbi. She said nothing about her debt to him—her debt of eight beans from a damned straight of tens that the old fox Leo Levin had managed to produce at the last moment.

People kept climbing up to the enormous ocean liner. This was the sixth in a row. To make the sixth and last voyage back to Europe.

Leaning against the railings, Theodore Weissberg looked up the stream of the great and eternal Yangtse toward Hongku, as it sank into the twilight mist. Then he turned around and cast a glance at Shanghai's mighty silhouette. Somewhere out there beyond Nantao was the German cemetery and the grave of Elisabeth Müller-Weissberg, the singer who had come here even though she could have chosen not to. Now she would remain in Shanghai forever, having put down her candle and quietly walked out of life.

He felt no joy that he was leaving this accursed Hongku. He was seized, rather, with sadness that one part of his life, one very important part, with a very precious person woven into it, was staying behind here, in Shanghai. Maybe because of that, maybe because of the mysterious logic of the soul, he was starting to be fond of this huge, confused, mad, cruel city. A man knows why he hates, but does he know why he loves?

Professor Mandel searched for his Japanese colleague, but did not find him among the crowd of those who had come to see everyone off. He would not find him: Colonel Hiroshi Okura at that moment was in the desolate Inner City, at the Jewish cemetery, where he had laid a big bouquet of tea roses on the grave of Hilde Braun. He remained there for some time, in silence, and then he took off along the utterly desolate, abandoned streets close to the bridge that, till recently, had marked the site of a whole aggregate of humiliations.

When he descended toward the harbor, the big ship was already floating away—white, with thousands of black spots filling all three of its decks. There were no more nuns to be seen at the dock, and no more well-wishers come to bid farewell to those who were leaving.

The colonel sat for some time on a bench, pensively looking out at the ship, which issued three mighty farewell blasts from its siren before disappearing behind the curve of the river. Then he again unfolded the crumpled telegram that he was clutching tightly in his fist, read the text that he already knew by heart, and laughed. In the chaos of defeat, the telegram had been stuck in the central Shanghai post office and only today had someone discovered it and brought it to him.

From the ministry in Tokyo they were ordering him to appear immediately for a briefing. Saneioshi-san had fulfilled his duty to the end—before committing hara-kiri. Doctor Okura felt no anger toward him for reporting him; after all, Captain Masaaki Saneioshi had not lacked a sense of honor and dignity, and had died as a samurai, and a true descendant of samurai, by ritually stabbing himself in the belly with the ancestral sword of his forefathers.

And those in Tokyo who'd sent the telegram were really jolly fellows! Despite Hiroshima and Nagasaki, despite the defeat and the capitulation signed on board the cruiser *Missouri*, the bureaucrats continued, diligently, in the Japanese manner, to fulfill their duties to the last moment. In just this way the nails of the dead keep growing for quite some time!

Could Colonel Okura be faulted for all that had happened during this monstrous war? Or for what Captain Masaaki Saneioshi had done to Hilde? For the hospital in Kwangju where he had silently treated the Korean girls forced into whorehouses for Japanese soldiers? For the lonely nights when he was writing gentle haiku poems, while at the very same time, in the nearby barracks, whole squads were passing through the bodies of those poor girls?

This is what the colonel was pondering without taking his eyes off the telegram.

The fault of Hiroshi Okura was a small fault, very minute, just like that of any number of his compatriots—simple, well-intentioned, decent Japanese people. Millions of small faults—composed of silence, indifference, obedience, myths of military honor. Now everyone had to redeem himself drop by drop, to redeem the motherland's big historic fault. The rising sun had to be washed and cleansed of its sin, if it were to continue its rise. . . .

The barefoot fisherman, sitting on the edge of the dock, heard, amid the screams of the cormorants, something like the distant dry sound of a breaking plank. He looked around but didn't see anything in particular; that Japanese officer without epaulettes continued to sit just like that on the bench by the river. From here you couldn't see the bullet hole in his temple.

In Shanghai that was the last shot fired of the Second World War.

*For the character of Vladek, the author has taken elements from the lives and destinies of three Bulgarians: Ivan Vinarov, Lieutenant Christo Boev, and Ivan Karaivanov. After the defeat of the anti-fascist uprising in Bulgaria in 1923, the three of them emigrated and put themselves in the service of Soviet intelligence. Vinarov and Boev at different periods of time were active in a number of European countries and in China; Karaivanov executed secret missions in Shanghai, Japan, and Africa. After the end of World War II, Ivan Vinarov achieved the rank of general in the new Bulgaria, and Christo Boev organized its military intelligence, after which he finished his career as a Bulgarian ambassador to Japan. The personality of Karaivanov is to this day veiled in mystery.*

*Hilde Braun has the characteristics of two of her contemporaries: Luise Klaas and Josepha Engelberg.*

*Colonel Okura is the actual Colonel Okura, Captain Saneioshi of the Kempeitai the actual Captain Saneioshi of the Kempeitai, and "King of the Jews" Go—the real Go. Those who passed through the camp at Dachau remember SS Scharführer Hansi Steinbrenner.*

*The real family name of Cheng Suzhin is Chan. Chan in reality was killed. But so many brave men and women fell in that fight that the author spared him and left him lying gravely wounded with the old Wu Laozian.*

*Kleinbauer, as well as all the other characters whose names have sometimes been modified for ethical considerations, is as real as the story that you have just read.*

Angel Wagenstein

## TRANSLATORS' ACKNOWLEDGMENTS

We are delighted to acknowledge those who, during the happy months of our collaboration in both Sofia and New York on the translation of *Farewell, Shanghai*, so generously gave us advice and suggestions on everything from the sometimes tricky challenges of turning Angel Wagenstein's richly colloquial Bulgarian into the idioms of contemporary American English to the finer points of Jewish religious practice, what's where in Paris, German prewar musical culture, the fascinating history of Shanghai, and both the perils and romance of World War II espionage: Ivan Angelov, Zlatko Anguelov, Florian Becker, Valentin Belinski, Susan Bernofsky, Jeni Bozhilova, Gina Brezini, Odile Chilton, Zdravka Eftimova, Yuval Elmelech, Franz Kempf, Barbara Korn, Marina Kostalevsky, Ivan Lidarev, Dragomir Marinov, Jacob Neusner, Joel Perlmann, and Maria Spirova.

We thank as well Mr. Wagenstein's American literary agent, Al Zuckerman, for steering us to Handsel Books and Other Press.

To Angel "Jacky" Wagenstein, we can only express affectionate gratitude for giving us the opportunity to live with his characters, and to experience, alongside them, their joys and griefs, their humanity, and their heroic struggles.

Elizabeth Frank   Deliana Simeonova
New York / Sofia
December 2006

# FAREWELL, SHANGHAI

*Reading Group Guide*

## ABOUT THE AUTHOR:

Angel ("Jacky") Wagenstein was born in the city of Plovdiv in 1922 and spent his early childhood in exile with his family in Paris. Upon his return to Bulgaria as a high school student, he joined an underground antifascist group. For taking part in anti-Nazi sabotage during World War II, he was sent to a labor camp from which he escaped to rejoin the Bulgarian partisans. Arrested, tortured, and condemned to death, he owes his life to the arrival of the Red Army in Bulgaria on September 9, 1944.

After studying filmmaking in Moscow, he went on to become one of the foremost screenwriters in Bulgaria, with more than fifty credits to his name, including the original screenplay for the film *Stars*, which in 1959 won the Cannes Prix Spécial du Jury, and tells the story of a German soldier's doomed attempts to rescue a young Greek-Jewish woman and her family, who are being transported to certain death in the "Eastern Territories" of the Reich.

Wagenstein has in recent years written three novels on the fate of European Jews in the twentieth century: *Isaac's Torah* (*Petoknizhie Isaakovo*), which has been translated into English (Handsel Books, 2008), French, and German; *Far From Toledo* (*Dalech Ot Toledo*), which has been published in French under the title *Abraham Le Poivrot* (*Abraham the Sot*) and was the winner of the Prix Jean Monnet de Littérature Européenne in 2004; and *Farewell, Shanghai* (*Sbogom, Shanghai*). Wagenstein wrote the screenplay for the film *After the End of the World* (1998) while simultaneously working on the novel *Far from Toledo* on which it is based—a singular case, it would seem, of an original screenplay's simultaneously giving birth to its adaptation as a novel and vice versa.

Wagenstein resides in Sofia, where he takes an active part in Bulgarian culture and politics.

## A NOTE FROM ANGEL WAGENSTEIN:

The Shanghai ghetto: a little-known page from the tragedy of the Jews during World War II. About thirty thousand refugees from Nazism, primarily German and Austrian Jews, sought asylum in Shanghai—according to a narrow statute still formally an open city, but in actuality under Japanese occupation. During these years, the great Far Eastern port was a hub of economic, political, and military interests, diplomatic intrigues, and international spy rings. For the fugitives from Europe, Shanghai initially conjured up illusions of joyous salvation; under pressure, however, by their German allies, the Japanese authorities quickly transformed a shabby section of town into a dismal Jewish ghetto. There its new inhabitants—of whom the greater part were intellectuals—experienced all the brutality of Japanese militarism and the bitterness of humiliation. But also the forces of civilian courage, solidarity, and intense human empathy.

Although the subject of the novel is developed against the background of colliding historical events, its essential fabric is woven from actual human destinies, documented facts, and those turbulent emotions—love and faith, hope and despair.

In *Farewell, Shanghai,* I have made use of rich archival material, including memoirs and personal contacts with surviving participants of actual events, various historical investigations, and repeated visits to China in search of traces of this Shanghai tragedy. Especially important material has been drawn from declassified secret intelligence archives, as well as recent research on the activities and the tragic end of the "Ramsay" espionage group, led by the legendary Soviet agent, Richard Sorge.

## DISCUSSION QUESTIONS:

1. What are some of the ways the Jews in Shanghai survive psychologically and maintain their dignity? Is humor one of their coping devices?

2. How do the Japanese and Chinese regard the Jews?

3. There is plenty of evidence for the "Law of Universal Disgustingness" in *Farewell, Shanghai*, but there are also numerous acts of unexpected kindness, generosity, and courage that undermine that law. Does the book give you hope despite its sometimes pessimistic tone?

4. Some of the more fragile characters survive while some of the strongest and most resilient break down. Why do you think this happens? Did the suicides come as a shock?

5. How does *Farewell, Shanghai* expose the "myth of Jewish solidarity"? Do you believe that Hitler and the Holocaust united Jews from around the world?

6. The narrator expresses cynicism about the leaders of governments in general. Does this seem accurate?

7. *Farewell, Shanghai* raises the question of whether Roosevelt knew in advance about the attack on Pearl Harbor. Do you think this may have been true? If it was, how do you understand his motivation for not acting on it?

8. Personal friendship overrides national and political allegiance in some cases in *Farewell, Shanghai.* What are the examples of this? In what sense do you find these ethical or understandable? In what sense do you find them objectionable?

9. What role does music play in *Farewell, Shanghai*?

10. Does the context of war create a moral ambiguity that produces some surprising actions, with decent people being forced to act against some of their principles while their cruel enemies sometimes act humanely? What seems to be the author's attitude toward the moral challenges of war?